David Gemmell's first novel, *Legend*, was published in 1984. He has written many bestsellers, including the Drenai saga, the Jon Shannow novels and the Stones of Power sequence. He is now widely acclaimed as Britain's king of heroic fantasy. David Gemmell lives in East Sussex.

Find out more about David Gemmell and other Orbit authors by registering for the free monthly newsletter at www.orbitbooks.co.uk

By David Gemmell

LEGEND
THE KING BEYOND THE GATE
WAYLANDER
QUEST FOR LOST HEROES
WAYLANDER II
THE FIRST CHRONICLES OF
DRUSS THE LEGEND
DRENAI TALES OMNIBUS ONE
DRENAI TALES OMNIBUS TWO

WOLF IN SHADOW
THE LAST GUARDIAN
BLOODSTONE

GHOST KING
LAST SWORD OF POWER

LION OF MACEDON
DARK PRINCE

IRONHAND'S DAUGHTER
THE HAWK ETERNAL

KNIGHTS OF DARK RENOWN

MORNINGSTAR

DARK PRINCE

David A. Gemmell

www.orbitbooks.co.uk

An *Orbit* Book

First published in Great Britain by Century 1991
Reprinted by Orbit 1998, 1999 (twice),
2000, 2002, 2003, 2005

© David A. Gemmell 1991

The moral right of the author has been asserted.

A CIP catalogue record for this book
is available from the British Library.

ISBN 1 85723 666 1

Typeset by Deltatype Ltd
Printed and bound in Great Britain by
Mackays of Chatham PLC, Chatham, Kent

Orbit
An imprint of
Time Warner Book Group UK
Brettenham House
Lancaster Place
London WC2E 7EN

This edition of *Dark Prince* is dedicated to all my friends at Random Century, past and present. And to all those who understand what is meant by 'The louder they spoke of their honour – the faster we counted the spoons.'

Acknowledgements

Grateful thanks to my editor Deborah Beale, who helped fuel the inspiration, my former editor Liza Reeves, for pointing the path to Parmenion, and to my current editor Oliver Johnson, who built the bridges.

Thanks also to Alan Fisher, Vikki Lee France, Valerie Gemmell, Stella Graham, Edith Graham, Tim Lenton, Jean Maund, Tom Taylor and Charon Wood for their help throughout the project.

Contents

Dark Prince

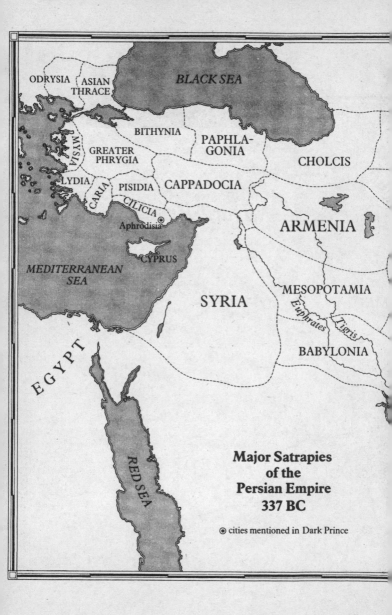

ODRYSIA
ASIAN THRACE
BLACK SEA
BITHYNIA
PAPHLA-GONIA
GREATER PHRYGIA
MYSIA
CHOLCIS
LYDIA
CARIA
PISIDIA
CAPPADOCIA
CILICIA
ARMENIA
Aphrodisia
CYPRUS
MEDITERRANEAN SEA
SYRIA
MESOPOTAMIA
Euphrates
Tigris
BABYLONIA
EGYPT
RED SEA

**Major Satrapies
of the
Persian Empire
337 BC**

⊙ cities mentioned in Dark Prince

Book One, 352 BC

Pella, Macedonia, Summer

The golden-haired child sat alone, as he usually did, and wondered whether his father would die today. Some distance away, across the royal gardens, his nurse was talking to the two sentries who guarded him during the hours of daylight. The soldiers, grim-eyed warriors, did not look at him and shifted nervously if he approached.

Alexander was used to this reaction. Even at four he understood it.

He remembered with sadness the day three weeks ago when his father, garbed for war, had walked along this same garden path, his cuirass gleaming in the sunlight. It was so beautiful that Alexander had reached out to touch the gleaming plates of iron, edged with gold, the six golden lions on the breast. But as his hand came forward Philip had moved swiftly back.

'Don't touch me, boy!' he snapped.

'I would not hurt you, Father,' whispered the prince, staring up at the black-bearded face, with its blind right eye like a huge opal beneath the savagely scarred brow.

'I came to say goodbye,' muttered Philip, 'and to tell you to be good. Learn your lessons well.'

'Will you win?' the child asked.

'Win or die, boy,' answered the King, kneeling to face his son. He appeared to relax, though his expression remained

3

stern. 'There are those who think I cannot win. They remember Onomarchus defeated me when last we met. But . . .' his voice dropped to a whisper, 'when the arrow tore into my eye at the siege of Methone they said I would die. When the fever struck me down in Thrace men swore my heart stopped beating. But I am Macedon, Alexander, and I do not die easily.'

'I don't want you to die. I love you,' said the child.

For a moment only Philip's face softened, his arm rising as if to reach out to his son. But the moment passed and the King stood. 'Be good,' he said. 'I will . . . think of you.'

The sound of children's laughter brought Alexander's thoughts back to the present. Beyond the garden walls he could hear the palace children playing. Sighing, he wondered what game they were enjoying. Hunt the Turtle perhaps, or Hecate's Touch. He watched them sometimes from the window of his room. One child would be chosen as Hecate, Goddess of Death, and would chase the others, seeking out their hiding-places, to touch them and make them slaves. The game would go on until all the children had been found and enslaved by Death.

Alexander shivered in the sunshine. No one would ask him to play such a game. He looked down at his small hands.

He had not meant the hound to die; he had loved the pup. And he had tried so hard, concentrating always, so that whenever he stroked the dog his mind was calm. But one day the playful hound had leapt at him, knocking him from his feet. In that moment Alexander's hand had snaked out, lightly slapping the beast on the neck. The hound collapsed instantly, eyes glazing, legs twitching. It had died within seconds, but what was worse it had decomposed within minutes, the stench filling the garden.

'It was not my fault,' the child wanted to say. But he knew that it was; knew that he was cursed.

Birds began to sing in the tall trees and Alexander smiled as he looked up at them. Closing his green eyes the boy allowed the bird-song to flow into him, filling his mind, merging with his own thoughts. The songs began to have

4

meanings then, that he could just decipher. No words but feelings, fears, tiny angers. The birds were screeching warnings to one another.

Alexander looked up and sang: 'My tree! My tree! Get away! Get away! My tree! My tree! I will kill you if you stay!'

'Children should not sing of killing,' said his nurse sternly, approaching where he sat but halting, as ever, out of reach.

'That is what the birds are singing,' he told her.

'You should come inside now, the sun is very hot.'

'The children are still playing beyond the wall,' he argued. 'And I like to sit here.'

'You will do as you are told, young prince!' she snapped. His eyes blazed and he could almost hear the dark voice within himself whispering: 'Hurt her! Kill her!' He swallowed hard, quelling the rising tide of anger.

'I will come,' he said softly. Rising to his feet he walked towards her, but she stepped quickly aside to let him pass, following him slowly as he returned to his own rooms. Waiting until she had gone, Alexander slipped out into the corridor and ran to his mother's apartments, pushing open the door to peek inside.

Olympias was alone and she smiled as he entered, opening her arms to him. He ran forward and embraced her, pushing his face against the soft flesh of her bosom. There was never anyone, he knew, so beautiful as his mother, and he clung to her fiercely.

'You are very hot,' said Olympias, pushing back his golden hair and stroking his brow. Filling a cup with cool water she passed it to him, watching as he drank greedily.

'Did your lessons go well today?' she asked.

'There were no lessons, Mother. Stagra is ill. If I had a pony, would it die?'

He saw the pain on her face as pulling him to her she patted his back. 'You are not a demon, Alexander. You have great gifts; you will be a great man.'

'But would the pony die?'

'I think that it might,' she admitted. 'But when you are

5

older you will know how to control . . . the Talent. Be patient.'

'I don't want to kill anything. Yesterday I made a bird fly to my hand. It sat for a long time before flying away. It didn't die. Truly!'

'When your father returns to Pella we will all go to the sea, and sail on boats. You will like that. The breeze is cool, and we will swim.'

'Is he coming back?' Alexander asked. 'Some people say he will die against the Phocians. They say his luck is finished, that the gods have deserted him.'

'Hush!' she whispered. 'It is not wise to voice such thoughts. Philip is a great warrior – and he has Parmenion.'

'The Phocians beat him before, two years ago,' said the boy. 'Two thousand Macedonians dead. And now the Athenians raid our coastline and the Thracians have turned against us.'

She nodded and sighed. 'You hear too much, Alexander.'

'I don't want him to die . . . even though he doesn't like me.'

'You must not say that! Ever!' she cried, seizing his shoulders and shaking him hard. 'Never! He loves you. You are his son. His heir.'

'You are hurting me,' he whispered, tears in his eyes.

'I am sorry,' she told him, drawing him into her arms. 'There is so much I wish I could tell you; explain to you. But you are very young.'

'I would understand,' he assured her.

'I know. That is why I cannot tell you.'

For a while they sat in silence, Alexander warm and sleepy in his mother's arms. 'I can see them now,' he said dreamily. 'There is a plain covered with flowers of purple and yellow. And there is Father in his golden armour. He is standing beside the grey gelding, Achea. And there are the enemy. Oh, Mother, there are thousands of them. I can see their shields. Look! There is the sign of Sparta, and there the Owl of Athens and . . . I don't know that one, but I can see the emblems of Pherai and Corinth . . . so many. How can Father beat them all?'

'I don't know,' whispered Olympias. 'What is happening now?'

'The battle begins,' answered the child.

The Crocus Field, Summer

Philip of Macedon rubbed at the scar above his blinded right eye and stared out over the Phocian battle-lines half a mile ahead. More than 20,000 infantry were massed on the plain, 1,000 cavalry behind and to the right of the main force. He transferred his gaze to the Macedonian lines, where 15,000 foot-soldiers waited in formation at the centre, his 3,000 cavalry to the left and right.

Everywhere there were flowers growing, some purple and yellow, others white and pink, and in that moment it seemed to the King almost inconceivable that within minutes hundreds – perhaps thousands – of men would lay down their lives, their blood soaking into the earth. And he felt, with sudden regret, it was almost as great a crime against the gods of beauty that these flowers would soon be trampled into the dust beneath the pale grass of the Crocian Plain. 'Don't be foolish,' he told himself. 'You chose this battle-ground.' It was flat and made for cavalry and Philip now commanded the Thessalian lancers, the finest horse-soldiers in Greece.

Two days ago, during a lightning march across the shallows of the River Penios, the Macedonian army surprised the defenders of the port city of Pagasai. The city had fallen within three hours. By sunset the Macedonians manning the ramparts had seen a fleet of Athenian battle

8

triremes sailing serenely across the gulf. But with Pagasai taken the triremes had nowhere to dock, and the soldiers they carried were lost to the enemy cause. The nearest shallow bay was a day's sailing and four days' march distant, and by the time the Athenian soldiers had come ashore the battle would be over.

Now, with the rear secured against an Athenian attack, Philip felt more confident of the coming battle. There was nowhere this time for Onomarchus to hide his giant catapults; no steep, tree-shrouded mountains from which he could send death from the skies. No, this battle would be fought man against man, army against army. Philip still remembered with sick horror the huge boulders raining down on the Macedonians, could still hear the awful cries of the crushed and dying.

But today it would be different. Today the odds were more even.

And he had Parmenion . . .

Glancing to his left Philip sought out the Spartan, watching him ride along the flank, talking to the riders, calming the younger men and lifting the spirits of the veterans.

A momentary anger touched Philip. The Spartan had come to Macedonia's aid seven years ago, when the nation was beset by enemies on all sides. His strategic skills had been vital then and he had trained Philip's fledgling army, turning them from farmers and peasants into the most feared fighting force in the civilized world.

'I loved you then,' thought Philip, remembering the heady days of victory over the Illyrians to the west, the Paionians to the north. City after city had fallen to Macedonia as her strength grew. But always the victories belonged to Parmenion, the *strategos*, the man whose battle plans had won victories for a quarter of a century, in Thebes, in Phrygia, in Cappadocia and Egypt.

Philip shaded his good eye and strained to see the Phocian centre, where Onomarchus would be standing with his bodyguard. But the distance was too great, the sun gleaming from too many breastplates, shields and helms for him to pick out his enemy.

'What I would not give to have your neck under my blade,' he whispered.

'Did you speak, sire?' asked Attalus, the King's Champion. Philip turned to the cold-eyed man beside him.

'Yes – but only to myself. It is time. Order the advance!'

Philip strode to the grey gelding, taking hold of the mane and vaulting to the beast's back. The gelding whinnied and reared, but Philip's powerful legs were locked to the barrel of its belly. 'Steady!' said the King, his voice soothing. A young soldier ran forward carrying Philip's high-crested helm of iron. It was polished until it shone like silver and the King took it in his hands, gazing down at the burnished face of the goddess Athena which decorated the forehead. 'Be with me today, lady,' he said, placing the helmet upon his head. Another man lifted Philip's round shield and the King slid his left arm through the leather straps, settling it in place on his forearm.

The first four regiments, 11,000 men, began the slow march towards the enemy.

Philip glanced to where Parmenion waited on the left with 2,000 cavalry and two regiments of reserves. The Spartan waved to his King, then transferred his gaze to the battlefield.

Philip's heart was hammering now. He could still taste the bitterness of defeat when last he had met Onomarchus. It was a day like this one – brilliant sunshine, a cloudless sky – when the Macedonians had marched against the enemy. Only then there were mountains on either side, and they had contained hidden siege-engines which hurled huge boulders down upon the Macedonians, smashing their formation, crushing bones and destroying lives. Then the enemy cavalry charged and the Macedonians had fled the field.

Long would Philip remember that day. For six years he had seemed invincible, victory following victory as if divinely ordained. And one terrible hour had changed everything. Macedonian discipline had reasserted itself by the evening and the army had re-formed in time for a fighting retreat. But, for the first time in his life, Philip had failed.

What was more galling even than defeat was the fact that Parmenion was not present at the battle. He was leading a force into the north-west to put down an Illyrian insurrection.

For six years the King had been forced to share his victories with his general, but the one defeat was his – and his alone.

Now Philip shook himself clear of the memories. 'Send out the Cretan archers,' he shouted to Attalus. The King's Champion turned his horse and galloped down to where the 500 archers were awaiting orders. Lightly armoured in baked leather chest-guards, the Cretans set off at a run to line up behind the advancing regiments.

Two hundred paces to the right of Philip's position the Second General, Antipater, was waiting with 1,000 cavalrymen. Philip tugged on the gelding's reins and rode to take his position alongside him in the front line. The horsemen, mostly Macedonian noblemen, cheered as he approached and he rewarded them with a wave.

Drawing his sword he led the cavalry forward at a walk, angling to the right of the advancing Macedonian infantry.

'Now they come!' yelled Antipater, pointing to the Phocian cavalry. The enemy horsemen, spears levelled, were charging towards them.

'Macedon!' bellowed Philip, kicking the gelding into a gallop, all his fears vanishing as the Macedonians thundered across the plain.

★

Parmenion's pale blue eyes narrowed as he scanned the battlefield. He could see Philip and his Companion Cavalry charging on the right, coming abreast now of the marching regiments of Macedonian infantry, with their shields locked, their eighteen-foot, iron-pointed *sarissas* aimed at the enemy ranks, the Cretan archers behind them sending volley after volley of shafts into the sky to rain down on the Phocian centre.

All was going according to plan, yet the Spartan was uneasy.

The King was the Supreme Commander of all Macedonia's forces, but Philip insisted always on riding into battle with his men, risking death alongside them, leading them from the front. His courage was both a blessing and a curse, Parmenion knew. With the King in their midst the Macedonians fought harder, yet were Philip to fall panic would sweep through the ranks faster than a summer fire over dry grass.

As always, with Philip at the heart of the fighting Parmenion took charge of the battle strategy, watching for signs of weakness, clues to the shifting changes in the fortunes of war.

Behind him the Thessalian cavalrymen awaited his orders, while before him the Fifth Regiment of infantry were standing calmly, watching the battle. Parmenion removed his white-crested helm, pushing his fingers through his sweat-drenched, short-cropped brown hair. Only one thought dominated his mind.

What was the Phocian planning?

Onomarchus was no ordinary general. During the past two years, since taking charge of the Phocian forces, he had moved his armies around central Greece with consummate skill, taking key cities in central Greece and sacking the Boeotian stronghold of Orchomenus. He was a wily and instinctive leader, respected by those who served him. But, more importantly to Parmenion, the man's strategy invariably relied on attack. Yet here his infantry regiments were positioned defensively, only his cavalry sweeping forward.

Something was wrong. Parmenion could feel it. Shading his eyes he scanned the battlefield once more. Here the Crocian Plain was virtually flat, save for a low line of hills to the far right and a small wooded area a half-mile to the left. There was no danger from the rear, now that Pagasai had been taken. So then, he thought again, what is the Phocian's battle plan?

Parmenion's concentration was broken as the Macedonian war-cry went up and the regiments broke into a run, the gleaming *sarissas* hammering into the Phocian ranks. Now the screams of the wounded and dying could be heard faintly above the clashing of shields. Parmenion turned to the rider beside him, a handsome young man in a red-crested helm.

'Nicanor, take five sections and ride towards the woods. Halt some two bow-lengths back from the trees and send in scouts. If the woods are clear, turn again and watch for any signal from me. If not, stop any hostile force from linking with Onomarchus. You understand?'

'Yes, sir,' answered Nicanor, saluting. Parmenion waited as the 500 riders cantered out towards the woods, then swung his gaze to the hills.

The Macedonian formation would not have been hard to predict – infantry at the centre, cavalry on either wing. Onomarchus must have known.

The infantry were now locked together, the Macedonians in tight phalanx formations sixteen ranks deep, one hundred and fifty shields wide. The First Regiment – the King's Guards, commanded by Theoparlis – had pierced the Phocian lines.

'Not too far!' whispered Parmenion. 'Swing the line and wait for support!' It was vital that the four regiments stayed in close contact; once separated they could be enveloped by the enemy's greater numbers. But the Spartan relaxed as he saw the King's Guards holding firm on the left, the right driving forward, the phalanx half wheeling, forcing back the Phocians. The Second Regiment had almost linked with them. Parmenion switched his concentration to the Third Regiment. It was coming under heavy pressure and had ceased to move forward, the fighting line beginning to bend back.

'Coenus!' yelled Parmenion. A broad-shouldered warrior at the centre of the reserve regiment looked up and saluted. 'Support the Third,' the general shouted.

The 2,500-strong Fifth Regiment began to move. They did not run but held to their formation, slowly crossing the field. 'Good man,' thought Parmenion. With emotions heightened by fear and excitement, it was all too easy for a commander to lead his men in an early charge, or run them hard to reach the battle. Coenus was a steady officer, cool

13

under pressure. He knew that his heavily armoured men would need all their strength when the fighting began – and not before.

Suddenly, on the left, the Macedonian line bulged and broke. Parmenion swore as he saw an enemy regiment burst clear of the centre, their shields tightly locked. He did not need to see the emblems on the enemy shields to know from which city they came: they were Spartans, magnificent fighting men feared across the world. The Third Regiment gave way before them and the Spartans moved out to encircle the Guards.

But Coenus and the Fifth were almost upon them. The *sarissas* swept down and the phalanx charged. Suddenly outflanked the Spartans fell back, the Macedonians regaining their formation. Satisfied the immediate danger was past, Parmenion swung his black stallion and cantered towards the right, the Thessalians streaming after him.

The King and his Companions were locked in a deadly struggle with the Phocian cavalry, but Parmenion could see the Macedonians were slowly pushing the enemy back. Glancing to the left he saw Nicanor and his 500 halted before the wood, the scouts riding into the trees.

Summoning a rider from his right Parmenion sent him to Nicanor with fresh orders, should the woods prove to be clear, then turned his attention to the hills.

If Onomarchus had planned any surprise strategy, then it was from here it must come. Returning his gaze to the centre, he saw Coenus and the Fifth had blocked the Spartan advance and were battling to link with Theoparlis and the Guards. The Third Regiment had merged with the Fourth and were once more cleaving at the Phocian lines.

Parmenion had two choices now. He could gallop in to aid the King, or swing his line to hit the enemy from the left. Touching heels to the stallion he rode further along the right flank. A rider detached himself from the battle and galloped to where Parmenion waited; the man had several shallow wounds on his arms, and his face was gashed on the right cheek.

'The King orders you to support the right. The enemy are almost beaten.'

The Spartan nodded and turned to Berin, the hawk-faced Thessalian prince. 'Take five hundred men and swing out to the right before linking with Philip.'

Berin nodded, called out his orders and – his men fanning out behind him – cantered across the battlefield. The wounded messenger moved closer to Parmenion. 'The King ordered *all* the reserves into action,' he whispered.

'You have done well, young man,' said Parmenion. 'Now ride back to camp and let the surgeon see to those wounds. They are not deep but you are losing a great deal of blood.'

'But, sir . . .'

'Do as you are bid,' said Parmenion, turning away from the man. As the messenger rode away a second Thessalian commander guided his mount alongside the general. 'What are we to do, sir?' he asked.

'We wait,' Parmenion answered.

★

Philip of Macedon, his sword dripping blood, swung his horse's head and risked a glance to the rear. Berin and his 500 Thessalians had circled to the right and charged in on the flanks of the Phocian cavalry, but Parmenion still waited. Philip cursed. A Phocian rider, breaking through the Macedonian outer line, swept towards him with lance levelled. Philip swayed left, the iron point slashing to his right and plunging into his gelding's side. The beast reared in pain but, even while clinging to its back, Philip's sword sliced out in a reverse cut which tore under the Phocian's curved helmet to rip open his throat. Maddened with pain Philip's gelding reared again, then fell. The King leapt clear of the beast's back, but a flailing hoof cracked against his hip and hurled him from his feet.

Seeing the King fall, the Phocians mounted a counter-charge. Philip rolled to his feet, hurled aside his shield and ran at the first rider. The man's lance stabbed out, glancing from the King's breastplate. Philip leapt, dragging the lancer from his horse and stabbing him twice in the belly

15

and groin. Leaving the dying man he ran to the horse, taking hold of the mane and vaulting to its back. But now he was surrounded by Phocian warriors.

A spear opened a long gash in Philip's right thigh, and a sword-blade glanced from his bronze wrist-guard to slice a cut on his left forearm. The King blocked a lunging sword, cleaving his own blade through the man's ribs.

Berin, Attalus and a score of riders attacked the Phocians, forcing them back from the King.

The enemy cavalry were split, the Macedonians surging forward now to engage the enemy infantry. In the brief respite Philip saw his enemy, Onomarchus, standing at the centre of the foot-soldiers, urging them on. 'To me!' yelled Philip, his voice rising above the clashing swords. The Macedonians gathered around him and the King kicked his horse into a run, charging at the first line of shields.

The Phocian line bent in on itself and almost broke, but Onomarchus ordered a second regiment forward to block the charge and Philip was pushed back. A lance plunged into his horse, skewering the heart. The beast collapsed, but once more Philip jumped clear.

'Where are you, Parmenion?' he bellowed.

*

The Spartan general could feel the increasing anxiety in the men behind him. Like all warriors, they knew that the balance of a battle could swing in a matter of moments. This one was teetering. If Philip's cavalry could be pushed back, Onomarchus would use the greater strength of his infantry to split the Macedonian centre and still achieve victory.

Parmenion looked to the left. A hidden force of foot-soldiers had charged from the woods, but Nicanor and his 500 were engaging them. From here it was impossible to gauge the numbers of men Nicanor and his troops were battling to hold, and the Spartan sent a further 200 men to his aid.

'Look!' shouted one of his Thessalians, pointing to the line of hills on the right.

Hundreds of cavalrymen had appeared on the crest.

Philip and his Companion cavalry were caught now between hammer and anvil.

The Phocians charged . . .

Parmenion's arm swept up. 'Forward for Macedon!' he shouted. Drawing his sword the Spartan kicked his stallion into a gallop, heading for the Phocian flank. Behind him the remaining 800 Thessalians drew their curved cavalry sabres and, screaming their war-cries, hurtled after him.

The two forces crashed together on the hillside above the surging mass of warriors fighting for control of the centre ground.

Onomarchus, seeing his cavalry intercepted, screamed out fresh orders to his men, who valiantly tried to form a shield-wall around him. But the Macedonians were pushing now on three sides: Theoparlis and the Guards at the front; Coenus and the Fifth forcing the Spartans back on the left; and the King, cutting and slashing a bloody pathway on the right.

Bodies lay everywhere, being trampled underfoot by the heavily armoured phalanxes, and no longer could a single bloom be seen on the churned earth of the battle site.

But Philip had long since ceased to think of the beauty of flowers. Mounted on his third horse he forced a path between the Phocian shields, hacking his blade down into a warrior's face, seeing the man disappear beneath the hooves of the Macedonian cavalry. Onomarchus was close now and the Phocian leader hurled a javelin which flew over Philip's head.

Suddenly the Phocians, sensing defeat was imminent, broke and fled in all directions. Onomarchus – his dreams of conquest in ruins – drew his sword and waited for death. Theoparlis and the Guards crashed through the last line of defence and, as Onomarchus turned to meet the attack, a *sarissa* clove through his leather kilt, smashing his hip and ripping the giant artery at the groin.

With the Phocian leader dead and his army fleeing in panic, the mercenary units and the contingents from Athens, Corinth and Sparta began a fighting retreat across the Crocus Field.

Philip dismounted before his dead enemy, hacking Onomarchus' head from his shoulders and thrusting the severed neck on to the point of a *sarissa*, which he held high in the air for all men to see.

The battle was over, the victory Philip's. A great weariness settled on the King. His bones ached, his sword-arm was on fire. Letting the *sarissa* fall, he pulled his helmet from his head and sank to the earth staring around the battlefield. Hundreds of men and scores of horses lay dead, the numbers growing even now as the Macedonian cavalry hunted down the fleeing Phocians. Parmenion rode to where Philip sat. Dismounting, he bowed to the King.

'A great victory, sire,' he said softly.

'Yes,' agreed Philip as his one good eye looked up into the Spartan's face. 'Why did you not come when I sent for you?'

Other men – Attalus, Berin, Nicanor and several officers – were close by, and they looked to the Spartan, awaiting his answer. 'You asked me to watch over the battle, sire. I believed Onomarchus would have men in reserve – as indeed he did.'

'Damn you!' Philip roared, surging to his feet. 'When the King gives an order it is obeyed! You understand that simple fact?'

'Indeed I do,' replied the Spartan, his pale eyes gleaming.

'Sire,' put in Nicanor, 'had Parmenion come to you earlier you would have been trapped.'

'Be silent!' thundered Philip. Once more he turned to Parmenion. 'I will not have a man serve me who does not obey my orders.'

'That is a problem easily solved, sire,' said Parmenion coldly. Bowing once he turned and, taking his stallion's reins, stalked from the battlefield.

*

Philip's anger did not abate during the long afternoon. His wounds, though shallow, were painful, his mood dark. He knew he had been unfair to Parmenion, yet in a strange way it only increased his irritation. The man was always so *right*. The King's wounds were bound with wine-soaked bandages and despite the remonstrations of the bald surgeon, Bernios, Philip supervised the removal of all severely wounded Macedonians to a hospital area outside Pagasai before retiring in the early evening to the captured palace at the centre of the deserted city. From here he watched the executions of the 600 Phocian prisoners captured by the cavalry. The killings lifted his mood. Onomarchus had been a strong enemy, a rallying point for all those who feared Macedonia. Without him the roads to central Greece were now open.

At dusk Philip made his way to the *andron*, a large room with nine couches. The walls were covered with murals by the Theban artist, Natiles; they were mostly hunting scenes, horsemen chasing down several lions, but Philip was impressed by the artistry and the vivid colours used. The painter was obviously a man who understood the hunt. His horses were real, the lions lean and deadly, the attitudes of the hunters reflecting both courage and fear. Philip decided to send for the man once this campaign was over. Such scenes would look spectacular in the palace at Pella.

One by one Philip's officers arrived with details of the day's losses. Theoparlis, commander of the Guards, had suffered 110 dead and 70 wounded. Antipater reported 84 dead among the Companion cavalry. In all the Macedonians had lost 307 killed, with 227 wounded.

The Phocians had been virtually annihilated. Two thousand had been slain on the battlefield, with at least another thousand drowning as they fled from the beaches, trying in vain to swim to the waiting Athenian triremes.

This last news cheered Philip considerably. Stretching his powerful frame on the silk-covered couch he drained his fifth cup of wine, feeling his tension evaporate. Glancing at his officers, he chuckled. 'A good day, my friends,' he said, sitting up and refilling his cup from a golden pitcher. But the mood was sombre and no one joined him in a toast. 'What is the matter with you all? Is this how to celebrate a victory?'

Theoparlis stood, bowing awkwardly. He was a burly man, black-bearded and dark-eyed. 'If you will excuse me, sire,' he said, his voice deep with the burr of the northern mountains, 'I wish to see to my men.'

'Of course,' answered Philip. Nicanor rose next, then Coenus and Antipater. Within minutes only Attalus remained.

'What in Hecate's name is wrong with them?' enquired the King, rubbing at his blinded eye.

Attalus cleared his throat and sipped his wine before answering, then his cold eyes met Philip's gaze. 'They want to see Parmenion before he leaves Pagasai,' Attalus told him.

Philip put down his wine-cup and leaned back against the cushioned couch. 'I was too harsh,' he said.

'Not at all, sire,' ventured Attalus. 'You gave an order and it was disobeyed. Now you may have to give another.'

Philip stared at his Champion and sighed. 'Ah, Attalus,' he said softly. 'Once an assassin always an assassin, eh? You think I should fear the man who has kept Macedonia safe all these years?'

Attalus smiled, showing tombstone teeth. 'That is for you to decide, Philip,' he whispered. The King's eye continued to stare at the Champion, remembering their first meeting in Thebes nineteen years before when Attalus was in the pay of Philip's uncle, the King Ptolemaos. The assassin had – for whatever reason – saved Philip's life then and had served him faithfully ever since. But he was a cold, friendless man.

'I shall not have Parmenion killed,' said Philip. 'Go and ask him to come to me.'

'You think that he will?'

Philip shrugged. 'Ask anyway.'

Attalus stood and bowed, leaving Philip alone with the pitcher of wine. The King wandered to the window. From here he could still see the twelve Athenian triremes at anchor in the gulf, moonlight glinting from their polished hulls. Sleek, beautiful craft, yet deadly in battle, with three banks of oars to propel them at the speed of galloping horses so that the bronze rams at the prows could smash to shards the timbers of lesser ships.

'One day,' thought Philip, 'I too will have a fleet to match them.'

His blind eye began to throb painfully and he turned away from the window, pouring yet another cup of wine. Slumping to the couch, he drank slowly and waited for his First General.

'Is it just envy, Parmenion?' he said aloud. 'I loved you once. But I was younger then and you were like a God of War – invincible, unbeatable. But now?' The sound of footsteps came to him and he stood, waiting at the centre of the room.

Parmenion entered, followed by Attalus. Philip moved to the assassin, laying his hand on the man's shoulder. 'Leave us, my friend,' he said.

'As you wish, sire,' answered Attalus, his eyes bleak.

As the door closed Philip turned. Parmenion was standing stiffly, his armour put aside, a pale blue tunic covering his slim frame, a grey riding-cloak hanging from his shoulders. Philip gazed into the tall Spartan's blue eyes.

'How is it, Parmenion, that you look so young? You seem no more than a man approaching thirty, and yet you are what . . . fifty?'

'Forty-eight, sire.'

'Is there some special food you eat?'

'You wanted to see me, sire?'

'You are angry with me, yes?' said the King, forcing a smile. 'Well, I can understand that. Join me in some wine. Go on.' For a moment it seemed the Spartan would refuse, but he picked up the pitcher and filled a cup. 'Now sit down and talk to me.'

'What would you have me say, sire? You gave me two orders. To obey the one, I had to disobey the other. When you are fighting it is I who lead the army. You made this clear to me. "Take whatever action is necessary", you said. What do you want of me, Philip? It is a long ride to Pella.'

'I do not want to lose your friendship,' said Philip, 'but you are making this hard for me. I spoke in haste. Does that satisfy your Spartan pride?'

Parmenion sighed, his tension sliding from him. 'You

will never lose my friendship, Philip. But something has come between us these last two years. What have I done to offend you?'

The King scratched his black beard. 'How many victories are mine?' he asked.

'I do not understand. They are all yours.'

Philip nodded. 'Yet in Sparta they tell all who will listen that it is a renegade Spartan who leads Macedonia to glory. In Athens they say, "Where would Philip be without Parmenion?" Where *would* I be?'

'I see,' said Parmenion, meeting the King's gaze. 'There is nothing I can do about this, Philip. Four years ago your horse won the Olympics. You were not riding him, yet he was still your horse and you took pride in that. I am a *strategos* – that is my calling and my life. You are a king – a fighting king. A Battle King. The soldiers fight the harder because you are alongside them. They love you. Who can say how many battles might have been lost without you?'

'But the only battle I have led alone ended in defeat,' Philip pointed out.

'And would have done so whether I was there or not,' Parmenion assured him. 'Your Paionian scouts were complacent; they did not search the mountains as they should. But there is something else, is there not?'

The King returned to the window, staring once more at the distant triremes. He was silent for a long while, then at last he spoke.

'My son is fond of you,' he said, his voice low. 'Sometimes in his nightmares the nurse tells me he calls your name. Then all is well. It is said that you can hug him – and feel no pain. Is this true?'

'Yes,' whispered the Spartan.

'The child is possessed, Parmenion. Either that or he is a demon. I cannot touch him – I have tried; it is like hot coals burning on my skin. Why is it that you can hold him?'

'I don't know.'

The King gave a harsh laugh, then turned to face his general. 'All of my battles were for him. I wanted a kingdom he could be proud of. I wanted . . . I wanted so much. You remember when we went to Samothrace? Yes? I loved Olympias then more than life. Now we cannot sit in the same room for twenty heartbeats without angry words. And look at me. When we met I was fifteen and you were a warrior grown, what . . . twenty-nine? Now I have grey in my beard. My face is scarred, my eye a pus-filled ball of constant pain. And for what, Parmenion?'

'You have made Macedonia strong, Philip,' said Parmenion, rising. 'And all your dreams should be within reach. What more do you want?'

'I want a son I can hold. A son I can teach to ride, without fearing that the horse will topple and die, rotting before my eyes. I remember nothing of the night on Samothrace when I sired him. I think sometimes he is not my son at all.'

Parmenion's face lost all colour, but Philip was not looking at him.

'Of course he is your son,' said Parmenion, keeping the fear from his voice. 'Who else could be the father?'

'Some demon sent from Hades. I will marry again soon; I will have an heir one day. You know, when Alexander was born they say his first sound was a growl, like a beast. The midwife almost dropped him. They say also that when his eyes first opened they were slitted, like an Egyptian cat. I don't know the truth of it. All I know is that I love the boy . . . and yet I cannot touch him. But enough of this! Are we still friends?'

'I will always be your friend, Philip. I swear it.'

'Then let's get drunk and talk of better days,' ordered the King.

*

Outside the door Attalus felt his anger rising. Silently he moved away down the torchlit corridor and out into the night, the cool breeze only fanning the flames of his hatred.

How could Philip not see what a danger the Spartan presented? Attalus hawked and spat, but still his mouth tasted of bile.

Parmenion. Always Parmenion. The officers adore him, the soldiers are in awe of him. Can you not see what is happening, Philip? You are losing your kingdom to this foreign mercenary. Attalus halted in the shadows of a looming temple and turned. I could wait here, he thought, his fingers curling round the hilt of his dagger. I could step out behind him, ramming the blade into his back, twisting it, ripping open his heart.

But if Philip found out . . . Be patient, he cautioned himself. The arrogant whoreson will bring about his own downfall, with all his misguided concepts of honesty and honour. No King wants honesty. Oh, they all talk of it! 'Give me an honest man,' they say. 'We want no crawling lackeys.' Horse-dung! What they wanted was adoration and agreement. No, Parmenion would not last.

And come the blessed day when he fell from favour it would be Attalus to whom Philip would turn, first to dispose of the loathsome Spartan and then to replace him as First General of Macedonia.

The *strategos*! What was so difficult about winning a battle? Strike at the enemy with the force of a storm, crushing the centre and killing the enemy king or general. But Parmenion had fooled them all, making them believe there was some wondrous mystery. And why? Because he was a coward, seeking always to hang back from the battle itself, keeping himself out of harm's way. None of them could see it. Blind fools!

Attalus drew his dagger, enjoying the silver gleam of moonlight upon the blade. 'One day,' he whispered, 'this will kill you, Spartan.'

The Temple, Asia Minor, Summer

Derae was weary, almost at the point of exhaustion, when the last supplicant was carried into the Room of Healing. The two men laid the child on the altar bed and stepped back, respectfully keeping their eyes from the face of the blind Healer. Derae took a deep breath, calming herself, then laid her hands on the child's brow, her spirit swimming into the girl's bloodstream, flowing with it, feeling the heartbeat weak and fluttering. The injury was at the base of the spine – the vertebrae cracked, nerve endings crushed, muscles wasting.

With infinite care Derae healed the bone, eliminating adhesions, relieving the pressure on the swollen nerve points, forcing blood to flow over the injured tissue.

Drawing herself back into her body, the priestess sighed and swayed. Instantly a man leapt forward to assist her, his hand brushing against her arm.

'Leave me be!' she snapped, pulling away from him.

'I am sorry, lady,' he whispered. Waving her hand, she smiled in his direction.

'Forgive me, Laertes. I am tired.'

'How did you know my name?' the man asked, his voice hushed. Derae laughed then.

'I heal the blind and no one questions my Gift. The lame walk and people say, "Ah, but she is a Healer." But so

25

simple a matter as knowing an unspoken name, and there is awe. You touched me, Laertes. And in touching me gave up all your secrets. But fear not, you are a good man. Your daughter was kicked by a horse, yes?'

'Yes, lady.'

'The blow injured the bones of her back. I have taken away the pain and tomorrow, when I have rested, I will heal her. You may stay here this evening. My servants will bring you food.'

'Thank you,' he said. 'I have money. . . ' Waving him to silence Derae walked away, her step sure. Two female servants pulled open the altar room doors as she approached, a third taking her arm in the corridor beyond and leading the blind Healer to her room.

Once inside, Derae sipped cool water and lay down on the narrow pallet bed. So many sick, so many injured . . . each day the queues beyond the Temple grew. At times there were fights, and many of those who finally reached her had been forced to bribe their way to the altar room. Often during the last few years Derae had tried to put a stop to the practice. But, even with her powers, she could not fight human nature. The people beyond the Temple walls had a need only she could satisfy. And, where there was need, there was profit to be made. Now a Greek mercenary called Pallas had thirty men camped before the Temple. And he organized the queues, selling tokens of admission to the supplicants, establishing some order to the chaos.

Unable to thwart him fully, Derae had demanded he allow five poor people a day to be led to her, against ten of the richer. He had tried to trick her on the first day, and she had refused to see anyone. Now the system worked. Pallas hired servants, cooks, maids, gardeners, to tend to Derae's needs. But even this irritated her, for she knew he merely wanted her time spent earning him money by healing the sick, and not engaged in *useless* pursuits like gardening, which she loved, or cooking or cleaning. And yet, despite the motive, it did mean that more people were being cured. Should I be grateful to him, she wondered? No. Greed was his inspiration, gold his joy.

She pushed all thoughts of him from her mind. Closing her blind eyes, Derae floated clear of her body. There was freedom here, with the flight of Spirit; there was even joy in the form of a transient happiness free of care. While her body rested Derae flew across the Thermaic Gulf, high above the trident-shaped lands of the Chalcidice and on across the Pierian mountains to Thessaly, her spirit called there by the lover of her youth.

So long ago now, she realized. Thirty years had passed since she and Parmenion lay together in Xenophon's summer home, lost in the exuberance of their youthful passion.

She found him in the captured city of Pagasai, walking from the palace. His step was unsteady and she saw that he had been drinking. But more than this, she sensed the sadness within him. Once Derae had believed they would spend their lives together, willingly locked into love, chained by desires that were not all of the flesh. Not all. . . ? She remembered his gentle touch, the heat of his body upon hers, the softness of his skin, the power in the muscles beneath, the warmth of his smile, the love in his eyes. . . . Despair whispered across her soul.

She was now an ageing priestess in a far-off temple, he a general in Macedonia's triumphant army. Worse, he had believed her dead for these last thirty years.

Sorrow followed the touch of despair, but she put it aside and moved closer to him, feeling the warmth of his spirit.

'I always loved you,' she told him. 'Nothing ever changed that. And I will watch over you as long as I live.'

But he could not hear her. A cold breeze touched her spirit and, with a sudden rush of fear, she knew she was not alone. Soaring high into the sky she clothed her spirit body in armour of light, a sword of white fire burning in her hand.

'Show yourself!' she commanded. A man's form materialized close by. He was tall, with short-cropped grey hair and a beard curled in the Persian manner. He smiled and opened his arms. 'It is I, Aristotle,' he said.

'Why do you spy on me?' she asked.

'I came to see you at the Temple, but it is guarded by money-hungry mercenaries who would not allow me to enter. And we must talk.'

'What is there to talk about? The child was born, the Chaos Spirit is within him, and all the futures show he will bring torment to the world. I had hoped to aid him, to help him retain his humanity. But I cannot. The Dark God is stronger than I.'

Aristotle shook his head. 'Not so. Your reasoning is flawed, Derae. Now how can I come to you?'

She sighed. 'There is a small side gate in the western wall. Be there at midnight; I will open the gate. Now leave me in peace for a while.'

'As you wish,' he answered. And vanished.

Alone once more, Derae followed Parmenion to the field hospital, watching as he moved among the wounded men, discussing their injuries with the little surgeon, Bernios. But she could not find the peace she sought and took to the night sky, floating beneath the stars.

It had been four years since the *magus* who called himself Aristotle had come to the Temple. His visit had led to tragedy. Together Derae and the *magus* had sent Parmenion's spirit into the vaults of Hades to save the soul of the unborn Alexander. But it had all been for nothing. The Chaos Spirit had merged with the soul of the child, and Derae's closest friend – the reformed warrior Leucion – had been torn to pieces by demons sent to destroy her.

Returning to the Temple, she rose from the bed and washed in cold water, rubbing her body with perfumed leaves. She did not allow her spirit eyes to gaze upon her ageing frame, could not bear to see herself as she now was – her hair silver, body thin and wasted, breasts sagging. Dressing in a clean full-length *chiton* of dark green, she sat by the window waiting for midnight. Outside the Temple the campfires were burning, scores of them. Some supplicants would wait half a year to see the Healer. Many would die before they could redeem their tokens. Once, before the arrival of Pallas, she had tried to walk among the sick, healing as many as she could. But she had been mobbed, knocked to the ground, saved only by her friend and servant Leucion who had beaten the crowds back with a club. Derae still mourned the warrior who had died defending her helpless body against the demons sent to destroy her.

She pictured his face – the long silver hair tied at the nape of the neck, the arrogant walk, the easy smile.

'I miss you,' she whispered.

Just before midnight, guided by her spirit sight, she crept down to the western gate, sliding back the bolt. Aristotle stepped inside. Locking the gate, she took him back to her room where the *magus* poured himself some water and sat on the narrow bed. 'Do you mind if I light a lantern?' he asked.

'The blind have no need of lanterns. But I will fetch you one.'

'Do not concern yourself, lady.' Reaching out he took a silver winecup, holding it high. The metal twisted, folding in on itself to form a spout from which a flame flickered and grew, bathing the room in light. 'You are not looking well, Derae,' he said. 'Your duties are leaving you overtired.'

'Come to the point of your visit,' she told him coldly.

'No,' he answered. 'First we must talk of the many futures. Has it occurred to you that there is a contradiction in our travels through time?'

'If you mean that the futures we see can change, of course it has.'

He smiled and shook his head. 'But do they change? That is the question.'

'Of course they do. I remember old Tamis telling me she saw her own deaths in many futures. In one, she said, she fell from a horse, even though riding was abhorrent to her.'

'Exactly my point,' said Aristotle. 'Now, let me explain: Tamis saw herself falling from a horse. But that is not how she died. So then – who fell from the horse?'

Derae sat down on a cushioned chair, her spirit eyes locked to the *magus'* face. 'Tamis,' she answered. 'But the futures were changed by events in the past.'

'But that is where the contradiction lies,' he told her. 'We are not talking of prophetic visions here, Derae. You and I – and Tamis once – can *travel* to the many futures, observing them. What we are seeing *is* happening . . . somewhere. All the futures are *real*.'

'How can they all be real?' she mocked. 'Tamis died but once – as will I.'

'I do not have all the answers, my dear, but I know this: there are many worlds, thousands, all akin to ours. Perhaps every time a man makes a decision he creates a new world. I don't know. What I do know is that it is folly to examine all these alternate worlds and base our actions upon events in them. I too have seen Alexander drag the world down into blood and chaos. I have seen him kill Philip and seize the throne. I have seen him dead as a child, from plague, from a dog-bite, from an assassin's blade. But, do you not see, none of it matters? None of the futures are ours. They are merely echoes, reflections, indications of what might be.'

Derae was silent, considering his words. 'It is an interesting concept. I will think on it. Now, to the point of your visit?'

Aristotle lay back on the bed, his eyes watching the flickering shadows on the low ceiling. 'The point – as always – concerns the boy in this world. You and I took Parmenion into Hades, where the child's soul merged with the Spirit of Chaos. We took it to be a defeat. But it may not prove to be so.'

'A curious kind of victory,' sneered Derae. 'The boy carries a great evil. It is growing within him worse than any cancer, and he does not have the strength to fight it.'

'He had the strength to stop it destroying Parmenion in the Void,' Aristotle pointed out. 'But let us not argue; let us instead think of ways of helping the child.'

Derae shook her head. 'I long ago learned the folly of seeking to change the future. Had I known then what I know now, there would have been no Demon Prince.'

'I think that there would, lady,' said Aristotle softly, 'but it does not matter. The child is no different from the many who are brought to you each day – only he is not crippled in the flesh, he is tormented in the spirit. Neither of us has the power to cast out the demon. But together – and with the boy's help – we might yet return the Dark God to the Underworld.'

Derae laughed then, the sound full of bitterness. 'I heal wounds, *magus*. I am not equipped to battle Kadmilos. Nor do I wish to.'

'What do you wish, lady?'

'I wish to be left alone,' she said.

'No!' he thundered, rising to his feet. 'I will not accept that from a woman of Sparta! What has happened to you, Derae? You are no lamb waiting for the slaughter. You are from a race of warriors. You fought the Dark Lady on Samothrace. Where is your spirit?'

Derae sighed. 'You seek to make me angry,' she whispered. 'You will not succeed. Look at me, Aristotle. I am getting old. I live here, and I heal the sick. I will do that until I die. Once I had a dream. I have it no longer. Now leave me in peace.'

'I can give you back your youth,' he said, his voice coaxing, his eyes bright with promise.

For a moment she stood silently, observing him without expression. 'So,' she said, at last, 'it was you. When I healed Parmenion of his cancer, I watched him grow young before my eyes. I thought it was the healing.'

'You can be young also. You can find your dream again.'

'You are a *magus* – and yet a fool,' she told him, her voice flat, her tone tired. 'Parmenion is married; he has three children. There is no place for me now. We may be able to meddle in the futures – but the past is iron.'

Aristotle stood and moved to the door. There he turned as if to speak, but shook his head and walked away into the darkness of the Temple corridor.

Derae listened until his footsteps faded, then sank to the bed, Aristotle's promise echoing in her mind: *'I can make you young again.'*

He was wrong, she knew. Oh, he could work his magic on her body, strengthening her muscles, tightening her skin. But youth was a state of mind. No one, god or man, could give her back her innocence, the joy of discovery, the

31

beauty of first love. Without that, what value would there be in a young and supple body?

She felt the rush of tears and saw again the young Parmenion standing alone against the raiders who had abducted her; lived once more the moment when he first held her.

'I love you,' she whispered.

And she wept.

★

Before allowing herself the luxury of sleep, Derae traced the lines of three protective spells on the walls, door and window of her room. They would not stop a seeress with the power of Aida, but any disruption to the spells would wake Derae in time to protect herself.

It was almost five years since the last attack, when Leucion had died defending her against the demons sent by the sorceress. Since then Derae had heard little of Aida. The Dark Lady had left her palace in Samothrace and journeyed back to the mainland – travelling, according to rumour, to the northern edges of the Persian empire, there to await Alexander's coming-of-age. Derae shivered.

The child of Chaos, soon to be a destroyer such as the earth had seldom witnessed.

Her thoughts turned to Parmenion and she climbed on to the bed, covering herself with a thin sheet of white linen. The night was warm and close, the merest breath of breeze drifting in through the open window. Seeking the sanctuary of sleep, Derae pictured Parmenion as he had been all those years ago – the bitter young man, despised by his fellows, who had found love in the tranquil hills of Olympia. Moment by moment she savoured the heady joys of their five days together, stopping her memories short of that awful morning when her father had dragged her from the house and sent her in shame back to Sparta. Slowly, dreamily, she drifted into a new dream where strange beasts –half-horse half-man – ran through forest trails, and dryads, beautiful and bewitching, sat by sparkling streams. Here was peace. Here was joy.

But the dream moved on and she saw an army marching, cities ablaze, thousands slain. The warriors wore black cloaks and armour, and carried round shields emblazoned with a huge sunburst.

At the centre of the horde rode a warrior in a black cuirass edged with gold. He was black-bearded and handsome, and she recognized him instantly. Yet there was something about him that was strange, different. Floating close to him, she saw that his right eye was made of gold, seemingly molten, and she felt the black touch of his spirit reaching out like ice and flame to freeze and burn.

Recoiling she tried to flee, seeking the peace of the enchanted wood where the centaurs roamed. But she could not escape and a new vision flowed before her spirit eyes.

She saw a palace, grim and shadow-haunted, and a child weeping in a small room. The King came to him there. Derae tried to block her ears and eyes to the scene. To no avail. The man approached the weeping child, and in his hand was a long, curved dagger.

'Father, please!' the child begged.

Derae screamed as the knife clove through the boy's chest. The scene shimmered and she saw the King leave the room, his mouth and beard streaming with blood.

'Am I immortal now?' he asked a shaven-headed priest who waited outside the room.

The man bowed, his hooded eyes avoiding the gaze of his King. 'You have added perhaps twenty years to your life-span, sire. But this was not the Golden Child.'

'Then find him!' roared the King, blood spraying from his lips and staining the man's pale robes.

The invisible chains holding Derae to the scene fell away and the Healer fled, coming awake in her darkened room.

'You saw?' asked Aristotle, his voice soft.

'So, it was your doing,' she answered, sitting up and reaching for a goblet of water from the table beside the bed.

'I sent you there,' he admitted, 'but what you saw was real. There are many sides to Chaos, Derae, in many worlds. In the Greece you saw there is already a Demon King.'

'Why did you show it to me? What purpose did it serve?'

Aristotle rose and walked to the window, staring out over the moonlit sea. 'You recognized the King?'

'Of course.'

'He has murdered all his children in a bid to achieve immortality. Now he seeks a child of legend, Iskander.'

'What has this to do with me? Speak swiftly, *magus*, for I am tired.'

'The enchantment in the world you saw is fading, the centaurs and other creatures of beauty dying with it. They believe that a child will come, a Golden Child, and that he will save them all. The King seeks that golden child; he believes that by eating his heart he will gain immortality. Perhaps he is right.' Aristotle shrugged. 'There are many ways of extending a life. However, even that is not the point. His priests can form small gateways between worlds, and now they are searching for that special boy. They think they have found him.'

'Alexander?' whispered Derae. 'They will take Alexander?'

'They will try.'

'And remove him from our world? Surely that is to be desired?'

Aristotle's eyes narrowed. 'You think it desirable that another child should have his heart cut from his body?'

'I do not think I like you,' whispered Derae. 'You are not doing this for the Source, or even to fight Chaos.'

'No,' he admitted. 'It is for me alone. My own life is in peril. Will you help me?'

'I will think on it,' she replied. 'Now leave me in peace.'

Pella, Macedonia, Summer

Alexander lifted his hand and stared at the blue and grey bird perched in the lowest branches of the tall cypress tree. The tiny creature fluffed out its feathers and cocked its head to one side, regarding the golden-haired child.

'Come to me,' the boy whispered. The bird hopped along the branch, then took to the air, swooping over the child's head. Alexander waited, statue-still, his concentration intense. With his eyes closed he could follow the bird's flight up over the garden wall, circling back to the palace and down, ever closer to the outstretched arm. Twice the finch sped by him, but the third time its tiny talons sought purchase on his index finger. Alexander opened his eyes and gazed down at the creature. 'We are friends then?' he asked, his voice gentle. Once more the bird cocked its head and Alexander could feel its tension and its fear. Slowly he reached over with his left hand to stroke the finch's back.

Suddenly he felt the surge of killing power swelling within him, his heartbeat increasing, his arm beginning to tremble. Holding it back, desperately he began to count aloud. But as he reached seven he felt the awful flow of death along his arm.

'Fly!' he commanded. The finch soared into the air.

Alexander sank to the grass, the lust for death departing as swiftly as it had come. 'I will not give in,' he whispered. 'I will reach ten – and then twenty. And one day I will stop it for ever.'

Never, came the dark voice of his heart. *You will never defeat me. You are mine. Now and always.*

Alexander shook his head and stood, forcing the voice away, deeper and deeper inside. The sun was beginning to drop towards the distant mountains and the boy moved into the cool shadows of the western wall. From here he could see the sentries at the gate, their armour bright, their bronze helms gleaming like gold. Tall men, stern of eye, proud, angry because they had been left behind when the King rode to battle.

The guards stiffened to attention, lifting their lances to the vertical. Excitement flared in the boy as the sentries saluted someone beyond the gate. Alexander began to run along the path.

'Parmenion!' he cried, his high-pitched voice disturbing scores of birds in the trees. 'Parmenion!'

*

The general returned the salute and walked into the gardens, smiling as he saw the four-year-old running towards him with arms outstretched. The Spartan knelt and the boy threw himself into his arms.

'We won, didn't we, Parmenion! We crushed the Phocians!'

'We did indeed, young prince. Now be careful you don't scratch yourself on my armour.' Detaching the boy's arms from around his neck, Parmenion loosened the leather thongs on the gilded ear-guards of his helmet, pulling it loose and laying it on the grass. Alexander sat down beside the helm, brushing his small fingers across the white horsehair crest.

'Father fought like a lion. I know, I watched it. He attacked the enemy flank, and had three horses killed under him. Then he cut the head from the traitor, Onomarchus.'

'Yes, he did all that. But he will tell you himself when he comes home.'

'No,' said Alexander softly, shaking his head. 'He won't

tell me. He doesn't speak to me often. He doesn't like me. Because I kill things.'

Parmenion reached out, drawing the boy close and ruffling his hair. 'He loves you, Alexander, I promise you. But, if it pleases you, I will tell you of the battle.'

'I know about the battle. Truly. But Father should beware of neck cuts. With his blind eye he needs to swing his head more than a warrior should, and that bares the veins of the throat. He needs to have a collar made, of leather and bronze.'

Parmenion nodded. 'You are very wise. Come, let us go inside. I am thirsty from the journey and the sun is too hot.'

'Can I ride your shoulders? Can I?'

The Spartan rose smoothly and, taking the prince by the arms, swung him high. The boy squealed with excitement as he settled into place. Parmenion scooped up his helm and walked back towards the palace. The guards saluted once more, the prince's nursemaids dropping to their knees as he passed. 'I feel like a King,' shouted Alexander. 'I am taller than any man!'

Olympias came out into the garden, her servants behind her. The Spartan took a deep breath as he saw her. With her tightly-curled red hair and her green eyes, she was the image of the Derae he had loved so many years before. The Queen was dressed in a sea-green gown of Asian silk, held in place at the shoulder by a brooch of gold shaped like a sunburst. She laughed aloud as she saw the Spartan general and his burden. Parmenion bowed, Alexander screaming with mock fear as he almost came loose.

'Greetings, lady. I bring you your son.'

Olympias stepped forward, kissing Parmenion's cheek. 'Always the welcome visitor,' she told him. Turning to her servants, she ordered wine and fruit for her guest and ushered him into her apartments. Everywhere there were fine silk hangings, brocaded couches, cushioned chairs, and the walls were beautifully painted with Homeric scenes. Parmenion lifted Alexander and lowered him to a couch, but the boy scrambled clear and took hold of the general's hand.

'Look, Mother. I can hold Parmenion's hand. There is no pain, is there, Parmenion?'

'No pain,' he answered.

'He saved Father's life. He led the counter-charge against the Phocian cavalry. They couldn't fool you, could they, Parmenion?'

'No,' the Spartan agreed.

Two female servants helped Parmenion from his breastplate and a third brought him a goblet of wine mixed with cool water. Yet another girl entered, bearing a bowl of fruit which she placed in front of him before bowing and running from the room.

The Spartan waited until the servants had been dismissed and then raised his goblet to the Queen. 'Your beauty improves with every year,' he said.

She nodded. 'The compliment is a pretty one, my friend, but let us talk of more serious matters. Are you out of favour with Philip?'

'The King says not,' he told her.

'But that is not an answer.'

'No.'

'He is jealous of you,' said Alexander softly.

The Queen's eyes widened in surprise. 'You should not speak of matters you do not understand,' she chided. 'You are too young to know what the King thinks.' Alexander met her gaze but said nothing, and the Queen looked back at the general. 'You will not leave us, will you?'

Parmenion shook his head. 'Where would I go, lady? My family are here. I will spend the autumn at my estates; Mothac tells me there is much to do.'

'How is Phaedra? Have you seen her?' asked Olympias, keeping her voice neutral.

Parmenion shrugged. 'Not yet. She was well when last I saw her. The birth of Hector was troublesome and she was weak for a while.'

'And the other boys?'

The Spartan chuckled then. 'Philotas is always getting into trouble, but his mother spoils him, giving way in everything. Nicci is more gentle; he is only two, but he follows Philo everywhere. He adores him.'

'Phaedra is very lucky,' said Olympias. 'She must be so happy.'

Parmenion drained his watered wine and stood. 'I should be riding home,' he said.

'No! No!' cried Alexander. 'You promised to tell me of the battle.'

'A promise should always be kept,' said the Queen.

'Indeed it should,' the general agreed. 'So, young prince, ask me your questions.'

'How many Macedonian casualties were there?'

Leaning forward, Parmenion ruffled the child's golden hair. 'Your questions fly like arrows to their target, Alexander. We lost just over three hundred men, with around two hundred badly wounded.'

'We should have more surgeons,' said the boy. 'The dead should not outnumber the wounded.'

'Most of the dead come from the early casualties,' the Spartan told him. 'They bleed to death during the battle – before the surgeons can get to them. But you are correct in that we need more skilled physicians. I will speak to your father.'

'When I am King we will not suffer such losses,' the boy promised. 'Will you be my general, Parmenion?'

'I may be a little old by then, my prince. Your father is still a young man – and a mighty warrior.'

'I will be mightier still,' promised the child.

*

The meeting with the Queen and her son disturbed Parmenion as he rode north towards his vast estates on the Emathian Plain. The boy, as all men knew, was possessed, and Parmenion remembered with both fear and pride the battle for the child's soul in the Valley of Hades five years before.

It was a time of miracles. Parmenion, dying of a cancer in the brain, had fallen into a coma – only to open his eyes to a world of nightmare, grey, soulless, twisted and barren.

Here he had been met by the *magus*, Aristotle, and together with the dead sorceress Tamis had tried to save the soul of the unborn Alexander.

Conceived on the mystic isle of Samothrace, the child was intended to be the human vessel of the Dark God, Kadmilos, destined to bring chaos and terror to the world. A small victory had been won in the Valley of the Damned. The child's soul had not been destroyed by the evil, but had merged with it, Light and Dark in a constant war.

Poor Alexander, thought Parmenion. A brilliant child, beautiful and sensitive, yet host to the Spirit of Chaos.

'Will you be my general, Parmenion?'

Parmenion had longed to say, 'Yes, my prince, I will lead your armies across the world.'

But, what if the Dark God won? What if the prince of beauty became the prince of demons?

The bay gelding crested the last hill before the estate and Parmenion drew rein and sat, staring down at his home. The white stone of the great house shone in the sunlight, the groves of cypress trees around it standing like sentries. Away to the left lay the smaller houses of the servants and farm-workers and to the right, the stables, paddocks and pastures to house Parmenion's growing herd of war-horses.

The general shaded his eyes, scanning the grounds of the great house. There was Phaedra, sitting by the fountain with Philo and Nicci beside her, little Hector in her arms. Parmenion's heart sank. Swinging his horse to the east he rode down onto the plain, skirting the great house and angling towards the stable buildings.

*

Mothac sat in the hay stroking the mare's long neck, whispering words of comfort. She grunted and struggled to stand. Mothac rose with her.

'No movement yet,' said his assistant, Croni, a wiry Thessalian who stood at the rear waiting to assist the birth of the foal.

'Good girl,' Mothac whispered to the mare. 'You'll do right. This is not the first, eh, Larina? Three fine stallions

40

you have borne.' Stroking the mare's face and neck, he ran his hands along her back and moved alongside the Thessalian.

The mare had been in labour now for several hours and was weary to the point of exhaustion. The old Theban knew it was unusual for a birth to be so delayed. Most mares foaled swiftly with few problems.

Always in the past Larina had delivered with speed, her foals strong. But this time they had covered her with the Thracian stallion, Titan, a huge beast of more than seventeen hands.

The mare grunted once more and lay down. Pushing Croni aside, Mothac gently eased his hand inside her, his fingers feeling for the water-sac.

'Be careful, master,' whispered the Thessalian. Mothac grunted and swore at the man, who chuckled and shook his head.

'Yes! It's coming. I can feel the feet.'

'Front or back?' asked Croni nervously. A breech birth, both men knew, would likely see the foal born dead.

'I can't tell. But it's moving. Wait! I can feel the head. By Zeus, it's big.' Easing his hand back Mothac stood and stretched. For the last two years his spine had been steadily stiffening, his shoulders becoming arthritic and painful. 'Fetch some grease, Croni. I fear the foal is tearing her apart.'

The Thessalian ran back to the main house, reappearing minutes later with a tub of animal fat, mostly used for the painting of hooves, to prevent sand-cracks and splitting. Mothac took the tub and smelt it.

'This is no good,' he grunted. 'It's almost rancid. Get some olive oil – and be quick about it!'

'Yes, master.'

He returned with a large jug in which Mothac dipped his hands, smearing the oil inside the mare, around the head and hooves of the foal. The mare strained once more and the foetal sac moved closer.

'That's it, Larina, my pet,' said Mothac. 'A little more now.'

41

The two men waited beside the mare for some time before the sac appeared, pale and semi-translucent. The foal's front legs could just be seen within the membrane.

'Shall I help her, master?' Croni asked.

'Not yet. Give her time; she's an old hand at this by now.'

The mare grunted and the sac moved further into view – then stopped. Bright blood spouted over the membrane, dripping to the hay. The mare was sweating freely now, and in some distress as Mothac moved to the rear and gently took hold of the foal's front legs, easing them towards him. At any time now the membranes would burst, and it was vital the foal's head should be clear, otherwise it would suffocate. Mothac pulled gently while the Thessalian moved to the mare's head, talking to her, his voice low, coaxing and soft.

With a convulsive surge the sac came clear, dropping to the hay. Mothac peeled away the membranes from around the foal's mouth and nostrils, wiping the body with fresh hay. The new-born was a jet-black male, the image of its sire down to the white starburst on its brow. It lifted its head and shivered violently.

'Aya!' exulted Croni. 'You have a son, Larina! A horse for a king! And such a size! Never have I seen a bigger foal.'

Within minutes the foal tried to stand and Mothac helped it to its feet, guiding it towards the mare. Larina, though exhausted, also rose, and after several unsuccessful attempts the new-born found the teat and began to feed.

Mothac patted the mare and walked out into the sunshine, washing his hands and arms in a bucket of water. The sun was high and he picked up his felt hat, covering the sensitive skin of his bald head.

He was tired, but he felt at peace with the world. Foaling always brought this feeling – the beauty of birth, the onward movement of life.

Croni moved alongside him. 'There is great loss of blood, master. The mare may die.'

Mothac looked down at the little man, noting his concern. 'Stay with her. If she is still bleeding in two hours, come and find me. I shall be in the western pasture.'

'Yes, master,' answered Croni. The Thessalian gazed up at the hills. 'Look, master, the lord is home once more.'

Glancing up, Mothac saw the rider. He was still too far away to be recognized by the old Theban, but the horse was Parmenion's second mount, a spirited bay gelding with a white face.

Mothac sighed and shook his head. 'You should have gone home first, Parmenion,' he thought sadly.

*

'Another victory for the Lion of Macedon,' said Mothac, pouring Parmenion a goblet of wine.

'Yes,' answered the general, stretching his lean frame out on the couch. 'How goes it here?'

'With the horses? Twenty-six foals. The last is a beauty. Larina's, the son of the Thracian stallion. Pure black he is, Parmenion, and what a size! Would you like to see him?'

'Not now, my friend. I am tired.'

The thick-set Theban sat opposite his friend, filling his own goblet and sipping the contents. 'Why did you not go home?'

'I shall. I wanted first to see how the farm fared.'

'I have to clear enough horse-dung all day,' snapped Mothac. 'Don't bring it into my house.'

Parmenion loosened the thongs of his riding-boots, pulling them clear. 'So tetchy, my friend! Maybe it is for the joy of your company. What difference does it make, Mothac? These are my estates and I go where I will. I am tired. Do you object then to my staying the night?'

'You know that I do not. But you have a wife and family waiting for you – and beds far more comfortable than any that I can offer.'

'Comfort, I find, is more to do with the spirit than the softness of beds,' said the Spartan. 'I am comfortable here. You are getting more irritable these days, Mothac. What is wrong with you?'

'Age, my boy,' answered the Theban, controlling his temper. 'But if you don't want to talk to me I won't press you. I will see you this evening.'

Mothac found his anger growing as he walked from the house and up the long hill to the western pasture. For more than thirty years he had served Parmenion, as both servant and friend, but these last five years had seen the Spartan become more distant, more secretive. He had warned him against marrying Phaedra. At seventeen the child was too young, even for the ever-youthful Spartan, and there was something about her . . . a coldness that radiated from her eyes. Mothac remembered, with an affection born of hindsight, Parmenion's Theban lover – the former whore, Thetis. Now there was a woman! Strong, confident, loving! But, like his own beloved Elea, she was dead.

He paused at the brow of the hill, watching the workers clear the dung from the first pasture. It was not a task his Thessalians enjoyed, but it helped control the worms which infested the horses. While grazing, a horse would eat the worm larvae in the grass. These would breed in the stomach and develop into egg-laying worms, the new eggs being passed in the droppings. After a while all pastures would be contaminated, causing stunted growth, or even deaths, among the young foals. Mothac had learned this two years before from a Persian horse-trader, and ever since had ordered his men to clear the pastures daily.

At first the Thessalians had been hard to convince. Superb horsemen, they did not take well to such menial tasks. But when the worm infestations were seen to fade and the foals grew stronger, the tribesmen had taken to the work with a vengeance. Strangely, it also helped to make Mothac more popular among them. They had found it hard to work for a man who rarely rode and, when he did, displayed none of the talents for horsemanship so prized among their people. But Mothac's skills lay in training and rearing, healing wounds and curing diseases. For these talents the riders grew to respect him, viewing even his irascible nature with fondness.

Mothac wandered on to the training field where young horses learned to follow the subtle signals of a rider, cutting left and right, darting into the charge, swerving and coming to a dead halt to allow the rider to release an arrow.

This was work the horsemen loved. In the evenings they would sit around communal camp-fires discussing the merits of each horse, arguing long into the night.

The training was being concluded when Mothac approached the field. The youngster, Orsin, was taking a two-year-old black mare over the jumps. Mothac leaned on a fence-post and watched. Orsin had rare talent, even among Thessalians, and he sailed the mare over each jump, turning her smoothly to face the next. Seeing Mothac, he waved and vaulted from the mare's back.

'Ola, master!' he called. 'You wish to ride?'

'Not today, boy. How are they faring?'

The youngster ran to the fence and clambered over it. On the ground the boy was ungainly to the point of clumsiness. 'There will be six of the stallions to geld, master. They are too high-spirited.'

'Give their names to Croni. When will the new pasture be ready?'

'Tomorrow. Croni says the lord is home. How did the stallion behave in battle?'

'I have not had time to ask him. But I will. There is a Persian trader due in the next few days. He seeks five stallions – the best we have. He is due to come to me at the house, but I don't doubt he will ride out to check the horses before announcing himself. Watch out for him. I do not want him to see the new Thracian stock, so take them to the High Fields.'

'Yes, master. But what of Titan? There is a horse even I would be glad to see the back of.'

'He stays,' said Mothac. 'The lord Parmenion likes him.'

'He is evil, that one. He will see his rider dead, I think.'

'The lord Parmenion has a way with horses.'

'Aya! I would like to see him ride Titan. He will fall very hard.'

'Perhaps,' agreed Mothac, 'but on the day you would be wise to consider placing a different bet. Now finish your grooming – and remember what I said about the Persian.'

*

Parmenion was mildly drunk, and at ease for the first time in months. The wide doors of the *andron* were open to the north winds and a gentle breeze filtered through the hangings, leaving the room pleasantly cool. It was not a large room, with only three couches, and the walls were bare of ornament or paintings. Mothac liked to live simply and never entertained, yet there was a warmth about his home that Parmenion missed when away from the estate.

'Are you happy?' asked the Spartan suddenly.

'Are you talking to me or yourself?' Mothac countered.

'By the gods, you are sharp tonight. I was talking to you.'

'Happy enough. This is life, Parmenion. I watch things grow, the barley and the grain, the horses and the cattle. It makes me part of the land. Yes, I am content.'

Parmenion nodded, his expression grave. 'That must be a good feeling.' He grinned and sat up. 'Do you still miss Persia and the palace?'

'No. This is my home.' The Theban leaned forward, gripping the Spartan's shoulder. 'We have been friends for a lifetime, Parmenion. Can you not tell me what is troubling you?'

Parmenion's hand came up to grip Mothac's arm. 'It is because we are friends that I do not. Five years ago I had a cancer in my brain. That was healed. But now there is a different kind of cancer in my heart – no, not a real one, my friend,' he said swiftly, seeing the concern in the old Theban's eyes. 'But I dare not talk of it – even to you – for it would put a heavy burden on you. Trust me in this, Mothac. You are my dearest friend and I would die for you. But do not ask me to share my . . . my sorrow.'

Mothac said nothing for a moment, then he refilled their goblets. 'Then let us get drunk and talk nonsense,' he said, forcing a smile.

'That would be good. What duties have you set yourself for tomorrow?'

'I have two lame horses I will be taking to the lake. Swimming helps to strengthen their muscles. After that I shall be horse-trading with a Persian named Parzalamis.'

'I will see you by the lake at noon,' said the Spartan.

The two men walked out into the night and Mothac saw a lantern burning in the foaling stable. Cursing softly he walked across to the building, Parmenion following. Inside Croni, Orsin and three other Thessalians were sitting round the body of the mare, Larina. The pure black foal was lying beside its dead mother.

'Why did you not call me?' thundered Mothac. Croni stood and bowed low.

'The bleeding stopped, master. She only collapsed a short while ago.'

'We must get the foal another milk mare.'

'Terias has gone to fetch one, master,' Orsin told him.

Mothac moved past the dark-haired boy and knelt by the mare, laying his huge hand on her neck. 'You were a fine dam, Larina. The best,' he said.

Croni sidled forward. 'It is the curse of Titan,' he said. 'He is a demon beast, and the son will be the same.'

'Nonsense!' said Parmenion, his voice harsh. 'Have Titan in the riding circle tomorrow. I shall tame him.'

'Yes, lord,' answered Croni miserably. 'It will be as you say.'

Turning on his heel Parmenion strode from the stable. Mothac caught up with him, grabbing his arm. 'You should not have said that,' he whispered. 'The Thessalians know their horseflesh. The beast is insane – and so are you if you attempt to ride him.'

'I have said what I will do,' Parmenion muttered. 'I have not seen a horse I cannot ride.'

'I hope you can say that tomorrow,' grunted Mothac.

*

The great house was silent as Parmenion rode through the cypress grove towards the main doors. Not a light showed at any window, yet as he reached the front of the house his manservant, Peris, ran forward to take the gelding's reins.

Parmenion leapt to the ground. 'Well met, Peris, does nothing escape your attention?' he asked, smiling.

The servant bowed. 'I saw you this afternoon, lord, on the hilltop. I have been waiting for you. There is cold meat and cheese in the *andron*, and some pomegranates. Eissa made cakes this afternoon. I will have some brought to you if you desire it.'

'Thank you. How is the arm?'

Peris lifted the leather-covered stump at the end of his right arm. 'It is healing well, lord. There is little pain now, but what there is seems to come from the fingers – as if they are still there. But – as you said – I am becoming more skilful with my left.'

Parmenion patted the man's shoulder. 'I missed you at the Crocus Field. I felt almost unsafe.'

Peris nodded, his dark eyes gleaming in the moonlight. 'I would like to have been there, lord.' Then he smiled and glanced down at his swelling belly. 'But, even had I the use of both hands, I fear no horse would carry me.'

'Too many of Eissa's honeycakes,' said the general. 'It was good of you to wait up for me.'

'It was less than nothing, lord,' replied Peris, bowing, his plump face reddening.

Parmenion walked on into the house. In the *andron* at the rear two lanterns were burning, casting a soft glow over the room. It was large, boasting twenty couches and thirty chairs, and L-shaped. When Parmenion entertained guests the full room was used, but now the lanterns glowed only in the alcove by the large doorway to the west-facing gardens. The general moved out onto the patio, breathing in the scent of the honeysuckle growing by the wall. The house was peaceful and only at times like this did he enjoy being here. The thought was depressing.

He heard a movement behind him and turned, expecting to see the crippled Peris.

'Welcome home, husband,' said Phaedra. He bowed stiffly. His wife was wearing a robe of shimmering blue that clung to her slender frame, her golden hair pulled back from her face and bound with silver wire into a pony-tail that hung to her narrow waist. Parmenion looked into her cold blue eyes and stiffened.

'I will not be here for long, lady,' he told her.

'Long enough to see your son, I would hope.'

'Sons,' he corrected her.

'There is only one for me,' she said, her face expressionless. 'Philotas – he who will be great; the greatest of all.'

'Do not say that!' he hissed. 'It is not true! You hear me?'

She laughed then, the sound chilling. 'I lost my powers when I gave myself to you, general, but I will never forget the vision I saw when first you touched me. Your first-born will rule the world. I *know* it. And he is Philotas.'

Parmenion felt his mouth go dry. 'You are a fool, woman,' he said at last. 'A fool to believe it, and doubly foolish to say it aloud. Think on this: if Philip or Olympias hear of your vision, will they not seek to have the child slain?'

All colour drained from her face. 'How would they hear?' she whispered.

'Who is listening now?' he asked. 'How do you know which servant may be walking in the gardens, or sitting within earshot?'

'You are just trying to frighten me.'

'Indeed I am, Phaedra. For they would not only kill the babe but the mother, brothers and father. And who would blame them?'

'You will protect him. You are the Lion of Macedon, the most powerful man in the kingdom,' she said brightly.

'Go to bed, woman,' he told her, his voice weary.

'Will you be joining me, husband?'

He wanted to tell her no, but always the sight of her body aroused him.

'Yes. Soon.' Her smile was triumphant and he swung away from it, listening to the soft sound of her footfalls as she left the room. For some time he sat in silence, his heart heavy, then he rose and moved through to the upper nursery where his children slept. Hector was lying on his side in his crib, sucking his tiny thumb. Nicci, as always, had climbed into bed with Philo and the two slept with arms entwined.

Parmenion gazed at his eldest son. 'What is she raising you to be?' he wondered.

He knew – had known for years – that Phaedra regarded

49

him with contempt. The knowledge hurt, but the greater pain was in the lie that bound them together. She had been a seeress and she had seen a golden future. But she had misread it. Parmenion could not tell her of her mistake, or even risk putting her aside; for Phaedra, in her vengeance, could cause incalculable harm. She had been the closest friend of Olympias, who had known of her virgin powers. If she went to the Queen and told her of the vision . . . Parmenion felt the swell of panic within him. No, at all costs the secret must be kept. The only final answer would be to kill Phaedra and this he would not, could not, do.

'Oh, Philo,' whispered Parmenion, stroking his son's head, 'I hope you will be strong enough to withstand your mother's ambitions for you.' The boy stirred and moaned in his sleep.

And Parmenion left the room, drawn by lust to a woman he despised.

*

Parmenion awoke in the hour before dawn. Silently rising from the large bed, careful not to wake Phaedra, he padded across the scattered rugs that covered the timbered floor. Back in his own rooms he washed himself down with cold water and then rubbed oil into the skin of his arms and chest, scraping it clear with an ivory knife.

Dressing in a simple *chiton* tunic, he walked down to the gardens. The birds still slept in the trees and not a sound disturbed the silent beauty of the pre-dawn. The sky was dark grey, streaked with clouds, but in the east the colour was lighter as Apollo and his fiery chariot grew ever closer. Parmenion breathed deeply, filling his lungs, before gently stretching the muscles of his thighs, groin and calves.

The garden gate lay open as he loped out in to the countryside. His muscles still felt stiff and his calves were beginning to burn long before he reached the crest of the first hill. It had been impossible to run during the months of the Phocian campaign, and now his body complained bitterly. Ignoring the discomfort he increased his pace, sweat gleaming on his face as the miles flowed by beneath him.

He had never understood the miracle of his healing, the tightening of his skin, the strength of youth once more surging through his body, but he did not need to understand it to glory in it. He had never found any activity to match the constant joy of running – the perfect communion between mind and body, the freeing of inhibition, the cleansing of spirit. When he ran his mind was free and he could think through his problems, finding solutions with an ease that still surprised him.

Today he was considering the Thracian stallion, Titan. He had cost a great deal of money and yet he was – by Persian standards – cheap. His pedigree was incredible, sired by the finest prize stallion in Persia and born to the fastest mare ever to win the Olympics. Two of his brothers had been sold for fortunes beyond the reach of all but the richest kings, yet Parmenion had acquired him for a mere 2,000 drachms.

Since then the stallion had killed two other horses and maimed one of his handlers, and now was kept apart from the main herd in a pasture ringed by a fence the height of a tall man.

Parmenion knew how foolhardy it was to boast of riding him, but all other methods had failed. The Thessalians did not believe in 'breaking' their horses in the Thracian manner, loading them with heavy weights and running them until they were near exhaustion before putting a rider on their backs. This method, said his men, could break a horse's spirit. It was always important, the Thessalians believed, to establish a bond between mount and man. But for a war-horse and his rider such a bond was vital. When trust was strong, most horses would willingly allow riders upon their backs.

Not so with Titan. Three handlers had been hurt by him, jagged bites or kicks cracking limbs. But on the last occasion he had thrown and then stomped the legs and back of a young Thessalian, who now had no feeling below the waist and was confined to his bed in the communal barracks. There, before long, according to Bernios, he would die.

Parmenion loped on along the line of the hills, his mind concentrating on the day ahead. The Thessalians believed Titan to be demon-possessed. Perhaps he was, but Parmenion doubted it. Wild, yes; untamed, certainly. But possessed? What profit would there be for a demon trapped inside a horse at pasture? No. There had to be a better explanation – even if he had not yet discovered it.

He ran until the dawn streaked the sky with crimson, then halted to watch the transient splendour of diamond stars shining in a blue sky, slowly fading until only the North Star remained, tiny and defiant against the arrival of the sun. Then that too was gone.

The breeze was cool upon the hilltop and his sweat-drenched body shivered. Narrowing his eyes he gazed over the lands that were now his, hundreds of miles of the Emathian plain, grassland, woods, hills and streams. No man could see it all from one place, but from this hilltop he looked down on the seven pastures where his herds grazed. Six hundred horses were kept here, and beyond the line of the eastern hills there were cattle and goats, five villages, two towns and a small forest that surrendered fine timber which was eagerly sought by the shipbuilders of Rhodes and Crete.

'You are a rich man now,' he said aloud, remembering the days of poverty back in Sparta when his tunic was threadbare, his sandals as thin as parchment. Swinging round he stared back at the great house with its high pillars, its twenty large guest-rooms. From here he could see the statues adorning the landscaped gardens and the score of smaller buildings housing slaves and servants.

A man ought to be happy with all this, he admonished himself, but his heart sank with the thought.

Picking up his pace again, he ran on towards the stables and pastures, his eyes scanning the hills, picking out the giant form of Titan alone in his pasture. The horse was running also, but stopped to watch him. Parmenion's scalp prickled as he ran alongside the fence under Titan's baleful glare. The stallion's domain was not large, some eighty paces long and fifty wide, the fence sturdily constructed of thick timbers. Not a horse alive could leap such an obstacle but even so, when Titan cantered towards him Parmenion involuntarily moved to his right to put more distance between himself and the fence. This momentary fear infuriated him, fuelling his determination to conquer the giant.

He saw Mothac talking to the slender Croni and the boy Orsin at the far gate, and more than twenty Thessalians had gathered to watch the coming contest. One of the men clambered up on to the fence, but Titan raced across his pasture, rearing to strike out at the man who threw himself backwards to safety, much to the amusement of his fellows.

'It is not a good day for such a ride,' Mothac told Parmenion. 'There was rain in the night and the ground is soft.'

Parmenion smiled. The old Theban was trying to give him an easy way out. 'It was but a smattering,' said Parmenion. 'Come, let us be starting our day. Which of you brave fellows will rope the beast?'

Mothac shook his head, his concern obvious. 'All right, my boys, let's be seeing some Thessalian skills!'

Several of the men gathered up long, coiled ropes. There was no humour evident now – their faces were set, their eyes hard. Two men ran to the right, keeping close to the fence, waving the coils and calling to Titan who charged at them, the fence-posts rattling as he struck. To the left, unnoticed by the enraged beast, Orsin and Croni climbed into the pasture, angling out behind the black stallion. Suddenly the beast swung and darted at Orsin. Croni's rope sailed over the stallion's great head, jerking tight as he reared to strike the youngster. Feeling the rope bite into his neck, Titan turned to charge Croni. Now it was Orsin who threw a loop over the stallion's head and neck, hauling it tight. Instantly the other Thessalians clambered over the fence, ready to help, but Titan stood stock-still, his great frame trembling.

The huge head slowly turned, his malevolent gaze fixing on Parmenion as he jumped down into the pasture.

'He knows,' thought Parmenion, with a sudden rush of fear. 'He is waiting for me!'

The Spartan moved towards the horse, always keeping in its line of vision until he stood beside the neck and head. Carefully his hand reached up to the top rope, loosening it and lifting it clear.

'Steady, boy,' he whispered. 'Your master speaks. Steady, boy.'

Still the stallion waited, like a black statue. Parmenion eased his fingers under the second rope, sliding it up along the neck, over the ears and down the long nose, waiting for the lunging bite that could tear away his fingers.

It did not come.

Stroking the trembling flanks, Parmenion took hold of the black mane, vaulting smoothly to the stallion's back.

Titan reared as the Spartan's weight came down, but Parmenion locked his legs to the horse's body, holding his position. Titan leapt high in the air, coming down on all four hooves with bone-crunching force, dipping his head and dragging his rider forward. Then he bucked. But Parmenion was ready for the manoeuvre, leaning back and holding to his point of balance.

The black stallion set off at a run, then rolled to his back, desperate to dislodge and crush his tormentor. Parmenion jumped to the ground as the stallion rolled, leaping over the belly and flailing hooves, and springing once more to Titan's back as the horse lunged to his feet. The Thessalians cheered the move.

The giant stallion galloped around the pasture, twisting, leaping, bucking and rearing, but he could not dislodge the hated man upon his back.

Finally Titan charged towards the fence. It was a move the Spartan had not anticipated, and instinctively he knew the stallion's intent. He would gallop towards the timbers and then swing his flanks to crash against the wood, smashing the bones of Parmenion's leg to shards, crippling the Spartan for life. Parmenion had only one hope – to leap clear – but if he did so the stallion would turn on him.

Seeing the danger the youngster Orsin clambered over the fence and leapt into the paddock, shouting at the top of his voice and waving his coiled rope around his head. The move disconcerted the stallion, who swerved and found himself running head-first at the timbers.

'Sweet Zeus, he'll kill us both!' thought Parmenion as Titan thundered towards the wooden wall.

But at the last moment Titan bunched his muscles, sailing high in the air, clearing the fence with ease and galloping across the hills. The horse herd grazing there scattered before him. Never had Parmenion known such speed, the wind screaming in his ears, the ground moving by below him like a green blur.

'Turn, my beauty!' he yelled. 'Turn and show me your strength.' As if the stallion understood him he swung wide and thundered back towards the pasture.

Mothac and Croni were pulling open the gate, but perversely Titan swerved once more, galloping straight at the highest point of the fence.

'Sweet Hera be with me!' prayed the Spartan, for here the highest bar of the fence was almost seven feet high. The stallion slowed, bunched his muscles and leapt, rear hooves clattering against the wood.

As Titan landed Parmenion swung his right leg clear and jumped to the ground. Immediately the stallion turned on him, rearing above him with hooves lashing down. The Spartan rolled and came up running, diving between the fence bars and landing head-first in a patch of churned earth. The Thessalians roared with laughter as Parmenion staggered to his feet.

'I think,' said the Spartan, with a grin, 'he may take a little breaking yet. But what a horse!'

'Look out!' yelled Croni. Titan charged the fence once more, leaping it without breaking stride. Parmenion dived out of the way, but the stallion swung, seeking him out. When Croni ran forward with his rope, Titan saw him and swerved towards the Thessalian, his huge shoulder crashing into the little man and punching him from his feet. Before anyone could move Titan reared above the Thessalian, his front hooves hammering down into Croni's face. The skull dissolved, the head collapsing in a sickening spray of blood and brains. Orsin managed to get a rope over the stallion, but twice more the hooves smashed down into the limp body on the grass. Titan felt the noose settle on his neck and jerked hard, tugging Orsin from his feet. Ignoring the boy he thundered towards Parmenion. The Spartan threw himself to his left but, as if anticipating the move, Titan reared high, his blood-spattered hooves plunging down. Parmenion dived again, this time to his right, his back striking a fence-post. Titan loomed above him.

Suddenly the stallion's neck arched back, an arrow jutting from his skull.

'No!' screamed Parmenion. 'No!' But a second shaft buried itself deep in Titan's flank, piercing the heart. The stallion sank to his knees, then toppled to his side.

Parmenion rose on unsteady legs, staring down at the dead colossus. Then he swung to see Mothac lay aside the bow.

'He was a demon,' the Theban said softly. 'No question.'

'I could have tamed him,' said Parmenion, his voice cold with rage.

'You would have been dead, lord,' put in the boy Orsin. 'As dead as my uncle, Croni. And, by all the gods, you rode him. And greatly.'

'There will never be his like again,' Parmenion whispered.

'There is the foal,' said Orsin. 'He will be bigger than his sire.'

Movement by Titan's dead eye caught Parmenion's attention. Thick white maggots were crawling from under the lid and slithering down the horse's face, like obscene tears. 'There are your demons,' said Parmenion. 'His brain must have been alive with them. Gods, they were driving him mad!'

But the Thessalians were no longer in earshot. They had gathered around the body of their friend Croni, lifting him and carrying him back towards the main house.

★

The death of the stallion left Parmenion's spirits low. Never had he seen a finer horse, nor one with such an indomitable

56

spirit. But worse than this, the slaying of Titan made him think of the child, Alexander.

Here was another beautiful creature, possessed by evil. Intelligent – perhaps brilliant – and yet cursed by a hidden malevolence. An awful image leapt to his mind: the child lying dead with fat, pale maggots crawling across his lifeless eyes.

Forcing the vision from his thoughts, he toiled alongside the men as they cleared the fields, helping them rope the young horses, getting them accustomed to the needs of Man.

Towards midday the Spartan wandered out to the lake where Mothac was exercising lame or injured mounts. The men had built a floating raft of timbers which was anchored at the centre of a small lake, a bowshot's length from the water's edge. A horse would be led out into the water, where he would swim behind the boat leading him until the raft was reached. Once there the lead rope would be thrown up to Mothac who would encourage the horse to swim around the raft. The exercise built up a horse's strength and endurance, while putting no strain on injured muscles or ligaments. Mothac, his bald head covered by an enormous felt hat, was walking the perimeter of the raft, leading a bay mare who struggled in the water alongside.

Removing his tunic Parmenion waded out into the cold water, swimming slowly towards the raft, his arms moving in long, lazy strokes. The cool of the lake was refreshing, but his mind was full of awful images: maggots and eyes, beauty and decay.

Hauling himself up to the raft he sat naked in the sunshine, feeling the cool breeze against his wet body. Mothac summoned the boat, throwing the lead rope to the oarsman.

'That's enough for today,' he shouted. The oarsman nodded and led the mare back to dry land. The old Theban sat beside Parmenion, offering him a jug of water.

'That hat looks ridiculous,' remarked Parmenion.

Mothac grinned and pulled the floppy hat from his head. 'It's comfortable,' he said, wiping sweat from the rim and covering his bald dome once more.

Parmenion sighed. 'It's a shame he had to die,' he said.

'The horse or the man?' snapped Mothac.

Parmenion smiled ruefully. 'I was talking of the horse. Though you are correct, I should have been thinking of the man. But Titan must have been in great pain; those maggots were eating his brain. I find it obscene that such a magnificent beast should have been brought low by such vile creatures.'

'He was only a horse,' said Mothac. 'But I shall miss Croni. He had a family in Thessaly. How much shall I send?'

'Whatever you think fit. How have the men taken his death?'

'He was popular,' Mothac answered. 'But they are hard men. You impressed them with your ride.' He chuckled suddenly. 'By Heracles, you impressed me!'

'I will never see another horse like him,' said Parmenion sadly.

'I think you might. The foal is the image of his sire. And he will be big – he has a head like a bull.'

'I saw him in the stables last night – with his dead mother. Not a good omen for the son of Titan – his first act in life to kill his dam.'

'Now you are sounding like a Thessalian,' Mothac admonished him. The Theban drank deeply from the water-jug and leaned back on his powerful forearms. 'What is wrong between you and Philip?'

Parmenion shrugged. 'He is a King in search of a glory he does not wish to share. I cannot say I blame him for that. And he has the lickspittle Attalus to whisper poison in his ear.'

Mothac nodded. 'I never liked the man. But then I never liked Philip much either. What will you do?'

The Spartan smiled. 'What is there to do? I will fight Philip's battles until he decides he has no more need of me. Then I will come here and grow old with my sons around me.'

Mothac grunted and swore. 'You would be a fool to believe that – and you are no fool. If you left Philip, every city in Greece would vie for your services. Within a season you would be leading an army. And, since there is only one great enemy, you would be leading it against Philip. No, Parmenion, when Philip decides he needs you no longer it will be Attalus who delivers the dismissal – with an assassin's knife.'

Parmenion's pale blue eyes grew cold. 'He will need to be very good.'

'And he is,' warned Mothac.

'This is a gloomy conversation,' Parmenion muttered, rising to his feet.

'Has the King invited you to the victory parade?' Mothac persisted.

'No. But then he knows I do not enjoy such events.'

'Perhaps,' said Mothac, unconvinced. 'So, where will the next war be fought? Will you march on the cities of the Chalcidice, or down through Boeotia to sack Athens?'

'That is for the King to decide,' answered Parmenion, his gaze straying to the eastern mountains. The look was not lost on the Theban.

'Then it is to be Thrace,' he said, his voice low.

'You see too much, my friend. I thank the gods you also have a careful tongue.'

'Where will his ambition end?'

'I don't know. More to the point, he does not know. He is not the man I once knew, Mothac; he is driven now. He had hundreds of Phocians executed after the Crocus Field, and it was said he stood and laughed as they died. Yet before we left Macedonia I watched him judge several cases at court. I knew, on this particular day, that he wanted to hunt and was hoping to conclude by early afternoon. At last he declared an end to the proceedings, telling the petitioners to come back on another day. But as he left the judge's chair an old woman with a petition came close to him, calling out for justice. He turned and said, "No time, woman." She just stood there for a moment and then, as he walked on, shouted: "Then you've no time to be King!" Everyone close by held their breaths. Was she to be executed? Or flogged? Or imprisoned? You know what he did? He cancelled the hunt and listened to her case for the rest of the day. He even judged it in her favour.'

Mothac rose and waved for the boat to come out to them. 'I did not say he was not a great man, Parmenion. I merely pointed out that I do not like him, and I do not trust him. Neither should you. One day he will order your death. Jealousy breeds fear, and fear sires hatred.'

'No one lives for ever,' replied Parmenion uneasily.

Pella, Macedonia, Autumn

'I shall walk ahead of the Guards. My people will see me,' said Philip.

'Madness!' snapped Attalus. 'What more can I say to you? There are killers in Pella, just waiting for the opportunity to come at you. Why are you set on this course?'

'Because I am the King!' thundered Philip.

Attalus sat back on the couch staring sullenly at his monarch. 'You think,' he asked finally, 'that you are a god? That cold iron cannot penetrate your body, cannot slice your heart?'

Philip smiled and relaxed. 'No delusions, Attalus. How could I?' he added, touching the scar above his blinded right eye. 'But if I cannot walk in the streets of my own capital, then my enemies have truly won. You will be there. I trust you to protect me.'

Attalus looked into the King's face, seeing no compromise there, and recalled the first time they had met, in Thebes nineteen years ago. The King had been merely a boy then, a frightened boy waiting for the assassin's blade. Yet in his eyes had been the same fierce glow. His uncle the King, Ptolemaos, had tried to have him quietly poisoned, but the boy outwitted him, saving his brother Perdiccas and killing Ptolemaos as he lay in his bed. This he had achieved as a thirteen-year-old. Now, at thirty-two, Philip had united Macedonia, creating a nation to be feared.

But such pride was double-edged, Attalus knew, bringing either greatness or an early grave. Macedonian spies in the Chalcidean city of Olynthos reported that an elite group of assassins had been hired to end the threat of Philip of Macedon. It took no genius to realize they would strike at the Festival of Thanksgiving when the King, dressed only in tunic and cloak, walked unarmed among the crowds to the Temple of Zeus.

'Think of Alexander,' urged Attalus. 'If you are slain, then he will be in great peril. You have no other heirs, which means the nobles will fight amongst themselves to succeed you. Alexander would be killed.'

For a moment only Philip wavered, stroking his thick black beard and staring from the wide window. But when he turned back Attalus knew the cause was lost. 'I will walk among my people. Now, have enough flowers been distributed along the route?'

'Yes, sire,' answered Attalus wearily.

'I want them strewn before my feet. It will look good; it will impress the ambassadors. They must see that Macedonia is with me.'

'Macedonia *is* with you – regardless of whether they throw flowers.'

'Yes, yes. But it must be *seen*. The Athenians are stirring up more trouble. They do not have the finance to mount a campaign themselves, but they are working hard on the Olynthians. I do not desire a war – yet – with the Chalcidean League. Now how do I look?'

Attalus curbed his temper and gazed at the King. Of medium height, he was broad-shouldered and powerful, his black tightly curled hair and beard shining like a panther's pelt, the tawny flecks in his single green eye highlighted by the crown of golden laurel leaves. His tunic was summer blue, his cloak night black.

'You look splendid – a King of legend. Let us hope you look as fine at the end of the day.'

Philip chuckled. 'Always so gloomy, Attalus. Have I not made you rich? Are you even now not content?'

'I will be content when the day is over.'

'I will see you in the courtyard,' said Philip. 'Remember, no more than ten Guards to walk behind me.'

Alone now, Philip moved back to the long table, spreading the goatskin map across the surface. For too long the great cities, Athens, Sparta and latterly Thebes, had fought to rule Greece; their own enmities causing war after bloody war. Athens against Sparta, Sparta against Thebes, Thebes against Athens, with all the minor states sucked in. Endless permutations of broken alliances, changing sides, shifting fortunes.

Macedonia had been covertly ruled by all three at different times.

Philip knew the endless wars were self-perpetuating, for the hundreds of cities and towns of northern Greece all paid homage to different masters. Any dispute between such cities could – and would – draw in the major powers. In Macedonia alone, when Philip came to power, there were more than twenty supposedly independent cities who offered no allegiance to the throne. Instead they formed alliances with Sparta, Athens, or Thebes, each city boasting its own small army or militia force. Many of them were coastal settlements, which meant safe landing for an invading army. One by one, during the seven years since he became King, Philip had taken these citadels, sometimes by force – as at Methone, where the population had been sold into slavery – but more often by coercion, bribery, or simply a careful blending of all three which men called diplomacy.

The plan was essentially simple: remove all threats from within the kingdom by stealth or war.

He had established an early treaty with Athens, which enabled him to concentrate on crushing his enemies in the west and north. Now he had forged strong links with Thessaly in the south by destroying the Phocian army, which had ravaged central Greece.

But the storm-clouds still gathered. Philip's army had

swept into the independent city of Amphipolis on his eastern border – a city Athens coveted. The shock invasion was not without its critics – including Parmenion.

'You promised Athens you would let them rule the city,' the general had pointed out.

'Not so. I told them I did not see it as Macedonian. There is a difference.'

'A small one,' replied Parmenion. 'You let them believe you meant them to take control. It will mean war with Athens. Are we ready for it?'

'It is a small risk, my friend. The Athenians are not rich enough to wage a full war at this distance. And I cannot allow Amphipolis to be a secret base for Athens.'

Parmenion had laughed then. 'There is no one else here, Philip. You do not need to take such a high tone. Amphipolis is rich; she controls the trade routes to Thrace, and all of the southern reaches of the River Strymon. You are running short of coin, and the army must be paid.'

'There is that,' answered Philip, his grin infectious. 'By the way, the army is not yet large enough. I want you to train me ten thousand more men.'

The smile vanished from the Spartan's face. 'You already have more than enough to secure the realm. From where will come the danger? Thrace is divided, the three kings warring among themselves; the Paionians are finished, and the Illyrians will never rise to their former glory. You are building an army now of conquest – not defence. What is it you want, Philip?'

'I want ten thousand more men. And before you ask another question, my Spartan friend, was it not you who once advised me to keep my plans more secret? Very well, I am following your advice. No one but Philip shall know. And was it not also my *strategos* who lectured me on the nature of empire? We remain strong, he said, only while we grow.'

'Indeed he did, sire,' admitted Parmenion, 'but as with all strategies there is the question of scale. Armies must be supplied, lines of communication need to be open and swift. Your greatest advantage over Athens is that your

64

commands are instantly obeyed, whereas the Athenians must gather their assembly and argue for days, sometimes weeks. And, unlike the Persians, we are not geared for empire.'

'Then we must learn, Parmenion, for the days of Macedon are here.'

Now Philip stared down at the map, his keen mind judging the areas of greatest danger. Parmenion had been right. The taking of Amphipolis and other independent citadels had struck fear into the hearts of his neighbours, who were busy enlisting mercenaries, *hoplites* from Thebes, javeliners from Thrace, archers from Crete.

And Athens, in the distant south, had declared war, sending agents to all northern realms and cities urging them to stand against the Macedonian aggressor. Now that the Phocians were crushed the game was becoming complex, for no single enemy would dare raise his head above the ramparts and no single battle could solve Philip's dilemma.

His enemies would wait for a sign of weakness – then strike together, coming from east, west and south. If he moved against any one foe the others would fall upon his back, causing a war on two or more fronts.

The greatest immediate danger lay to the east, from Olynthos, the leader of the Chalcidean League of cities. Philip's finger traced over the trident-shaped lands of the Chalcidice. Between them the cities could raise 20,000 *hoplites* armed with spear, sword and shield, more than 3,000 cavalry and, perhaps, a further 7,000 – maybe 8,000 – javeliners. A war with Olynthos would be costly and dangerous. Whoever won would be so weakened they would fall to the next aggressor. That was why the Olynthians were relying on the assassins they had sent to Pella.

The King heard the sounds of the Guards marching into the courtyard below his window. 'Walk with care today, Philip,' he warned himself.

*

Attalus gathered the ten members of the Royal Guard,

inspecting their bronze breastplates and helms, their scabbards and greaves. They shone like burnished gold. Moving behind the lines, he glanced at their black cloaks. Not a trace of dust or grime showed. Satisfied, he walked back to stand before them.

'Be aware,' he said slowly, 'that the King is always in danger. *Always*. It does not matter that he walks in the heart of his realm. It is immaterial that the people love him. He has enemies. As you march behind him, keep your eyes on the crowd. Do not look at the King. Watch for any sudden movement. Is that understood?' The men nodded.

'May I speak, sir?' asked a man to his right.

'Of course.'

'Are you speaking in general terms, or is there a particular threat today?'

Attalus looked closely at the man, trying to remember his name. 'As I said, the King is always in danger. But it is a good question. Be vigilant.'

Taking his place at the centre, he waited for the King. The route would take them along the main Avenue of Alexandros, through the market-place and on to the Temple of Zeus. A walk of no more than a thousand paces, perhaps less, but the crowd would be pressing in. Attalus had stationed soldiers along the line of the parade, but they would be stretched to keep back the thousands of citizens. Philip's popularity was high and that made for great danger on a day such as this, for the people would be excitable – straining to touch him, pushing against the thin line of soldiers. Sweat dripped into Attalus' eyes. A trained assassin himself, he knew how easy it was to kill a man no matter how well protected. At no time would Philip be more than five paces from the throng. A sudden dash, the flash of a knife, the spurting of royal blood . . .

For the hundredth time he pictured the route, the white-walled buildings and narrow alleyways.

Where would you make the attempt? he asked himself again. Not at the start when the guards would be at their most alert, but towards the end. Not near the temple, where open ground would prevent the assassins' escape. No. The attack would come close to the market-place with its scores of alleyways. Two hundred paces of sheer terror awaited him.

Damn you, Philip!

The King walked from the palace doors, the ten guards beating their fists upon their breastplates in greeting. Attalus was slow to follow, his mind preoccupied. 'I see you, Coenus,' said Philip, smiling at the man whose name Attalus had been struggling to remember. 'And you, Diron. I would have thought you'd have had enough of my company.' One by one Philip greeted each of the men. It never ceased to amaze Attalus how the King memorized the names of the men under his command. Coenus – now Attalus remembered him. He had been promoted by the whoreson Parmenion to command the reserve phalanx at the Crocus Field.

'Are we ready?' asked the King.

'Yes, sir,' Attalus answered.

Two soldiers opened the gates and Philip strode from the palace grounds to be greeted by a thundrous roar from the citizens beyond. Attalus kept close behind him. Brushing the sweat from his eyes, he scanned the crowd. There were hundreds waiting here on both sides of the avenue. Flowers of every kind rained in on the King as he waved to his people. At the cross section the main parade was waiting: cavalrymen from Thessaly, ambassadors from Thebes, Corinth, Pherai, Olynthos and Thrace. Behind them were jugglers and acrobats, jesters and actors in masks of gleaming bronze. At the rear of the parade two white bulls, garlanded with flowers, were led on their last walk to the sacrificial altar of Zeus.

Philip marched to the head of the parade and began the walk along the Avenue of Alexandros.

Attalus, hand on his sword-hilt, saw the crowd surge forward against the thin line of soldiers on either side who fought to keep the way open. Philip walked on, waving and smiling. A small boy dashed from the left, running up to the King. Attalus' sword was half drawn. He slammed it back into its scabbard as Philip swept the child from his feet and stopped as the boy gave him a pomegranate.

'Where is your mother?' Philip asked him. The child pointed to the right and the King walked the boy back, handing him to a woman in the crowd.

Attalus cursed. One thrust now and it was all over. . . .

But Philip moved back into the centre of the avenue and continued on his way at the head of the parade.

As they approached the market-place, Attalus' gaze flickered left and right over the crowd, watching faces, looking for signs of tension. Still the flowers came, the avenue carpeted with myriad colours.

Suddenly the crowd surged again. Three men broke clear, running towards the King.

Knives flashed in the sunlight, as Attalus sprinted forward.

A long dagger plunged into the King's side.

'No!' screamed Attalus. Philip staggered, his hand sweeping aside his cloak and coming up with a hidden sword. The blade smashed through the first assassin's neck. A second knife lunged for the King's throat, but Philip parried the blow, sending a reverse cut that opened the man's arm from elbow to shoulder. Attalus killed the third man as he tried to stab Philip in the back.

The crowd were screaming now. As Philip advanced on the wounded assassin, the man flung himself to his knees.

'Spare me. I will tell you all!' he pleaded.

'You have nothing of worth to say,' said the King, his sword plunging between the man's collar-bones.

'Get a surgeon!' yelled Attalus, moving alongside Philip and taking his arm.

'No!' countermanded the King. 'It is not necessary.'

'But I saw him stab you.'

Philip made a fist and tapped at his tunic. A metallic ring sounded. 'There is a breastplate beneath it,' he said. 'I may be reckless, Attalus, but I am not stupid. Let the parade continue,' he bellowed.

Later that night as the King relaxed in his chambers, growing steadily more drunk, Attalus asked the question that had been gnawing at him all day.

'Why did you kill the last assassin? He could have named the people who hired him.'

'It would have achieved nothing. We both know the men came from Olynthos. If such news became public I would be forced into a war with the Chalcideans; the people would demand it. But it was a good day, was it not? A good day to be alive?'

'I enjoyed it not at all,' snapped Attalus. 'I aged ten years out there.'

Philip chuckled. 'All life is a game, my friend. We cannot hide. The gods use us as they will, then discard us. Today my people saw their King; they watched him march, they saw him fight and conquer. Their pride was fed. So, then, the Olynthians only helped my cause. I feel grateful to them – and to you for protecting my back. I trust you, Attalus, and I like you. You make me feel comfortable – and safe. You remember that first day in Thebes? When I held my knife to my breast and offered you the chance to ram it home?'

'Who could forget it?' answered Attalus. The young prince, fearing Attalus had been sent to kill him, gave him the chance in an alleyway where there were no witnesses. And Attalus had been tempted. At the time he served King Ptolemaos, and Philip was but a boy the King desired dead. Yet he had not struck the blow. . . and still did not know why.

'What are you thinking?' asked Philip.

Attalus jerked his mind to the present. 'I was re-living that day, and the journey back to Macedonia. Why do you trust me, Philip? I know myself, and all my failings. I would not trust me – so why do you?'

The smile left the King's face as, leaning forward, he gripped Attalus' shoulder. 'Do not question it,' he advised. 'Enjoy it. Few men ever earn a King's trust, or his friendship. You have both. It does not matter why. Perhaps I see in you a quality you have not yet found. But, were I beset by enemies, you are the man I would most want by my side. Let that be enough.' The King drained his wine, refilling the cup. He stood – staggered – and wandered to the window, staring out to the west.

Attalus sighed. Exhausted by the tension of the day, he

took his leave and walked slowly back to his own rooms in the new barracks. His servants had lit lanterns in the *andron* and bedchamber. Attalus untied the thongs of his breast-plate, removed it and sank to a couch.

'You are a fool to trust me, Philip,' he whispered.

Too tired to climb the stairs to his bed, he lay back on the couch and slept.

*

'An impressive herd, my dear Mothac. How is it that a Theban develops such a talent for horses?' The Persian stroked his golden beard and leaned back in his chair.

'I listen and I learn, noble Parzalamis. Is the wine to your taste?'

The Persian smiled thinly, but his pale eyes showed no trace of humour. 'Of course – it is from my country, and I would guess at least ten years old. Am I correct?'

'It would surprise me if you weren't.'

'A kind compliment,' said Parzalamis, rising from the chair and walking to the open doorway where he stood looking out over the western hills. Mothac remained on the couch, but his gaze followed the silk-clad Persian. Such clothes, he thought! What was the point of such luxury? Parzalamis wore loose trousers of blue silk, edged with silver wire which in turn held small pearls. His shirt was also silk, but the colour of fresh cream, the chest and back embroidered with gold thread forming the head of a griffyn, part-eagle part-lion. He had no cloak, but his heavy coat of embroidered wool had been flung carelessly across a couch. Mothac's gaze moved down to the man's boots. They were of a skin he had never seen, scaled and uneven, yet with a sheen that made a man want to reach out and touch them.

Parzalamis swung and walked back to his seat. Rich Persian perfume wafted to Mothac as the man crossed the room and he chuckled. 'What amuses you?' asked his guest, his expression hardening.

'Not amusement – embarrassment,' said Mothac swiftly. 'Happy as I am to see you, your magnificence makes my

70

home feel like a pig-sty. Suddenly I see all the cracks in the wall, and notice that the door-frame has warped.'

The Persian relaxed. 'You are a clever man, Theban. Your tongue moves faster than a cheetah. So, I have bought your horses and now let us move to more serious matters. What are Philip's plans?'

Swinging his legs from the couch, Mothac refilled his goblet. 'Parmenion assures me he is still securing his borders against his enemies. The Great King has nothing to fear.'

'The Great King fears nothing!' snapped Parzalamis. 'He is merely interested in his vassal king.'

'Vassal?' queried Mothac. 'As I understand it, Philip sends no tribute to Susa.'

'The point is immaterial. All Macedonia is part of the Great King's empire. Indeed, the same can be said for all of Greece. Athens, Sparta and Thebes all accept the sovereignty of Persia.'

'If Macedonia is indeed a vassal,' said Mothac, choosing his words carefully, 'then surely it is strange that the Phocians paid their army with Persian gold when all men knew the army would march against Philip.'

'Not at all,' answered Parzalamis. 'The general Onomarchus travelled to Susa and knelt before the Great King, offering his allegiance to the empire. For this he was rewarded. And let us not forget it was Philip who marched against the Phocians, not the reverse. And I am unhappy with this idea of securing borders. Where does it stop? Philip already controls Illyria and Paionia. Now the Thessalians have made him their King. His borders grow with every season. What next? The Chalcidice? Thrace? Asia?'

'Not Asia,' said Mothac. 'And Parmenion maintains the Chalcidice is safe for the time being. Therefore it is Thrace.'

'What does he want?' hissed Parzalamis. 'How much territory can any one man hold?'

'An interesting question from a servant of the Great King.'

'The Great King is divinely blessed. He is not to be

71

confused with a barbarian warrior. Thrace, you say? Very well, I will bear that intelligence to Susa.' Parzalamis leaned back, staring at the low ceiling. 'Now tell me of the King's son.' The question was asked in a tone altogether too relaxed and Mothac let it hang in the air for a moment.

'He is said to be a brilliant child,' the Theban answered. 'When barely four he could read and write, and even debate with his elders.'

'Yet he is possessed,' said Parzalamis. Mothac could feel the tension in the man's voice.

'You see a four-year-old child as a threat?'

'Yes – not of course to Persia, which is beyond fear, but to the stability of Greece. You lived for many years in Persia and no doubt came to understand the true religion. There is Light which, as Zoroaster informed us, is the root of all life, and there is Darkness, in which nothing grows. Our wise men say that this Alexander is a child of Darkness. You have heard this?'

'Yes,' agreed Mothac, shifting uncomfortably under the Persian's gaze. 'Some talk of him being a demon. Parmenion does not believe it.'

'And you?'

'I have seen the child only once but, yes, I could believe it. I touched his shoulder when he came too close to a stallion. The touch burned me. I could feel it for weeks.'

'He must not live,' whispered Parzalamis.

'I'll have no part in this,' answered Mothac, rising and walking to the door. Stepping outside into the gathering twilight he looked around. There was no one in sight and he returned to the room. The light was failing and Mothac lit three lanterns. 'It would be madness to kill the child. Philip's anger would be colossal.'

'That is true. But we must consider where best such anger could be directed. In Athens the orator Demosthenes speaks out against Philip with great vehemence. If the assassin were to be in the pay of Athens then Philip would march south, yes?'

'Nothing would stop him,' agreed the Theban.

'And it is well known that central Greece is a burial

ground for ambition. All the great generals have fallen there.'

'How will the deed be done?'

'The matter is already in hand. A Methonian slave named Lolon will kill the child; he has been bribed to do so by two Athenians in our service. He will be taken alive, of course, and will confess that he was hired on the instructions of Demosthenes, for he believes such to be the case.'

'Why are you telling me this?'

'The two Athenians have been told to flee north from Pella. It will not be expected. You will hide them here for some weeks. After that they can make their way to Olynthus.'

'You ask a great deal,' Mothac told him.

'I agree, my dear Mothac, but then – as you know – we pay very well.'

*

Parmenion sat in the western alcove of his *andron*, eyes fixed on a honey-bee as it settled on a flowering yellow rose. The bloom slowly bent as the bee shuffled inside seeking pollen.

'Is that all he said?' asked the Spartan.

'Is it not enough?' Mothac countered.

Parmenion sighed and stood, stretching his back. It had taken three years to infiltrate Mothac into the Persian spy system, and at last it was beginning to justify the effort. At first they had been wary of him, knowing him to be Parmenion's friend. Then slowly, as his information proved accurate, they had begun to trust him more. But this sudden sharing of such a powerful secret would need some serious consideration. 'I will have the servant watched, and put extra guards in the garden beneath Alexander's window.'

'But you must tell the King,' put in Mothac.

'No, that would not be wise. There is great fear in Persia that – ultimately – Philip will lead his forces into Asia. It is making them reckless. The attack on Philip at the Festival – the Olynthians would never attempt anything so rash. No, it was the Persians, and I don't think it wise to tell Philip.

But equally I do not want Parzalamis to know that you are no traitor.'

'Why is that so important?' asked the Theban.

Parmenion grinned. 'I do not wish to find you with a knife between your ribs. And there is no doubt in my mind that Persia will one day be the enemy. It is the richest kingdom in the world – and Philip spends recklessly. Despite the mines and cities we have captured there is still not enough wealth in Macedonia to pay for the army. No, Persia is the ultimate prize, therefore it is vital to maintain contact with Parzalamis. But how do we save the prince – without compromising you?'

'The Methonian servant could have an accident – break his neck?' offered Mothac.

Parmenion shook his head. 'Too obvious. And the Athenians –whose names we do not know – would only hire someone else. It is a thorny problem. But I will work on it.'

'He gave no indication of how soon Lolon will strike. It could be tonight!' said Mothac.

'Yes,' answered Parmenion, holding his voice even, not allowing a flicker of emotion to betray his concern. 'I will ride for Pella tomorrow. Now, tell me, how is Titan's foal?'

'Suckling well with a milk mare. He is strong. He will survive.'

'Good. Now you should get home and rest. I need to think.'

Mothac stood. 'This game is growing in complexity, my friend. I am not comfortable with it.'

'Nor I. But kingdoms are at stake and nothing remains simple.'

When the Theban had gone Parmenion strolled in the gardens, halting at the marble fountain. There were three statues at the centre representing Aphrodite, Goddess of Love, Athena, Goddess of Wisdom and War, and Hera, the Queen of the Gods. In their midst stood a handsome youth holding an apple.

'Kingdoms are at stake and nothing remains simple.'

The youth was Paris, a Prince of Troy, and the three goddesses had commanded him to present the golden apple to the most beautiful among them. Parmenion gazed at the youth's stone face, reading the emotion the sculptor had so exquisitely carved there. It was the look of the lost. If he gave the apple to one then the others would hate him, not resting until they saw him dead.

'*Kingdoms are at stake and nothing remains simple.*'

Paris had presented the prize to Aphrodite, and she had rewarded him by making the most beautiful woman in the world love him. His happiness was complete. But the woman was Helen, wife of Menelaus, King of Sparta, and Athena, allied with Hera, conspired to bring a Greek army seeking vengeance. Paris saw his city conquered, his family slain, and was himself stabbed to death as Troy burned.

Foolish boy, thought Parmenion. He should have ignored beauty and presented it to the strongest. How could Paris have believed that Love alone could save him? Pushing such thoughts from his mind he stayed by the fountain pool until dusk, concentrating on the problem set by Parzalamis.

Servants brought him food and wine which he left untouched on the marble bench where he sat beneath a flowering tree that offered shade from the setting sun. As the hours passed he was no nearer to a solution and this galled him.

Loosen your mind, he told himself. Think back to your days with Xenophon, and the advice the Athenian general offered so freely.

'If a problem cannot be tackled by a frontal assault,' Xenophon had said, 'then try a flank attack.' Parmenion smiled at the memory.

Very well, he thought. Let us examine all that we know. The Persians wish to kill Alexander. They gave Mothac two reasons. Firstly their *magi* believe him to be possessed. Secondly, if Athens could be implicated in the child's murder, it would set Philip on the road to revenge. What facts do I possess, he asked himself?

The name of the assassin.

He sat upright. Why would Parzalamis have revealed the name? Why not just tell Mothac that a servant had been bribed? It would be safer that way. A mistake, perhaps? No, Parzalamis was too wily to fall victim to a loose tongue. The answer was suddenly chillingly obvious – they were still testing Mothac. Parzalamis did not need a hiding-place for the Athenians. What he needed was to know whether his finest Macedonian spy could be trusted. Yet to tell him of the assassination attempt was perilous indeed, for if news came to Philip he would certainly go to war with Persia.

Therefore Parzalamis must have taken steps to prevent the information reaching the Macedonian King.

It was as if sunlight had speared through the clouds of Parmenion's troubled thoughts. Mothac would have been . . . must have been . . . followed. Once they had seen him rushing to Parmenion, they would know he had betrayed them.

The unarmed Spartan lurched to his feet. Parzalamis would have only one option now. Eliminate the danger. Kill Mothac and the man to whom he had confided the secret.

With a whispered curse he started to run back towards the house.

A figure leapt from the shadows, moonlight gleaming on an upraised knife-blade. Parmenion ducked and hammered his left fist into the man's face, hurling him off balance. A second attacker grabbed him from behind, but Parmenion dropped to one knee, taking hold of the assassin's arm and pitching him into his comrade. A third man ran at him with a short stabbing sword in his hand. Surging to his feet Parmenion swayed left, the blade slashing past his hip. His fist cannoned against the assassin's chin, staggering him. The other men had regained their feet and were advancing. Parmenion backed away. They came at him in a rush. With a savage scream the Spartan launched himself feet first into their midst, smashing one of the attackers from his feet. The sword cut a shallow wound in his thigh, a knife sliced his scalp. Parmenion rolled to his left. The sword-blade clanged against the stone of the path, sending up a shower of sparks. Parmenion's right leg swept out, knocking the swordsman to the ground. The Spartan's hand fell against a large stone, which he threw into the advancing knifeman's face. Blood spurting from his crushed nose the man cried out, dropping his knife. Parmenion dived for it and rolled to his feet.

The swordsman aimed a wild cut at his head. Parmenion ducked once more and then stepped inside, ramming the knife into the man's belly and ripping it up through the lungs. As the assassin screamed and fell, his comrades turned to run. Parmenion's arm swept up, the blood-covered knife slicing through the air to plunge into one assassin's back. The man stumbled but ran on. Scooping up the fallen sword, the Spartan gave chase. The fleeing warriors ran to the western gate, where their mounts were tethered. The first man vaulted to his horse but his wounded comrade, blood streaming down his back, could not summon the strength to mount. 'Help me, Danis!' he begged. Ignoring him, his companion kicked his horse into a gallop.

Parmenion raced through the gateway and hacked the sword through the wounded attacker's neck. Seizing the reins of the assassin's horse, he swung himself to the beast's back and set off after the third man.

The fleeing rider had a good start, but he was no horseman and steadily Parmenion gained. His mount, a sway-backed dun gelding, was not quality but he had staying power and slowly Parmenion closed the distance. His erstwhile attacker, a slim bearded man, cast a nervous glance over his shoulder as the horses thundered up the hillside heading east. Suddenly the assassin's horse stumbled, pitching his rider to the earth. The man hit hard, but pushed himself to his feet and started to run. Parmenion galloped his horse alongside the man, the flat of the sword-blade rapping his skull and toppling him to the ground.

Reining in the gelding, Parmenion leapt down. His would-be killer backed away.

'Speak swiftly,' said the Spartan. 'Your life depends on it.'

The man's face hardened. 'I'll tell you nothing, you Spartan scum-bucket.'

'Unwise,' said Parmenion, plunging the sword into the man's belly. The warrior died without a sound, toppling face-first to the grass. Parmenion remounted and galloped the gelding down past the paddocks and stables, leaping to the ground outside Mothac's house.

The Theban walked out to greet him. His face was ashen and a dagger jutted from his shoulder. 'I think you should forget about keeping contact with Parzalamis,' Mothac grunted.

Parmenion walked into the house where the Persian was lying on the floor, his head twisted at an impossible angle.

'He was waiting for me,' said Mothac, 'but I don't think he expected an old man to be so strong. And like so many of his ilk he wanted to talk before he fought, to make me feel fear, to force me to beg, perhaps. He knew of my meeting with you; he called me a traitor. I think he was truly offended by my duplicity.'

'We must get that knife out,' Parmenion said.

'No time, my friend. Before we fought he taunted me with the fact that the assassination of Alexander is set for tonight. Take Bessus – he's the fastest we have.'

Parmenion ran to the stable. But even as the stallion galloped clear of the buildings, the Spartan felt an icy terror.

There was no way he could reach the capital in time . . .

Pella, Macedonia, Autumn

Alexander's dreams were troubled. He saw a dark mountainside and a stone altar around which black-robed priests were chanting, calling out a name, summoning . . .

'Iskander! Iskander!'

The voices were sibilant, like storm winds through winter branches, and he felt a terrible pull on his chest. Fear swept through him.

'They are calling me,' he realized, and his dream eyes fixed on the sharp knives they carried and the blood channels carved into the altar.

A figure moved forward, the moonlight shining on his face. Alexander almost screamed then, for the man was his father, Philip, dressed for war in a cuirass the boy had never seen.

'Well?' asked the King. 'Where is the child?'

'He will come, sire,' answered the chief priest. 'I promise you.'

The King turned and Alexander saw that his blind eye was no longer like an opal. Now it shone pure gold and seemed to burn with a yellow fire.

'I see him!' yelled the King, pointing directly at Alexander. 'But he is so faint!'

'Come to us, Iskander!' the priests chanted.

The pull grew stronger.

'No!' screamed the child.

79

And woke in his bed, his body trembling, sweat covering his tiny frame.

*

Lolon crept into the royal gardens, keeping to the shadows of the trees, ever watchful for the sentries. His hand strayed to the dagger at his side, taking comfort from the cold hilt.

The child was possessed, he reminded himself. It was not like killing a real child. Not as the Macedonians had done to his own two sons back at Methone, when the troops poured through the breached wall, killing all who stood in their way. The mercenaries guarding the walls had been the first to die, alongside the city militia. But then it was the citizens – cut down as they fled, the women raped, the children butchered.

The survivors had been herded together in the main square. Lolon had tried to protect his wife, Casa, and his sons. But what could he do against armed men? They dragged Casa and the other women away, killing the children and making a mound of their tiny bodies. Then they marched the men north, the women east, where the ships waited to take them to the slave markets of Asia.

The city had been destroyed, razed utterly, every surviving man and woman sold into slavery.

Lolon felt the weight of his heartache and sank to the soft ground, tears welling in his eyes. He had never been rich. A maker of sandals, he eked out a living, often going hungry himself so that Casa and the children could eat. But the Macedonians had come with their siege-engines, their long spears and their stabbing swords.

There was no place in the tyrant's heart for an independent city within Macedonia. Oh, no! Bend the knee or die.

I wish they'd given me the chance to bend the knee, thought Lolon.

But now – thanks to the Athenians – he had a chance to repay the tyrant in blood. A simple thrust with the knife and the Demon Prince would die. Then Philip would know the anguish of loss.

Lolon's mouth was dry and the cool night breeze made him shiver.

He had been marched first to Pelagonia in the northwest, where the new slaves were put to work building a line of fortresses along the borders of Illyria. For a year Lolon had toiled in the stone quarries. He had spent his evenings making sandals for other slaves before his handiwork was observed by a Macedonian officer. After that he was removed from the work-force and given a better billet, with warm blankets and good food. And he made sandals, boots and shoes for the soldiers.

In Methone his work had been considered fair, but among the barbaric Macedonians he was an artist. In truth his talent did swell, and he was sold on at great profit – to the household of Attalus, the King's Champion.

It was then that the Athenians had come to him. He had been walking in the market-place, ordering leather and hide, and had stopped for a cool drink.

'Surely I know you, friend,' came a voice, and Lolon turned. The speaker was a short, stout man, bald and beardless. Lolon did not remember him, but glanced down at the man's sandals. These he knew; he had made them two years before – a month before the Macedonians came.

'Yes, I remember you,' he answered dully.

As the weeks passed he saw the man, Gorinus, more often, at first talking of better days, and then – the floodgates of his bitterness giving way – speaking of his hatred. Gorinus had been a good listener, becoming a friend.

One morning, as they met in the market-place, Gorinus introduced a second man and they took Lolon to a small house behind the *agora*. Here the plot was hatched: kill the demon child, said Gorinus, and then come with us to Athens.

At first he had refused, but they fed his bitterness, reminding him of how the Macedonians had killed the children of Methone, taking the youngest by their ankles and dashing their brains to the walls.

'Yes! Yes!' cried Lolon. 'I will have my revenge!'

Now he cowered beneath the trees, staring up at Alexander's window. Easing himself from the shadows, he ran to the wall, his heart beating wildly. Slipping through a side door into the corridor beyond he moved carefully in the darkness, climbing the stairs, stopping every few steps to listen for the sentries. There was no guard on Alexander's door, the Athenians had assured him, but two warriors were stationed at the end of the corridor.

Reaching the top of the stairs, he glanced out. The soldiers were standing some twenty paces away, talking in hushed voices, their whispers carrying to the waiting assassin. They were discussing a coming horse-race. Neither was looking in Lolon's direction. Swiftly he crossed the corridor, pushing his back against the door to Alexander's room.

Slowly he drew the dagger.

*

Alexander swung his legs from the bed and jumped to the floor, the dream still strong in his mind, his golden hair lank with sweat. Moonlight streamed through the open window of his room, bathing the ceiling with a pale, white light.

He could still hear the voices, like whispering echoes in his mind.

'Iskander! Iskander! Come to us!'

'No,' he whispered, sitting down at the centre of a goatskin rug and pressing his hands to his ears. 'No, I won't! You are dreams. You are not real!'

The rug was warm and he lay down upon it, staring up at the moonlit ceiling.

Something was wrong in the room. He gazed around, the dream forgotten, but could see nothing amiss. His toy soldiers were still scattered about the floor, with his small siege-engines. His books and drawings were on the tiny table. Alexander stood and walked to the window, climbing up on the bench seat below it so that he could look out into the gardens. Leaning out on the sill he gazed down . . . at the moon.

The gardens had disappeared and stars shone all around

the palace, above and below, to left and right. In the distance there were no mountains, no plains or hills, no valleys and woods. Only the dark of an all-consuming sky.

The boy's fear was forgotten, lost as he was in the wonder of this miracle. He did not often wake in the night. Perhaps it was always this way, but no one had bothered to tell him. The moon was an incredible sight, no longer a silver disc but a scarred and pitted shield that had seen many battles. Alexander could see the marks of arrows and stones upon the surface, the dents and cuts.

And the stars were different also, perfectly round, like a slinger's stones, glowing, pulsing. In the distance he saw a movement, a flashing light, a dragon with a tail of fire . . . then it was gone. Behind him the door opened, but he was aware of nothing but the beauty of this colossal night.

*

Lolon saw the boy at the window. Softly closing the door, he swallowed hard and advanced across the room. His foot came down on a wooden soldier, which broke with a loud crack. The prince glanced round.

'Look,' he said, 'isn't it wonderful? The stars are everywhere.'

Lolon drew his dagger, but the boy had turned back to the window and was leaning out over the void.

One thrust and it would be over. Lolon tensed, aiming the dagger point at the small back. He was no older than Lolon's youngest. . .

Don't think that way, he cautioned himself. Think of revenge! Think of the pain you will cause the tyrant!

Suddenly Alexander cried out and fell forward, losing his grip on the sill. Without thinking Lolon's hand snaked out, grabbing the prince by the leg and hauling him back. A terrible, soul-searing pain swept through the slave and he staggered, clutching his chest. The agony coalesced into a burning ball in his heart and he sank to his knees, gasping for air.

'I'm sorry! I'm sorry! I'm sorry!' wailed Alexander, the stars forgotten. Lolon began to tremble, then pitched face-first to the floor. 'I'll get help,' shouted the prince, running to the door and pulling it open. But there was no corridor, no stone walls, no familiar hangings. The door opened on to the vault of the night, huge, dark and irresistible. The boy teetered on the edge of the abyss, his balance failing him. With a last despairing cry he fell . . . tumbling among the stars.

The voices came roaring back to him as he hurtled through the sky, and he heard a shout of triumph from the priest: *'He is coming! The Golden Child is coming!'*

Alexander screamed and saw again the face of the man who looked like his father – a malevolent grin on his bearded face, his golden eye gleaming like a ball of fire.

The Temple, Asia Minor

The man's heart was weak, the valves hard and inelastic. His lungs were huge now, distorting his rib-cage, and he could move only a few paces before exhaustion forced him to rest. Derae sat beside his bed, her hand resting on his chest, and gazed down into his tired eyes.

'I can do nothing for you,' she said sadly, watching the light of hope fade from his eyes.

'Just . . . give me . . . a few more days,' he begged, his voice weak.

'Not even that,' she told him, taking his hand.

Beside the bed his wife began to weep. 'So . . . soon . . . then?' he whispered.

Derae nodded and his head sagged back to the pillow.

'Please help him!' begged the wailing woman, throwing herself to her knees before the Healer.

The man on the bed tensed suddenly, his face darkening. His mouth opened but no words came forth, only a long, broken sigh. 'No!' screamed the woman. 'No!'

Derae eased herself to her feet and walked slowly from the altar room, waving away the servants who moved to assist her. The corridors were cold and she shivered as she made her way to her room.

A man stepped into her path. 'They have taken him,' said Aristotle.

Derae closed her eyes. 'I am tired. I can be of little use to you. Go away.' Pushing past him, she forced her weary body on. Behind her Aristotle dipped his hand into the pouch at his side, lifting clear a golden stone.

Derae walked on, her mind locked to the merchant whose death she could not prevent. She took a deep breath. The air felt good in her lungs, refreshing, invigorating. How strange, she thought, as her weariness evaporated. She felt better than she had in years and remembered how cool it was in the sea, how good to run down to the beach and wade out into the crystal-clear waters, feeling the sun warm on her back.

Suddenly she laughed. It was too long since she had last left the temple to walk the cliff path. And she was hungry. Ravenous!

Pushing open the door to her room, she wandered to the window. How clear the air, she thought as she stared out over the sea. White gulls circled the cliffs and she could see each bird as it wheeled and dived. Even the clouds were sharply defined. Then she realized she was not using her spirit eyes. Her blindness had gone. Glancing down, she looked at her hands. The skin was smooth and unlined. Anger flared in her and she swung to face the *magus* who stood, silently, in the doorway.

'How dare you!' she thundered. 'How dare you do this to me!'

'I need you,' he responded, moving into the room and pushing shut the door behind him. 'And what is so terrible about youth, Derae? What is it you fear?'

'I fear nothing!' she stormed, 'unless it be the suffering I cannot heal. Did you see the man they carried in? He was a prince; he was kind, caring. But his heart had rotted within him, moving far beyond my capacity to heal. That is what I fear – living long enough to see another thousand like him. You think I want to be young again? Why? For what purpose? Everything I ever desired has been denied me. Why should I want to live any longer?'

Aristotle moved further into the room, his face reflecting his sorrow.

'If you wish then I will return your body to its former . . . glory? But first will you help me? Will you aid Parmenion?'

Derae moved to the mirror and stared at her youthful reflection. A deep sigh came from her and she nodded. 'I will go. But first you must change my face. He must not know me – you understand?'

'It will be as you say,' he promised.

*

'I think it was rash to execute the sentries,' said Parmenion, struggling to hold his temper.

'And what would you have done, Spartan?' sneered Attalus. 'Promoted them, perhaps?'

Parmenion swung away from the man, focusing on the King who sat hunched on the throne, his face grey from exhaustion, his eyes dull. In the two days since the disappearance of the prince, Philip had not slept. The 3,000 Guards had scoured the city, searching every house, attic and cellar. Riders had swept out into the countryside, seeking news of anyone travelling with a child or children.

But there was no sign of Alexander.

'Sire,' said Parmenion.

The King looked up. 'What is it?'

'The sentries who were executed. Did they say anything?'

Philip shrugged. 'They told us nonsense, an incredible fabrication. I don't even remember it all. Something about stars . . . Tell him, Attalus.'

'To what point, sire? It will bring us no closer to recovering the prince. He is being held somewhere for ransom; someone will contact us.'

'Tell him anyway,' said Philip.

'They said that the corridor disappeared and a great wind swept them from their feet. All they could see were stars, and they heard the prince cry out as if from a great distance. They both swore to it; it was lunatic.'

'Perhaps so, Attalus,' said Parmenion softly, 'but if your life was at stake would you invent such a ridiculous tale?'

'Of course not. You think they were telling the truth?' Attalus chuckled and shook his head.

'I have no idea what the truth is . . . yet. But the guards at the gate say no one passed them. The sentries on the walls outside reported no screams or shouts. Yet the prince is gone. Have you identified the corpse?'

'No,' answered Attalus. 'He had rotted almost to nothing.'

'Have you checked the household slaves to see who might be missing?'

'What makes you think he was a slave?' asked Philip.

'All that was left was his tunic. It was poor cloth – even a servant would have worn better.'

'That is a good point,' said the King. 'See to it, Attalus. Now!' he added, as the warrior made to speak. Attalus, his face reddening, bowed and left the throne-room.

'We must find him,' Philip told Parmenion. 'We *must*.'

'We will, sire. I do not believe him dead. If that was the purpose, his body would have been found by now.'

Philip glanced up, his single green eye gleaming with a savage light. 'When I find those responsible they will suffer as no one has ever suffered before. I will see them die – and their families, and their city. Men will talk of it for a thousand years. I swear it.'

'Let us first find him,' said Parmenion.

The King did not seem to hear him. Rubbing at his blind eye he rose from the throne with fists clenched, knuckles ivory-white. 'How could this happen?' he hissed. 'To me? To Philip?' Parmenion kept silent, hoping the murderous rage would pass. In this mood Philip was always unpredictable. The Spartan had not told him of the Persian, Parzalamis, and had sworn Mothac to secrecy. No matter what Philip believed, Parmenion knew the Macedonians were not yet ready for a war against the Persian empire. Parzalamis' body had been secretly buried on the estate, and while the slaying of the three assassins could not be kept from the King, no one knew where they came from nor who had sent them.

The wound on Parmenion's thigh itched as he stood silently watching the King, and he idly scratched at it through the linen bandage. Philip saw the movement – and smiled.

'You did well, Spartan,' he said, the tension seeping from him. 'To kill three was no mean feat. How many times have I urged you to have guards at your estate?'

'Many times, sire, and I shall listen to your advice from now on.'

Philip sank back to the throne. 'I thank the gods Olympias is not here. And I hope to Zeus that we find him before news reaches Epirus. She will return like an avenging Harpy, threatening to rip my heart out with her bare hands.'

'We will find him,' promised Parmenion, forcing a confidence into his voice that he did not feel.

'I should not have killed the sentries,' said Philip. 'It was foolish. You think there may be sorcery in this?'

'There is too much we do not know,' Parmenion answered. 'Who was the man in the room? Why did he carry a dagger? Was his mission to kill? If it was, was he alone? As to the sentries . . . what did they mean about the stars? There is little sense in this, Philip. If the boy had been killed we would have found the body. Yet, why would he be taken? Ransom? Who would live to spend such wealth? Let us, for argument's sake, assume that the Olynthians were responsible. They are not fools. They know Macedonia's army would descend on them with fire and sword; the lands of the Chalcidice would run with blood.'

'Athens,' muttered Philip. 'They would do anything to cause me pain. Athens . . .' Parmenion saw again the gleam in the eye, and spoke swiftly.

'I do not think so,' he said softly. 'Demosthenes makes great play about your *tyranny* and your supposed evils. His honeyed words seduce many of the lesser cities. How would he appear if named as a child killer? No. If Athens sent assassins their victim would be you, not Alexander. What did the priestess say when you saw her?'

'Pah!' snorted the King. 'She is an old fool. She walked around the boy's room pretending to talk to the spirits. But, at the end, she could tell me nothing.'

'But what did she say?'

'She told me the boy's spirit was not in Macedonia. Nor

in Hades. Now you tell me how that could be true. He had not been gone more than half a day. Even if he was carried away by an eagle he would still have been in Macedonia when she spoke. Senile old hag! But I tell you this, she was frightened. She trembled when she entered his room.'

'You should rest,' Parmenion advised him. 'Go to bed. Send for one of your wives.'

'That's the last thing I need, my friend. They are hard-pressed to keep the glee from their eyes. My son and heir is missing – maybe dead. All they can think of is opening their legs and supplying me with another. No. I shall not rest until the truth is known.'

Attalus entered the throne-room and bowed. 'There is a slave missing, sire,' he said, his face ashen. 'His name is Lolon; he is a sandal-maker, a Methonian.'

'What do we know of him?' asked Parmenion, keeping his expression even.

'I bought him from the commander of Pelagonia some months ago. He was a good worker. The other slaves say he was a quiet man, keeping to himself. I know no more.'

'What was he doing in my son's room?' thundered Philip. 'He must have had a reason.'

'He told Melissa – one of my slave-girls – that he had a family in Methone. His children were slaughtered, his wife taken from him.' Attalus cleared his throat and swallowed hard. 'I think he wanted revenge.'

Philip surged from the throne. 'He must have had accomplices – or else where is the boy? How many other Methonians have you brought into the palace?'

'There are none, sire. And I did not know he was Methonian, I swear it!'

'Attalus is not at fault, sire,' said Parmenion. 'We have stormed many cities and flooded the land with slaves. That is why the price per man is only forty drachms against two hundred three years ago. Almost every slave in Pella would have reason to hate you.'

'I care nothing for their hate!' snapped Philip. 'But you are right, Parmenion, Attalus is blameless.' Turning to his

Champion, he patted the man's shoulder. 'Forgive my anger, my friend.'

'There is nothing to forgive, sire,' answered Attalus, bowing.

Later, as Parmenion sat alone in one of the forty palace guest-rooms, Attalus came to him. 'Why did you speak for me?' he demanded. 'I am no friend to you – nor desire to be.'

Parmenion gazed into the man's cold eyes, seeing the tension there and in the tight lines of his hatchet face, the grim gash of his almost lipless mouth. 'It is not a question of friendship, Attalus,' he said, 'merely of truth. Now I do not enjoy your company and, if you have nothing else to say, be so kind as to leave me in peace.'

But the man did not leave. Walking further into the room, he sat in a high-backed chair and poured a goblet of watered wine, sipping it slowly. 'This is good,' he said. 'Do you think the story about the stars is important?'

'I don't know,' admitted the Spartan, 'but I intend to find out.'

'And how will you accomplish this?'

'When first I came to Macedonia I met a *magus* – a man of great power. I will seek him out. If there is sorcery involved, he will know of it – and its source.'

'And where will you find this . . . man of magic?'

'Sitting upon a rock,' the Spartan answered.

The Empire of Makedon

Alexander opened his eyes and shivered, feeling cold mud beneath his rain-soaked body. He had fallen, screaming and lost, through the star-filled sky, losing consciousness as bright lights and myriad colours blazed across his eyes. Now there were no colours, only a bone-numbing coldness and the dark of a mountain night.

He was about to move when he heard the voices and instinctively he crouched down, staring at the shadow-haunted tree-line from where the voices came.

'I swear to you, sire, the child is here. The Spell took him and drew him to this hillside. I did warn you that it might not be precisely to this spot. But he must be within a hundred paces in any direction.'

'Find him – or I'll feed your heart to the Vores.'

Alexander shivered again – though this time not from the cold. The second voice was like his father's, though deeper and more chilling. He could not yet see the speakers but he knew they were coming closer. There were bushes nearby and the child crept into them, hunching his naked body down.

The glittering light of many torches flickered in the trees and Alexander saw the man with the golden eye walk out on to the mountainside, the dark-robed priest alongside him. Behind him came a score of warriors holding torches aloft, scanning the undergrowth, searching, pushing aside the bracken with long lances.

The leaf-covered soil was damp and soft beneath the boy and he dug his fingers deep into it, rolling silently to his back and pulling earth and rotted vegetation over his legs and chest. He could feel small insects scurrying in panic over his skin, and a soft worm slid over his left calf. Ignoring the discomfort, he smeared mud on his face and hair and waited, heart beating wildly, for the searchers.

'One thousand drachms to the man who finds him!' called the King.

'Aya!' roared the men, raising their torches in salute.

From where he lay, Alexander could see the legs and feet of the searchers as they neared him. They were barefoot, but their calves were protected by greaves of bronze, showing intricate designs. But each one that he saw had a central motif, a stylized sunburst. This surprised the child, for the sunburst was the symbol of Macedonia and yet the armour the men wore was neither Macedonian nor Phrygian – the breastplates more elaborate, the helms bearing raven's wings, rather than the horsehair plumes sported by his father's soldiers.

Even through his fear, Alexander was puzzled. These soldiers were like none he had ever seen, in life or in paintings or murals.

An enormous clap of thunder sounded, lightning forking across the sky.

A lance-point sliced through the bush above him, the branches parting. Then the lance pulled clear and the man moved on.

Alexander stayed where he was until all sounds around him faded away. At last, as the rain stopped, he moved his frozen body, crawling from the shelter of the bush and standing on the mountainside.

Glancing up, he gazed at the stars in the now clear sky – realizing with a sharp stab of fear that he knew them not at all. Where was the Bowman, and the Great Wolf, the Spear Carrier and the Earth Mother? Seeking out the North Star he scanned the heavens. Nothing was remotely familiar.

The searchers had moved down the mountain behind him and the boy decided to walk in the opposite direction.

The trees were shrouded in darkness, but Alexander swallowed his fear and moved on, deeper into the wood. After a little while he saw the altar of his dream, gaunt and stark in a small clearing, broken columns of stone around it. It was here that they had tried to summon him.

The clearing was deserted, but under a spreading oak a small fire still smouldered. Alexander ran to it, kneeling down and blowing flames to life. He searched for dry wood, but there was none and he sat by the dying blaze, holding his trembling hands to the fading heat.

'Where is this place?' he whispered. 'How can I get home?' Tears welled and he felt the beginning of panic. 'I will not cry,' he said. 'I am the son of a King.'

Gathering wet twigs, he laid them in the hot ashes at the edge of the fire to dry, then rose and began to scout the area. He needed fuel for the fire; without it he could die in this cold. The altar yielded nothing and he walked further into the wood. Here the darkness was deeper, the tree branches interlaced like a great domed roof. But the ground was dryer underfoot, and Alexander found several broken branches which he gathered in his arms before returning to the fire.

Patiently he worked at the small blaze, careful not to smother it, feeding small twigs to the dancing fingers of flame until at last his trembling body began to feel the growing heat.

Three times he returned to the heart of the wood, gathering fuel, building up a store which he hoped would last the night. On his fourth journey he thought he heard a sound in the darkness and paused. At first there was silence, then came a stealthy padding that filled him with terror. Dropping the wood he ran for his fire, sprinting across the clearing and crouching beside the blaze, seizing a burning branch and hoisting it above his head.

From the woods came a hunting pack of grey wolves, padding out to circle him – yellow eyes gleaming, fangs bared. They were huge beasts, taller even than the war-hounds of his father, and he had no weapon save the burning branch.

He could feel their hunger beating upon his mind, coming at him in waves. They feared the fire, but their empty bellies were fuelling their courage.

Alexander stood very still and closed his eyes, reaching out with his Talent, sliding through the haze of hunger and fury, seeking the pack leader, touching his soul fire and merging with his memories. The child saw a birth in a dark cave, tumbling tussles with brothers and sisters, more bitter fights and battles as he grew – scars and pain, long hunts, victories.

At last the boy opened his eyes. 'You and I are one,' he told the great, grey wolf. The beast cocked its head and advanced on him. Alexander returned the branch to the fire and waited while the wolf came closer, his jaws level with the boy's face. Reaching out slowly, Alexander stroked the grizzled head and the matted fur of its neck.

Puzzled, the other wolves moved uneasily around the clearing.

The boy let his mind wander further, scouring the mountainside and the woods beyond until at last he felt the beating of another heart – a doe sleeping. Alexander shared the image with the wolf-leader and pointed to the south.

The wolf padded silently away, the pack following. Alexander sank to his knees by the fire – tired, frightened, yet exultant.

'I am the son of a King,' he said aloud, 'and I conquered my fear.'

'A fine job you made of it,' said a voice from behind him. Alexander did not move. 'Do not fear me, lad,' said the man, moving out into the boy's range of vision and squatting by the fire. 'I am not your enemy.' The newcomer was not tall, his hair short-cropped and grey, his beard tightly curled. He was wearing a kilt of leather and a bow was slung across his broad shoulders. A horse moved out into the clearing; it wore no chabraque or bridle but came close to the man, nuzzling his back. 'Be at ease, Caymal,' he whispered, stroking the stallion's nose. 'The wolves are gone. The young prince dismissed them in search of a doe.'

95

'Why did I not sense your presence?' asked Alexander. 'And why did the wolves not pick up your scent?'

'The two answers are one: I did not wish to be found.'

'You are a *magus*, then?'

'I am many things,' the man told him. 'But despite all my virtues I have one irritating vice: I am by nature curious, and I find this current situation irresistibly intriguing. How old are you, boy?'

'Four.'

The man nodded. 'Are you hungry?'

'I am,' admitted Alexander. 'But I see you have no food.'

The newcomer laughed and dipped his hand into a leather pouch by his side. The pouch was small, yet – impossibly – the man drew from it a woollen tunic which he tossed to the boy. 'What we see is not always the complete truth,' he said. 'Put on the tunic.' Alexander stood, lifting the garment over his head and settling it into place. It was a perfect fit, the material soft and warm, edged with leather. When he sat down again the man was turning an iron spit over the flames, on which meat was sizzling.

'I am Chiron,' said the man. 'Welcome to my woods.'

'I am Alexander,' responded the boy, the smell of the roasting meat filling his senses.

'And the son of a King. Which King would that be, Alexander?'

'My father is Philip, King of Macedonia.'

'Wonderful!' said Chiron. 'And how did you come here?'

The prince told him of the dream and the night of stars followed by the long fall into darkness. Chiron sat silently as the boy talked, then questioned him about Macedonia and Pella.

'But surely you know of my father,' said Alexander, surprised. 'He is the greatest King in all of Greece.'

'Greece? How interesting. Let us eat.' Chiron lifted the meat from the spit, pulling it apart and handing a section to the boy. Alexander took it gingerly, expecting the hot fat to burn his fingers. But although well-cooked the food was only warm, and he devoured it swiftly.

'Will you take me to my father?' he asked when the meal was finished. 'He will reward you well.'

'I am afraid, my boy, that what you ask is beyond even my powers.'

'Why? You have a horse. I cannot be far from home.'

'You could not be further. This is not Greece, but a land called Achaea. And here the great power is Philippos, Lord of the Makedones – the Demon King. It was he who stood upon this hillside, his priests calling you from your home. It is he who hunts you even now. And, though my power temporarily blocked the magic of his golden eye, no, Alexander, I cannot take you home.'

'I am lost then?' whispered the boy. 'I will never see my father again?'

'Let us not leap to conclusions,' advised Chiron, but his grey eyes avoided Alexander's gaze.

'Why would this . . . Philippos want me?'

'I . . . am not sure,' replied Chiron.

Alexander looked at him sharply. 'I think you are . . . not telling me the truth.'

'You are quite right, young prince. And let us leave it that way for the moment. We will sleep now, and tomorrow I will take you to my home. There we can think and plan.'

The child looked into the grey eyes of the man, not knowing whether to trust him nor how to arrive at a decision concerning him. Chiron had fed him and clothed him, offering him no harm, but this in itself gave no indication of his longer-term plans. The fire was warm and Alexander lay down beside it to think . . .

And slept.

He was awoken by the man's hand on his shoulder, gently shaking him, and it was some moments before he realized that the killing power he had come to dread had not touched the grey-haired *magus*.

'We must leave – and swiftly,' said Chiron. 'The Makedones are back!'

'How do you know?' asked Alexander sleepily.

'Caymal kept watch for us,' the *magus* answered. 'Now listen to me, this is most important. You are about to meet another friend. He will surprise you, but you will trust him. You must. Tell him that Chiron wants him to go home. Tell him the Makedones are upon us and he must run – not fight. You understand?'

'Where are you going?' asked the boy fearfully.

'Nowhere,' answered Chiron, handing his bow and quiver to the prince. 'Watch and learn.' Rising swiftly, he ran to the stallion and turned to face the boy. The stallion's great head rested on the man's shoulder, and the two stood as still as statues. Alexander blinked, and it seemed that a heat-haze danced over man and horse. Chiron's chest swelled, his head thickening, beard darkening. Great bands of muscle writhed over his chest, while his legs stretched and twisted, his feet shrivelling into hooves.

Alexander sat transfixed as horse and *magus* became one. Gone was the stallion's head. Now the torso of a man reared up from the shoulders of the stallion. The centaur stamped his front hoof and reared, then, seeing the boy, trotted forward.

'Who are you?' boomed a voice deep as distant thunder. Alexander stood looking into the distorted face. Nothing of Chiron remained. The eyes were wide-set and brown, the mouth full, the beard chestnut-coloured and straight.

'I am Alexander – and I have a message from Chiron,' he said.

'You are very small. And I am hungry.'

'Chiron told me to warn you that the Makedones are near.'

Leaning back his head the centaur gave a great cry, a mixture of rage and anger. He saw the bow in the boy's hand and reached out.

'Give to me. I will kill Makedones.'

'Chiron also said that you are to go home. He needs you. You must not fight the Makedones.'

The centaur moved closer, dipping his torso until he looked over the prince. 'You are friend to Chiron?'

'Yes.'

'Then I will not kill you. Now give me the bow, and I will go home.'

'Chiron said for you to take me with you,' lied the boy swiftly, handing him the bow and quiver.

The centaur nodded. 'You may ride me, Human, but if you fall Camiron shall not stop for you.'

Reaching out, he swung Alexander to his back and cantered from the clearing. The boy slipped and almost fell. 'Hold to my mane,' called Camiron. Alexander looked up. Long hair grew from the centaur's spine and he took hold of it with both hands. The centaur broke into a run, and then a gallop, coming clear of the tree-line and thundering into the open.

Directly ahead of them were some fifty cavalrymen. Camiron dug in his front hooves, skidding to a stop that almost dislodged the prince. The riders saw them and fanned out in a wide circle to trap them. Camiron notched an arrow to his bow. 'I kill Makedones,' he said.

'No!' shouted Alexander. 'Home. Go home. Chiron needs you!'

The centaur grunted and leapt to the gallop. An arrow sliced the air by his head. At full run Camiron loosed his own shaft; it hammered into a warrior's chest, toppling him from his mount. More arrows flew at them and one slashed through the muscles of Camiron's hip. He shouted in pain and rage, but continued to run.

They were almost encircled now and Alexander felt a growing sense of despair. Just as it seemed they would be run down the centaur swerved and cut to the right, loosing an arrow into a second rider. The man fell, and for a brief moment a gap appeared in the Makedones' line. Swift as a storm wind Camiron leapt through it, his hooves thundering on the plain as he swept clear of the riders, who streamed after them.

The centaur increased his speed, his laughter carrying back to the warriors who screamed curses after him.

'I fool them!' shouted Camiron. 'The greatest am I.'

'Yes,' agreed Alexander, clinging to the mane. 'You are great. How far is home?'

'Long way for you to walk,' said the centaur. 'Not far for Camiron to run. Are you truly friend to Chiron?'

'Yes, I told you.'

'It better be truth,' the centaur told him. 'If Chiron is not there – I will kill you, Human, and dine on your marrow.'

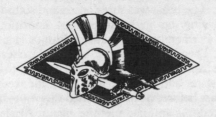

The Thracian Border, Macedonia

Parmenion reined in the gelding and swung to look back over the hills towards the distant River Axios. He could no longer see the rider, but he knew without a shred of doubt that he was still being followed. The Spartan found this irksome, but not as yet worrying.

He had spotted him on his second day from Pella, a distant dot on the horizon, and had changed his course, veering north-east before cutting back to the main trail. From a heavily wooded hill-top Parmenion had then watched the rider also change direction.

The distance was too great for identification. All Parmenion could see was that the man wore a burnished helm and breastplate and was riding a tall, dappled grey. The Spartan rode on, wary now for Thrace was close and he wished no confrontation with the border guards.

The land stretched ahead in a series of folds, gulleys and hollows, thinly wooded and undulating. There were shallow streams here, sparkling in the sunlight, offspring of the great River Nestos that flowed through the land to merge with the sea north of the island of Thasos.

Parmenion guided the chestnut gelding into a small wood and dismounted by a stream. The gelding stood quietly with ears pricked, nostrils quivering with the sweet smell of mountain water. Parmenion removed the lionskin chabraque from the horse's back and rubbed him down with a handful of dry grass. Mothac had urged him to take the stallion Bessus, but instead the Spartan had chosen the chestnut. The beast was sure-footed and sound of temperament, having no great speed but enormous levels of stamina. Parmenion stroked the gelding's face and led him to water. There was no need to hobble the chestnut and the Spartan strolled to a nearby boulder and sat listening to the rushing water and the bird-song from the trees.

Six years before, he had travelled this route heading west into Macedonia and had met the *magus*, Aristotle.

'Seek me out when you have need,' Aristotle had told him. Well, thought Parmenion, the need could not be greater. Untying the chinstraps of his baked leather helm Parmenion pulled it clear, running his fingers through his sweat-soaked hair. Despite the imminence of winter the weather remained hot and dry and he could feel sweat trickling down his back under the leather breastplate.

Phaedra could not understand why he had clothed himself like a poor mercenary. Worse still, she had asked openly why he should embark on such a quest at all.

'You are the real power in Macedonia,' she whispered. 'You could seize the throne. The army would follow you – and then Philo would have the future the gods ordained for him. Why should you care what happens to the demon child?'

He had not answered her. Settling his chabraque over the gelding, he had ridden from the great house without a backward glance.

Skirting the villages on his estate, his first stop had been in a small town in the shadows of the Krousian Mountains. Here he bought supplies, dried meat and fruit, grain for the gelding. The town was expanding – new buildings being erected on the outskirts, evidence of Macedonia's growing wealth. Many of the new settlers were mercenaries, buying land with their wages from Philip's campaigns. Others were crippled ex-soldiers who had earned good pensions from the King's service. The town bustled with activity and Parmenion had been glad to ride from it, heading for the sanctuary and peace of the countryside.

Now, as he sat by the stream, he considered again the problems facing him. He had no idea where Alexander was being held – nor why – and his hopes were resting on the promise of a *magus* he had met in the flesh only once. And what if the Persians had smuggled Alexander out of Macedonia? Suppose he was being held hostage in Susa? How could one man hope to rescue him? And if he did would not Philip, hungry for revenge, take his armies east into the heart of the Persian kingdom?

These sombre thoughts fluttered around Parmenion's mind like irritating moths and angrily he brushed them aside, remembering Xenophon's advice:

'When asked to move a mountain, do not look upon its size. Merely move the first rock.'

The first rock was to find Aristotle.

Allowing the gelding to rest, Parmenion walked to the crest of the hill and stared out over his back-trail, seeking the rider who was following him. But a heat-haze shimmered over the land and he could see no sign of movement.

Riding until dusk, Parmenion made camp in a hollow in the mountains, setting a small fire against a boulder and enjoying the reflected heat. Tomorrow he would reach the pass where first he had met the *magus*. Praying that Aristotle would be there, he slept fitfully.

Two hours before dawn he reached the foothills of the Kerkine Mountains. The breeze was colder here as he urged the gelding up the scree-covered slope towards the pass, and he pulled his black cloak more tightly about him. As he crested the slope he saw four mounted men blocking the narrow pass. Beyond them were two more horses. Parmenion flicked his gaze to the rocks on the left, where two archers waited with arrows notched.

'A fine day to be riding,' said a swarthy warrior on a sturdy black stallion. The man touched heels to his mount and rode forward. He was hatchet-faced, a thick black beard failing to disguise the pockmarks on his cheeks. His eyes were dark and deep-set. His comrades hung back, waiting silently, hands on their swords.

'Indeed it is,' agreed Parmenion. 'What do you require of me?'

'You have entered Thracian lands, Macedonian, and we require a toll. Be so kind as to hand over the contents of that pouch by your side.'

'Firstly,' said Parmenion, 'I am no Macedonian, and secondly it should take no great mind to reason that a mercenary has no coin when he is riding *towards* Persia. Only when he returns.'

'Ah, well,' answered the man, smiling, 'you do have a fine horse. That will have to do.'

The warrior suddenly tensed. Instantly Parmenion kicked the gelding into a run. Two arrows slashed through the air where the Spartan had been. The gelding's shoulder cannoned into the stallion, who bucked violently, throwing his rider. Drawing his sword the Spartan charged at the remaining men, but they scattered before him and then re-formed to give chase.

The pass curved to the right. Out of sight of his pursuers Parmenion hauled on the reins, turning the gelding back the way he had come. It was the last move the robbers had considered. As they rounded the bend, expecting to see their quarry running away from them, they found themselves instead facing a charge.

The gelding hurtled fearlessly into their midst. Parmenion hacked his blade into one rider's neck, spilling him to the ground with blood spurting from his open jugular. The gelding reared, kicking out at a second man whose horse stumbled and fell.

The swarthy leader screamed a battle-cry and lunged at the Spartan. But Parmenion blocked the wild cut, sending a riposte that sliced the skin of the man's face, tearing out his right eye.

The other robbers galloped clear. Parmenion dismounted and approached the fallen leader. The man was struggling to rise, his hand pressed against his ruined eye, trying in vain to stop the flow of blood.

'You whoreson!' he shouted, lifting his sword and running at Parmenion. The Spartan side-stepped, his own blade cleaving into the man's groin, and with a cry of anguish the Thracian toppled to the ground. Parmenion slashed his sword through the man's neck, then stepped over the body to gather the reins of the gelding.

'Neatly done,' came a familiar voice and Parmenion cursed softly.

'What do you want here, Attalus?'

The King's Champion leapt lightly down from the dappled grey and walked across to where Parmenion waited. 'Not overjoyed to see me? Ah, well, that is I suppose understandable. But you intrigued me with your tale of sorcerers and rocks; I thought it might amuse me to meet the man.'

Parmenion shook his head. 'I would as soon sleep with a poisonous snake as entertain your company on the road. Go back to Pella.'

Attalus smiled at the insult, but there was malice in his cold eyes. 'You are known as a man who thinks well, Spartan. I respect you for that. But you are not thinking now. Suppose this . . . wizard . . . can lead you to the child – do you think you will be able to rescue him alone? You may not like me, Parmenion, but you cannot argue against the fact that I am the finest swordsman in Macedonia.'

'That is not at issue,' Parmenion snapped.

'Then what is?'

'I cannot trust you,' answered the Spartan.

'Is that all? Gods, man, what do you expect me to do – cut your throat while you sleep?'

'Perhaps. But you will not have the opportunity for I will travel alone.'

'I do not think that wise,' came a third voice and both men swung to see a grey-haired man sitting cross-legged on a flat-topped boulder.

'You move silently,' whispered Attalus, easing his sword from its scabbard.

'Indeed I do, young Attalus. Now put your sword away – it would be bad manners to attack a man who is arguing on your behalf.' Aristotle looked to Parmenion. 'I think you may find that the King's Champion will be an aid to you on this quest. And believe me, you will need help to recover the prince.'

'Where is he held?' asked Parmenion.

'In a kingdom of the damned,' answered the *magus*. Jumping down from the boulder, he walked back towards a towering rock-face and disappeared. Ignoring Attalus, Parmenion tugged the gelding's reins and followed Aristotle. As before, the seemingly solid wall of rock proved no more substantial than mist, and man and horse found themselves in a cold cavern where great stalactites hung like dragons' teeth from the domed roof. The gelding did not like this dank, cold place and began to tremble. Parmenion patted the beast's neck, whispering soothing words. Attalus came through the wall behind him.

'Not seen enough to amuse you?' asked Parmenion.

'Almost,' the swordsman answered. 'Where did he go?'

Parmenion pointed to a distant shaft of golden sunlight and the two men headed towards it, emerging at last from a wide cave-mouth which overlooked a verdant valley. At the bottom of the slope was a white-walled house, built alongside a mountain stream. Mounting their horses, the two warriors rode down to the house where Aristotle was waiting beside a table laden with food and wine.

'Now to the point of your visit,' said Aristotle as the meal was concluded. 'The child, Alexander, is no longer in this world.'

'You mean he is dead?' hissed Attalus. 'I do not believe it!'

'Not dead,' said Aristotle patiently. 'He was drawn through a portal into a parallel world – that is why his guards reported seeing stars in the corridor. In order to rescue him, you must travel into that world. I can show you the way.'

'This is nonsense,' stormed Attalus, rising from the table. 'Are you going to sit and listen to this horse-dung?' he asked the Spartan.

'Before making judgements,' Parmenion told him, 'look about you. Where are the mountains we rode through? Where is the River Nestos? Can you not see that we are already in another world?'

'It's a trick of some kind,' muttered Attalus, swinging round to stare at the unfamiliar horizon.

Ignoring him, Parmenion turned back to Aristotle. 'Why did they take the boy?'

Aristotle leaned forward, resting his elbows on the broad table-top. 'There is a King there, a man possessed. He desires immortality. To win such a prize he must devour the heart of a special sacrifice. His priests told him of a golden child . . . a special child.'

'This world – is it like our own? Can we find our way through it?' asked the Spartan.

'I cannot fully answer that,' the *magus* told him. 'There are great similarities and yet enormous differences. There are centaurs there, and all the creatures you would hear of only in myth – werebeasts and Harpies, gorgons and beasts of darkness. It is a world of magic, my friend. And yet it is Greece.'

'The King you spoke of – he has a name?'

'Philippos, King of the Makedones. And, before you ask, yes, he is Philip, the image of the man you serve.'

'This is insane,' sneered Attalus. 'Why do you sit and listen to such gibberish?'

'As I told you before,' said Parmenion coldly, 'you are more than welcome to return to Pella. As for myself, I will travel into this other Greece. And I will find the prince. Will you come with me, Aristotle?'

The *magus* shook his head and looked away. 'I cannot . . . not yet. Much as I would wish it.'

'Too dangerous for you, wizard?' Attalus mocked.

'Indeed it is,' agreed Aristotle with no trace of rancour. 'But I will come to you when I can, to lead you home. If you survive.'

Book Two, 352 BC

The Forests of Olympus

The pursuing Makedones were not far behind as Camiron climbed the slopes of the mountains. Alexander looked up at the snow-crested peaks and shivered.

'How high will we go?' he called out.

'To Chiron's caves,' replied the centaur, 'on the roof of the world.'

Alexander glanced back. The Makedones were close enough now for him to see the bright sunburst emblems on their black breastplates, and their lance-points glittering in the sunlight. Camiron galloped on, seemingly tireless, while the boy held fast to the chestnut mane. 'How much further?' shouted Alexander.

Camiron paused in his climb and pointed to a forest that clung to the mountain-sides like green mist. 'There! The Makedones will not follow. If they do, they will die.' Bunching the muscles of his hind legs the centaur leapt forward, almost dislodging the boy as he galloped at great speed towards the trees.

As they neared the forest four centaurs rode out to meet them. All were smaller than Camiron, and only two were bearded. Armed with bows, they formed a line and waited. Camiron halted before them.

'What do you want here, outcast?' asked the leading centaur, his beard white, his flanks golden.

111

'I am riding to Chiron's cave,' Camiron answered diffidently. 'We are pursued by Makedones.'

'You are not welcome here,' said another. 'You will bring us trouble.'

'It is the order of Chiron,' protested Camiron. 'I must obey.'

'Lickspittle!' snorted a third centaur. 'What is the Human to you? Are you a slave to his bidding?'

'I am no man's slave,' said Camiron, his voice deepening. Alexander could feel the centaur's muscles tensing. Leaning back, the boy lifted his hand, catching the attention of the newcomers.

'Would you surrender one of your own to his enemies?' he asked.

'Speak when you are spoken to, Human!' snapped the white-bearded leader.

'No,' replied Alexander. 'Answer my question – or does your cowardice shame you to silence?'

'Let me kill him, Father!' shouted a youngster, notching an arrow to his bow.

'No!' thundered White-beard. 'Let them pass!'

'But, Father . . .'

'Let them pass, I say.' The centaurs moved aside and Camiron galloped into the trees. There were more horse people here, all armed with bows. Alexander swung to see the Makedones toiling up the slope, and he heard their screams as the first volley of arrows tore into them.

But the sounds of battle faded as they rode deeper into the forest.

Camiron was silent as they moved on, but Alexander could feel the deep well of his anguish. The boy could think of nothing to say and settled down once more against the broad back. At last they came to a clearing and an open cave-mouth. Camiron trotted inside and lifted Alexander to the ground.

'There is no sign of Chiron,' said the centaur, his eyes brooding and angry.

'May I thank you?' asked Alexander, moving close to the beast. 'You saved my life, and you were very courageous.'

112

'I am the bravest of them all,' said Camiron. 'And the strongest,' he added, lifting his arms and tensing the huge muscles of his biceps.

'You are indeed,' the boy agreed. 'I have never seen anyone stronger.'

The centaur swung his head. 'Where is Chiron, boy? You said he would be here.'

'No,' said Alexander slowly. 'I said he asked you to come here – to bring me to safety. He told me you could be trusted; he talked of your courage.'

'I hurt,' said Camiron suddenly, touching his hand to the shallow gash in his flanks. The blood had already begun to congeal around the wound, but it had flowed down the right foreleg, matting the hair.

'If there is water, I will clean it for you,' offered the boy.

'Why is Chiron not here? Why is he never here? I need him.' The tone was suddenly plaintive, with an edge of panic. 'Chiron!' he bellowed, the sound echoing in the cave. 'Chiron!'

'He will come,' promised Alexander. 'But you must rest. Even one as strong as you must be tired after such a ride.'

'I am not tired. But I am hungry,' he said, his dark eyes fixing on the child.

'Tell me about yourself,' urged Alexander. 'I have never met a centaur, though I have heard tales of them.'

'I don't want to speak. I want to eat,' snapped Camiron, turning and trotting from the cave. Alexander sat down on a rock. He too was hungry and tired, but he dared not sleep while the unpredictable Camiron was close by. After a while he decided to explore the cave. It was not deep, but there were small alcoves that appeared man-made. Entering the first, Alexander noticed that the right-hand wall was a slightly different shade of grey from the stone around it. Reaching out he tried to touch the rock – only to see his hand pass through it. Edging forward he passed through the wall to find himself inside a beautifully furnished room, hung with silks, the walls painted with delicate scenes from Homer, the wooden horse at the gates of Troy, the ship of Odysseus by the island of Sirens, the seeress Circe turning men into swine.

Walking to a window, Alexander gazed out over a sparkling ocean. From here he could see that the building was of white marble, supported by many columns. It was larger than his father's palace at Pella, and infinitely more beautiful. Slowly the boy wandered from room to room. There were many libraries, hundreds of scrolls on scores of shelves, and rooms full of paintings or statues. In yet another room he found sketches of animals, birds, lions and creatures of impossible shapes, some with necks twice as long as their bodies, others with noses that hung to the ground. At last he found the kitchens. Here honey-roasted hams hung from hooks and there were barrels of apples, sacks of dried apricots, pear and peach and other fruits Alexander had never seen. Sitting down at a wide table he tried them all, then remembered the centaur. Finding a silver tray, he loaded it with fruit and meats of all kinds, carrying it back to the first room and through the insubstantial wall into the cave.

'Where were you?' shouted Camiron. 'I looked for you everywhere.'

'I was fetching you some food,' answered Alexander, approaching the centaur and offering the tray. Without a word Camiron took it and began stuffing the food into his cavernous mouth, meats and fruits together. Finally he belched and threw the tray aside.

'Better,' he said. 'Now I want Chiron.'

'Why do the other centaurs not like you?' asked Alexander, changing the subject swiftly.

Camiron folded his legs and settled down on the cave-floor, his dark eyes fixed on the golden-haired boy. 'Who says that they don't? Who told you that?'

'No one told me. I saw it when they rode from the forest.'

'I am stronger than they are,' the centaur said. 'I don't need them. I need no one.'

'I am your friend,' Alexander told him.

'I need no friends,' thundered Camiron. 'None!'

'But are you not lonely?'

'No . . . Yes. Sometimes,' admitted the centaur. 'But I would not be if only I could remember things. Why was I in the wood where I found you? I don't remember going there. I am so confused sometimes. It used not to be like this, I know it didn't. Well, I think it didn't. I am so tired.'

'Sleep for a while,' said Alexander. 'You will feel better for some rest.'

'Yes. Sleep,' whispered the centaur. Suddenly he looked up. 'If Chiron is not here in the morning, I will kill you.'

'We will talk about that in the morning,' said Alexander.

Camiron nodded, his head sinking to his chest. Within moments his breathing deepened. Alexander sat quietly watching the creature, feeling his loneliness slowly subside. Once more the haze began around the beast, shimmering, changing, until the human form of Chiron could be seen asleep on the floor beside the horse, Caymal.

Alexander moved to the *magus*, lightly touching his shoulder. Chiron awoke and yawned.

'You did well, boy,' he said. 'I knew it was a risk leaving you with . . . him, but you handled the situation with skill.'

'Who is he?' asked the prince.

'Like all centaurs, he is a blend of horse and man: partly me, partly Caymal. It used to be that I could control him. Now he grows stronger and I rarely allow him life. But I had to take the risk, for Caymal alone could not have carried us both free of the Makedones.'

'The other centaurs called him an outcast. They hate him.'

'Ah, well, that is a longer story. When first I tried the spell of Merging, I lost control of Camiron and he rode into their village.' Chiron smiled and shook his head. 'I had not considered the timing of the Change. Caymal was in season, and hot for the company of a young mare. Camiron, full of almost childish enthusiasm, tried to force his attention on several of the village females. The males did not take kindly to such advances and chased him from the forest.'

'I see,' said the boy.

'You do? You are a surprising four-year-old.'

'But tell me why Camiron seeks you. You can never have . . . met. Why should he even know of you?'

'A good question, Alexander. You have a fine mind.

115

Caymal knows me and, after his own fashion, has regard for me. When the Merge takes place the end result is a creature – Camiron – who is both of us, and yet neither of us. The part – the greater part – that is Caymal longs to be reunited with his master. It was a sad experiment, and one that I will not repeat. And yet Camiron is an interesting beast. Just like a horse, he is both easily frightened and yet capable of great courage.'

Pushing himself to his feet, Chiron led the boy back through the alcove wall into the palace beyond. 'Here we will be safe for a while. But even my powers cannot stand for long against Philippos.'

'Why does he want me, Chiron?'

'He has the powers of a god, yet he is mortal. He desires to live for ever. So far he has sired six children and has sacrificed each of them to Ahriman, the God of Darkness. But he is not yet immortal. I would imagine his priests sought you out, and you are to be the seventh victim. I can see why. You are a brilliant child, Alexander, and I feel the dark power within you. Philippos wishes to feed on that power.'

'He can have it,' said the youngster. 'It is nothing but a curse to me. Tell me, how is it that I can touch you and yet you feel no pain?'

'That is not easy to answer, young prince. The power you possess – or that possesses you – is similar to that which dominates Philippos. Yet they are different. Individual. Your demon – if you will – desires you, but he needs you to live. Therefore he lies dormant when I am close, for he knows I am your hope for survival.'

'You speak about my power as if it is not of me.'

'Nor is it,' said the *magus*. 'It is a demon, a powerful demon. It has a name. Kadmilos. And he seeks to control you.'

Alexander found his mouth suddenly dry, and his hands began to tremble. 'What will happen to me if he wins?'

'You will become like Philippos. But that is a mountain you must climb on another day. You have great courage, Alexander, and an indomitable spirit. You may be able to hold him at bay. I will help you in any way that I can.'

'Why?'

'A good question, my boy, and I will answer it.' The *magus* sighed. 'A long time ago, by your reckoning – twenty years or more – I was instructed to teach another child. He too was possessed. I taught him all that I could, but it was not enough. He became the Demon King. Now there is you.'

'But you failed with Philippos,' Alexander pointed out.

'You are stronger,' Chiron told him. 'Now tell me this, is there anyone from your world with the wit to seek you out?'

Alexander nodded. 'Parmenion. He will come for me. He is the greatest general and the finest warrior in Macedonia.'

'I will watch for him,' said Chiron.

The Stone Circle, Time Unknown

Aristotle led the Macedonian warriors to an ancient wood in a valley so deep as to seem subterranean. Massive trees grew here, with trunks ten times thicker than the oaks of Macedonia, their branches interlaced and completely blocking the sky. The ground was ankle-deep with rotted vegetation and the warriors led their mounts for fear that a horse might catch his hoof in a hidden pothole or leaf-covered root, snapping the leg.

No birds sang in the forest and the air was cold, without hint of breeze. The trio moved silently on, Aristotle in the lead, coming at last to an open section of land. Attalus sucked in a deep breath as sunlight touched his skin, then stared around at the huge columns of stone. They were not round, nor made of blocks, but single wedges of granite, roughly hewn and three times the height of a tall man. Some had fallen, others had cracked and split. Parmenion moved to the centre of the stone circle where an altar was raised on blocks of marble. Running his fingers down the blood channels, he turned to Aristotle.

'Who built this . . . temple?'

'The people of Akkady. They are lost to history . . . gone. Their deeds like dust on the winds of time.'

Attalus shivered. 'I do not like this place, *magus*. Why are we here?'

'This is the Gateway to that other Greece. The two of you remain here, by the altar. I will prepare the Spell of Opening.'

Aristotle strode to the outer circle and sat cross-legged on the grass, hands clasped to his breast and eyes closed.

'What excuse do you think he will give when no Gateway opens?' asked Attalus, forcing a smile. Parmenion looked into the swordsman's cold blue eyes, reading the fear there.

'Now would be a good time for you to lead your horse from this circle,' he said softly.

'You think I am frightened?'

'Why should you not be?' countered Parmenion. 'I am.'

Attalus relaxed. 'A Spartan afraid? You hide it well, Parmenion. How long . . .' Light blazed around the circle and the horses reared, whinnying in terror. The warriors tightened their grip on the reins, calming the frightened animals. The light faded into a darkness so absolute both men were blind. Parmenion blinked and gazed up at the sky. Gradually, as his eyes became accustomed to the night, he saw stars shining high in the heavens.

'I think,' he said, keeping his voice low, 'that we have arrived.'

Attalus hobbled the dappled grey and walked to the edge of the circle, staring out over the mountains and valleys to the south. 'I know this place,' he said. 'Look there! Is that not Olympus?' Swinging to the north, he pointed to the silver ribbon of a great river. 'And there, the River Haliakmon. This is no other world, Parmenion!'

'He said it was like Greece,' the Spartan pointed out.

'I still do not believe it.'

'What does it take to convince you?' asked Parmenion, shaking his head. 'You have passed through the solid stone of a mountain, and moved within a heartbeat from noon to midnight. Yet still you cling to the belief that it is all trickery.'

'We will see,' muttered Attalus, returning to the grey and removing the hobble. 'Let us find somewhere to camp. It is too open here for a fire.' The swordsman vaulted to the grey, riding from the circle towards a wood to the south.

As the Spartan was about to follow Attalus the voice of Aristotle whispered into his mind, echoing and distant. 'There is much I wish I could tell you, my friend,' said the *magus*, 'but I cannot. Your presence in this world is of vital importance – not only for the rescue of the prince. I can safely give you only two pieces of advice: first, you should remember that the enemies of your enemy can be your friends; and second, make your way to Sparta. Treat it like a beacon of light to a ship in jeopardy. Sparta is the key!'

The voice faded and Parmenion mounted his horse and rode after Attalus. The two riders made their camp by a small stream that meandered through the wood. Hobbling the horses the warriors sat in silence, enjoying the warmth of the blaze. Parmenion stretched out on the ground, closing his eyes, his mind working at the problem facing him: how to find a single child in a strange land.

Aristotle had known only that the boy was not held by the Makedones. Somehow he had escaped. Yet despite his skills the *magus* could not locate him. All he knew was that the child had appeared close to Olympus and the Makedones still searched for him.

Wrapping himself in his cloak, Parmenion slept.

He awoke in the night to hear a whispering laughter echoing in the woods. Sitting up he looked towards Attalus, but the swordsman was asleep beside the dead fire. Easing himself to his feet, Parmenion tried to locate the source of the laughter. Some distance away he saw twinkling lights, but the trees and undergrowth prevented him from identifying their nature and source. Moving to Attalus, he tapped the man's arm. The swordsman awoke instantly, rolling to his feet with sword in hand. Gesturing him to silence, Parmenion pointed to the flickering lights and began to edge his way towards them. Attalus followed him, sword still drawn.

They came at last to a circular clearing where torches had been set in iron brackets on the trees. A group of young women, dressed in shimmering *chitons*, were sitting in a circle drinking wine from golden goblets.

One of the women rose from the circle, calling out a

name. Instantly a small creature ran forward, bearing a pitcher of wine and refilling her goblet. Parmenion felt Attalus tense beside him, for the creature was a satyr, no taller than a child – ears pointed, upper body bare of hair, his legs those of a goat, his hooves cloven.

Touching Attalus' arm, Parmenion backed away and the men returned to their camp.

'Were they nymphs, do you think?' asked Attalus.

Parmenion shrugged. 'I don't know,' he admitted. 'I took little note of myths and legends when a child. Now I wish I had studied them more carefully.'

Suddenly the distant laughter faded, to be replaced by screams, high-pitched and chilling. Drawing their swords, the two men ran back through the trees. Parmenion was the first to burst into the clearing.

Armed men were everywhere. Some of the women had escaped, but at least four had been borne to the ground, black-cloaked warriors kneeling around them. A girl ran clear, pursued by two soldiers. Parmenion leapt forward, slashing his sword through the neck of the first man, then blocking a savage cut from the second. Hurling himself forward he crashed his shoulder into his assailant, spinning him from his feet.

Hearing the sound of clashing blades, the other warriors left the women and ran to the attack. There were at least ten of them and Parmenion backed away.

'Who in Hades are you?' demanded a black-bearded soldier, advancing on Parmenion with sword extended.

'I am the name of your death,' the Spartan answered.

The man laughed grimly. 'A demi-god, are you? Heracles reborn, perhaps? You think to kill ten Makedones?'

'Perhaps not,' agreed Parmenion, as the soldiers formed a semi-circle around him, 'but I'll begin with you.'

'Kill him!' the man ordered.

At that moment Attalus emerged behind the circle, stabbing one man through the back with his dagger and sending a slicing cut across the face of a second. Parmenion leapt forward as the men swung to face this new threat. The black-bearded leader parried his first lunge, but the second plunged through his leather kilt to slice open the artery in his groin.

Attalus was in trouble, desperately fending off four attackers, the remaining three turning on Parmenion. The Spartan backed away once more, then sprang forward and left, engaging a warrior and slashing his sword towards the man's neck; he swayed back and Parmenion almost lost his balance. A soldier ran at him. Dropping to one knee Parmenion thrust his sword into the man's belly, ripping the blade clear as the other two closed on him.

'Help me, Parmenion!' yelled Attalus. Diving to his left, Parmenion rolled to his feet and ran across the clearing. Attalus had killed one man and wounded another, but now he was fighting with his back to an oak tree, and there was blood on his face and arm.

'I am with you!' shouted Parmenion, seeking to distract the attackers. When one turned towards him, Attalus' blade licked out, plunging into the man's throat. Attalus shoulder-charged the warriors before him, ducking as a slashing sword tore the helm from his head.

Parmenion reached his side and the two Macedonians stood back to back against the remaining four warriors.

A deafening roar sounded from the trees and the Makedones, terror in their eyes, fled from the clearing.

'By Zeus, that was close,' said Attalus.

'It's not over yet,' Parmenion whispered.

Emerging from the tree-line came three colossal men, each over seven feet tall. One had the head of a bull and was carrying a huge double-headed axe. The second had a face that was almost human, save that it boasted a huge double-pupilled single eye in the centre of the forehead; this one carried a club into which iron nails had been half hammered. The third had the head of a lion; he carried no weapon, but his hands ended in talons the length of daggers. Behind them the women gathered together, fear still showing in their eyes.

'Sheathe your sword,' ordered Parmenion.

'You must be insane!'

'Do it – and swiftly! They are here to protect the women. It may be we can reason with them.'

'Dream on, Spartan,' whispered Attalus as the demonic beasts shuffled forward, but he returned the stabbing sword to its scabbard and the two men stood before the advancing monsters. The cyclops moved closer, raising his pitted club.

'You . . . kill . . . Makedones. Why?' he asked, his voice deep, the words coming like drum-beats from his cavernous mouth.

'They were attacking the women,' Parmenion answered. 'We came to their aid.'

'Why?' asked the monster again, and Parmenion looked up at the club hovering above his head.

'The Makedones are our enemies,' he said, tearing his eyes from the grisly weapon.

'All . . . Humans . . . are . . . our . . . enemies,' replied the cyclops. To the right the lion-headed monster squatted down over a dead soldier, ripping loose an arm at which he began to gnaw. But all the while his tawny eyes remained fixed on Parmenion. The minotaur moved closer on the left, dipping his horned head to look into the Spartan's face. His voice whispered out, surprising Parmenion, for it was gentle, the tone perfect. 'Tell me, warrior, why we should not kill you.'

'Tell me first why you should?' Parmenion responded.

The minotaur sat down, beckoning the Spartan to join him. 'Everywhere your race destroys us. There is no land – save one – where our lives are safe from Humans. Once this land was ours; now we hide in woods and forests. Soon there will be no more of the Elder races; the sons and daughters of the Titans will be gone for ever. Why should I kill you? Because even if you are good and heroic your sons, and the sons of your sons, will hunt down my sons, and the sons of my sons. Is that an answer?'

'It is a good one,' agreed Parmenion, 'yet it is flawed. Should you kill me, then my sons would have reason to hate you, and that alone will make your vision true. But should we become friends, then my sons would come to know you and look upon you with kindly eyes.'

'When has that ever been true?' the minotaur asked.

'I do not know. I can only speak for myself. But it seems to me that if an act of rescue can result in summary execution then you are little different from the Makedones. Surely a son of the Titans will show more gratitude than that?'

'You speak well. And I like the lack of fear in your eyes. And you fight well too. My name is Brontes. These are my brothers, Steropes and Arges.'

'I am Parmenion. This is my . . . comrade Attalus.'

'We will not kill you,' said Brontes. 'Not this time. Our gift is your lives. But if ever you walk in our woods again your lives will be forfeit.' The minotaur pushed himself to his feet and turned to walk away.

'Wait!' called Parmenion. 'We are seeking a child from our land who was abducted by the King of the Makedones. Can you help us?'

The minotaur swung his great bull's head. 'The Makedones gave chase to a centaur two days ago. It is said that the centaur carried a child with golden hair. They travelled south to the Woods of the Centaurs. That is all I know. The woods are forbidden to Humans, save Chiron. The horse people will not allow you to pass. Nor will they speak with you. Your greeting will be an arrow through the heart or eye. Be warned!'

*

Attalus' fist slammed into Parmenion's chin, spinning him from his feet. The Spartan hit the ground hard, then rolled to his back, staring up at the enraged Macedonian who loomed above him with fists clenched, blood still seeping from the shallow gash in his cheek.

'You miserable whoreson!' hissed Attalus. 'What in Hades were you thinking of? Ten men! By Heracles, we should be dead.'

Parmenion sat up and rubbed his chin, then pushed himself to his feet. 'I was not thinking,' he admitted.

'Excellent!' sneered Attalus. 'But I do not want that engraved on the walls of my tomb: "Attalus died because the *strategos* wasn't thinking." '

'It will not happen again,' promised the Spartan, but the swordsman would not be mollified.

'I want to know why it happened this time. I want to know why the First General of Macedonia rushed to the aid of women he did not know. You were at Methone, Amphipolis and a dozen other cities when the army sacked them. I did not see you racing through the streets protecting the women and children. What is so different here?'

'Nothing,' replied the Spartan. 'But you are wrong. I was never in those cities when the rapes and murders took place. I organized the attacks, but when the walls were breached my work was done. I do not seek to avoid responsibility for the barbarism that followed, but it was never perpetrated in my name, nor have I ever taken part in it. As for my actions today, I accept they were inexcusable. We are here to rescue Alexander – and I put that in jeopardy. But I have said it will not happen again. I can say no more.'

'Well, I can – if you ever decide to act the romantic fool do not expect me to be standing beside you.'

'I did not expect it in the first place,' said Parmenion, his expression hardening, his eyes holding to the swordsman's gaze. 'And know this, Attalus – if you ever strike me again I shall kill you.'

'Enjoy your dreams,' replied the swordsman. 'The day will never dawn when you can best me with blade or spear.'

Parmenion was about to speak when he saw several of the women moving across the clearing towards them. The first to arrive bowed low before the warriors, then looked up with a shy smile. She was slim and golden-haired, with violet eyes and a face of surpassing beauty.

'We thank you, lords, for your help,' she said, her voice sweet and lilting, almost musical.

'It was our pleasure,' Attalus told her. 'What true men would have acted differently?'

'You are hurt,' she said, moving forward and reaching up to touch his face. 'You must let us tend your wounds. We have herbs and healing powders.'

Ignoring Parmenion the women closed around Attalus, leading him to a fallen tree and sitting beside him. A young

125

girl in a dress of shimmering blue sat upon the swordsman's lap, lifting a broad green leaf which she placed over the wound on his cheek. When she pulled the leaf clear the gash had vanished, the skin appearing clean and unbroken. Another woman repeated the manoeuvre with the cut on the warrior's left forearm.

The satyr reappeared from the edge of the trees and skipped forward to Parmenion bearing a goblet of wine. The Spartan thanked him and sat down to drink. Smiling nervously, the satyr moved away.

The attempt to rescue the women was everything that Attalus implied: romantic, stupid and, considering the odds, suicidal, and Parmenion's spirits were low as he sat apart from the group. Thinking back he remembered the quiet joy he had felt watching the women, and the sudden explosive anger that had raced through him when he heard their screams. Images leapt to his mind, like a window thrown open in a corner of his soul, and he saw again the children of Methone piled carelessly one upon another in a grisly hill of the dead.

The city was being prepared for destruction and Parmenion had ridden through it, overseeing the demolition. He had stopped in the main market square, where wagons were drawn up to remove the bodies.

Nicanor was riding beside him. Turning to the blond warrior, Parmenion had asked a simple question.

'Why?'

'Why what, my friend?' replied Nicanor, mystified.

'The children. Why were they slain?'

Nicanor had shrugged. 'The women go to the slave markets of Asia, the men to Pelagonia to build the new fortresses there. There is no price any more for young children.'

'And that is the answer?' whispered the general. 'There is no price?'

'What other answer is there?' the warrior responded.

Parmenion rode from the city without a backward glance, determined never again to view the aftermath of such victories. Now, here in this enchanted wood, the realization struck him with sickening force that he was a coward. As a general he set in motion the events that led to horror, and had believed that by not allowing himself to witness the brutality he was somehow freed from the guilt of it.

Sipping his wine, he found the weight of his grief too powerful to bear and tears spilled to his cheeks, all sense of self-worth flowing from him.

He did not know at which point he fell asleep, but he awoke in a soft bed in a room with walls of interlaced vines and a ceiling of leaves.

Feeling rested and free of burdens, his heart light, he pushed back the covers and swung his legs from the bed. The floor was carpeted with moss, soft and springy below his feet as he rose. There was no door in the vines and he approached them, pushing his hands against the hanging wall and moving the leaves aside. Sunlight streamed in, almost blinding him, and he stepped out into a wide glade bordered by oak trees. Standing still for a moment, as his eyes grew accustomed to the light, he heard the sound of rushing water and turned to see a waterfall gushing over white marble, filling a deep pool around which sat a group of women. Others were swimming through the crystal-clear water, laughing and splashing each other, tiny rainbows forming in the spray.

As Parmenion strolled towards the group a looming figure moved from his right and he saw the minotaur, Brontes. The creature bowed clumsily, his great bull's head dipping and rising.

'Welcome to my home,' he said.

'How did I come here?'

'I carried you.'

'Why?'

'You drank the wine, Human. It made you sleep and gave you dreams. Then more Makedones came and the Lady bade me bring you.'

'Where is Attalus?'

'Your companion still sleeps – and will continue so to do. Come, the Lady waits.' The minotaur strode on, past the waterfall, angling to the right through the trees and coming at last to another wall of vines. Two women stood by them, pulling them apart for the minotaur to enter. Parmenion followed, finding himself in a natural hall columned by tall cypress trees and roofed by flowers. Birds of all kinds were flying here, swooping and diving high among the multi-coloured blooms.

There were many pools within the hall, surrounded by white marble boulders from which grew enormous flowers of salmon-pink and crimson. Yellow-stoned paths had been set around the pools, curving across the moss-covered floor of the hall, all leading to the dais at the far end.

Ignoring the women and satyrs who sat by the water's edge, Brontes marched on until he stood before the dais. His brothers, Steropes and Arges, were sitting here, but Parmenion barely glanced at them; his eyes were drawn to the naked woman who sat upon a throne carved from a huge block of shining marble. Her hair was white – but not the tired, listless colour of the aged, more the proud, unconquered white of mountain snow. Her eyes were grey, her face ageless, unlined and smooth, but not young. Her body was slim, breasts small, hips boyish.

Parmenion bowed low. The woman rose from the throne and climbed from the dais, taking the Spartan's arm and leading him deeper into the hall, then out through the vines to a hollow in the hills bathed in sunshine.

'Who are you, Lady?' he asked, as she sat beneath a spreading oak.

'Men have given me many names,' she answered. 'More than the stars, I think. But you may continue to call me Lady. I like the sound of it upon your tongue. Now sit beside me, Parmenion, and tell me of your son, Alexander.' It was a moment before he realized what she had said, and a cold thrill of fear whispered through his soul.

'He is the *son* of my King,' he told her, as he stretched out on the grass beside her. 'He has been abducted by Philippos. I am here to return him to . . . his father.'

She smiled, but her knowing eyes held his gaze. 'He is your child, sired during a night of Mysteries. It is a shame you bear – with many other guilts and despairs. I know you, Man, I know your thoughts and your fears. You may speak openly.'

Parmenion looked away. 'I am sorry that you have seen so much, Lady. It grieves me to bring my . . . darkness . . . to this place of beauty.'

Her fingers touched his face, stroking the skin. 'Do not concern yourself with such shame – your guilt is all that kept you alive after you drank my wine. For only the good can know guilt and you are not evil, Parmenion. There is kindness in your heart and greatness in your soul – which is more than can be said for your companion. I have let him live only because you need him. But he will sleep on until you leave, and will never see my land.' Rising smoothly, she walked to the crest of a hill and stood staring at the distant mountains. Parmenion followed her and listened as she pointed out the landmarks. 'There, far to the west, are the Pindos Mountains, and there, across the plains to the south, is River Peneios. You know these places, for they exist in your own world. But further south there are cities you will not know: Cadmos, Thospae, Leonidae. They fight in a league against Philippos – and will soon fall. Athens was destroyed during the spring. Soon only one city state will stand against the Tyrant: Sparta. When you find Alexander, take him there.'

'First I must find him,' said the warrior.

'He is with the *magus*, Chiron, and safe for the moment. But Philippos will find him soon, and the Wood of the Centaurs will prove no barrier to the Makedones.'

Turning to him she took his arm, leading him back through the glades to the hall of vines.

'Once upon a time,' she said, her voice soft and sorrowful, 'I could have helped you in this quest. No longer. We are the people of the Enchantment, and we are slowly dying. Our magic is failing, our sorcery faint against the bright swords of the Makedones. I give you my blessing, Parmenion. There is little else.'

'It is enough, Lady, and a gift I am unworthy of,' he told her, taking her hand and kissing it. 'But why give me even that?'

'Our interests may yet be mutual. As I said, the Enchantment is fading. Yet there is a legend here that all of us know. It is said that a golden child will come among us, and the land will shine once more. Do you think Alexander is that golden child?'

'How could I know?'

'How indeed? Once I could see into the future – not far, but far enough to be able to protect my people. Now I see only the past and lost glories. And perhaps I too cling to foolish legends. Sleep now – and awake refreshed!'

He awoke wrapped in his cloak at the camp-site, the horses grazing by the stream. Across from the dead fire Attalus slept on, no signs of wounds upon his face and arms.

Parmenion stood and walked through the woods to the clearing. There were no bodies here, but dried blood still stained the earth.

Back at the camp-site he woke Attalus.

'I had the strangest dream,' said the swordsman. 'I dreamt we rescued a group of nymphs. There was a minotaur and . . . and . . . damn, it's fading now.' Attalus rolled to his feet and brushed dirt from his cloak. 'I hate forgetting dreams,' he said. 'But I remember the nymphs – wonderful women, beautiful beyond description. What of you? How did you sleep?'

'Without dreams,' answered the Spartan.

*

Derae watched Parmenion and Attalus ride west, then stepped from the shadows of the trees to the centre of the camp-site. Her hair was no longer flame-red but a deep brown, close-cropped. Her face was more square, her nose long, her eyes, once sea-green, now hazel beneath thick brows.

'You are certainly no beauty now,' Aristotle told her, as they stood in the Stone Circle following the departure of the Macedonians.

'I will not need beauty,' she answered, her voice deep and almost husky.

She had stepped through the portal in time to see

Parmenion and Attalus riding into the woods and had followed them, settling herself down a little way from their camp-site. At first she had intended to introduce herself that same night but, reaching out with her Talent, she touched the souls of both men, learning their fears. They were uneasy with one another. Parmenion did not trust the cold-eyed Macedonian warrior, while Attalus had no love for the man he considered an arrogant Spartan. They needed time, she realized and, wrapping herself in her cloak, she slept.

She was awakened by the sound of laughter and heard the two Macedonians creeping through the undergrowth. Soaring from her body, she viewed the scene from above and was the first to see the dark-cloaked Makedones warriors making their way through the woods towards the women.

When the first screams came, Derae sped to Parmenion. His emotions were surging. Part of him yearned to rescue the maidens, but a stronger desire was to stay safe and think of Alexander. Instinctively Derae used her power, filling him with a new sense of purpose. Even as she did so she knew it was a mistake. One against ten would mean the death of the man she loved. Transferring her spirit to Attalus, she swiftly read his intent. There was no way he would go to Parmenion's aid. His mind was locked to a single thought: Protect yourself! With nothing else to work on Derae made his fear swell. If Parmenion was to die Attalus would be trapped in this world for ever, all his riches counting for nothing. Never would he see his palaces and his concubines. He would spend his life as a mercenary soldier in a world that was not his own. His anger was colossal as he drew his sword and raced to Parmenion's aid.

The two warriors fought magnificently, but Derae was sickened by the slaughter and, when it was over, withdrew to her body, carrying with her a sense of shame.

The deaths were on her conscience. She had manipulated the events, and that was contrary to all her beliefs. Long into the night she tried to rationalize her actions. The Makedones were intent on rape and murder. Had she not intervened the women would have been abused and slain. But their deaths would not have been your fault, she told herself. Now the blood of the Makedones was on her hands.

What could I have done, she asked herself? Whatever action or inaction she had chosen would still have resulted in tragedy, for there had been no time to influence all of the Makedones. But you did influence them, she thought. You slowed their reflexes, giving Parmenion and Attalus an edge.

Filled with self-doubt the Healer slept, dreaming of centaurs and a Demon King. In the midst of her dream she was awoken by the touch of a hand and sat up to see a naked white-haired woman sitting on a fallen tree. Behind her stood the minotaur she had seen at the clearing. The moon was high and a shaft of light bathed the woman, making her seem almost ethereal.

'You did well, seeress,' the woman said. 'You saved my children.'

'It was wrong of me to interfere,' Derae told her.

'Nonsense. Your actions saved not only my people but the two men you follow. Had they not acted as they did, then Brontes and his brothers would have slain them while they slept.'

'Why?' asked Derae. 'What harm have they done you?'

'They are Humans,' answered the woman. 'It is enough.'

'What do you want of me?'

'Your blood is of the Enchantment. That is why you have the Talent. Parmenion also is a man of Power. You are strangers to this world, and I need to know if you come to do good or to work evil.'

'I will never knowingly help the cause of Chaos,' answered Derae. 'But that does not necessarily mean that I will always do good. For many years I fought the Chaos Spirit, seeking to prevent him becoming flesh. But I was responsible for his birth.'

'I know. Parmenion sired Iskander, and now the Demon King seeks him.' The woman was silent for a time, her expression distant. Then she turned her gaze once more to the Healer. 'The Enchantment is dying. Can you help to save it?'

'No.'

The woman nodded. 'Neither can I. But, if the child is truly Iskander . . .' She sighed. 'I have no choice.' Turning to the minotaur she laid a slender hand on his huge shoulder. 'Go with her, Brontes, and help where you can. If the child is not Iskander, then return to me. If he is, then do what you must to get him to the Gateway.'

'I will, Mother,' he answered.

The moonlight faded, and with it the white-haired woman, but the minotaur remained. Derae reached out with her spirit – but was met by an invisible wall.

'You do not need to read my thoughts,' he told her, his voice impossibly sweet. 'I am no danger to you.'

'How can there be no danger when there is so much hate?' she countered.

He did not reply.

The Wood of the Centaurs

Alexander sat in the warm sunlight at the mouth of the cave, high on the mountain, staring out over the roof of the forest and the plains beyond. Despite his fear he felt wonderfully free in the Wood of the Centaurs. Here he could touch without killing and sleep without dreams. Yesterday a silver-grey bird had landed on his hand, sitting there warm in the security of his friendship, and not once had the killing power threatened to flow. It was a form of bliss Alexander had never known. He missed his home, and his mother and father, but the longing was eased by this new-found joy.

Chiron wandered out into the open. 'A fine day, young prince,' he said.

'Yes. It is beautiful. Tell me of the centaurs.'

'What would you wish to know?' asked the *magus*.

'How do they survive? I know something of horses, and the amount they must eat and drink. Their throats and stomachs are made for digesting grass and vast quantities of liquids. And their lungs are huge. I cannot see how the centaurs can function. Do they have two sets of lungs? Do they eat grass? And if so how do they manage it, for they cannot bend like the neck of a horse?'

Chiron chuckled. 'Good questions, Alexander. Your mind works well. You saw me with Caymal and it is the same with the true centaurs. They live like men and

134

women, but they have formed special bonds with their mounts. They Merge in the hours of daylight, but at dusk they separate.'

'What happens if a horse dies? Can the centaur find another?'

'No. If the horse dies the man – or woman – will fade and pass away within a day, occasionally two.'

'Would that happen to you if Caymal died?' Alexander asked.

'No, for I am not a true centaur. Our Merging is born of external magic. That is why Camiron feels so isolated. Lost, if you will.'

Chiron passed the boy a chunk of sweet bread and, for a while, the companions ate in silence. Then the boy spoke again. 'Where did it begin?' he enquired.

'What an enormous question that is,' the *magus* answered. 'And who am I to attempt an answer? The world once brimmed with natural magic, in every stone and brook, every tree and hill. Many thousands of years ago there was a race of men who harnessed that magic. They strode the earth like gods – indeed they were gods, for they became almost immortal. They were bright, imaginative, inquisitive. And their children were the Titans, giants if they chose to be, poets if they wished to be. Times of wonder followed, but they are difficult to describe – especially to a four-year-old, albeit one as brilliant as Alexander. I would imagine you saw, at your own court, how men and women seek out the new – cloaks in different colours, dresses of different shape and design. Well, in the Old World the Titans sought out different shapes in the cloak of life. Some wished to be birds, having wings to soar into the sky. Others wished to swim in the depths of the sea. All manner of hybrids graced the earth.' Chiron lapsed into silence, his eyes focused on the past.

'What happened then?' whispered Alexander.

'What always happens, boy. There was a great war, a time of astonishing cruelty and carnage. A vast amount of the world's magic was used up in that terrible confrontation. Look around you and see the trees. It would seem impossible that they could all be cut down. But if Man sets his mind to a matter he will achieve it, no matter how destructive. What I am saying is that all things are finite – even magic. The war went on for centuries, and now there are only pockets of true power. This wood is one, but out there in the New World of Men the stones are empty, the brooks and hills devoid of magic. So the children of the Titans – those who survive anyway – are drawn to these few areas of Enchantment, held to them by chains stronger than death.'

'You make it sound so sad,' said Alexander. 'Will the magic not come back?'

'Perhaps. One day, like a perfect flower, it might seed itself and grow again. But I doubt it.' Chiron sighed. 'And even if it does, Man will corrupt it. It is the way of all things. No, better for it to fade away.'

'But if it does, will not the centaurs die with it?'

'Indeed they will, and the nymphs and satyrs, the dryads and cyclopses. But so also will the Vores and the gorgons, the hydras and the birds of death. For not all the creatures of Enchantment are benign. However,' he said, rising, 'that is enough of my world for one day. Tell me of yours.'

They talked on for some time, but Alexander could tell him little of interest and became aware of a growing irritation within the *magus*. 'What is wrong?' the boy enquired at last. 'Does my lack of knowledge displease you?'

'Pah! It is not you, child,' replied Chiron, rising and walking away down the mountainside. Alexander ran after him, taking his hand.

'Tell me!' pleaded the prince. Chiron stopped and knelt before the boy, his expression softening.

'I have a dream, Alexander. I hoped you could help me in my pursuit of it. But you are very young and you know so little. It is not your fault. Indeed, I cannot imagine any other four-year-old who would know so much.'

'What are you seeking?'

'A world without evil,' answered Chiron sadly, 'and other impossibilities. Now wait for me at the cave. I need to walk for a while, to think and to plan.'

Alexander watched him walk away down the mountain to vanish into the trees, then the boy climbed up to the cave-mouth and sat for a while enjoying the sunshine.

Hunger at last forced him to move and he walked through the wall of illusion, entering the palace beyond and making his way to the kitchens where he ate honey-cakes and dried fruit. He had seen no servants here, yet the food was replenished every day. His interest aroused, Alexander strolled out into the palace grounds, seeking signs of life. But there were no tracks in the soft earth, save those that he made himself, and he returned to the palace where he wandered aimlessly from room to room, bored and lonely.

For a time he looked at the scrolls and books in one of the many library rooms. But these were of little interest, inscribed as they were with symbols he could not read. At last he came to a small room, western-facing, where he found a circular table covered with a velvet cloth. At first he thought the table was cast from solid gold, but as he examined the six ornate legs he realized they were carved from wood and overlaid with thick gold-leaf. Climbing on a chair he pulled aside the velvet and gazed down on a jet-black surface, so dark it reflected no light, and it seemed he was staring down into an enormous well. Reaching out he tentatively touched the table – and recoiled, as dark ripples spread across the surface, lapping at the raised perimeter.

Fascinated, he touched it again. It was colder than snow and yet curiously comforting.

The surface lightened, becoming blue. Then a cloud moved across it. Alexander laughed aloud. 'There should be birds,' he shouted. Obedient to his wishes the scene rolled on and he saw swans flying in formation across the sky. 'Wonderful!' he cried. 'Now where is the land?' The image rolled once more, making the boy dizzy so that he gripped the edges of the table to steady himself. But now he saw the forest as if from a great height, the trees clinging to the mountains like green smoke. 'Show me Chiron!' he commanded.

A figure loomed into life. It was the *magus* sitting beside a stream, flipping stones into the water. His expression was sorrowful and Alexander felt a sudden stab of guilt for intruding on Chiron's solitude.

'Show me Philippos!' he said.

The mirror table darkened and he saw an army camped before a burning city, dark tents highlighted by the distant flames. The image settled on a huge tent at the centre of the camp, moving inside to where the King was seated on a black throne of carved ebony.

Around him, kneeling at his feet, were dark-robed priests. One of them was speaking, but the boy could hear nothing. Pale shapes moved at the edge of the mirror, and Alexander felt an icy touch of dread as creatures of nightmare crept forward to surround the King. Their skin was fish-white, their eyes dark and hooded, their heads bald, the crown of the scalp raised in ridges of sharp bone. Scaled wings grew from their shoulder-blades and their hands were hooked into talons.

'Closer!' ordered the boy.

A ghastly face, in silhouette, filled the mirror and Alexander could see that the teeth inside the lipless mouth were pointed and sharp, rotting and green at the purple gums. Suddenly the creature's head turned – the dark shining eyes, with their slitted pupils, staring up at the child.

'He cannot see me,' Alexander whispered.

The mirror exploded outwards as a taloned hand flashed up, sinking into the boy's tunic and scoring the flesh beneath. The prince found himself dragged forward into the mirror and screamed, his hands scrabbling at the scaled arm.

The killing power surged from his fingers with such power that the arm holding him was turned instantly to dust.

Throwing himself back Alexander toppled to the floor, the taloned hand still clinging to his tunic. Ripping it loose, he flung it across the floor and then swiftly gathered the velvet covering, hurling it over the mirror table.

As he did so there came a sound like a low groan, which formed into a terrible sentence.

'I know where you are, child,' came the voice of Philippos, 'and there is no escape.'

*

Alexander sped from the room. His foot caught the edge of a flagstone and he tumbled to the floor, grazing his knees. Tears fell now as this fresh pain unleashed his fears. *They are coming for me*, his mind screamed at him. Up the long stairs he ran, heart beating wildly, until at last he emerged from the cave-mouth into the sunshine.

Scanning the skies for signs of the scaled creatures he sank to a rock in the sunshine, shivering uncontrollably.

A centaur carrying a bow and quiver trotted from the tree-line, saw him and cantered up the mountainside. It was the white-bearded leader with the palomino flanks. He halted before the child.

'Why do you cry?' he asked, leaning forward to touch his thumb to Alexander's cheek, brushing away a tear.

'My enemies are coming for me,' said Alexander, struggling to halt the surging panic.

'Where is the outcast who carried you here?'

'He is gone. I am with Chiron now.'

The centaur nodded, his dark eyes thoughtful. 'These enemies you speak of, child – are they men, or of the Enchantment?'

'They have wings and scales. They are not men.'

'Vores,' hissed the centaur. 'Their touch is disease, their breath is the plague. Why does the Demon King seek you?'

'He wants to kill me,' the child answered. 'He wants to live for ever.' The shivering was worse now and sweat bathed his face. He felt dizzy and nauseous.

'Are you Iskander then?' asked the centaur, his voice echoing from a great distance as if whispering across the vaults of Time.

'That is . . . what they . . . called me,' answered Alexander. The world spun and he toppled from the rock to the soft grass. It felt cool against his face, but his chest was burning and a dark mist rolled across his mind . . .

*

Dropping his bow and arrows Kytin bent his front forelegs and leaned down, lifting the child in his arms. The small boy was burning with fever. The centaur pulled aside the boy's torn tunic, cursing as he saw the marks of talons on the slender torso. Already pus was seeping from the wounds, the flesh around them puckered and unhealthy. Leaving his weapons where they lay Kytin galloped down the mountainside, cutting along a narrow path through the trees and splashing across a shallow stream.

Two other centaurs rode alongside him.

'Why do you have the child?' asked one.

'He is Iskander,' replied Kytin, 'and he is dying!' Without waiting for a response he galloped on, lungs burning with the effort of the sustained pace, breath coming in ragged gasps. On he ran, deep into the heart of the woods. It was almost dusk when he arrived at a village on the banks of a broad river. The homes here, perfectly round and windowless, with huge, gaping doorways, were built of wood and straw. Beyond the scores of buildings were wide pastures and treeless hills, and already there were horses grazing, their bondsmen sitting around fires. Kytin felt the *Need* upon him. Not yet, he cautioned himself. Hold to the *Form*. Iskander needs you!

Halting before a roundhouse set apart from the rest, he called out a name. But there was no reply and he stood waiting, knowing she was inside. Yet he would not – indeed could not – disturb her at this time, and felt with sick dread the life of the child ebbing away like water passing through sand.

Finally an ancient pony stepped from the large doorway, tossed its head and trotted towards the hills.

'Gaea,' called the centaur. 'Come forth. I need you.'

An old woman, supporting herself with a staff, hobbled into the doorway. 'I am tired,' she said.

'This is Iskander,' Kytin told her, extending his arms. 'He has been touched by a Vore.'

The old woman's head sank down to rest on the tip of the staff. 'Why now,' she whispered, 'when I am so weak?' For a moment she was silent, then she drew in a deep breath and raised herself to her full height 'Bring him in, Kytin. I will do what I can.'

The centaur eased past her, laying the unconscious boy on a narrow pallet bed. Alexander's lips and eyelids were blue now, and he scarcely seemed to breathe. 'You must save him,' urged Kytin. 'You must!'

'Hush, fool,' she told him, 'and go to your privacy. Your flanks are trembling and the *Need* is upon you. Go now, before you shame yourself in public.'

Kytin backed away, leaving the old woman sitting on the bed beside the dying child. Taking his hand, she felt the fever raging. 'You should have come to us twenty years ago,' she whispered, 'when my powers were at their height. Now I am old and near useless. My pony is dying and will not see out the winter. What would you have me do, Iskander –if you are truly Iskander?'

The boy stirred, moaning in delirium. 'Par . . . menion!'

'Hush, child,' said Gaea, her voice soothing. Pulling open the tunic she laid a wrinkled, bony hand upon the festering scars. The heat scalded her skin and her mouth tightened. 'That the Enchantment should have sired such creatures . . .' she said, her voice acid and bitter. Her hand began to glow, the bones standing out like dark shadows below the skin as if a lantern was hidden under her palm. Smoke writhed from the boy's chest, flowing through her outstretched fingers, and the wounds sealed, pus oozing to the skin of his chest. The smoke hung in a tight sphere above him, dark and swirling. 'Begone!' hissed the old woman. The sphere exploded and a terrible stench filled the roundhouse. Alexander groaned, but the colour flowed back to his pale cheeks and he sighed.

Gaea stood, staggered and reached for her staff. An elderly man, stooped and bent, edged his way into the room.

'Does he live?' he asked, his voice thin, whispering through rotted teeth.

'He lives, Kyaris. You brought him in time. How can you be sure he is Iskander?'

The old man moved slowly to a chair by a burning brazier, sitting and holding his hands to the blaze. 'He told me. And the Tyrant seeks him, Gaea, to kill him and become immortal. Who else can he be?'

'He could be a human child – and that is all. The Tyrant is not infallible; he has been wrong before.'

'Not this time. I can feel it.'

'In your bones, I suppose,' she snapped. 'I swear your horse has more sense than you. The Vores marked him; that means they know where he is. How long before their wings are beating the wind above this wood? Eh? How long?'

'But if he is Iskander we must protect him. He is our hope, Gaea!'

'Hopes! Dreams!' snorted the old woman. 'They are like smoke in the breeze. I once dreamt of Iskander. But no more. Now I wait for my pony to die, and to leave this world of blood and pain. Look at him! How old is he? Four, five? You think he will lead us from peril? His mouth still yearns for his mother's tits!'

Kyaris shook his head, his wispy white hair floating like mist against his face. 'Once you had belief. But you are old, and your faith has gone. Well, I too am old, but I still have hopes. Iskander will save us. He will restore the Enchantment. He will!'

'Cling to your nonsense if you will, old man – but tomorrow be ready with bow and spear. For the Vores will come, and after them the Makedones. Your stupidity will see us all destroyed.'

Kyaris struggled to his feet. 'Better to die than to live without hope, Gaea. I have sons, and sons of my sons. I want them to see the return of the Enchantment. I will fight the Vores; they will not take the child.'

'Find a mirror, you old fool,' she taunted him. 'Once the words of Kyaris-Kytin echoed like thunder across the world. Now you can scarce stand without support. Even Merged you cannot run far.'

'I am sorry for you,' he told her. Moving to the bedside, he laid his hand on the sleeping child's brow. 'Sleep well, Iskander,' he whispered.

'Sell him to Philippos,' she advised. 'That would be true wisdom.'

'There is no wisdom in despair, woman,' he answered.

*

Parmenion and Attalus rode from the woods, angling down towards the plain and the distant, shimmering River Peneios. Clouds were bunching in the sky, huge and rolling, promising a storm, but the wind was still warm, the rain holding off. Attalus eased his grey alongside Parmenion.

'Where do we go, *strategos*?'

'Across the plain and into those woods,' answered the Spartan, pointing to the western hills on which the tree-line curved like the crest of a giant helmet.

The first drops of rain began to fall, then a crack of thunder sounded. Attalus' stallion reared, almost dislodging the Macedonian. Lightning forked across the sky and the deluge began. The horses walked now, heads bowed, the riders drenched and conversation impossible.

Glancing to his left, Attalus saw a body lying on the grass, the legs stripped of flesh. Beyond it was another, then another. Attalus leaned to his right, tapping Parmenion's arm and pointing to the corpses. The Spartan nodded, but said nothing. For most of the morning they rode on through the deserted battlefield and at last the rain died away, the sun streaming through the broken clouds.

'There were thousands of them,' said Attalus, swinging to stare back over the plain. 'They weren't even stripped of weapons.'

Parmenion reined in the gelding. 'I would guess the main battle was fought there,' he said, indicating a low range of hills. 'But – judging by the way the corpses are grouped – the left broke and the defeated army ran west. They were cut down by cavalry and tried to make a stand. No prisoners were taken and they were massacred to a man.'

'A world not unlike our own,' said Attalus, forcing a smile. But it faded swiftly.

'You are wrong. This is a war unlike any I have seen,' muttered the Spartan, his pale eyes scanning the battlefield. 'This is not just conquest; this is butchery. I would not wish to be part of such a conflict.'

Attalus dismounted and walked to a nearby corpse, kneeling to lift the dead warrior's shield. It was fashioned of wood, reinforced by bronze, and painted blue. At the centre two snakes were depicted, held in a man's fist. 'Have you ever seen anything like it?' he asked, passing the shield up to Parmenion.

'No. It is obviously meant to be Heracles killing the snakes in his crib. It could be Theban; their shields carry the club of Heracles.'

'I see nothing I recognize,' said Attalus, nudging his foot under the corpse and flicking the body to its back. Picking up a dented helm, he turned it in his hands. It was of leather, covered by thin sheets of what appeared to be bright bronze. There was no crest or plume, no cheeks-flaps to protect the face, merely two badly-cast raven's wings, loosely riveted to the temples, and a slender metal bar that dropped vertically from the brow. 'Badly made,' said Attalus, 'and these wings serve no purpose,' he added. 'Look at the nasal guard. It is too thin to protect the face. The entire piece is useless – as I think he found.'

Tossing the helm to the ground, Attalus remounted. 'These bodies have been here for weeks, maybe months. Why have they not been stripped?'

'Perhaps there is no one left alive to strip them,' said Parmenion.

Dark shadows flowed along the grass. Parmenion gazed up to see a score of pale shapes soaring high in the sky, moving westward, their great wings beating slowly. Despite the height at which they flew, and the brightness of the sun, there was no doubt as to their semi-human shape.

'What in the name of Hecate. . . ?' whispered Attalus.

The creatures were joined by a second group coming from the north. Shading his eyes, Parmenion saw more of the beasts flying in from south and west. 'They are coming from all sides,' he said.

'They seem to be heading for the woods. I tell you, Parmenion, I do not like this world.'

'Nor I,' agreed the Spartan, kneeing the gelding into a canter. Attalus was about to follow when he spotted another corpse, a bowman lying on his back, his face torn away by crows. Dismounting, the Macedonian removed the man's leather quiver, hefting his short, curved bow of horn. Looping the quiver over his shoulder, Attalus vaulted to the grey and rode after the Spartan.

It felt good to have a bow in his hands again. Such a fine weapon. Silent death, with little risk to the killer. The Spartan's back was to him and Attalus pictured a shaft lancing into Parmenion's brain. No, he thought. There is no way I will kill him like that. I want to see the expression on his face. I want to watch the arrogance and pride drain away.

And I will, he promised himself. Once we find the boy – and a way home.

*

Chiron strolled beside the stream, his thoughts sombre. The world's Enchantment was fading fast. Now there were fewer than a hundred areas across the globe where primal magic oozed from rock and tree. Only seven remained in Achaea.

Kneeling by the water, he cupped his hands and drank. Philippos had been a bright, intelligent child, swift to learn, swifter to laugh. But the evil within him, the Spirit of Chaos, had finally won him, destroying all that was human, all that had knowledge of kindness and beauty.

Sorrow descended on Chiron like a terrible weight. His shoulders sagged and he lifted his eyes to the heavens. 'Perhaps it is time to die,' he said softly. 'Perhaps I have lived too long.' Rising, he walked from the trees to the slopes of his mountain and began the long climb to the cave.

He saw Caymal grazing nearby and waved, but the horse did not see him. Chiron's legs ached by the time he reached the cave and he stopped to rest for a moment, drawing the healing stone from the pouch at his side and holding it in his hand.

Strength flowed in his limbs and once more the desire came to let the magic stream into his blood, bringing him the full power of youth. But the once golden stone was

145

almost drained of Enchantment and he dared not exhaust it. Dropping it back in the pouch, he strode through the cave and on into the palace, seeking Alexander.

The boy was nowhere in sight. At first Chiron was unworried. The palace was large, with a score of rooms; all children loved to explore and many of the rooms here contained artefacts that would fascinate a child like Alexander. But as time passed Chiron's concern grew. Surely the boy would have more sense than to wander away into the forest, he thought.

Then he came to the room of the mirror table and saw the severed hand on the cold marble floor, the talons stained with blood.

'No!' he whispered. 'No!' Moving to the table, he saw that the cloth had been hastily thrown over it. With trembling hands Chiron eased it clear and found himself staring down into the tent of Philippos. The King was sitting upon an ebony throne. He looked up, his golden eye gleaming in the firelight.

'Ah, you are back, my friend,' said the King. 'How are you faring?'

'Better than you, I fear,' answered Chiron.

'How can that be? I am Makedon, and my armies conquer all who stand in my way. Better than that, I am invulnerable.'

'You are inhuman, Philippos. There is nothing left of the boy I knew.'

The King's laughter filled the room. 'Nonsense, Chiron! I am he. But, as a man, it is necessary to put aside childish ways. Where am I different from the kings who ruled before me?'

'I will not debate with you. You are no longer human. Your soul is long dead; you fought a brave battle against the Dark, and it defeated you. I pity you.'

'Save your pity, Chiron,' said the King, no trace of anger in his tone. 'It is misplaced. I did not suffer defeat – I overcame the Chaos Spirit and now he serves me. But you have something that I desire. Will you give it to me – or must I take it?'

Chiron shook his head. 'You must take it . . . if you can. But it will serve no purpose. The child will not bring you immortality. He is not Iskander; he is the son of a King in another land.'

Philippos stood. 'If he is not the One, then I will keep searching. I will have what I desire, Chiron. It is my destiny.'

'There is no more to say,' said Chiron. 'Begone!' His hand swept across the surface of the table and, for a moment only, the mirror shimmered into darkness. Then the face of Philippos returned.

'You see,' hissed the King, 'you no longer even have the power to dismiss my image. Send me the boy – or I will see your blood flow upon my altar. You know that I can do it, Chiron. All your centuries of life will be gone. You will be no more. That frightens you, doesn't it? I can see it in your eyes. Bring me the child and you will live. Defy me and I will make your death last as long as your life.'

The mirror darkened. Chiron covered it and backed from the room, running up the stairs and out through the cave.

Then he saw Kytin's bow and quiver lying where the centaur had left them, and heard the beating of wings from the sky above him.

*

Kytin galloped across the sunlit clearing, reared, and sent an arrow flashing into the heart of a hovering Vore whose wings collapsed, its pale form crashing to the grass. A black dart narrowly missed Kytin's head and the centaur swung to send a second arrow winging its way into his assailant's belly.

Eleven centaurs were down and more than thirty Vores, but still they came – their great wings flapping, their deadly missiles slashing through the air.

'Back under the trees!' shouted Kytin. 'They cannot fly there!' Several centaurs made a dash for the forest, but amid the stamping hooves, the beating of wings and the screams of the dying many others could not hear him and fought on. A Vore dropped from the sky to Kytin's back, sharp talons cutting into the centaur's shoulder. The old man bellowed in rage and pain, bucking and flinging the creature into the air. Its wings spread wide, halting its fall. Kytin leapt forward, his huge hands grabbing the scrawny neck and twisting savagely, snapping the hollow bones of the Vore's throat.

A dart sliced into Kytin's back, the poison streaming into his blood like acid. The imminence of death galvanized the centaur. Twisting and rearing he galloped to Gaea's hut, ducking inside the doorway and stepping over the dart-pierced body of the old healer to gather up the still-sleeping child. Kytin's legs almost buckled, but with a supreme effort of will he raced back out into the daylight with the boy held safe in his arms, and thundered towards the trees. Two more darts struck him, one piercing the flesh beside his long spine, the other glancing from his hind-quarters. Then he was past his attackers and on to the mountain path.

Vores soared up above the trees, but they could not easily follow him, for the branches were interlaced like a canopy over the trail. Several of the creatures flew low, but the undergrowth was thick, overhanging limbs hampering their flight.

Kytin galloped on, the poison spreading through his limbs. Twice he stumbled and almost fell, but drew on his reserves of strength and courage, holding himself alive by the power of his dream.

Iskander! He had to rescue the boy. The Enchantment had to be saved.

He ran on deeper into the forest, seeking a cave, a hollow tree – anywhere he could hide the boy. But his eyes were veiled by a grey mist that swirled across his mind, and so many thoughts flitted by him, old memories, scenes of triumph and tragedy. He saw again the fight with Boas, the great ride to Cadmos, his marriage to Elena, the birth of his first child . . .

The boy awoke and struggled in his arms.

'It is all right, Iskander,' he told him, his voice slurred now. 'I will save you.'

'There is blood on your chin, staining your beard,' said the boy. 'You are hurt.'

'All . . . will . . . be well.'

The centaur slowed, his front legs buckling, Alexander tumbling from his arms and landing on his back with the breath knocked out of him.

A Vore swooped down between the high branches with arms outstretched, a rope dangling from his hands. The boy tried to run, but he was still winded and the loop dropped over his shoulders, pulling tight. Alexander screamed as he was pulled into the air.

An arrow plunged into the Vore's side. Letting go the rope the creature tried to escape, but his wings crashed against a branch and he somersaulted through the air before falling to his death.

Two horsemen galloped into sight and Alexander looked up.

'Parmenion!' he cried. The Spartan leapt to the ground and drew his sword. A black dart flashed towards him but his sword-blade batted it aside. Another arrow lanced through the air, bringing a screech of pain from a hovering Vore. Parmenion picked up the boy and ran back to the gelding.

'No!' shouted Alexander. 'We mustn't leave! My friend is hurt!'

'Your friend is dead, boy,' Attalus told him, notching another arrow to his bow. 'Where to now, *strategos*? I can hear more of them coming.'

'The cave,' Alexander told them.

'Which way?' asked Parmenion, lifting the boy to the gelding and vaulting to sit behind him.

'There on the mountainside!' shouted Alexander, pointing to a break in the trees.

'Can we outrun them?' Attalus asked.

'I would doubt it,' answered Parmenion. 'But we must try.'

Urging their mounts to a run, the Macedonians raced along the narrow trail and out onto the mountainside.

'Up there!' yelled Alexander. Parmenion glanced up. The black mouth of the cave was less than two hundred paces from them. Looking back, he saw the Vores closing fast. They would not reach it in time.

Attalus was ahead; the powerful grey, with less of a load, was surging on towards the sanctuary of the cave. A black dart lanced into the stallion's back. For a few moments the beast ran on, then its front legs gave way, pitching Attalus to the earth. The swordsman hit hard, but rolled to his knees. He still held the bow – but it was snapped at the tip. Flinging it aside, he drew his sword.

Parmenion leapt down beside him, slapping the gelding's rump and urging the beast towards the cave. With less to carry the gelding sped on, Alexander clinging to his mane.

Suddenly a flash of lightning exploded into the hovering ranks of the Vores, scattering them and killing more than twenty. In the momentary confusion Parmenion saw their chance to escape. 'Run!' he yelled, turning to sprint up the mountainside.

A grey-haired man stepped into their path, but he did not look at them. Instead his hands were raised, pointing at the skies. Blinding white light leapt from his fingers, and the air was filled with the smell of burning flesh and the echoing death-cries of the Vores.

Without looking back, the Macedonians scrambled into the cave where Alexander waited. 'Follow me!' ordered the boy, leading them through the illusory wall and into the palace.

'Can the beasts follow us here?' asked Parmenion.

'Chiron says no enemies can pass through the wall,' the boy answered.

'We'll see,' said Parmenion, hefting his sword and waiting, Attalus beside him.

Chiron appeared. 'I must offer you my thanks,' said the *magus*, smiling.

'That's why you sent us here,' replied Parmenion. 'It is good to see you again, Aristotle.'

'I fear there is some mistake,' the *magus* told them. 'I do not know you.'

'What game is this?' hissed Attalus, moving forward to lay his sword on Chiron's shoulder, the blade resting against his throat. 'You send us into a world of madness and now claim we are strangers? No jests, *magus*! I am not in the mood for them.'

'Wait!' said Parmenion, stepping in and lifting Attalus' blade clear. 'What is your name, friend?'

'I am Chiron,' the *magus* told him. 'The name Aristotle is not known to me. But this is truly fascinating. I exist – in another form – in your world. And in how many others, I wonder?'

'Are you believing this?' stormed Attalus. 'We can see who he is!'

'No,' said Parmenion. 'Look closely. He is more thick-set, and Aristotle has a small scar on his right temple. Other than that they could be twins. But, before we enter into a debate, let us first ascertain how safe we are here. Can the creatures enter?'

'Not immediately,' replied the *magus*. 'But the Enemy has many allies, and my power is not what it was.'

Parmenion strolled to the window, staring out at the sparkling ocean. 'Are we still in your world, *magus*, or is this yet another?'

'It is the same – merely in a different place. There are seven centres of Power in Achaea. I can travel between them. This palace is on the Gulf of Malin.'

'Malin? Malia, perhaps,' whispered Parmenion. 'Is there a pass close by, with a name similar to Thermopylae?'

'Exactly that. Two days' ride to the south.'

'Then Thebes will be the closest major city.'

'There is no city of that name,' the *magus* told him.

'The White Lady spoke of Cadmos.'

'What White Lady?' put in Attalus, but the other two men ignored him.

'Yes, there is Cadmos, the strongest city of central Achaea,' agreed Chiron, 'but the Makedones have it besieged. They will not hold out against Philippos. What is it you plan?'

'We must get to Sparta,' said Parmenion.

'Why there?' asked Attalus. 'And who is this Lady? Will someone tell me what is going on?'

'A good question, my friend,' said Chiron, laying his hand on the swordsman's shoulder. 'Let us go to the kitchens, where I will prepare food and we can sit and talk. There is much here I also do not understand.'

Later, as they sat in the open air, Parmenion told Attalus of the meeting with the lady of the glade, and of her advice. 'It was no dream. We fought the Makedones, and were then drugged. I do not know who the Lady was, but she treated me well and I believe her advice to be sound.'

'I would not know about that,' snapped Attalus, 'since she did not have the good manners to wake me. Why you, Spartan? Am I seen as some lackey running in your footsteps?'

'I cannot answer your questions. The glade was a place of magic and beauty. I do not think they desired the presence of men. But we rescued the nymphs and therefore, I suppose, earned their gratitude.'

'They showed it well, leaving me asleep on the cold earth. Well, a curse on them! I care nothing for them, nor any of the deformed monsters of this place. I have only one question: How do we get home?' he asked, turning to the *magus*.

Chiron spread his arms. 'I do not know.'

'Does anyone know anything here?' stormed Attalus, rising and stalking out into the gardens and down the steps to the wide beach.

'Your friend is frightened,' said Chiron. 'I cannot say that I blame him.'

Parmenion nodded. 'He is a powerful man back in Macedonia and he needs to feel in control of his surroundings. Here, he is like a leaf in a storm.'

'I sense you are not friends. Why did he accompany you on this quest?'

'He has his own reasons,' said Parmenion. 'The first among them is to see that I do not rescue Alexander alone. He wishes to share in that glory, and will risk his life to that end.'

'And what of you, Parmenion? Are you frightened?'

'Of course. This world is strange to me; I have no place in it. But I am a hopeful man. I have found Alexander and, for the moment, we are safe. That is enough.'

Alexander walked out into the sunshine and clambered on to Parmenion's lap. 'I knew you'd come, Parmenion. I told you, didn't I, Chiron?'

'Yes you did, young prince. You are a good judge of men.'

'Why is Attalus here? I don't like him.'

'He is here to help you,' said Parmenion. 'Now, why don't you go down to the beach and make friends with him?'

'Must I?'

'He is your father's most trusted warrior, and Philip does not give such trust lightly. Go. Speak to him. Then make your judgements.'

'You are just trying to get rid of me so that you can talk to Chiron.'

'Exactly right,' Parmenion admitted, with a broad smile.

'Very well then,' said the boy, easing himself to the ground and walking away.

'He's a fine child,' said Chiron, 'and he loves you dearly.'

Ignoring the comment, Parmenion stood and stretched his back. 'Tell me something of this world, *magus*. Make me feel less of a stranger.'

'What do you wish to know?'

'The balance of power. Begin with Philippos. When did he come to the throne – and how?'

Chiron poured a goblet of wine, sipping it before answering. 'He murdered his brother Perdikkas ten years ago and seized the crown. Then he led his troops into Illyria and the north, conquering their cities and stealing their mines. Athens declared war, as did the cities of the Trident . . .'

'The Trident?'

'The lands of the Halkidike?'

'Ah yes. The Chalcidice. Go on.'

'Philippos crushed the armies of the Trident three years ago, then conquered Thrace.'

'What about the Persian empire?'

'What empire?' asked Chiron, chuckling. 'How could such uncouth barbarians have an empire?'

153

Parmenion leaned back. 'Then who rules the lands of Asia?'

'No one. It is a wilderness populated by nomadic tribes who slaughter and kill each other in scores of meaningless wars. There are Greek cities on the coastline, once ruled by Athens or Sparta, but no . . . empire. Is there such where you come from?'

'Yes,' Parmenion told him. 'The greatest the world has ever seen. The Great King rules from the borders of Thrace to the edge of the world. Even Greece . . . Achaea as you call it . . . pays homage to Persia. But you were telling me about the conquest of Thrace.'

Chiron nodded. 'The army of Makedon moved through the country like a forest fire, destroying everything, every city, every town. The entire population was sold into slavery, or slain. Then, last year, Philippos marched south into Thessalonika. The battle was fought near here against the combined forces of Cadmos and Athens. They were crushed utterly. Then the King skirted Cadmos and struck at Athens, burning the acropolis and killing all the citizens save those who escaped to sea. Now Cadmos faces his wrath. It will not stand long. After that it will be Sparta.'

'Why is he so invincible?' asked Parmenion. 'Surely it is possible to defeat him?'

Chiron shook his head. 'When he was a child he was . . . like Achilles before him . . . dipped into the River Styx. He is invulnerable to wounds. Unlike Achilles his mother did not neglect to cover his heel. No arrow can mark him, nor sword cut him. Then when he was twenty, and newly crowned, he asked a sorcerer of great power to create for him an eye of gold, an all-seeing eye that would allow him to read the hearts of men. The sorceror did as he was bid. Philippos took the eye and then tore his own right eye from its socket, replacing it with the magical orb. So you see, Parmenion, no one can either outfight him or outthink him. He knows in advance all the plans of his enemies.'

'What happened to this sorcerer of great power? Perhaps he will know of a way to destroy his creation.'

'No, my friend. I am that sorcerer, and I can help you not at all.'

*

Attalus sat on the beach, feeling the warmth of the sun on his face, yet even this was not as hot as his anger. To be forced to travel with the loathsome Spartan was bad enough, but he had expected a ride into Thrace or the Chalcidice in order to rescue the prince. Not this appalling place of deformity and madness.

Picturing the flying creatures, he shivered. How could a warrior hope to combat such beasts?

Unbuckling his breastplate, he put aside his clothes and waded out into the sea, enjoying the sudden cool on his body. Hurling himself forward he ducked under the water, swimming with long easy strokes to surface some way from the shore. Small translucent fishes swam by him in glittering shoals and he splashed his hand in the water, laughing as they scattered in all directions.

This at least was a reality he knew, and he revelled in the feeling.

At last he began to tire of the sea and headed back for the shore, pushing himself upright in the soft sand and flicking the water from his long hair.

Alexander was waiting beside his armour. 'You swim well,' said the boy.

Attalus swallowed a curse. He did not like the child. A demon, they said, barely human, who could kill at a touch. The swordsman nodded a greeting and sat down on a rock, waiting for the sun to dry his skin.

'Are you frightened?' asked the prince, his expression disarmingly innocent, head cocked to one side.

'I fear nothing, my prince,' Attalus answered. 'And any man who says differently will answer to me with a blade.'

The child nodded solemnly. 'You are very brave to come so far to find me. I know my father will reward you.'

Attalus laughed. 'I have three estates and more wealth than I can spend in a lifetime. I need no rewards, Prince

155

Alexander. But I would give a king's ransom to see Macedonia again.'

'We will. Parmenion will find a way.'

Attalus bit back an angry retort. 'It is good to have faith in one's heroes,' he said at last.

'You do not like him, do you?'

'I like no man – save Philip. And you see too much. Beware, Alexander, such gifts can be double-edged.'

'Do not ever go against him,' warned the prince. 'He would kill you, Attalus.'

The swordsman made no reply, but he smiled with genuine humour. Alexander stood silently for a moment, then looked up into the Macedonian's eyes. 'I know you are said to be the best swordsman in the land, and also my father's most trusted . . . assassin. But know this, if ever Parmenion dies in mysterious circumstances it is to you I will come. And your death will follow soon after.'

Attalus sighed. 'I did not enter this world of the bizarre to hear your threats, boy. I came to rescue you. You do not have to like me – why should you, after all? I am not a likeable man. But – should I ever have cause to fight Parmenion – your threats will not sway me. I am my own man and I walk my own path. Remember that.'

'We will both remember,' said Alexander.

'There's truth in that,' the swordsman agreed.

*

'Do not try to think of a way to defeat Philippos,' said Chiron. 'It is not possible.'

'Nothing is impossible,' Parmenion assured him, as the two men strolled through the palace grounds in the last lingering light of the fading sun.

'You misunderstand me,' continued Chiron. 'There are greater issues here. Why do you think such a being of enormous power would wish to house himself in the frail human shell of a man – even a king?'

Parmenion halted by a stream and sat on a wooden bench. 'Tell me,' he said.

Chiron stretched himself out on the grass and sighed. 'It

is not a simple matter. The Chaos Spirit has no natural form. He is . . . *IT* is . . . of spirit, apparently both immortal and eternal. So then, the real question is *how* he exists. Do you follow me?'

'Not yet, *magus*, but I am ever the willing learner.'

'Then let us take it slowly. What is the single greatest moment of your life?'

'What has this to do with anything?' asked Parmenion, suddenly uncomfortable.

'Bear with me, warrior,' urged Chiron.

Parmenion took a deep breath. 'Many years ago – a lifetime, it seems – I loved a young woman. She made the sun shine more brightly. She made me live.'

'What happened to her?'

The Spartan's expression hardened, his blue eyes gleaming with a cold light. 'She was taken from me and slain. Now make your point, *magus*, for I am losing patience.'

'Exactly my point!' said Chiron, pushing himself to his feet and sitting beside the Spartan. 'I want you to think back to how you felt at the moment you pictured your love and your days together, and then how those thoughts changed when touched with bitterness. The Chaos Spirit may seem to be immortal and eternal, but it is not entirely the truth. He needs to feed. I do not know if pain, anguish and hatred sired him, or whether he is the father and mother of all bitterness. In a way it does not matter. But he needs Chaos to keep him alive. In the body of Philippos he strides the world, birthing oceans of hatred. Every slave, every widow, every orphaned child will know hate; they will lust for revenge. Long after Philippos is dust the Makedones will be despised. Do you see? He cannot be beaten, for even in destroying Philippos you only continue to feed the spirit that possesses him.'

'What then do you suggest, that we meekly lie down before the Tyrant, offering our lives with a smile and a blessing?'

'Yes,' answered Chiron simply, 'for then we would be countering Chaos with a greater force – love. But that will never be. It would take a greater man than any I have met who could answer violence with forgiveness, evil with love. At best all we can do is to fight him without hatred.'

'Why did you make the eye for Philippos?' asked Parmenion suddenly.

'I had a vain hope that he would use it to see himself, the true soul within. He did not. It has always been a problem for me, Parmenion, for I seek to see the good in every man, hoping it will conquer. Yet it happens so rarely. A strong man will seek to rule; it is his nature. And to rule he will need to conquer others.' Chiron sighed. 'All our heroes are men of violence, are they not? I do not know the names of such heroes in your world. But it will be the same story.'

'Yes,' agreed Parmenion. 'Achilles, Heracles, Agamemnon, Odysseus. All men of the sword. But surely if evil men choose sword and lance, then good men must do the same to combat them?'

'Would that it were that simple,' snapped Chiron. 'But good and evil are not so easily distinguished. Good does not wear golden armour, nor does evil always dress in black. Who is to say where evil lies? You are a general in your own world. Did you ever sack a city? Kill women and children?'

'Yes,' answered Parmenion, uncomfortable now.

'And were you serving the forces of good?'

The Spartan shook his head. 'Your point is well made. You are a good man, Chiron. Will you come with us to Sparta?'

'Where else would I go?' answered the *magus* sadly. Rising, he made as if to walk away, then turned. 'There is a legend here – a fine legend. It is said that one day the Enchantment will return, that it will be brought back to us by a golden-haired child of the gods. He will restore peace and harmony, and the world will shine again. Is that not a beautiful idea?'

'Hold to it,' advised Parmenion, his voice gentle.

'I do. I hoped Alexander was the Golden One. But he too is cursed by Chaos. How many other worlds are there, Parmenion? Does a version of the Dark God stalk them all?'

'Never give in to despair,' the Spartan advised. 'Think on this: If you are correct, then perhaps in most of those worlds the Golden Child has already come.'

'That is a good thought,' agreed Chiron. 'And now I must leave you for a while. You are safe here – for the moment. But watch the sea. Philippos will be using all his powers to locate Alexander.'

'Where are you going?'

'Back to the wood. They will need me there.'

*

Parmenion found the sorcerer's mood infectious and his spirits were sombre as he strolled along the line of cliffs overlooking the beach. Far below he could see Attalus and Alexander sitting on the white sand, deep in conversation, and he stopped for a while to watch them.

My son, he thought suddenly, and sadness struck him like a blow. Philotas, Nicci and Hector were his sons, yet his feelings for them were ambivalent. But this boy – this golden child – was everything to him. There is no profit in regret, he reminded himself, but the words, though true, offered no comfort. For this one regret lived on in his own private Hall of Shame. On the wedding night in Samothrace, when Philip was awaiting the arrival of his bride, Parmenion had betrayed him. There was no other word to suit the occasion. With the King lying in a drunken stupor, it was Parmenion who had donned the ceremonial full-faced helm and cloak of Kadmilos and walked into the torchlit room where Olympias lay waiting; Parmenion who had climbed to the bed, pinning her arms beneath him; Parmenion who had felt her soft thighs slide over his hips . . .

'Enough!' he said aloud, as the memory brought fresh arousal. It was a form of double betrayal, and even now he could not understand it. His pride and powerful sense of honour had led him to believe that he would never betray a friend. Yet he had. But what was worse, and continued to torment him, was how even now, while his mind reeled sick with the shame of his deed, his body continued to react to the memory with arousal, lust and delight.

It was why he endured Philip's anger, and his occasional taunts. Guilt tied him to the Macedonian King with bonds stronger than love, as if by serving Philip faithfully he could in some way even the balance, eradicate the shame.

'You never will,' he whispered.

Olympias had been so much like Derae, slim and beautiful, her red-gold hair glinting in the torchlight. She had tried to remove the helm, complaining that the cold metal was hurting her face, but he held her hands down against the soft sheets, ignoring her pleas. She had spent the first part of the night in the Woods of the Mysteries, inhaling the Sacred Smoke. Her pupils were enormously dilated and she lost consciousness while he lay upon her. It did not stop him.

Guilt came later when he crept back into Philip's rooms, where the King lay naked on a couch, lost in a drunken sleep. Pulling clear his helm, Parmenion gazed down on the man he had sworn to serve and felt then the sharp pain of regret. He dressed the unconscious monarch in the cloak and helm and carried the King into the bedroom, laying him alongside Olympias.

Back in his own rooms he had tried to justify his actions. The Lady Aida, in whose palace they were guests, had told Philip that if he did not consummate the wedding within what she termed the Holy Hour, then the marriage would be annulled. Philip had laughed at that. Faced with a beautiful woman, he had never been found wanting, and felt no concern at the threat. Yet, as he waited through the long night, he had continued – despite Parmenion's warnings – to drain goblet after goblet of the heavy Samothracian wine. Philip's capacity for alcohol was legendary, and it still surprised Parmenion how swiftly the King had succumbed to its influence on this special night.

At first Parmenion tried desperately to rouse Philip, but then he had gazed into the bedroom where Olympias lay naked on the broad bed. He tried to convince himself that his first thought had been of Philip, and the hurt to his pride in the morning when all of Samothrace heard of his failure in the marriage bed. But it was a lie. That excuse came later, as he lay awake watching the dawn.

Now he lived with a constant torment, as double-edged

as any dagger. Firstly he feared the truth becoming known, and secondly he had to endure the sight of his beloved son being raised by another.

'I hope you are thinking of a plan to get us home,' said Attalus, moving silently alongside the Spartan.

'No,' admitted Parmenion, 'my thoughts were on other matters. Did you enjoy your swim?'

'It cooled me for a while. Where is the sorcerer?'

'He will be back soon. He has gone to see if the centaurs need his help.'

Alexander climbed into view, the steps on the cliff path almost too high for him. He waved as he saw Parmenion and moved alongside him, sitting close. Instinctively the Spartan put his arm around the boy. Attalus said nothing, but Parmenion felt his gaze.

'We must make our way down to the Gulf of Corinth,' said Parmenion swiftly, 'and then to Sparta. We can only hope that Aristotle will find a way to us there.'

'Hope?' sneered Attalus. 'I would like something stronger than that. But why Sparta? Why not return to the Circle of Stones and wait? That is where he sent us. Surely that is where he will expect us to be?'

Parmenion shook his head. 'The enemy are everywhere – and they have used sorcery to locate Alexander. We could not hope to survive alone against them. Sparta holds out. We will be safe there. And Aristotle is a *magus*; he will find us.'

'I am not convinced. Why not wait here?' argued Attalus.

'I wish that we could, but Chiron does not believe we are safe even here. The King's reach is long, his powers great. Are you beginning to regret your decision to accompany me?'

Attalus chuckled. 'I began to regret it the moment we rode from the Circle. But I will stay the course, Spartan.'

'I did not doubt it.'

'Look! A ship!' cried Alexander, pointing out to sea where a trireme was sailing gracefully into view, its black sail furled, its three banks of oars rising and dipping into the sparkling blue water. Slowly the prow turned until the craft was pointing to the shore.

Closer it came until the watchers could see clearly the hundred or so armed men gathering on the great deck.

'Friendly, do you think?' asked Attalus as the ship was beached, the warriors clambering to the sand.

'They are Makedones,' said Alexander, 'and they are coming for me.'

'Then some of them will die,' said Attalus softly.

*

'Back into the palace,' ordered Parmenion, sweeping Alexander into his arms and moving away from the cliff-edge. Far below them the Makedones soldiers began the long climb up the steep path, sunlight glinting from spear and sword.

Parmenion ran into the palace kitchens where he had put aside his breastplate, helm and sword. Donning the armour, he lifted Alexander and made his way swiftly to the wide stairway, taking the steps two at a time.

'What if those flying creatures are still on the other side?' asked Attalus as they reached the illusory wall.

'We die,' muttered Parmenion, drawing his sword and stepping through to Chiron's cave. It was empty. Lowering Alexander to the ground the Spartan moved to the cave-mouth, scanning the mountainside. The dead grey stallion lay where it had fallen, black crows squabbling over the carcass. Beyond the stallion lay the corpses of more than thirty Vores, but these the crows avoided. Of Parmenion's gelding there was no sign.

'We'd be safer in the woods,' said Attalus. Parmenion nodded and the trio crossed the open mountainside, reaching the sanctuary of the trees without incident.

The woods were unnaturally silent. No bird-song sweetened the air, and not a trace of breeze disturbed the canopied branches above. The silence made both warriors uneasy, but Alexander was happy walking beside his hero, holding Parmenion's hand. They walked deeper into the woods, keeping to a narrow game trail that twisted, rose and fell until it reached a shallow stream where cool mountain water rippled over white stones.

'Do we cross it – or follow it?' asked Attalus, keeping his voice low. Before Parmenion could answer they heard sound of movement from the trail ahead, the snapping of dried wood underfoot. Then came voices, muffled by the undergrowth.

Gathering the child, Parmenion backed away towards the bushes, Attalus beside him. But before they could find a place in which to hide, a warrior in a raven-winged helm appeared on the other side of the stream.

'Here!' he bellowed. 'The child is here!'

More than a score of dark-cloaked soldiers carrying spears and swords ran to join him. Attalus' blade hissed from its scabbard.

Parmenion swung round. Behind them was a narrow track. On either side were thick stands of thorn bushes and brambles. From where he stood the Spartan could see no end to the track, but glancing down he saw cloven hoofprints of deer leading away up the slope.

The Makedones surged forward into the water, the woods echoing with their screams of triumph.

'Run!' shouted Parmenion, holding Alexander tight to his chest as he set off along the track. Thorns cut into his calves and thighs as he ran, and twice he almost stumbled as dry dust shifted beneath his sandalled feet. The slope was steep, the track meandering, but at last he emerged to a wider trail bordered by huge, gnarled oaks. Glancing over his shoulder he saw Attalus some ten paces back, the pursuing Makedones closing on him. A soldier paused in his run to hurl a spear.

'Look out!' shouted Parmenion and Attalus swerved left, the weapon slashing past him to bury itself in the ground in front of the swordsman. Attalus grabbed the shaft as he ran, pulling it from the earth. Turning suddenly, he launched the spear back at the thrower. The soldier threw himself to the ground, the missile taking the man behind him full in the throat.

Spinning on his heel, Attalus raced after Parmenion. The Spartan ran on, seeking always narrow tracks that would keep the enemy in single file behind them, and as he ran his anger grew. There was no strategy here for victory, no subtle plan to swing a battle. Outnumbered, they were being hunted through an alien wood by a deadly enemy. All that was left was to run. But where? For all Parmenion knew they were heading towards an even greater enemy force, or worse perils.

It was galling to the point of rage. All his life the Spartan had survived by outthinking and outplanning his enemies. He was the *strategos*, the general. Yet here he had been reduced to the level of the panic-stricken prey, running for his life.

No, he realized, not panic-stricken. Never that!

In his youth he had been a distance runner, the fastest and the best in Sparta and Thebes, and now – even burdened by the child – he knew he could outlast the Makedones. But the problem was where to run. Glancing up at the sky, he tried to establish his position in the woods. The cave would be to the left. Yet what purpose would be served by returning there? They could pass the wall and escape their immediate pursuers, only to be caught by the soldiers searching the palace beyond. No, the cave was no answer.

A fallen tree lay across his path and he hurdled it effortlessly. Ahead the trail forked, one path rising, the other dipping down into a shadow-haunted glen. A spear flashed by him. Cutting right, he made for the glen.

Three soldiers ran into his path some thirty paces ahead. Cursing, he twisted to his left and leapt a low bush, scrambling up a steep rise to emerge in a circular clearing in a hollow ringed by cypress trees. Attalus came alongside, his face red from exertion, sweat glistening on his skin.

'I . . . can run . . . no further,' said the swordsman.

Ignoring him, Parmenion moved to a nearby tree, lifting Alexander to the lowest branch. 'Climb into that fork and crouch down,' ordered the Spartan. 'You will not be seen from the ground.' The boy pushed his small body through the pine needles and lay, hidden from view.

Drawing his sword, Parmenion ran back to the edge of the slope and waited. The first Makedones warrior scrambled up – and screamed as Parmenion's blade smote his neck. The soldier tumbled back amongst his comrades.

Three more Makedones entered the clearing from the left and Attalus ran to meet them, blocking a sword-thrust and sending a reverse cut that opened one man's throat in a spray of crimson.

But then the main body of the enemy appeared, spreading out around the Macedonians. Parmenion backed away, Attalus joining him, the spears of the Makedones closing around them in a wall of pointed iron.

'I should have taken your advice,' whispered Attalus.

'Where is the child?' asked a swarthy, dark-eyed warrior with a pockmarked face.

Attalus chuckled. 'It is hard to believe anything so ugly could have learned the power of speech.'

'Where is the child?' asked the man again, the spear-points moving closer.

A spearman toppled forward, an arrow jutting from his skull. Then another screamed as a shaft pierced his thigh.

'Down!' shouted Parmenion, seizing Attalus' arm and dropping to the earth.

From all sides arrows hissed across the open ground. A dead Makedones fell across Parmenion with two shafts in his back, a third through his eye. Everywhere the soldiers were dying. Several men tried to run back to the trail, but the huge form of the minotaur Brontes appeared, his double-headed axe slicing through their breastplates and helms.

Two warriors managed to pass him and disappeared down the slope, but their screams echoed back and Parmenion watched as the minotaur's brothers – Steropes the lion-headed, and Arges the cyclops – emerged from the trees.

A terrible silence descended on the clearing. Parmenion eased himself clear of the corpse that had fallen across him and rose, sheathing his sword. Bodies lay everywhere. From the trees came centaurs carrying bows and quivers, their faces grim, their eyes fierce.

'It is good to see you again,' Parmenion told Brontes as the minotaur approached. The great bull's head nodded.

'You run well,' said the minotaur, moving past him to the cypress tree where Alexander was hidden. Dropping his axe, the creature raised his arms. 'Come to me, Iskander!' he called.

Alexander wriggled clear of the branches, dropping into the minotaur's arms. 'Are you truly Iskander?' the beast whispered.

'That is what I was called,' answered the boy.

'And you can open the Giant's Gateway?'

'We shall see,' said Alexander, choosing his words with care. With the boy in his arms, Brontes walked back to where Parmenion and Attalus waited.

'The centaurs brought word that Iskander had come. The Lady bade us protect him. This we will do, with our lives if necessary. Yet it may not be enough. The Makedones are many, and we are few.'

'We must get to Sparta,' said Parmenion. 'There the boy will be safe.'

'The Spartan King is said to be a great man,' said Brontes. 'He does not hunt down the people of the Enchantment. And the Giant's Gateway is close by. Yes, we will come with you to Sparta.'

Parmenion nodded, then swung his gaze over the centaurs. 'How many are with us?' he asked.

'These twenty are all that survive.'

'Then who is scouting the woods to watch for the enemy?'

'No one,' admitted Brontes.

The Spartan walked across the clearing, stepping over the corpses, until he stood before a young centaur, a deep-chested creature with chestnut hair and beard. 'Who commands here?' he asked.

'I am Kheops, the son of Kytin-Kyaris. No one commands.'

'Well, Kheops, I am the guardian of Iskander, and I will command and be obeyed.'

'We will not suffer the orders of a Human,' replied Kheops, his face reddening.

'Then leave us,' said Parmenion softly, 'and we will try to save Iskander alone.'

166

The centaur's front hooves stamped the earth, a low growl rumbling in his throat. Parmenion waited, holding to the creature's gaze. 'We must see that Iskander lives,' said Kheops. 'We cannot go.'

'Then you will obey me,' Parmenion told him. 'Send five of your . . . fellows to watch for the Makedones. We must not be surprised by them again.'

'It will be as you say,' answered Kheops, as if the words were torn from him.

Parmenion swung away from the centaur to see Chiron moving carefully across the clearing, avoiding the blood-stains on the earth. The sorcerer took Parmenion's arm, leading him away from the others.

'This is wrong,' whispered Chiron. 'The child is not Iskander. I know it; you know it.'

Parmenion sighed. 'What I know, *magus*, is that we must reach Sparta to save Alexander. I will take all the aid I can find.'

'But these creatures . . . what of their hopes? Don't you see, Iskander is everything to them? He is the promise that keeps them alive, the one who will return magic to the world and end the reign of Man.'

'What is this Giant's Gateway?' the Spartan asked.

'There is a wood a day's ride south of Sparta. There, on a hill, stand two colossal pillars linked by a great lintel stone. That is the Gateway.'

'To where?'

'To nowhere,' replied Chiron. 'But the legend says that Iskander will open it, that he will grow to the height of the tallest tree and rest his hands on each pillar. Only then will the Enchantment return, bathing the world. But Alexander cannot do it; he is not the Golden Child.'

'What would you have me do, *magus*? Lose the only allies we have in this strange world of yours? Condemn Alexander to death? No, I will not do it. They have made their choice. I did not force it upon them.'

'That is not an argument you can use,' said Chiron. 'You know they are wrong, but you allow them to continue in their error because it suits your purpose. What you are doing will, in all likelihood, condemn them all to death.'

'Is there a problem here, Chiron?' asked Brontes, ambling forward to join them.

'Is there a problem?' the *magus* enquired of Parmenion.

The Spartan's cold blue eyes met his gaze. 'No,' he answered. 'Tomorrow we will take Iskander to his destiny.'

Then he turned and saw the woman.

*

Derae took a deep breath as the Spartan turned. Her legs felt weak and boneless and her hands trembled. So close, she thought. They had talked on Samothrace, but then Derae had been hooded and veiled, her mind locked to the task ahead. But now, as he walked slowly towards her, she felt sixteen again – remembering the softness of his touch, the sweetness of his breath.

'Do you know me, lady?' he asked. It was not the voice of the youth she had loved, but still the sound sent a shiver through her. Her spirit flickered out, touching his mind, sensing the emotions surging through him: curiosity, empathy, and – though her body was now plain and unmemorable – arousal. Swiftly she withdrew from him.

'I know you,' she answered, her voice steady, her hazel eyes meeting his gaze.

He stood for a moment, silent, indecisive. Brontes strolled across to them. 'She is a friend to the Goddess, my mother,' said Brontes. 'She is of the Enchantment.'

Parmenion nodded, but his gaze remained on the dark-haired woman. 'We must get away from this place,' he said, turning to Brontes. 'You know these woods. Where can we go?'

'Do not answer,' said Derae swiftly. 'We are being observed.'

Brontes' huge hand closed around the haft of the axe hanging from his belt and Parmenion swung to scan the clearing. 'There is no one here,' Derae told them. 'We are being watched from afar.'

'By whom?' the minotaur asked.

'By a priest of Philippos.'

168

'Can you shield us? My mother says you are a mystic.'

'Perhaps.' Derae sat down on the grass and closed her eyes, her spirit flying free. A lance of light swept towards her. Her hand flashed up, the lance splitting into a thousand sparks which floated around her like fireflies.

'You will die,' shouted the shaven-headed priest as he floated before her.

'We will all die one day,' she answered. Her hands came up and the fireflies streamed back to the priest, linking to form a golden ribbon that wound about his head and face to blind him. 'Go back to your master,' said Derae. The priest disappeared.

She opened her eyes and stood. 'He is gone,' she told Brontes. 'Now you may speak freely.'

'There are only two ways we can travel to Sparta, southeast to the Peleponnese and through Korinthos, or northwest to the sea and take a ship around the coast to Gytheum.'

'What about west?' asked Parmenion. 'Surely we can cross the Pindos Mountains and make our way to the gulf?'

'No – that way lies death,' said Brontes. 'You cannot pass through the Forest of Gorgon. The Vores dwell there, and Gorgon himself. He is the most vile beast and his heart is corruption. I could speak of his evil, but I swear my tongue would blacken and your soul be shrivelled by what you hear. We might just as well drink poison now as consider that route.'

'Tell me of it anyway,' ordered the Spartan.

'Why? It is out of the question.'

'Because he is the *strategos*,' said Derae, 'and he needs to know.'

Brontes sighed. 'The forest stretches south to the Gulf of Korinthos. It is vast and deep, and unexplored by Man. But every hill and hollow, every dark glen, teems with the creatures of Chaos.'

Derae watched the Spartan. His expression was set and unreadable, and this time she did not reach out to read his thoughts. 'What can you tell us, lady?' he asked suddenly.

'The forces of Makedon are all around you,' she told him.

'They are coming from north, south and east. They have creatures . . . Vores? . . . in the sky and men, and beasts that walk like men, upon the ground.'

'Can we skirt them?'

Derae shrugged. 'Not with twenty centaurs. They are seeking the child. Philippos is linked to him. Whichever route we take will draw peril to us. I have the power to shield us from the Demon King for a little while. But not long, Parmenion; he is too strong for me.'

'So, we are being herded towards the west whether we wish it or no?'

'Yes,' she agreed.

'I will think on it. But first let us find a place to spend the night.'

The Pindos Mountains

Brontes led the way to a cluster of shallow caves, leaving Parmenion, Alexander, Chiron and Attalus in one while he and his brothers took shelter nearby, the dark-haired woman remaining with them. The centaurs drifted away at dusk, returning as men when night fell. They also chose to stay in a separate cave a little to the north of the others.

Chiron was silent as Attalus prepared a fire by the far wall and Parmenion walked out into the night to satisfy himself that the glow did not reflect any light past the cave entrance. Wrapped in Parmenion's cloak, Alexander slept peacefully by the small blaze and the Spartan sat alone in the cave-mouth, watching the stars.

'Are you making plans?' asked Attalus, moving alongside him and sitting with his back to the wall.

'No, I was thinking about my youth.'

'I hope it was misspent.'

'Indeed it was,' answered Parmenion, sighing. The night sky was clear, the moon bright, bathing the trees in silver light. A badger shuffled out into the open, then loped away into the undergrowth.

'It is said you were a champion in Sparta,' said Attalus. 'With all the rewards, why did you leave?'

Parmenion shook his head. 'Where do these stories start? A champion? I was a hated half-breed, a mix-blood,

171

derided, beaten. All I carried from Sparta was my bruises, and a hatred that was all-consuming and ultimately self-defeating. Have you ever been in love, Attalus?'

'No,' admitted the Macedonian, suddenly uncomfortable.

'I was . . . once. And for that love I broke the law. I slept with an unmarried girl of good family. Because of it she was killed, and I slew a fine man. Worse, I brought about the downfall of my own city and with it the death of the only friend I had ever had. His name was Hermias, and he was killed at Leuctra, fighting alongside the King he adored.'

'All men die,' said Attalus softly. 'But you surprise me, Spartan. I thought you were the ice-cold general, the fighting man who had never lost a battle. I thought your life was charmed – blessed, if you like.'

Parmenion smiled. 'The other man's life often looks that way. There was a rich merchant in Thebes. Men would look at him with envy, cursing his luck, jealous of the gold rings he wore and the huge house he built upon a hill high above the stench of the city. But then they didn't know he was once a slave, working in a Thracian mine; that he had toiled for ten years before purchasing his freedom, and then had worked for another five to build a small amount of coin which he gambled on a risky venture that made him rich. Do not envy me, Attalus.'

'I did not say I envied you,' said the swordsman. Suddenly he grinned. 'But I suppose that I do. I could never like you, Parmenion, but I respect you. Now that is enough of compliments. How are we going to get to Sparta?'

Parmenion rose, stretching his back. 'We'll travel west, crossing the Pindos Mountains, then move down to the coast, keeping to the high ground and forests.'

'You are talking of a journey of some weeks. I do not wish to sound defeatist, but do you think that a party including three monsters and twenty centaurs can travel the length of Greece – even this Greece –without being noticed?'

'Centaurs are not uncommon here,' said Parmenion, 'but we will travel mostly by night when they appear as men. As to Brontes and his brothers, I agree with you. But their strength is prodigious and they may prove invaluable if there is trouble on the road.'

'And you are expecting trouble, no doubt?'

'Yes. We have one great problem that no amount of thinking will overcome. Philippos used sorcery to locate Alexander in another world, therefore it seems likely he will be able to find him in this one. Wherever we go – however well we hide – the enemy will always be close.'

'Drawn to the boy like flies to a cowpat?' offered Attalus.

'A disgusting observation, though one that is close to the truth,' agreed the Spartan. 'But the priestess claims she can protect us for a while.'

'So then your plan – such as it is – entails leading a small force of half-human beasts across a war-torn land and arriving at a destination where we may – or may not – be welcome, in the hope that Aristotle will have the necessary power to find us and bring us home?'

'Succinctly put. Do you have a better plan?'

'I must admit that nothing of brilliance springs to mind,' said Attalus, 'but there is something else that concerns me. The question of Alexander. Is he the Iskander these . . . creatures . . . have been waiting for?'

'No.'

'Then what happens when the beasts find out? They are likely to be just a little angry.'

'Perhaps,' said Parmenion. 'But that is a problem for another day.'

'Something else to look forward to,' grunted Attalus. 'I'll say this for you, Spartan – life in your company is seldom dull.'

*

Towards dawn, as he sat lost in thought, Parmenion saw the monstrous figure of Brontes emerging from the trees at the foot of the mountainside. The creature walked forward, then dropped to his knees. Light, ghostly and pale, shimmered around him, and Parmenion watched, awestruck, as the huge bull's head disappeared, leaving the features of a young man, pale-skinned, with hair the colour of polished bronze.

Looking up, the young man saw Parmenion and froze, holding his position for some moments before sitting back and turning away from the Spartan's gaze.

Parmenion strolled out into the moonlight, walking down the slope to sit beside the former minotaur.

'It is not considered polite to view the Change,' said Brontes. 'But then you are not of this world and cannot be expected to understand our customs.'

'Why do you need to assume another form?'

'Why do you Humans need to eat, or breathe? I do not know the answer. I only know what is, and what is necessary. Without the Change I would die. And, as the Enchantment lessens day by day, the Change becomes more difficult, more fraught with pain. That is what Iskander will rectify; he will bring back the Enchantment.'

'Unless Philippos captures him,' pointed out Parmenion.

'Exactly so. How do you propose escaping him?'

'By travelling through the Forest of Gorgon.'

'Then we are all dead.'

'Now it is for you to trust me, Brontes. I am not a man who understands your mysteries, or the power of the Enchantment, but I know the ways of war and the nature of enmity.'

'Gorgon will kill you, Parmenion. He hates Humans even more than I.'

'I am counting on that,' answered the *strategos*. 'We have a saying, Brontes: The enemy of my enemy must be my friend.'

'Gorgon has no friends. Not now . . . not ever.'

'You know him?' asked Parmenion softly.

'I do not wish to speak of it.'

*

Derae lay awake, her spirit floating in the night sky, seeking signs of hidden watchers. But there were none, and this worried her. Did it mean that they feared her powers, or that they had somehow found a way to neutralize them and were even now spying on the caves? The thoughts were not comforting.

You need sleep, she told herself, settling down and covering herself with the rust-coloured cloak Aristotle had supplied. It was thick wool, warm at night, cool in the heat of the day, and she snuggled under it. But sleep would not come.

She had not known what to expect in this strange new world and had prepared herself for surprises. But Chiron had astonished her. He was almost a twin of Aristotle. Derae had gently reached out, touching the man's memories, and in the same moment he became aware of her. He did not close off his thoughts but greeted her with a mind-smile.

He was not Aristotle, having no memories of Macedonia or the Greece she knew. Yet the halls of his memory were vast, full of vanished nations, changed worlds. He had walked in Akkady and Atlantis, in many forms – warrior and mystic, demi-god and demon, made immortal by the magic of the same golden stones possessed by Aristotle.

'Are you satisfied?' he had asked, jerking her back to the present.

'Yes,' she told him. That had been earlier in the day when Brontes and his hideous brothers had met with the centaurs and planned the ambush that saved the two Macedonians. Brontes had been scouting ahead and had seen the chase, judging quite rightly where it must end. Even so it was close-run and had left Derae trembling.

'Where are you from, my dear?' Chiron asked her as they walked from the battle site to the caves.

'I am a priestess – a Healer,' she answered. 'A friend urged me to come here to aid Parmenion.'

'This friend . . . does he look like me?'

'Indeed he does.'

'Curious. I wonder how much of our history is shared? I would like to meet him. Will he be following you through?'

'I do not think so. There is something here which frightens him greatly.'

Chiron chuckled. 'There are things here which frighten *me* greatly. Have you known Parmenion for long?'

'We have met – but briefly,' she answered, with honesty.

175

'Now that is a surprise. I notice your gaze is never far from him. Is it merely that he is a handsome warrior?'

'There are some subjects we should avoid, sir,' she told him primly.

'As you wish.' He had left her then and walked back to join Brontes at the rear.

As the night wore on Derae slept fitfully, waking with the dawn. The child Alexander peeked in at the cave-mouth, smiling as he saw her. 'Good day,' he said, moving into the cave and squatting down beside her.

'And to you, young prince. You are awake early.'

'Yes, I don't need much sleep. What is your name?'

'You may call me Thena.'

'Ah, but it isn't your name, is it?'

'I did not say that it was. I said that is what you may call me.'

'Then you must call me Iskander.'

'I shall . . . Iskander. Are you frightened?'

'No,' he replied with a wide grin. 'Parmenion is here. There is no greater warrior in all of Greece – and he's the best general too.'

'You have much faith in him, Iskander. You must admire him greatly.'

'After my father he is the man I love best. Where are you from?'

'I am a Healer. I dwell in a Temple across the sea, near the ruins of Troy.'

'Have you always been a Healer?'

'No. Once I was just a girl, who dreamt of marrying the man she loved. But it was not to be.'

'Why?' The question was asked so simply that Derae laughed and reached out to ruffle his hair. As her hand was about to touch him she felt a burning pain in her palm and jerked back. His face crumpled. 'I'm sorry. It hasn't done that for a long time; I thought I was free.'

Steeling herself she reached out again, her fingers pushing back the golden fringe above his green eyes. The pain touched her once more, but she showed nothing. 'It was just a cramp,' she assured him. But he shook his head.

176

'You are very kind, but please do not touch me. I do not wish to see you in pain.'

A dark shadow fell across the cave-mouth and Parmenion entered. 'There you are,' he said, kneeling down beside the prince. 'Come, we must prepare for the march.'

'Her name is Thena,' said Alexander. 'She's very nice.' Then he scampered from the cave and Derae looked into Parmenion's eyes.

'You have chosen your route, *strategos*?'

'Yes.' He settled down beside her. 'Are you sure we have not met, lady?'

'What makes you think so?' she countered.

'I cannot say. Your face is not familiar to me, but I feel I know you.'

'We have met,' she admitted, 'on the isle of Samothrace.'

'You!' he whispered. 'You were hooded and veiled; I thought you were in mourning.'

'I was. And I am. Now,' she said, rising smoothly to her feet, 'you said we must prepare for the march.'

'Yes, of course. You know where I plan to go?' he asked, pushing himself upright.

'To the Forest of Gorgon.'

He smiled then, his face becoming remarkably boyish. Derae was forced to look away. 'There is no other way,' he said.

'I know. What is your plan?'

'We will walk to the edge of the forest. Brontes says it will take three days. I will leave the others there and make my way to Gorgon.'

'Why must you risk this? What can you gain?'

Parmenion's smile faded. 'We can go no other way. In the open we will be hunted down: nowhere to hide, nowhere to run. The forest offers sanctuary and a chance to reach the Gulf.'

'Brontes says the evil there is worse than the Makedones.'

'Yes, and I believe him.'

'Then how can you bargain with them? What can you offer?'

'The dream of Iskander: to open the Giant's Gateway and

177

bring back the magic. Evil or not, they are still creatures of Enchantment.'

'I will go with you,' she said.

'There is no need to risk yourself. I am capable of negotiating with the Forest Lord.'

'Even so, I will accompany you. I have many talents, Parmenion. They will prove useful.'

'I do not doubt it.'

*

For two days the group moved on, heading west, higher into the mountains, seeking the long pass that snaked down into the Forest of Gorgon spreading out below them in an ocean of trees. On the morning of the third day, as they sheltered from a sudden storm under a wide overhang of rock, they heard the sound of hoofbeats on the path. Attalus and Parmenion drew their swords and walked out into the storm, followed by Brontes and Chiron.

A stallion came trotting along the path, lifting its great head and whinnying as it saw the *magus*. 'Caymal!' shouted Chiron, running forward and stroking the horse's neck. 'It is good to see you, boy.'

Taking the beast's mane, Chiron vaulted to the stallion's back. The rain eased and the *magus* rode Caymal alongside Parmenion. 'I shall scout on ahead,' said Chiron. 'I will find you before nightfall.'

'Be careful, *magus*, we will need you and your magic if the Vores return,' Parmenion warned him.

The storm passed overhead, the clouds breaking up behind it, allowing sunshine to bathe the mountains as the group moved on, the centaurs riding ahead. Parmenion ran back up the slope, shading his eyes and studying their back-trail.

Attalus joined him. 'You see anything?' the Macedonian asked.

'I'm not sure. Look over there, beyond the pines. There is a cleft in the rocks. I thought I saw a man moving between them.'

'I see nothing. Let's move on.'

'Wait!' urged Parmenion, grabbing Attalus' arm and hauling him down. 'Look now!'

A line of men was moving down the slope several miles to the east, sunlight glinting from helms and spear-points. Above them a Vore circled. 'How many?' Attalus whispered.

'More than fifty. Happily they are afoot and that means they could not come up to us before dark. Even so we must hurry.'

'Why? They'll have a difficult task trying to track us in the forest.'

'First we need permission to enter the forest,' said Parmenion.

'From whom?'

'The monsters who dwell there,' answered the Spartan, moving back from the rim and loping down the pass.

'Monsters? You said nothing of monsters,' shouted Attalus, running after him.

Parmenion slowed and grinned. 'I like to surprise you, Attalus.' The smile faded and he gripped the other man's shoulder. 'I may not come back. If that be the case, do whatever you can to bring Alexander to Sparta.'

'I'll come with you. I'm getting used to your company.'

'No. If we both die, what hope is there for the boy? You stay with him.'

It was dusk when the travellers came to the foot of the mountains. The centaurs rode off to find their own private places while Brontes, Steropes and Arges prepared a fire in the centre of a cluster of white boulders. Attalus and Alexander settled down beside the blaze to rest, while the woman Thena strolled from the camp to stand alongside the Spartan as he studied the forest.

'When will you go in?' she asked.

'I would prefer it to be dawn,' he told her. 'But the Makedones are close behind and we may not have that long. Where in Hecate's name is Chiron?'

'It would be best if we entered the forest before nightfall,' advised Thena.

Parmenion nodded. 'Then let us be about it.' Striding to the boulders, he outlined his plan to the others.

179

'You are a madman,' stormed Brontes. 'I thought you would realize your folly. Don't you understand? Gorgon will kill you – and if he doesn't, he will betray you to Philippos.'

'You may be correct, my friend, but our choices are limited. If I am not back by the dawn, you must make your own way to the Gulf as best you can.'

Without another word he swung on his heel and walked across the open ground towards the dark wall of trees.

Thena came alongside him. 'Are we being observed?' he asked, his voice low.

'Yes. There are several beasts in the trees watching us. They are thinking of murder,' she said.

She felt Parmenion stiffen, his stride faltering, his hand easing towards his sword. 'We could go back,' she whispered.

'These creatures,' he said softly, 'you can read their thoughts?'

'Yes – such as they are.'

'Can you talk to them?'

'No, but I can influence them. What do you wish them to do?'

'Take me to the Lord Gorgon.'

'Very well. Count up to twenty and then shout his name. That will give me time to work on them.'

Derae took several deep breaths, calming herself, then sent her spirit into the trees. The first creature she touched – part reptile, part cat – made her recoil. His thoughts were of blood, and rending flesh. There was little intelligence here and she moved on, coming at last to a Vore who sat in the highest branches of an oak, his pale eyes staring at the two humans. He also relished thoughts of murder, but Derae sensed curiosity too.

'Gorgon!' yelled Parmenion. 'I wish to speak to the Lord Gorgon!'

The Vore tensed, unsure what to do. Derae's voice whispered deep within his mind, sending up thoughts from his subconscious. 'I must take them to the Lord. He will be angry if I do not. He will kill me if I do not. One of these

180

others will tell him the man called for him. He will blame me.'

Spreading his wings, the Vore launched himself into the air, gliding down to land some twenty paces from the Humans.

Derae opened her eyes and instinctively reached out to take Parmenion's hand.

The Vore moved closer, its taloned feet uncomfortable on flat ground. 'You wish to see the Lord?'

'I do,' answered Parmenion.

'You are from Philippos?'

'I will speak only to the Lord Gorgon,' Parmenion said.

'I will lead you, Human.'

The Vore swung round and began to walk clumsily towards the trees, its treble-jointed feet making it stoop as it moved. Several times it slipped, but its wings flashed out to steady its balance.

Still holding Derae's hand, Parmenion followed the creature. 'What are the others thinking?' he whispered.

'One of them plans to leap upon you the moment you reach the shadows of the trees. Beware! But do not kill it. Leave it to me!'

Letting go of her hand Parmenion walked on, gripping the hilt of his sword. Sweat bathed his face and his heart was beating wildly. Yet not all his thoughts were of fear. The touch of the woman's hand had been like fire moving through his blood, lifting him. The trees came closer, dark and forbidding, no sound emerging from the forest, no bird-song, not even the chitter of bats.

A reptilean creature sprang from an overhead branch and Parmenion leapt aside, but the beast plummeted to the ground and lay without moving. The Vore hissed out a warning to the other beasts nearby, then walked stiff-legged to the unconscious creature. 'Is it dead?' he asked.

'Sleeping,' Derae answered.

The Vore knelt over the body, ramming its talons through the creature's neck and wrenching clear the head. 'Now it is dead,' he hissed, licking the blood from his claws.

Slowly they walked on through the gathering gloom.

Derae could hear the sounds of beasts moving on either side of them and in the branches above, but no further violence threatened them.

'Sweet Hera!' whispered Derae.

'What is it?'

'The Lord of the Forest . . . the Gorgon. I touched him. Such hatred.'

'Against whom is it directed?'

'Everyone.'

The track widened and the Vore led them down into a huge hollow where a score of fires were lit and a monstrous figure waited, seated upon a throne of skulls. His skin was dark green, mottled with brown, his head enormous, his mouth cavernous and rimmed with fangs. But upon his head, in place of hair, writhed a score of snakes. Parmenion walked forward and bowed.

'Death to your enemies, sire,' he said.

The Hills of Arcadia

Far to the south, across the Gulf of Korinthos in the low hills of Arcadia, a bright light blazed briefly across the marble Tombs of the Heroes. It shone like a second moon, flickered and then died.

A shepherd boy saw the light and wondered if it presaged a storm, but his sheep and goats were undisturbed and there were no clouds in the night sky – the stars bright, the moon shining clear.

For a moment or two the boy thought about the light, then pushed it from his mind and huddled into his cloak, switching his gaze to his flock, eyes scanning the perimeters of the pasture to seek signs of wolf or lion.

But there was only one wolf close by, and the boy did not see him, for he was nestled down behind a marble gravestone in the nearby hills; and he too saw the light. As it flared up all around him, dazzling, terrifying, his thoughts of hunger fled before it.

The wolf was old, banished from the pack. Yet once he had been mighty, a leader to be feared, cunning and deadly. But never in his long life had such a light blazed around him and it left him confused, uncertain. He lay still, lifting his grizzled head to sniff the air. Here was something he knew – and feared. The scent of Man.

And close by.

The wolf did not move. The scent was from his left and he slowly turned his head, yellow eyes watching for movement.

A man was lying on a slab of marble, his naked skin pale in the moonlight. He groaned and moved. Only moments before, the wolf had leapt to that same slab to look out over the flock, selecting his victim. There had been no scent of Man then. Yet there he was, stretched out.

The wolf had survived his many years by knowing when to be cautious and when to be brave. Men who appeared from the air, amid bright unnatural light, did not inspire courage in the old beast. And though he was hungry he slunk away towards the northern woods, far from the scent of Man.

*

Helm stirred. The stone was cold and uncomfortable on his back and he groaned as he woke, rolling to his side and swinging his powerful legs over the side of the slab. Sitting up, he yawned and stretched. The night was cool, but not unpleasant, and he saw a wolf loping away down the hillside towards the trees. Helm's hand reached for his sword, and it was then he realized he was naked and unarmed.

'Where is this place?' he said aloud. 'How did I come here?'

In those first few moments Helm was not concerned. He was a warrior – strong, tested in the heat of many battles, confident in his power. But as he searched his memories, fear akin to panic flared within him. He did not know how he had come to this strange place, but worse than this – so much worse – he realized with a shock which sent his heart hammering wildly that the corridors of his memory were silent and deserted.

'Who am I?' he whispered.

Helm. I am Helm.

'Who is Helm?' The name was small comfort, for with it came no memories of times past. Looking down at his hands, he saw they were broad and calloused, the fingers short and powerful. His forearms showed many scars, some jagged, others straight cuts. Yet how he had come by them was a mystery.

Be calm, he warned himself. Look around this place. It was then that he realized he lay within a graveyard, full of silent statues and marble tombs. Quelling his panic, he leapt lightly from the slab and explored. Some of the tombstones had cracked and fallen, others were overgrown with weeds. No one tended this place then, he thought. A cool wind hissed over the stones and he shivered. Where are my clothes, he wondered? Surely I have not walked across the land naked like a field slave? A gleam of light came from his left. For a moment only he thought a warrior stood there, moonlight gleaming from a full-faced helm of bronze and a gilded breastplate. He tensed, his hands curling into fists; then he saw that there was no silent soldier, only a suit of armour placed on a wooden frame.

He approached it warily, eyes scanning the graveyard around it.

The helm was beautifully crafted, save that it had no plume or crest. The skull was clear, showing no sign of the armourer's hammer, nor a single rivet. The face-guard had been shaped into the features of a man, bearded and stern of eye, with high curved brows and a mouth set in a terrible smile. The breastplate was also of superb design, the shoulders padded with bronze-reinforced leather, the chest fashioned in the shape of a strong man's musculature, curving pectorals and well-developed muscles at the solar plexus. Beneath it was a kilt of leather strips edged with bronze, and below that a pair of doeskin riding boots.

Beside them lay a scabbarded sword. Helm reached down and drew the weapon. His heartbeat slowed, confidence returning. The blade was of polished iron, double-edged and keen, the balance perfect.

The armour is mine, he realized. It has to be.

Swiftly he dressed. The breastplate was a perfect fit, as were the boots. The kilt sat well on his waist, the sword scabbard sliding easily into a loop of bronze at his left hip. Lastly he lifted the helm, easing it down over his short-cropped hair. As it settled into place a searing pain flowed over his features, burning like fire. He screamed and tried to pull the helm loose, but molten metal ate into his skin, pouring into his nostrils and mouth and anchoring itself to the bones of his face.

The pain passed.

Opening his eyes he saw that he had fallen to his knees. He rose and tried once more to remove the helm, but it would not budge. The breeze whispered across the graveyard – and he felt it upon his face, even as he had felt his hands when they tried to remove the helm. Lifting his right hand, he touched the metal mouth. It was cold, yet yielding. His finger probed further, touching his tongue; this too was metallic and yet still soft.

His face was now bronze; the helm was more than joined to his skin, it had become part of him.

'What is happening to me?' he bellowed, his own voice strange in his ears.

'Nothing is happening,' replied a soft voice. 'You are merely preparing yourself for the task ahead.'

Helm swung, his sword flashing into his hand. But there was no one in sight. 'Where are you?'

'Close by,' came the voice. 'Do not be alarmed, I am a friend.'

'Show yourself, *friend*.'

'That is not necessary. You are in the hills of Arcadia. Your quest lies to the north, at the Gulf of Korinthos.'

'I am not your slave!' stormed the warrior.

'You do not know what you are, all you know is the name I gave you.' The voice pointed out, the tone equable, even friendly. 'But all your answers lie ahead. You must seek out the Golden Child.'

'And if I don't?'

There was no reply. 'Are you still there? Speak to me, curse you!'

But the graveyard was silent.

*

Attalus sat back, resting his shoulders against a boulder and surveying his companions. Brontes was sitting opposite, his great brown eyes staring into the fire. Beside him the lion-headed Arges was stretched out, his maned head resting on his hugely muscled arm, his tawny eyes watching Attalus. The cyclops, Steropes, was asleep, breath hissing through his fangs. Attalus transferred his gaze to the cliff path where a single centaur watched for signs of the Makedones. Beside him Alexander stirred, moaning in his sleep. Attalus glanced back at Arges; still the creature watched him.

'Do you have to lie there and stare?' Attalus asked. The lion's mouth opened, a low growl issuing forth.

Brontes looked up from the fire. 'He does not like you,' he said.

'I'll lose no sleep over that,' retorted Attalus.

'From where does your anger come, Human?' queried Brontes. 'I feel it in you – a bitterness, a frustration perhaps?'

'Leave me in peace,' snapped Attalus. 'And make sure your hairy brother keeps his distance, or he's likely to wake up with a length of Macedonian steel in his heart.' And he stretched out on the ground, turning his back on the brothers.

Bitterness? Oh yes, Attalus knew where the seeds had been planted for that. It had been on the day when his father killed his mother. The death had not been easy and the boy had listened to her screams for hours. He had been young then, merely twelve, but after that day he had never been young again. At fourteen he had crept into his father's bedchamber with a razor-sharp skinning knife, running the blade expertly across the man's throat and standing back to watch the sleeping man wake with blood bubbling into his lungs. Oh, he had thrashed his arms, struggling to rise, his fingers scrabbling at his throat as if to bind the slashed arteries. Bitterness? What could these creatures know of his bitterness?

Unable to sleep, Attalus rose and walked from the camp. The moon was high, the night breeze chill. He shivered and glanced up at the cliff path. The centaur was nowhere in sight. Uneasy now the swordsman scanned the high rocks, seeking any sign of movement.

There was nothing, save the breeze rustling the dry grass on the sides of the cliff. Swiftly he returned to the circle of boulders where the three brothers were asleep. Lightly he tapped Brontes on the shoulder. The minotaur groaned and raised his massive head. 'What is it?'

'The sentry is gone. Wake your brothers!' whispered Attalus. Moving to Alexander he lifted the boy to his shoulder and set off for the forest. As he reached open ground there came the sound of screams from the north. Several ponies ran from the rocks, but spears and arrows sliced into them. A young man riding a pale pony almost got clear, but a Vore swooped down from the night sky, a dart thudding into the pony's neck. The beast went down, throwing the boy clear. He rose, staggered, and fell as a second dart lanced his body.

Attalus started to run. Alexander woke, but he did not scream or shout. His arms moved around Attalus' neck and he held on tightly.

From behind came the sound of a galloping horse and Attalus swung, dragging his sword clear. A huge centaur carrying a curved bow ran towards them.

'Camiron!' shouted Alexander. The centaur slowed.

'Many Makedones,' he said. 'Too many to kill. The centaurs are dead.'

Sheathing his sword, Attalus took hold of Camiron's mane and leapt to his back. 'Make for the trees!' he commanded. Camiron surged forward, almost unseating the Macedonian, but then they were away. Dark-cloaked warriors were closing in from the south, north and east. But the way west, to the forest, was still clear. Camiron thundered across the open ground as arrows slashed the air around him.

A Vore swooped down from the sky and Camiron swerved and reared as a dart sliced in to the ground beside him. Notching an arrow to his bow the centaur sent a shaft winging through the air, taking the Vore in the right side and piercing its lung. The creature's wings folded and it crashed to the earth.

Camiron broke into a gallop and headed for the trees,

leaving the Makedones far behind. The forest closed around them but still Camiron ran, leaping fallen trees and boulders, splashing across streams, until he crested a hill that led on to a small hollow circled by tall pines. Here he slowed.

'This place no good. This is Gorgon's Forest.'

Attalus lifted his leg and slid to the ground. 'It's safer than where we were,' he said, releasing Alexander. The boy sank to the earth, his hands clasped to his temples.

'Are you ill?' Attalus asked, dropping to his knees beside the boy. Alexander looked up and the swordsman found himself staring into yellow eyes, the pupils slitted.

'I am well,' came a deep voice. Attalus recoiled and Alexander laughed, the sound hollow and cruel.

'Do not fear me, assassin. You have always served me well.'

Attalus said nothing. At Alexander's temples dark skin erupted, flowing, swelling, curling back over his ears and down to his neck, forming into twin ram's horns, ebony-dark and gleaming in the moonlight.

'I like this place,' said the Chaos Spirit. 'It suits me.'

*

'Death to your enemies, sire,' said Parmenion, bowing low.

'You are an enemy,' hissed Gorgon. The Spartan straightened and smiled, looking into the pale eyes of the monstrosity before him.

'Indeed I am – for I am Human. But I have the capacity to give you all that you desire.'

'You can have no understanding of what I desire. But speak on, for you amuse me – as your imminent death will amuse me.'

'Long ago you were a warrior,' said Parmenion softly, 'a child of the Titans. You had the ability to change your shape, to fly, or to swim below the sea. But when the Great War ended you were banished here, trapped in the last form you chose. Now the Enchantment is dying, all over the world. But you will survive, Gorgon; you know that. You will live for a thousand years, here in this place of dark

189

magic. But one day even this forest will fall to the axes of men.'

Gorgon surged to his feet, the snakes of his hair hissing and thrashing. 'You came here to tell me what I already know? You are no longer amusing, Human.'

'I came to offer the answer to your dreams,' Parmenion told him.

'And what is my dream?'

'Be careful, Parmenion,' came the voice of Thena in his mind. 'I cannot read him.'

'You have many dreams,' said Parmenion. 'You dream of revenge, you nurse your hatreds. But the one dream, the one great dream, is to see the Enchantment restored, to be free of Man.'

Gorgon sank back on to the throne of skulls. 'And this you can give me?' he asked, his cavernous mouth stretching into an obscene smile.

'Iskander can bring the dream to life.'

For a moment the King was silent, then he leaned forward, his pale eyes glittering. 'You speak of the child Philippos seeks. He has offered much for this child – many women, not plain like the one with you, but beautiful, soft and sweet. He promises to accept my sovereignty over the forest. I think his is the offer I will accept.'

'Why does he want the child so desperately?' countered Parmenion.

'For immortality.'

'An immortal Human? Is that to be desired? And what else?'

'What else is there?'

'The death of Enchantment. Without Iskander you have no hope. You will all wither and die. That is the ultimate aim of Philippos – it has to be.'

'And the child is Iskander?'

'He is,' Parmenion replied.

'And he can lift the curse from me and my people?'

'He can.'

'I do not believe it. Now it is time to die, Human.'

'Is this all that you want?' asked Parmenion, his arm

190

sweeping out to encompass the clearing, 'or have you lived so long as a monstrosity that you can no longer remember what it was like to live as a god? I pity you.'

'Save your pity!' thundered the King. 'Save it for yourself and the bony woman beside you!'

'What was your name?' asked Thena suddenly, her voice clear and sweet.

'My name? I am Gorgon.'

'What was your name before, in the bright golden days?'

'I . . . I . . . what has this to do with anything?'

'Can you not remember?' she asked, moving forward to stand before him.

'I remember,' he answered. 'I was Dionius.' The King sagged back on the throne, the taut muscles of his shoulders relaxing. 'I will think more on what you say. You and your man may stay with us tonight; you will be safe while I consider your words.'

Thena bowed and walked to Parmenion, leading him away to the edge of the clearing.

'What was that about his name?' asked the Spartan.

'His mind was too powerful to read, but one image kept flickering in his thoughts when you spoke of the return of the Enchantment. It was of a handsome man with clear blue eyes. I guessed it must be him.'

'You are a good companion to have,' he told her, taking her hand and kissing it. 'Wise and intuitive.'

'And bony and plain,' she replied, with a smile.

'Not at all,' he whispered. 'You are beautiful.'

Snatching her hand from his, she pulled back. 'Do not mock me, Spartan.'

'I spoke only the truth. Beauty is more than skin, flesh and bone. You have courage and spirit. And, if you doubt my words, then read my mind.'

'No. I know what is there.'

'Then why are you angry?'

'I had a lover long ago,' she said, turning away from him. 'He was young, as was I. We did not have long together, and I have missed him for many years.'

'What happened?'

'I was taken from him, across the sea, and held captive in a temple until I agreed to become a priestess.'

'And he made no attempt to find you? His love could not have been as great as yours.'

'He thought me dead.'

'I am sorry,' said Parmenion, taking her hand once more. 'I know the scars you carry; I have them too.'

'But you are married now, with three children. Surely you have forgotten your first love?'

'Never,' he replied, his voice so soft the word was barely a sigh.

The Forest of Gorgon

For much of the night the creatures of the forest sat around the campfires. There was no laughter or song and they huddled together in grim silence as Gorgon sat upon the throne of skulls. Thena was asleep, her head resting on Parmenion's shoulder, but the Spartan stayed awake. The silence was unnatural; he sensed the creatures were waiting for something and he remained tense and watchful as the hours passed.

Towards dawn the creatures climbed to their feet, moving to left and right of the throne in two lines. Easing Thena to the ground, Parmenion rose. His limbs were stiff and he stretched the muscles of his back. Tension hung in the air as Gorgon rose from the throne and stared to the east.

A dozen weird beasts emerged from the trees, dragging a prisoner, roped and tied. There was blood upon the prisoner's body and the marks of many wounds. Parmenion cursed softly.

The prisoner was Brontes.

His captors – part-reptile, part-cat, their limbs covered in fur, their faces scaled – pulled Brontes between the waiting lines. Jagged knives and swords hissed into the air.

'Wait!' called Parmenion, striding out to stand above the bound minotaur. Brontes looked up at him, his expression unreadable. Swiftly Parmenion drew his dagger, slicing the razor-sharp blade through the thongs binding him. 'Stay down,' ordered the Spartan, then rose to face the Forest King.

'This is my friend – and my ally,' he said. 'He is under my protection.'

'Your protection? And who protects you, Human?'

'You do, sire – until you have reached a decision.'

'So,' hissed Gorgon, pacing forward to stand over the minotaur, 'you have a human friend now, Brontes. Do you remember the last one? You don't learn, do you?'

The minotaur said nothing but he lowered his head, avoiding Gorgon's gaze. Then a sound came from the Forest King that could have been laughter. 'He was a prisoner on Creta,' he told Parmenion. 'The King penned him in a labyrinth below his city, feeding him on the entrails of pigs and other vile meats. One day the King threw a *hero* into the labyrinth. But Brontes did not kill him, did you, brother? No, he befriended him and together they escaped. Imagine Brontes' surprise when the hero returned home to brag of his battle with the deadly, man-eating minotaur. Did he become King, Brontes? Yes, I believe that he did. And spent his days – as all kings do – hunting down the people of the Enchantment. Thus do they build their legends.'

'Kill me,' said Brontes, 'but pray do not bore me to death.'

'Ah, but how can I kill you, Brontes? You are under the protection of the Human. How fortunate for you.' Suddenly Gorgon's foot lashed out, cracking against Brontes' jaw and hurling him to the ground.

'How many enemies do you need, sire?' asked Parmenion.

'Do not try my patience, Human! This is my realm.'

'I do not question that, sire. But when the Enchantment is restored, it will be restored for all the children of the Titans. All . . . including my friend Brontes.'

'And if I kill him?'

'Then you will need to kill me. For I will surely strike you down.'

Gorgon shook his head, the snakes convulsively rising, then he knelt by Brontes. 'What are we to make of this, brother?' he asked. 'A Human is prepared to die for you. How far have we fallen that we should earn their pity?' Glancing up at Parmenion he shook his head once more. 'You will have my answer come the dawn. Enjoy the moments before then.'

Parmenion moved to Brontes, helping the minotaur to his feet. His chest and back showed a score of shallow cuts and he was bleeding freely.

'What happened?' asked Parmenion as he led the minotaur back to where Thena slept.

'The Makedones surprised us. The centaurs are dead – as are my brothers. I managed to reach the forest, but there I was captured. All is lost, Parmenion.'

'What of the boy!'

'Your friend carried him clear – but I don't know if they escaped.'

'I am sorry for your brothers, my friend. I should have led us all into the forest and taken the chance.'

'Do not blame yourself, *strategos*. And I thank you for speaking for me. Sadly it will delay our deaths only a little while. Gorgon is playing with us, allowing hope to build. At dawn we will see his true evil.'

'He called you brother.'

'I do not wish to speak of it. I will sleep these last hours. It will annoy him dreadfully.' The minotaur sank back to the grass, lowering his huge head to the ground.

'I will tend your wounds,' Parmenion offered.

'No need. They will be healed by the time we face our doom.' Brontes closed his eyes.

Parmenion touched Thena's shoulder and she woke instantly. 'Alexander is lost somewhere. Can you find him?'

'I cannot soar here. The Dark Enchantment is too strong. What will you do?'

Parmenion shrugged. 'I will use my wits to the last and, if that fails, I'll stab the snake-headed bastard through the heart and order his men to surrender.'

'I believe that you would,' she said, smiling.

'Spartan training. Never admit defeat.'

'I too am Spartan,' she said. 'We are a very stupid people.' They both laughed and he put his arm around her.

'Go back to sleep,' he advised, his smile fading. 'I will wake you for the dawn.'

'If you do not object, I would like to sit with you. You can tell me of your life.'

'There is nothing in my life to interest a priestess.'

'Tell me of your first love, how you met. I would like to hear that.'

*

The horned child moved to the centre of the clearing and gazed through slitted eyes into the darkness of the forest. 'Come to me!' he called, his voice echoing into the trees. Slowly, one by one, the beasts came forth until they formed a huge circle around him. Attalus stayed close to the centaur, Camiron, who stamped his feet nervously, his brown eyes wide, almost panic-stricken.

'Stay calm,' advised Attalus.

'I am not frightened,' the centaur lied.

'Then stand still, damn you!'

'I want to leave. I will run to the open ground. I cannot breathe here. I need Chiron; I must find him.'

'Wait!' commanded Attalus. 'Do nothing rash. If you run they will drag you down. And, more importantly, me with you.'

More and more creatures filed slowly forward, silently kneeling before Alexander. The stench was appalling and Attalus almost gagged. A scaled beast pushed past him, its rough skin grazing the swordsman's arm. But the beasts showed little interest in man or centaur; their eyes were fixed on the Golden Child.

Alexander walked back to Attalus. 'Lift me to the centaur's back,' he said. The swordsman did so and Camiron shifted uneasily. Alexander patted Camiron's shoulder and Attalus saw that his fingernails were now black and pointed. 'Such a puny body,' said the Chaos Spirit, staring at his hands. 'But it will grow. Come, let us find Parmenion. Head south, Camiron.'

'I do not wish to carry you. You are hurting me,' said the centaur.

'Your wishes do not concern me. But you may die here if you desire it.'

Camiron cried out as fresh agony lanced through his frame. 'That is true pain,' said the Chaos Spirit. 'Now move – and slowly. Attalus, you will walk beside me. My servants can smell your blood. It makes them hungry. Stay close to me.'

'Yes, my prince. But where are we going?'

'To war and slaughter. There cannot be two kings in the forest.'

*

The sun rose slowly over the trees, but no birds sang. The creatures of Gorgon had remained in two lines before the throne, unmoving, unspeaking, waiting for the dawn. Parmenion stood and stretched. Thena rose with him. Brontes groaned and stirred as the first rays of sunshine touched him. His wounds had healed in the night; now only dried blood remained on his massive torso.

'Now we await Gorgon's pleasure,' whispered Brontes. 'It would be a kind act were you to kill the woman now.'

'No,' said Parmenion softly. 'We'll play out the game to the end.'

'As you wish.'

The trio walked forward between the waiting lines and halted before the throne. Gorgon's huge head lifted, his pale eyes glaring balefully at Parmenion.

'I have given thought to your words, warrior. I find them unconvincing.'

'Naturally,' said Parmenion. 'When one is cursed for so long, a dream is hard to hold. So many disappointments, so much bitterness and hatred. Why should you find it easy to believe?'

'I mean to kill you,' continued the King, as if he hadn't heard. 'I will ensure your death is long in coming.'

'Does this mean that you will accept the offer of Philippos?' asked Parmenion calmly.

'Yes. I will find the child and deliver him to the Makedones King.'

'In return for what? A few women? Sovereignty over the forest? Do you sell yourself so cheaply? Philippos grants you what you already have, and you take it as a gift. What of your people here? What do they get? You turn down their chance of removing the curse upon them. What is there for them?'

'They serve me!' bellowed Gorgon, rising from his throne. 'They will do as I command. You think your sweet words have swayed them? Yes, we are cursed, but there is no Iskander to rescue us. He is a dream, an invention, created by those without the courage to live without hope. But you can serve a purpose, Human. Your screams can amuse us for a little while.'

The lines of monsters began to move, curling around the trio. Brontes gave a low growl and Parmenion drew his sword. Derae stood still, her gaze resting on the Forest King, her spirit reaching out.

'To live without hope,' she said, her voice high and clear and unafraid, 'is not courageous. It is the worst form of cowardice. It means you have given up the struggle. Have you always been such a man, Dionius? Or was there a time when your dreams were golden and the joy of love filled your soul?' Through the waves of bitterness surging from the Forest King she saw, suddenly, the briefest vision – a young woman and a man, hand in hand before the ocean. Then the image was savagely cut off.

'I never knew love!' he roared.

'You lie! There was Persephone!'

Gorgon reeled as if struck, then cried out, his scream high-pitched and chilling. Derae saw it all then, as the gates of Gorgon's memory fell away. The beautiful young woman and the handsome child of the Titans – walking together, laughing, touching, loving. She saw them in many shapes, sea birds, dolphins and other exquisite creatures she could not name. But Persephone was human, and not all the Titan's magic could hold back her final hours when the dark plague swept in from the north.

198

Gorgon fell to the ground, beating at the earth with his fists. The monsters of the forest stood back, silent and uncertain. Slowly Gorgon rose, the snakes hanging lank and lifeless from his scalp. From his belt he drew a long dagger, its edge serrated, and advanced on Derae.

'Would Persephone enjoy this scene?' she asked.

Gorgon sighed and dropped the knife. 'I will see the child,' he whispered. 'If he is Iskander, I will help you. If he is not, then your screams will last an eternity.'

*

For a moment Parmenion stood still, his gaze moving from the tall woman to the snake-headed monster before her. Then he sheathed his sword. Thena's voice whispered in his mind. 'Do nothing and say nothing,' she urged.

Gorgon turned away from the scene, returning to his throne and slumping upon it with his head in his hands.

Thena touched Parmenion's arm and walked back to the shade of the tree where they had spent the night. The Spartan followed her. 'What is wrong?' he asked. 'Is he lying? Will he truly help us?'

'Gorgon is not the concern,' she whispered. 'The Demon Prince has gathered an army. He is moving towards us, intent on destroying the Forest King.'

'What Demon Prince?' asked Parmenion. 'What are you saying?'

'The Chaos Spirit has taken control of Alexander. He has become a horned creature, with fangs and talons. It is these woods, Parmenion, so full of Dark Enchantment. They swelled his power. Attalus is with him, and a centaur called Camiron. But the Spirit now controls hundreds of Gorgon's followers.'

'I don't understand. How do you know this? You said you could not release your spirit here.'

'I can still reach out, touching those I know if they are not too far distant. I can feel the thoughts and fears of Attalus. They will be here very soon.'

'From which direction do they come?'

'The north,' she answered, pointing to a break in the trees.

'Is the demon in full control of the boy?'

'Yes.'

Parmenion sighed, then cursed softly. 'I will go to them,' he said.

'The Demon Prince will kill you!'

'I have no choice,' he replied wearily. A Vore swooped down over the trees, landing before the Forest King. Parmenion strode back to the throne. Gorgon listened as the Vore spoke, then came to his feet – eyes angry, fists clenched.

'This child of yours comes to me for war!' he thundered.

'As you would expect, my lord,' answered Parmenion. 'He does not know whether we are prisoners or guests. I shall go to him, and bring him to you alone.'

'This Iskander,' said the King, 'is horned and cat-eyed. The legends do not speak of this.'

'He is a shape-changer, as you once were, sire. His powers, as you now know, are very great. Let me go to him.'

Gorgon nodded, then his hand stabbed out, pointing to Thena and Brontes. 'They stay,' he hissed, 'and if you lie they will suffer.'

Parmenion bowed. 'As you wish, lord,' he said, holding his voice even. Bowing once more, the Spartan swung to the north and walked from the clearing. Once in the cover of the trees he ran – long, loping, effortless strides along the narrow trail, his mind concentrating on the problem ahead. How could he deal with a god? What arguments could he use?

Thena's voice whispered once more into his brain. 'I can feel Alexander now. He is not wholly overcome. And there is something else . . . the demon and the boy are linked. The Chaos Spirit is not yet whole. He is still . . . I don't know . . . child-like?'

The words faded and the Spartan ran on, up a hillside and on to a wider track. 'More to your left!' came the voice of Thena. 'No more than two hundred paces.'

The undergrowth was too thick to change direction, and Parmenion ran back along the way he had come before turning to a new trail. He could hear them now, just ahead. Slowing to a walk the Spartan stepped out before them and waited, keeping his face emotionless despite the shock of seeing the Demon Prince sitting upon the giant centaur. Alexander's face was now a pallid grey, mottled black ram's horns sprouting from the temples. His hair was white, the golden eyes slitted beneath heavy brows, his mouth was twisted and wide with teeth long and protruding. There was nothing left of the beautiful child.

'Ah, my general approaches!' came a deep voice. 'Welcome, Parmenion!'

Beyond the Prince the monstrous army waited, and beside him stood Attalus, his face a mask, his expression unreadable.

'This is neither your time nor your world,' said Parmenion softly. 'Give us back the boy.'

'Serve me or die!' answered the Chaos Spirit.

'No, you will die,' Parmenion told him. 'You think this display of . . . power . . . can win you a world? Gorgon will fight you, and even if you defeat him what will you have? A pitiful forest in a world where another Spirit rules. And that Spirit controls an army of countless thousands. You are playing a child's game in a man's world. Now give us back the boy!'

The Demon swung to Attalus. 'Kill him!' he ordered. Attalus said nothing, but drew his sword and walked to where Parmenion stood waiting. Once there the Macedonian turned and faced the Demon. 'You betray me!' shouted the prince. 'Then you will both die.'

'Wait!' called Parmenion. 'Your world is a long way from here. Only I can return you to it. Without me you will be trapped here, in the body of a child. How will you survive?'

'I have my army,' answered the Demon, but his voice wavered as he looked upon the beasts around him.

'You will conquer nothing with those,' said Parmenion. 'You might not even best the Forest King.'

'And if I give you the boy?'

'I will return him to his own world.'

'How so?' sneered the Demon. 'By trusting Gorgon? He will kill him . . . me.'

'Then you must decide – and swiftly. You may have this forest . . . or a world. Decide, damn you!'

For a moment the Demon sat very still, his slitted eyes fixed on Parmenion, then he seemed to relax. 'One day I will kill you both,' he said, his voice echoing as if from a great distance. The horns began to shrink, Alexander cried out and fell from the centaur. Parmenion ran forward, lifting the boy and pushing back the golden hair. There was no sign now of the Demon, save in the fading brown patches of skin at the temples. Once more his hair was golden, his face beautiful.

'I couldn't . . . stop him . . . Parmenion,' wailed the child. 'I tried!'

'You did enough. Believe me! You did not allow him his full strength. That confused him.'

'Look out, Parmenion!' shouted Attalus. All around the man and the boy the beasts were rising, their eyes baleful. Without the Demon to control them they saw only three Humans and a centaur, four enemies for the slaughter.

Parmenion surged upright, holding Alexander tightly to his shoulder. 'Back!' he shouted, but the beasts ignored him. His sword snaked out as a creature with the head of a lizard sprang forward. His blade slashed across its throat, hurling it back.

Suddenly an eerie wailing filled the air and the creatures fell to their knees. Parmenion swung to see Gorgon striding from the forest, Thena and Brontes behind him.

A horned beast of prodigious size lifted a huge club and ran at the Forest King. Gorgon's eyes glowed. The beast staggered – and began to shrink, its muscles wasting away. Thinner and thinner it became until at last it fell to the earth, breaking into many pieces. A slight wind blew, raising a cloud of dust where the beast had fallen. Not even bones were left.

Gorgon turned towards Parmenion. 'Bring the child to me!' he commanded. The Spartan's legs were unsteady as he walked to the King, but his sword was still in his hand and he was ready to plunge it into the King's belly at the first sign of treachery.

'Be brave!' he whispered to the boy. Alexander nodded. Parmenion lowered the prince to the ground and the boy approached the Forest King, staring up into the green snake-shrouded face.

'Show me your power,' said Gorgon.

'I will show you,' Alexander told him. 'But at the Giant's Gateway.'

'Then you are truly Iskander.'

'I am,' Alexander answered.

*

The prince stood silently with head cocked to one side, his green eyes watching the writhing snakes. 'Are they real snakes?' he asked suddenly.

'Reality depends upon your perspective,' answered Gorgon, kneeling down and dipping his head. The snakes rose up, hissing, their forked tongues darting forward under sharp fangs.

The boy did not flinch. 'They are not alive,' he said.

'If they bite you, you will die,' Gorgon pointed out.

'That does not make them real. Their eyes are blind. They cannot see, they cannot feel. They move because you order it.'

'So does my arm – and that is real.'

'Indeed,' agreed the boy, 'and that is precisely what the snakes are – an extension of your body, like arms or legs. They merely look like snakes.'

'Are you not frightened of me?'

'I fear nothing,' lied Alexander, straightening his back and lifting his chin defiantly.

'But you find me monstrous and ugly.'

'I find you fascinating. Why did you choose such a countenance?'

A sound resembling laughter roared from the Forest King. 'I chose it to instil fear in my enemies. It did so. It still does so. But then the war was lost and the losers were . . .

punished? A spell was cast upon us, forcing us to hold our forms. You, Iskander, will wash away this spell.'

'Are you evil?' asked the boy.

'Of course. We lost. The losers are always evil, for it is the victors who sing the songs that become history. And in these forms they have left us what choices do we have? Look at the Vores! Their touch is death, their breath the plague. How many good works can they accomplish? The victors left us with hate and bitterness in our hearts. They called us evil, and made us evil. Now we live up to their expectations. You believe me?'

'It would be discourteous to admit that I did not,' answered the boy.

'True,' agreed the King, 'but I will allow you one discourtesy.'

'Then I must say that I do disagree. Parmenion says that every man has choices. If what you say is true, then all ugly men would be evil and all handsome men good.'

'Well said, child,' commented the minotaur, Brontes. 'My brother omits to mention that he – and his allies – began the war, bringing death and slaughter to thousands.'

Gorgon rose and shook his head, the snakes hissing and writhing. 'Just when it seemed I could have an intelligent conversation . . . Ah well, let us not rake over the ashes of history, Brontes. As I recall there were many thousands on both sides who died, brother killing brother. Let it end with the coming of Iskander.'

'I do not believe you will ever let it end, Dionius,' said Brontes sadly. 'It is not in your nature.'

'We shall see, brother. How is our mother? Does she still pine for me?'

A low growl came from Brontes, his fists clenching, the muscles of his shoulders bunching into tight ridges. 'Do not even think of it,' whispered Gorgon, his pale eyes glowing like lanterns.

'Please do not fight,' pleaded Alexander.

'No one is going to fight,' said Parmenion, moving between Brontes and the Forest King. 'We are allies now, against a common enemy. Is that not correct, Brontes?'

'Allies?' hissed the minotaur, shaking his head. 'I cannot bring myself to believe so.'

'You can,' argued Parmenion, 'because you *must*. This war you speak of was fought eons ago. There must come a time when it can be put aside. Let that time be now. Let it be here in this forest.'

'You have no idea what he did!' stormed Brontes.

'No, I have not. Nor do I need to. It is the way of war to bring out both the best and the worst in the combatants. But the war is over.'

'As long as he lives it will never be over,' said Brontes, turning away and stalking back into the forest. Alexander switched his gaze to the Forest King and thought he saw a look of disappointment, almost sadness on the twisted features. Then the grim, sardonic expression returned.

'Your mission has not begun well, Iskander,' said the King.

'Nothing of worth comes easily,' the boy answered.

'You are a wise child. I could almost like you – were I able to remember what such an emotion feels like.'

'You can remember,' said Alexander, with a bright smile. 'And I like you too.'

*

Alexander moved away from the Forest King and saw Camiron standing apart from the monsters who filled the clearing. The centaur was trembling, his front hooves pawing at the ground. The prince walked towards him but Camiron, seeing him, backed away several steps.

'You hurt me,' said the centaur, his huge eyes blinking rapidly.

'It was not me,' said Alexander soothingly, reaching out his hand. 'Did it look like me?'

'Except for the horns,' said Camiron. 'I don't like this place; I don't want to be here.'

'We will be leaving soon,' the boy told him. 'Will you let me ride you?'

'Where will we go?'

'We will find Chiron.'

'I'll never find him,' muttered the centaur. 'He has abandoned me. And I will always be alone.'

'No,' said Alexander, stepping close and taking Camiron's hand. 'You are not alone. We will be friends, you and I. Until we find Chiron.'

The centaur bent his torso forward and whispered, 'This is an evil place. It has always been so. If you get on my back, I will run from here like the wind. I can carry you to the far mountains. They will not catch us.'

'There is evil everywhere, my friend,' Alexander told him, 'and we are safer here than in the mountains. Trust me.' Camiron said nothing, but fear still shone in his eyes and his flanks trembled. 'You are mighty Camiron,' said the boy suddenly, 'the strongest of centaurs. You fear nothing. You are the fastest, the bravest, the finest of warriors.'

The centaur nodded. 'Yes, yes, I am all those things. I am! I am a great fighter. I am not frightened.'

'I know. We will journey to the sea and then to Sparta. I will ride you and you will protect me.'

'To the sea, yes. Will Chiron be there? Is he close?'

'He is very close. Tell me, where were you when you . . . awoke last?'

'It was in a wood, close to the mountains. I heard shouts and screams. It was the Makedones killing the centaurs. That's when I saw you.'

'Was anything around you when you woke?'

'Just trees and rocks and . . . a stream, I think. I don't remember going there. I don't remember things very well.'

'The first time I saw you, you had a pouch of leather on a belt. In it there was a golden stone. But you do not have it now.'

'A pouch? Yes . . . there was. But I left it behind. The screams startled me. Is it important?'

'No, I just wondered where it was. We will leave soon, but first I must speak with Parmenion.'

The Spartan was deep in conversation with the priestess Thena and Attalus, but when Alexander joined them the group fell silent. 'I need to speak with you,' said the boy.

206

'Of course,' Parmenion answered, kneeling to face the prince.

'It is about Chiron.'

'I think he is lost to us.'

'No. He is the centaur, Camiron.' Swiftly he told Parmenion of his first meeting with the *magus*, and how he had become a centaur. 'But now Camiron has lost the magic stone. I don't think he can change back.'

'There is little we can do for him,' said Parmenion, 'save keep him with us. But, more importantly, how are you faring?'

Alexander looked into the Spartan's eyes, reading the concern there. 'I am well. He took me by surprise. The Enchantment in these woods is very strong – and very dark.'

'Do you recall any of it?'

'All of it. In a strange way it was very peaceful. I could see everything and yet I was not in command. I needed to make no decisions. He is very strong, Parmenion. I felt it when his mind reached out and touched the beasts. He brought them to his will instantly.'

'Can you still feel his presence?'

'No. It is as if he is sleeping.'

'Do you have the strength to stop him, should he try to . . . control you once more?'

'I think so. But how can I know?'

'Do the best that you can,' advised the Spartan, 'and tell me when he returns.'

'I will. What happens now?'

'The King is going to lead us to the sea. Once there we will find a way to cross the Gulf of Korinthos . . . Corinth. From there we will travel south through Arkadia to Sparta. After that . . . I don't know.'

'I can open the Giant's Gateway,' said Alexander softly.

'Do not think of it,' whispered the Spartan. 'You are not who they think you are.'

'Oh, but I am,' answered the boy. 'Believe me, Parmenion, I am Iskander.'

*

For three days the small group moved south through the forest, led by Gorgon and guided by three Vores who swooped and dived in the sky above the trees, watching for signs of pursuit. Alexander rode Camiron, whose spirits had soared on the second morning.

'I can remember,' Camiron told the prince. 'It is wonderful. I went to sleep and woke up in the same place.'

'That is good,' replied the boy distantly.

Parmenion walked often beside the Forest King, Derae and Attalus bringing up the rear behind the centaur and his rider.

For the first two days the priestess said little to the swordsman, walking in silence and spending her evenings in deep conversation with Parmenion. But on the morning of the third day Attalus hung back from the group, allowing some thirty paces to grow between them.

'You are walking very slowly,' said Derae.

'I want to talk to you,' he told her.

'Why? What am I to you?'

'I need . . . I want . . . advice.'

Derae looked at him closely, reaching out to touch his spirit, feeling the surging, complex emotions raging within him. Swiftly she withdrew. 'How may I help you?'

'You are a seeress, are you not?'

'I am.'

'And you can see the future?'

'There are many futures, Attalus; they change day by day. Tell me what troubles you.'

'The Demon said that he would see Parmenion and me both slain. Did he speak the truth?'

Derae looked into the swordsman's troubled face. 'What would you do if I told you that he did?'

'I don't know. All my known enemies are dead; there is safety in that. But he is the son of the only friend I have ever had. I could not . . .' His voice trailed away. 'Will you tell me my future?'

'No, it would not be wise. You carry great hatred and bitterness, Attalus. And the events of your past have twisted your soul. Your love for Philip is the only redeeming quality you have.'

'Will you tell me whether the boy is a danger to me?'

For a moment only she hesitated. 'Give me your hand,' she commanded. He obeyed her, offering his left, his right resting on his sword-hilt. Emotions flooded her – strong, harsh and almost overpowering. She saw his mother slain by his father, saw the father murdered by the young Attalus. Then, in the years that followed, she saw the bitter young man send scores of people to their deaths, using knife or bow, sword or poison. At last she sighed and released his hand.

'Well?' he demanded.

'You have many enemies,' she told him, her voice low and sorrowful. 'You are hated by almost all who know you. Believe me, assassin, at this time the prince is the least of your foes.'

'But he will be an enemy, will he not?'

'If he lives,' she replied, holding to his gaze. 'If any of us live.'

'Thank you,' he said, moving past her and walking on.

That night, as the others slept, Derae sat with Parmenion on the brow of a hill and told the Spartan what had occurred with Attalus. 'You think he will try to kill the boy?' he asked.

'Not immediately. But he is a sad, twisted man. There is little good in him.'

'I will watch him with care. But tell me, lady, why did Aristotle send you?'

'He thought I could help you. Have I not done so?'

'Of course – but that is not what I meant. Why did he send *you*? Why not another?'

'Is my company so painful to you?' she countered, her unease growing.

'Not at all. You are like a cool breeze on a summer's day. You make my soul rest. I am not good with women, Thena. I am clumsy and short of temper.' He chuckled. 'The ways of your race are alien to me.'

'You make us sound like another species.'

'Sometimes I think that you are,' he admitted. 'When I was very young I used to watch Derae run. I would hide on a

209

hilltop and observe the girls in their races. Their grace made me feel ungainly and awkward – and yet the memories have a certain glow.'

'It is good to talk of fine memories,' she told him. 'They are all that makes life a joy. Tell me of your family.'

'I thought you wanted good memories,' he snapped, looking away.

'You do not love your wife?'

'Love Phaedra?' he answered, shaking his head. 'She married me for one purpose . . . and I do not wish to talk of it.'

'Then we will not.'

Suddenly he gave a wry smile. 'Why did you ask me that question? You are a seeress, Thena; you know the answer already.' The smile faded, his expression hardening. 'Do you know all my secrets?'

The thought of lying flitted across her mind, but she dismissed it. 'Yes,' she told him softly.

He nodded. 'I thought so. Then you know why she married me.'

'To rid herself of the unwanted gift of prophecy.'

'And?' he pressed – his eyes, cold now, holding to her gaze.

'Because her gift told her you would sire a god-king to rule the world. She wanted that boy to be her son.'

'And now,' said Parmenion sorrowfully, 'she raises poor Philotas, filling his mind with thoughts of future glories. It is a terrible illusion – and I can do nothing to stop it. Is this the price I must pay for my . . . betrayal?'

'You are not an evil man,' she told him, taking his hand. 'Do not allow one mistake to poison your feelings of self-worth.'

'It could all have been so different, Thena, if Derae and I had been allowed to wed. Maybe there would have been no riches – but we would have had a home and children.' Pushing himself to his feet, he stared out over the moonlit treetops. 'But then there is little advantage in trying to reshape the past. We didn't marry. They killed her. And I became Parmenion, the Death of Nations. I can live with it.

Come, let us get back to the camp. Perhaps tonight I can sleep without dreams.'

*

By the fifth day of their journey the trek south had slowed. The Vores had flown away the night before and not returned, and Gorgon seemed to Parmenion to have grown more cautious, constantly scouting ahead, leaving the others behind. Brontes had been unusually silent for the past two days, wandering away from his companions and sitting alone, his huge bull's head in his hands. And Attalus was growing surly, his pale eyes constantly flickering towards Alexander.

Parmenion felt a growing unease. The forest was thicker here, little light breaking through the thick canopy of intertwined branches high above, the air filled with the stench of rotting vegetation. But it was not just the sickening smell or the lack of light that left the Spartan on edge; in this place there was an aura of evil that entered the mind, touching the soul with dread.

That night, for the first time, Parmenion built a fire. Attalus and Thena sat down beside it, the swordsman staring gloomily into the dancing flames. Brontes moved away and sat with his back to a broad oak and Parmenion followed him.

'Are you in pain?' asked the Spartan.

Brontes' head came up. A thin trickle of blood was dripping from his right nostril.

'I need . . . the Change,' whispered Brontes. 'But it cannot be . . . accomplished . . . in this place. If we do not move clear of this forest in the next two days I shall die.'

'You knew this would happen?'

'Yes.'

'And yet you came with us? I don't know what to say, Brontes.'

The minotaur shrugged. 'Iskander is all-important; he must arrive at the Giant's Gateway. Leave me, my friend. It is hard to speak through the pain.'

At that moment Gorgon returned, easing his giant bulk

through the undergrowth. He ran across the small clearing and kicked earth upon the fire, scattering sparks that swept across Thena's robes.

'What in Hades are you doing?' stormed Attalus.

'No fires!' hissed Gorgon.

'Why? Is this not your forest?' responded the swordsman. 'What should we fear?'

'Everything,' answered Gorgon, stalking towards Parmenion. 'The Makedones have entered the forest,' he said, his eyes glittering. 'There are more than a thousand warriors, split into five groups. Two are behind us, two to the east and one ahead.'

'Do they know where we are?'

'I believe that they do. Many of the Vores have deserted me and joined the Makedones. There is little loyalty in this forest, Human. I rule because I am the strongest, and my crown is secure only so long as I am feared. But the Vores fear Philippos more. So they should, for his power is greater than mine.'

'When will we reach the sea?'

'Two days – if we travel fast. Three if we are careful.'

Parmenion shook his head. 'Brontes will not survive three days.'

Gorgon's mouth stretched into the parody of a smile, the snakes on his head rising with fangs bared.

'What does that matter? All that is important is that Iskander reaches the Gateway. And that is now doubtful. This forest is my domain and my strength – yet it is taxing my powers to the limit to keep Philippos from finding us. The bony woman with you is also nearing exhaustion, shielding us. But we are tiring, Human. And when our magic is drained there will not be a place in this forest to hide. Do you understand? At this moment the priestess and I have covered the forest with a spirit mist, and we are hidden within it. But every hour that passes sees the Demon King cutting away at our defences. Soon it will be like a storm wind dispersing our mist, and we will stand in the full view of the golden eye. I cannot concern myself with the small problem of Brontes' life.' Gorgon lay down, closing his eyes. 'We will rest for two hours,' he said softly, 'then push on through the night.'

Parmenion walked back to the dead fire where Alexander was sleeping peacefully beside the centaur, Camiron. Removing his cloak Parmenion covered the child, pausing to stroke the boy's head.

Attalus saw him, his eyes narrowing, but he masked his feelings as Parmenion joined him. 'Why is the beast so nervous?' asked the Macedonian, flicking his hand towards the sleeping Gorgon.

'A thousand Makedones have entered the forest.'

'Only a thousand? Surely they will prove no problem for the *strategos*? What will you do this time? Summon the birds from the trees to our aid? Or perhaps the trees themselves will uproot and march to your orders?'

'Your anger is misdirected,' Parmenion pointed out. 'I am not your enemy.'

'Ah! A friend, I suppose? That is an amusing thought.'

Parmenion turned away to see the tall priestess watching them both. Her voice whispered into his mind:

'We are being watched by a priest of Philippos. They have broken through our defences and he is listening to your words, relaying them to the Demon King.'

Parmenion gave no sign that he had heard her and swung back to Attalus. 'I know you find this hard to believe, Attalus, but, I say again, I am not your enemy. And here, in this dread place, I am indeed your friend. We will stay here for two more days, then strike east – back across the mountains. Once clear of this forest you will feel more easy in your mind. It is the evil that gnaws at you. Believe me.'

'What gnaws at me is none of your concern,' hissed Attalus.

'He is gone!' pulsed Thena. 'Gorgon drove him back.'

Parmenion leaned in close to the Macedonian. 'Now you listen to me, there are enemies all around us and – if we are to survive – we must be together in spirit and strength. You think me your foe? Perhaps I am. But here I must depend on you. And you must trust me. Without that our hopes – slender as they are – will prove to be for nothing. We were

213

both threatened by the Chaos Spirit. But I choose to ignore his words. He does not know the future – and I will always be the master of my fate. As will you – for we are men of strength. Now . . . can I trust you?'

'Why ask the question? You would not believe me if I told you what you wanted to hear.'

'You are wrong, Attalus. Say the words and I will believe them.'

The swordsman smiled. 'Then you can trust me,' he said. 'Does that satisfy you?'

'Yes. Now we will rest for two hours – and then find a path west and south.'

'But you said . . .'

'I changed my mind.'

'*You cannot trust him,*' Thena pulsed, but Parmenion ignored her.

Stretching out on the cold ground, he closed his eyes. All around them, as he had said, there were deadly enemies, moving in from three sides and guided by the malevolent power of the Makedones King. The Spartan considered his allies: a dying minotaur, a priestess, a twisted assassin and a Forest King steeped in evil.

His thoughts were not hopeful, his dreams full of torment.

*

Attalus lay awake, his thoughts confused. The threat from the demon nagged at him, burning in his mind with fingers of fire. It would be so easy to creep across the camp-site and draw his dagger across the boy's throat. Then the threat would be neutralized. And yet the child was the son of Philip – the only man whose friendship Attalus had ever desired.

I need no friends, he told himself. But the words echoed in his mind, flat and unconvincing. Life without Philip was worth nothing. He was the sun, the only warmth the swordsman had known since childhood.

He need not know you slew his child. Now this thought was tempting. At some point he could lure Alexander away

214

from the others and kill him silently. *Breaking Philip's heart in the process.*

As Attalus rolled to his side the darkness was lifting, thin beams of moonlight piercing the overhanging trees. There came a sound, a soft swishing, like a stick cutting the air, and Attalus looked up to see a Vore gliding down from the upper branches of a tall pine. The creature landed lightly, moving silently towards the sleeping Alexander.

The swordsman did not move. Wings folded, the Vore leaned over the child, reaching out . . .

Here, thought Attalus exultantly, was deliverance!

The creature's taloned hands dropped towards Alexander. Attalus' dagger flashed through the air, glittering in the moonlight to plunge into the Vore's back. The beast let out a high-pitched shriek. One wing flared out, but the second was pinned to its back by the jutting dagger. Gorgon surged to his feet and ran towards the Vore. The dying creature stumbled, pitching face-first to the ground. Parmenion and the others, awakened by the Vore's screams, gathered around the still twitching corpse.

Attalus stepped past them, ripping clear his dagger.

'Be careful,' snapped Gorgon, 'the blood is poisonous. One touch and you will die.' Attalus plunged the blade into the earth at his feet cleaning the dagger on the moss before returning it to its sheath.

Gorgon flipped the Vore to its back. 'He was one of mine,' he said. 'It is time to leave.'

'You saved me,' said Alexander, moving alongside Attalus and gazing up into the swordsman's face.

'Are you surprised, my prince?'

'Yes,' answered the boy.

'Are you?' Attalus asked Parmenion.

The Spartan shook his head. 'Why should I be? Did you not give me your word?'

'Spoken words are small noises that vanish in the air,' said Attalus softly. 'Do not put your faith in words.'

'If that were true, you would not have intervened,' countered Parmenion.

Attalus had no answer and swung away, his thoughts full

215

of guilt and self-loathing. How could you be so stupid, he railed at himself? Moving back to his bed he gathered the cloak he had used for a blanket, brushing the dirt from it and fastening it once more to his shoulders with the brooch of *turkis* given to him by Philip.

The others were all preparing to leave – save the priestess, who was sitting quietly beneath a spreading oak.

Gorgon's voice broke the silence. 'Stay close to me, for where we travel it is very dark and the dangers are many.' But still Thena sat beneath the tree. Attalus walked across to her.

'We are ready,' he said.

'I will not be travelling with you,' she whispered.

'You cannot stay here.'

'I must.'

Parmenion joined them and the seeress looked up at the Spartan. 'You go on,' she said, forcing a smile. 'I will join you when I can.'

'Why are you doing this?' asked Parmenion, kneeling down beside her.

'I must delay the Makedones – and fool the Demon King.'

'How?' Attalus asked.

'Like that!' she said, pointing back across the camp. Attalus and Parmenion turned . . . to see themselves apparently still sleeping by a fire that now burned brightly. Across the clearing the form of Gorgon could be seen, lying beside the minotaur Brontes, while Alexander snuggled against the sleeping centaur. 'You must go swiftly – before the spirit of Philippos returns.'

'I will not see you in danger,' said Parmenion.

'We are all in danger,' she insisted. 'Go now!'

Attalus could see Parmenion had more to say and seized his arm. 'No more foolishness, remember? The boy must be saved. Now come on!' Parmenion pulled clear of his grip, but moved away to stand alongside Gorgon.

'She has great power,' said the Forest King, gazing at his own sleeping form several paces away.

The Spartan did not answer and Gorgon led the way into

216

the depths of the forest; Parmenion and Brontes followed, Attalus bringing up the rear just behind the centaur and the boy.

As Gorgon had said, the trail was dark, and they made slow progress for the first two hours. Then the dawn light began to seep through the intertwined branches, though no bird-song greeted the morning and all was silent.

But towards mid-morning Gorgon, at the front of the small column, suddenly waved his hand and darted into the undergrowth, moving with surprising speed for all his bulk. Swiftly the others followed him, Parmenion grabbing Camiron and pulling the centaur to his side. For a moment the beast's hooves flailed in the air. 'Quiet!' hissed the Spartan. From the north came the sounds of many men trampling through the undergrowth. Dropping to his belly, Attalus eased back the bush before him and saw a troop of soldiers emerging from the trees some thirty paces away. They were marching in single file, their spears held carelessly to their shoulders.

After they were gone Gorgon rose from his hiding place and the group set off once more, this time angling to the north.

Parmenion dropped back alongside Attalus. 'How many did you count?' asked the Spartan.

'Eighty-five. You?'

'The same. That means there are more ahead of us.' Parmenion glanced back. 'I hope she escapes them.'

Attalus nodded, but said nothing.

*

Derae sat in the moonlight, her thoughts sorrowful. This, she knew with calm certainty, would be her last night alive. In order to keep the Makedones away from Parmenion she needed to hold the spell, but in so doing was forced to remain in the clearing, drawing the warriors of the Demon King towards her.

The night was cool, the trunks of the nearby trees bathed in silver. A fox moved out into the clearing, drawn to the carcass of the Vore. Carefully it moved around the body and

217

then, catching the putrid scent of the dead beast, it slunk away into the undergrowth.

Derae took a deep breath. The golden stone was warm in her hand and she gazed down at it, marvelling at its beauty and its power. Aristotle had given it to her as they stood in the Stone Circle.

'Whatever you wish – within reason – the stone will supply,' he had told her. 'It will turn stones to bread, or bread to stone. Use it with care.' The stone was but a fragment of gold, veined with slender lines of jet. But as she held the spell in place the black lines thickened, the power in the fragment fading.

'Where did you come by it?' she had asked the *magus*.

'In another age,' he answered, 'before the oceans drank Atlantis and the world changed.'

Closing her fist around the stone, she looked across the clearing at the sleeping image of Parmenion. It was a surprising thought that these five days in Achaea had doubled their time together.

Her thoughts sped back over the years, her mind's eye picturing the gardens of Xenophon's home near Olympia where she and Parmenion, uncaring of danger, had kissed and touched and loved. Five days: the longest and shortest five days of her life. The longest because her memories dwelt in them, seizing on every passionate moment, the shortest because of the weight of the barren years that followed.

The seeress Tamis was the source of all the pain Derae had endured, yet in truth it was impossible to hate her for it. The old woman had been obsessed by a dream, her mind dominated by one ambition – to prevent the birth of the Dark God. Walking the paths of the many futures, Tamis had discovered all the identities of the men who could be used by Chaos to sire the demon. What she needed was a man to use as a weapon against them – a Sword of the Source.

In order to achieve her desire she caused Derae to be taken from Sparta and hurled into the sea off the coast of Troy, her hands bound behind her. When Parmenion discovered her fate it unleashed within him a terrible hatred, changing his destiny and setting him on the path of revenge. All this had been planned by Tamis, in order that Parmenion would become the man of destiny she longed for.

It would have been better, thought Derae, had I died in that sea. But Tamis had rescued her, keeping her prisoner in the Temple, filling her head with lies and half-truths.

And for what?

Parmenion did kill all the possible fathers save one. Himself.

'I will not miss this life,' she said aloud.

She shivered as fear touched her soul. Gazing up with her spirit eyes she saw the image of Philippos hovering in the air above the camp-site, his golden eye staring at her and probing her thoughts. Filling her head with memories of the past she obscured all her fears of the present, while the power of the Eye whispered through her mind like a cold, cold breeze.

In the distance she could hear the stealthy sounds of men creeping through the forest and her fear swelled. She licked her lips, but there was no moisture on her tongue. Her heart began to hammer.

Just then she felt the elation of Philippos as he gazed down on the sleeping child. Anger flared in Derae and she let fall the spell, revelling in the King's shock and disappointment as the bodies disappeared.

Rising from her body, she faced Philippos. 'They have escaped you,' she said.

For a moment he did not reply, then a smile appeared on his handsome, bearded face. 'You have been clever, witch. But no one escapes me for long. Who are you?'

'The enemy,' she answered.

'A man is judged by the strength of his enemies, Derae. Where is the boy?'

The golden eye glowed, but Derae fled for the sanctuary of her body, her hand closing around the golden stone and shielding her thoughts.

'I do hope you will gain some enjoyment from your last

219

hours alive,' came the voice of the King. 'I know my men will.'

Soldiers burst clear of the bushes surrounding the clearing. Derae stood – and waited for death, her mind suddenly calm.

Two men ran forward to pin her arms, while a third strode out to stand before her. 'Where are they?' he asked, his right hand on her throat, his fingers digging into her cheeks.

'Where you will not find them,' she answered icily. Releasing her chin he struck her savagely with his open hand, splitting her lip.

'I think you would be wise to tell me,' he warned her.

'I have nothing to say to you.'

Slowly he drew his dagger. 'You will tell me all I wish to know,' he assured her, his voice deepening, his face flushing. 'If not now – then later.' His fingers hooked into the neck of her tunic, the dagger slicing through the material, which he ripped clear to expose her breasts and belly. Sheathing the blade he moved in, his hand sliding over her skin, fingers forcing themselves between her legs.

She felt her emotions swamped by the surging lust of the men all around her, then the soldier whispered an obscenity in her ear.

All her adult life Derae had followed the path of the Source, knowing with cold certainty that she would rather die than kill. But in the moment he spoke all her training fled away, taking with it the years of devotion and dedication. All that was left was the girl from Sparta – and in her ran the blood of a warrior race.

Her head came up, her eyes meeting his. 'Die,' she whispered. His eyes widened. The stone in her hand grew warmer. Suddenly he gasped and fell back with blood spurting from his eyes, ears, nose and mouth.

'She's a witch!' someone shouted, as the officer's lifeless body slumped to the earth. The men holding her tightened their grip on her upper arms, but she raised her hands – which transformed themselves into cobras, hooded and hissing. The soldiers leapt back from her. Spinning on her heel she pointed the snakes at them. Lightning leapt from the serpents' mouths, smashing the men from their feet.

Derae swung once more, as the remaining soldiers drew their weapons and rushed at her. A flash of brilliant light seared across the clearing, blinding the warriors, causing them to stumble and fall.

In the confusion that followed Derae strode from the camp-site and into the woods.

*

Derae moved silently towards the south, drawing her cloak tightly around her naked frame. The trees were thinner here, the stars bright above them, and she broke into a loping run, following a path that sloped down to where a dark stream rippled over black stones.

In the distance behind her she could hear the shouts of the soldiers, but she knew they would not catch her now. They were blundering around in the dark, with no idea of the direction she had taken.

Come daylight it would be different, when they could send the Vores soaring above the trees to hunt her in the sunshine. But this was the night – and it was hers! She had waited for the enemy, fooled them and killed at least one. A savage joy flowed through her, filling her body with strength as she ran.

Suddenly she faltered and slowed.

I killed a man!

The joy vanished, to be replaced by a numbing sense of horror. *What have you become?* she asked herself.

Her gaze flickered to the silent trees, her spirit recoiling from the malevolence of the forest. This place of evil had touched her, eroding all her beliefs, all the years of her dedication.

Falling to her knees Derae prayed for forgiveness, sending her thoughts up and out into the void and beyond. But she felt them echoing in a vast emptiness, seemingly unheard and certainly unanswered. Wearily she rose and walked on toward the south, making herself one promise

221

that she swore to keep for as long as she lived. Never would she kill again.

Never.

*

On the morning of the third day since they had left the priestess, Parmenion awoke to see Gorgon kneeling over the sleeping form of Brontes. The minotaur was not moving and Gorgon's hand was resting lightly on the creature's chest. Parmenion's heart sank. For the last two days the minotaur had stumbled on, unspeaking, his eyes weary and bloodshot, his limbs leaden.

'You can make it,' Parmenion had told him the previous afternoon. But Brontes had not replied, his huge bull's head sagging forward, his gaze locked to the ground at his feet. The group had made camp early, for Brontes had been unable to keep up with the pace. Now Parmenion rose and moved alongside Gorgon.

'Is he dead?' he asked.

'Soon,' answered Gorgon. Parmenion knelt by the minotaur. Blood was seeping from both nostrils and he was barely breathing.

'What can we do?' the Spartan asked.

'Nothing,' grunted Gorgon.

'How soon will we be clear of the forest?'

'Not for another day.'

'In any direction?' queried the Spartan.

Gorgon shook his head. 'No. We could move directly east; then we would be at the edge of the forest, but maybe a day's march from the sea. It is the kingdom of Aetolia – close to the town of Calydon. But the King of Aetolia is a vassal of Philippos, and he keeps a force of over three hundred men at Calydon. They will be watching the forest.'

'Can you carry Brontes?'

Gorgon's huge hand snaked out, his fingers curling around Parmenion's cloak and dragging the Spartan forward. 'Are you insane? I have given up a kingdom for this quest of yours. Many of my own people have turned against me. And why? So that I can bring the Golden Child to the

222

Giant's Gateway. Now you would risk it all for *this*?' he demanded, pointing to the dying minotaur.

'No, I will not risk it all. But the men watching the forest cannot be everywhere. And there is something else, Gorgon,' said Parmenion softly. 'There is friendship. There is loyalty. Brontes has risked his life on this quest, saving mine in the process. I owe him a debt – and I always repay.'

'Ha! What if it was me lying there? Would you risk your life for me?'

'Yes.'

Gorgon relaxed his grip and smiled, his pale eyes glowing, his expression unreadable. 'I believe you would. You are a fool . . . as Brontes is a fool. But then what is one more foolishness? Yes, I will carry him to the sunlight, if that is your wish.' The Forest King pushed his great hands beneath the minotaur, lifting him with ease and draping the body over his shoulder.

Parmenion shook the others awake and they followed Gorgon to the east. Within the hour the trees thinned out and bird-song could be heard in the distance. At last they reached the edge of the forest and emerged on to a hillside overlooking a walled town.

Gorgon laid the minotaur on the grass and backed away. Parmenion knelt beside Brontes, his hand resting on the creature's shoulder. 'Can you hear me, my friend?' he whispered.

A low groan came from Brontes, but his eyes opened. Blood was seeping over the lids in crimson tears.

'Too . . . late.'

'No. Use whatever strength you have. *Try*.'

The minotaur's eyes closed as Gorgon moved alongside Parmenion. 'Come away. He needs privacy. The sun will feed him and there is a little Enchantment left here. I can feel it burning my feet.'

Parmenion stepped back into the shade of the trees, turning his eyes from the body on the grass.

'Will he live?' asked Alexander, taking Parmenion's hand.

'If he has the will,' the Spartan answered.

'I am very hungry,' said Camiron. 'Will we eat soon?'

'We are all hungry,' snapped Attalus. 'My belly thinks my throat has been cut. So stop complaining!'

'I will hunt something,' announced Camiron. Before anyone could speak the centaur, bow in hand, galloped down the hillside, heading south-east.

'Come back!' yelled Parmenion, but Camiron carried on running – in full view of the sentries on the walls of Calydon. Within minutes the gates opened and a score of riders issued forth, racing in pursuit of the centaur.

'At least they are heading away from us,' observed Attalus. Parmenion said nothing. Glancing back to Brontes he saw the body bathed in dazzling sunlight, the minotaur's skin glowing like gold. The great head began to shrink, the horns disappearing. Brontes' right arm twitched and he groaned. The light faded. Parmenion and Gorgon moved alongside him; once more he was a golden-haired young man, handsome and blue-eyed.

'Thank you,' he said, reaching up and gripping Parmenion's hand.

'Give your thanks to Gorgon,' answered the Spartan, pulling Brontes upright. 'He carried you here.'

'I don't doubt he had his own reasons,' Brontes remarked.

'You overwhelm me with your gratitude, brother,' said Gorgon, the snakes hissing on his skull and baring their fangs. He turned to Parmenion. 'Now we must move on – unless of course you wish to rescue the centaur. Say the word, general, and I will surround the city.'

Parmenion smiled. 'That will not be necessary. Lead on!'

'But we cannot leave Camiron behind,' wailed Alexander.

'We cannot help him, my prince,' said Parmenion sadly.

A dark shadow flickered across the grass and Gorgon glanced up. High above them a Vore circled, then flew off towards the north.

'We have been seen,' said Gorgon. 'Now it will be a race to the sea.'

The march south-west was slow. For the past few days the companions had lived on sour berries and foul-tasting mushrooms, forced to drink brackish water from dark pools. Parmenion's strength was fading, while Attalus twice vomited beside the trail. Only Gorgon seemed unaffected and tireless, striding on ahead with Alexander perched upon his shoulders.

They made camp at dusk beneath an overhang of stone, Gorgon permitting a fire which lifted the spirits of the Macedonians.

'Once across the Gulf, how long until we reach Sparta?' asked Attalus.

'If we can find horses – three more days,' Parmenion answered.

'Why Sparta?' put in Gorgon. 'Why not straight to the Gateway?'

'We are hoping to meet a friend there,' the Spartan told him. 'A *magus* of great power.'

'He will need to be – for Sparta will not stand for long against Philippos. Even as you entered the forest my Vores were telling me of the Makedones' march to the south. Korinthos has declared for the Demon King. Cadmos is overthrown and destroyed. Only one army stands now against Philippos. And they cannot defeat him. Sparta may already have fallen before we cross the Gulf.'

'If that proves to be true,' said Parmenion, 'then we will make our way to the Giant's Gateway. But Philippos has not yet faced a Spartan army and he may find it a punishing experience.'

Towards midnight, when the blaze had flickered down to coals, Parmenion awoke from a light sleep to hear the sounds of stealthy movement from the undergrowth to his left. Drawing his sword he woke Attalus, and the two men moved silently away from the fire.

The bushes parted and Camiron trotted towards the camp, carrying a dead doe across his shoulders. The centaur spotted the Macedonians and gave a broad smile. 'I am a great hunter,' he said. 'Look what I have!'

Gorgon strode from the camp-site, moving away to the east. Attalus took the doe, skinning it and hacking away the choicest sections with his sword. Within minutes the air was rich with the smell of meat roasting over the freshly-built fire.

'I swear by Zeus I never smelt anything finer,' whispered Attalus, as the fat oozed into the flames.

'You are magnificent,' Alexander told the centaur. 'I am very proud of you. But what happened to the men chasing you?'

'No one is as fast as Camiron,' replied the centaur. 'I ran them until their horses were bathed in lather, then cut back to the west. Mighty is Camiron. No rider can catch him.'

The meat was tough and stringy, but no one cared. Parmenion felt strength seeping back into his muscles as he devoured his third portion and licked the fat from his fingers.

'You realize,' remarked Attalus, lying back replete, 'that in Macedonia we would have flogged a hunter who tried to sell us meat as tough as that?'

'Yes,' said Parmenion, 'but was it not wonderful?'

'Beyond description,' the swordsman agreed.

'It would need to be,' muttered Gorgon, stepping forward from the darkness. 'The centaur has left a trail a blind man could follow. And the enemy are already close enough to smell the feast.' Lifting Alexander to his shoulders, he set off towards the south.

'Did I do wrong?' asked Camiron nervously. Parmenion patted the centaur's shoulder.

'We needed to eat,' he said. 'You did well.'

'Yes, I did, didn't I?' exclaimed Camiron, his confidence returning.

Refreshed, the companions walked on through the night and by dawn had reached the last line of hills before the Gulf of Korinthos. The pursuers were close behind now and twice, looking back, Parmenion had seen moonlight gleaming from armour or lance-point.

As they cleared the trees Gorgon took hold of a jutting tree-root, ripping it clear and holding it above his head. He stood, statue-still, and began to chant in a language unfamiliar to the Macedonians.

'What is he doing?' Parmenion asked Brontes.

'He is drawing on the evil of the forest,' answered the former minotaur, turning away and walking to the crest of the hill to gaze down on the dawn-lit sea.

Finally Gorgon ceased his chanting and, the root in his hand, strode past Brontes to begin the long descent to the beach below. The others followed him on the sloping path. Camiron found the descent almost impossible, slithering and sliding, cannoning into Brontes and knocking him from his feet. Parmenion and Attalus moved to either side of the centaur, taking his hands and supporting him.

At last they reached the shore. High above them the first of the enemy appeared.

'What now?' demanded Attalus. 'Do we swim?'

'No,' answered Gorgon, lifting the tree-root above his head. Closing his eyes the Forest King began to chant once more. Parmenion glanced back up the cliff path. More than a hundred Makedones warriors were slowly making their way down the treacherous slope.

Smoke poured from the tree-root in Gorgon's hand, floating out over the sea and down into the waves. The water turned black and began to boil, yellow gases erupting from the surface and flaring into flame. Then a dark shape broke clear of the waves and an ancient trireme – its hull rotted, its sails rags – floated once more to the surface of the Gulf. Parmenion swallowed hard as the ship glided in to shore. There were skeletal corpses still seated at the oars, and rotted bodies lay upon the shell-encrusted decks. Glancing back, he saw the Makedones were almost within bowshot.

The ship beached close in, a narrow gangplank sliding from the upper deck to thud against the sand.

'If you want to live, climb aboard!' yelled Gorgon, carrying Alexander up to the deck. Parmenion and Attalus followed, then Camiron cantered up the plank, his hooves slipping on the slimy wood.

The trireme glided back on to the currents of the Gulf,

leaving the Makedones standing, horror-struck, on the beach. Several arrows and spears flew at the vessel, but most of the enemy warriors just stood and stared as the death ship disappeared into a grey mist seeping up from the night-dark sea.

*

Derae hid behind the trunk of a huge oak as the soldiers came into sight. The sea was so close, yet the way was barred. She scanned the cliff-tops looking for a way to slip past the Makedones, but the warriors had spread out, seeking other paths to the beach.

It was galling to have come so far and be thwarted. She had managed to evade the many patrols searching the forest and had emerged from the trees just as Parmenion and the others reached the shore.

Ducking back into the forest, Derae ran towards the west until the soldiers were far behind. Then she moved out along the line of the cliffs, looking for a way down. But, sometime in the recent past, the sea had finally clawed away at the last foundations of the cliff edge until great sections had sheared into the water. No paths were left. Derae slowed to a walk, then peered over the edge, seeking handholds that would enable her to climb down. But there were none that looked safe.

'There is the witch!' came a shout.

Derae spun, to see more soldiers running from the tree-line, fanning out to cut off her escape. Turning to the cliff-face, she looked down at the breakers far below as they swept over partially submerged rocks. Taking a deep breath, she loosed her cloak and stood naked on the clifftop.

Then she launched herself out over the dizzying drop. Her body arched, then began to fall. Throwing her arms out to steady herself she felt herself spinning out of control and fought to stay calm, angling her body into a dive. The sea and the rocks rushed towards her and she fell for what seemed an age. At the last moment she brought her hands together, cleaving an opening into the water. The force of the impact drove all air from her lungs, but she missed the rocks and plunged deep below the waves, striking the sandy seabed with bone-crushing force. Pushing her legs beneath her she kicked for the surface, her lungs close to bursting. Up, up she moved towards the sunlight sparkling on the water above her.

I'm going to die! The thought gave her the strength of panic and she clawed her way upwards. As she came clear she only had time for one swift breath before a breaker hammered her down, hitting her body against a rock. This time she was calmer and swam under water, surfacing in the swell and allowing her bruised body to float gently for a while safe from the crashing waves. A spear splashed into the water alongside her, followed by a score of arrows. Ducking below the surface, she swam out to sea towards a thick white mist that seemed to seep up from beneath the waves.

Then she saw the ship of the dead gliding across the water.

'Parmenion!' she yelled. 'Parmenion!'

The Spartan saw her and – incredibly – the ghost ship slowed, its broken prow swinging towards her. As it neared she reached up to grasp an oar-blade, but it snapped, pushing her below the waves. She surfaced to see Parmenion climbing down over the side of the ship, holding to an oar-port and stretching his arm towards her. Grasping his wrist, she felt herself lifted from the sea. Scrabbling for a foothold her heel came down on a rotting skull which cracked and rolled into the water, but then she was up beside Parmenion. His arm went around her, pulling her into a hug as he kissed her brow tenderly.

'It is good to see you,' he said.

'And now you are seeing too much of me,' she answered, pulling away and climbing to the deck.

Attalus removed his cloak, wrapping it around her shoulders. 'Welcome back, lady,' said the swordsman. 'You are a most welcome sight.'

'Thank you, Attalus.' The warmth of his greeting surprised her and she returned his smile. Parmenion clambered over the deck rail and was about to speak when Gorgon's voice rang out.

'There is a ship to the west! A trireme!'

The companions moved to the deck rail and stared at the oncoming vessel. It was almost forty lengths back, but all three banks of oars were dipping smoothly into the water, the ship moving at ramming speed towards them.

'Fascinating craft,' observed Attalus to Derae. 'See the bronze ram just ahead of the prow? That can rip a ship's hull worse than a reef.'

'Can we outrun them?' Parmenion asked Gorgon.

The Forest King chuckled and pointed to the corpses all around them. 'My crew have seen better days,' he said, 'but we shall see.'

From below decks came a terrible groaning and the oars lifted and dipped into the swell. Attalus looked over the side to see skeletal hands gripping the rotted wood. The ship picked up speed – but not enough to escape the chasing trireme.

'Swing her left!' bellowed Parmenion.

The corpse at the tiller rolled to the right, the death ship veering left. The attacking trireme slid past them, her rowers desperately dragging in their oars. Most were saved but the death ship clove into twenty or more, snapping them like sticks.

Arrows flashed from the decks of the trireme. Parmenion threw himself at Derae, pulling her to the deck. A shaft glanced from Attalus' helm. Then the ships drew apart once more. The mist thickened around them as the death ship glided into the ghostly cloud.

For an hour or more they sailed on in silence, listening to the calls of the enemy as they searched the mist-shrouded sea. The clouds above them darkened, lightning forking across the sky as the sound of thunder boomed across the gulf.

Rain lashed down – the death ship was faltering, slowing.

'My magic is almost gone,' confided Gorgon. 'Soon she will break up and sink – for the second time.'

They were less than a mile from land, but the storm was against them.

The mist fled against the force of the storm winds. As Parmenion glanced back, the trireme hove into view.

Lightning flashed once more, glinting from the bronze ram at the prow as it clove the water towards the death ship's hull.

*

Alexander crouched down on the windswept deck, holding hard to a wooden post as the death ship rose and fell in the surging storm-tossed sea. From here he could only see the chasing trireme when the huge swell lifted the prow. A massive wave hit the death ship, a section of the upper deck collapsing under the weight of the water. Camiron lost his grip on the broken mast and was swept towards the raging sea. Alexander screamed, but no one heard him above the roar of the storm. Seeing Camiron in peril, Brontes threw himself across the rain-lashed deck, grabbing the centaur's hand. For a moment it seemed as if the former minotaur had succeeded, but the ship rolled and a second wave broke over them, plucking both from the deck.

Alexander tried to stand, hoping to reach Parmenion at the stern, but he slipped and almost lost his grip on the post. Thena made her way to him, holding him tightly.

'Camiron is gone!' wailed the prince. Thena nodded, but said nothing. Another section of deck, close to the prow, sheared away into the sea.

Alexander reached out with his spirit, trying to locate Camiron.

At first there was nothing, but then his mind was filled with the sweetest music he had ever heard. High-pitched and joyous, it forced all thoughts of the centaur from his mind. The ship shuddered, the rotten wood groaning under the onslaught of the storm, but Alexander heard nothing save the ethereal song from below the sea. He let the music drift across his thoughts, waiting for his talent to translate it. But it was almost beyond his powers. There were no words, merely emotions, rich and satisfying. Reaching out further he sought the source, but the sound came from all around him in a harmony beyond imagining. When he had heard birds singing in the trees he had been able to fasten to each, for they were individual. But this music was different. The singers were empathically linked.

The death ship foundered, water gushing in through the open oarports. The deck split in half, the sea roaring around the child and the priestess. Alexander's hands were torn from their grip on the post.

Thena tried to hold on to him but the ship rolled, spilling them both into the water. Alexander felt the sea close over him, but still the music filled his soul.

As he sank beneath the waves he felt a soft, curiously warm body alongside him, bearing him up. His head broke clear of the surface and he sucked in a deep breath, his hands thrashing out at the water as he struggled to stay afloat. A dark grey form surfaced alongside him, a curved fin on its back. He grabbed for the fin, holding to it with all his strength. The dolphin flicked its tail and swam towards the distant shore, the music of its song washing over the child and soothing all his fears.

*

The trireme's ram smashed through the timbers of the death ship's stern, the force of impact hurling Parmenion from his feet. Sliding across the rain-lashed deck he caught hold of a section of rail and struggled to rise. He saw Gorgon hurl the tree-root high into the air, watched it caught by the storm winds and carried to the trireme's deck.

Locked together now, the two ships wallowed in the swell. The rowers on the trireme tried to back oars, in an attempt to pull away from the doomed vessel. But the magic which kept the death ship afloat was gone and the full weight of the saturated timbers dragged down on the enemy trireme, pulling the prow down, the stern rising up from the water.

The death ship rolled, pitching Parmenion towards the sea. But he clung on grimly with his left hand, while his right scrabbled at the fastenings of his breastplate. He would never be able to swim with its weight upon his torso. A massive wave crashed over the decks, pulling the Spartan loose and carrying him over the side.

His helm was ripped from his head – and still the breastplate was in place. Staying calm Parmenion drew his

232

dagger, cutting away the last thongs holding the armour in place. Shrugging free of the breastplate, he surfaced in time to see the doomed ships vanish beneath the waves.

To his right, for a moment, he saw Attalus desperately trying to keep his head above water. Dropping his dagger Parmenion struck out towards the Macedonian. Still in full armour, Attalus sank beneath the waves. Parmenion dived deep, his powerful legs propelling him towards the drowning swordsman.

It was pitch-dark, but a flash of lightning speared the sky and, for a heartbeat only, Parmenion saw the still struggling Macedonian. Grabbing hold of Attalus' shoulder-guard, Parmenion swam for the surface. His lungs were close to bursting as his head came clear. Attalus came up alongside him, but sank almost immediately under the weight of his breastplate. Parmenion dived once more, feeling for the dagger Attalus wore on his left hip. It was still in place. The Spartan drew it and sawed at the breastplate thongs. The blade was razor-sharp and the wet leather parted. Attalus ducked his head, pushing the breastplate up and away from him. Free of its weight, he rose to the surface.

A wave lifted the warriors high and Parmenion saw the distant shoreline. Keeping his movements slow and preserving his strength, the Spartan angled his body towards the beach, allowing the currents to carry him to safety.

He did not look back for Attalus, nor allow his mind to dwell on the fate of Alexander and the others. Alone against the might of sea and storm he anchored his thoughts to a single objective.

Survival.

Book Three, 352 BC

The Cliffs of Arkadia

Ektalis sat apart from his men under a small overhang of rock, watching the rain on the grey stone cascading down before him. He was drier here, but the wind occasionally blew the curtain of water against his bare legs, where it trickled behind the bronze greaves he wore. Staring gloomily out over the storm-lashed gulf, Ektalis wished he were back in Korinthos with his wife and sons.

He glanced to his left where the remaining ten men of his detachment sheltered in a shallow cave, then looked to his right where the five Makedones sat in the open, watching the sea.

Ektalis felt his hatred rise like bile in his throat. Loathsome barbarians! How such a cultured city as Korinthos could form an alliance with the Demon King was beyond him. But form it they had, and now he rode with the devil's army.

If you were a man, he told himself, you would have stood against the decision in the *agora* when the councillors put the question to the public vote. But you did not . . . and stayed alive. The debate had been heated. Leman, Parsidan and Ardanas – good friends all – had spoken heroically, denouncing the alliance. All had been murdered within a day of the meeting. Now Philippos ruled.

Ektalis shivered as the wind hurled more rain over his

drenched white cloak. 'Find the Golden Child,' his general had told him. 'It is the King's order.'

He is not my King, Ektalis wanted to say. But he had not. Instead he had saluted, gathered his century and set off for the west. The priests first said the boy was in the Forest of Gorgon. Now a message had been received saying he was aboard a ship heading towards the coast. There were ten bays where a ship could come in close to the shore and Ektalis ordered men to guard them all.

Then the five Makedones had arrived – grim, cold-eyed warriors, proud and haughty. What have they to be proud about, wondered Ektalis? Ten years ago they were mating with sheep in the barbarous hills of their native land. They have no culture – no history. But now they strode among civilized men, looking down upon them, treating them like slaves. Treating *us* like slaves, he corrected himself.

But then that is what we are, he realized. Slaves to the dreams of a child-murdering madman.

A patch of blue appeared in the sky to the east, sunlight shining on the distant hills. For a moment only, Ektalis felt his spirits lift; then he saw the Makedones rise to their feet, one of them pointing at the shoreline. Ektalis glanced down to see a small child emerging from the water.

His heart sank. Everyone knew the boy's intended fate – to be sacrificed to the Demon King.

The rain petered out, the clouds breaking. Ektalis moved back to his men. Sending two of them to fetch the soldiers from the other bays, the Korinthian led his warriors down the cliff path to the beach, following the five Makedones who had already drawn their swords.

Then came a sight which Ektalis would long remember. A dolphin swam into view, with a naked woman alongside it holding to its fin. It moved close to the shore, allowing the woman to find her feet and walk through the swell.

'I praise thee, Poseidon, Lord of the Deep,' whispered a man alongside Ektalis. The other Korinthians took up the prayer. 'Look upon us with favour, bless our families and our city.'

The goddess moved forward, kneeling down beside the

boy and putting her arms around him. The Makedones reached the sand and advanced upon her.

'Stop!' cried Ektalis, but the Makedones ignored him and he began to run, his men following. A lean Makedones warrior pulled back his sword, ready to ram it into the woman's belly. Ektalis hurled himself at the man, knocking him from his feet.

'What in Hecate's name do you think you are doing?' stormed the Makedones officer, a tall, broad-shouldered warrior with a trident beard.

'She is one of Poseidon's daughters, Canus. Did you not see her riding through the waves upon a dolphin?'

Canus shook his head. 'You fool! She is a witch, that is all. Now stand aside.'

'No!' cried Ektalis, drawing his own sword. 'She will not be harmed. Take the child, but the woman is not to be harmed.'

'If you go against me in this,' hissed Canus, his dark eyes gleaming, 'then you go against my King. And that is treason.'

'Even so,' answered Ektalis, trying in vain to suppress his fear.

Canus saw his terror and laughed. The sound of his laughter ripped into Ektalis worse than a blade, and he felt his new-found courage melting before it.

'Say the word, captain, and we'll cut the dogs into pieces,' said a Korinthian warrior. Ektalis was amazed. He knew the men held him in low regard – as well they might, for he had never been a man of action. Canus turned and stared at the eight Korinthians.

'You think to thwart me? You believe five Makedones could not kill you all? Well, think on this, you worthless scum. My thoughts are linked to the High Priest, and his to the King. Everything that happens here is known already. And if you persist in this, then not only you will die but all your families. You understand?' Canus saw the Korinthians relax, hands moving away from sword-hilts, and turned back to the woman. But as he moved towards her Ektalis leapt to stand before her.

Canus lunged at the Korinthian but Ektalis parried the blade, sending a reverse cut at the Makedones' face. Canus swayed back, the sword slashing harmlessly by him. Then he sprang forward, his sword plunging into Ektalis' groin. The Korinthian knew he was finished, but with his last strength he rammed his blade into Canus' neck, slicing it up under the jaw-line, through mouth and tongue, before burying it in Canus' brain. The Makedonian fell forward, his weight tearing the blade from Ektalis' grasp as the dying Korinthian fell to his knees.

The goddess moved alongside him, pulling clear the sword. But his vision was failing and he fell against her.

'I . . . am . . . so sorry,' he whispered.

*

Derae eased the dying man to his back, ignoring the remaining Makedones. Her spirit flowed into him, moving through arteries and veins until she reached the terrible wound that had ripped into his lower belly. As swiftly as she could she began to work on the severed artery at the groin, closing it, increasing by tenfold its ability to heal. Moving on to the muscle wall she first slowed the flow of blood, then brought the tissue together in a perfect join. The Korinthian was wearing a leather kilt and this had prevented the blade from making deep penetration. The worst wound was to the groin, but with this now sealed the warrior would live.

Derae returned to her body and opened her eyes.

'The woman may live,' said a tall Makedones, 'but the boy is ours.'

'Take him and go,' said the Korinthian who had first spoken in support of Ektalis.

'The boy stays,' said another voice, deep and metallic, and Derae swung to see a warrior walk into sight. His face was masked by a bronze helm, and his armour was bright in the sunlight. He moved smoothly across the sand and, as he came closer, she saw that the bronze covering his features was no mask but living metal; bronze lids above bronze eyes, a bronze beard and mouth.

240

'Who are you?' asked the new Makedones leader, a hatchet-faced warrior called Plius.

'I am Helm. And the boy is mine.'

'Take him!' yelled Plius. The four warriors sprang at the newcomer, but Helm's sword slashed through the throat of the first man and came up to block a wild cut from the second. Helm spun on his heel, ramming his elbow into Plius' face, smashing his nose and hurling him back into the path of the fourth attacker. The bloody sword rose and fell – and a second Makedones died. Helm leapt at Plius, who tried to block the deadly thrust; but the pain from his broken nose had partly blinded him and Helm's sword slid home in his throat. The last Makedones threw himself at Helm, but the newcomer sidestepped, slashing his sword through the back of the man's neck as he stumbled past. The soldier fell face-first into the sand and struggled to rise. Helm struck him again, the blade almost decapitating the man.

'The boy is mine,' said Helm again, turning to face the Korinthians.

At that moment Ektalis woke and stared up into Derae's face. 'Is this death?' he asked.

'No. You are healed.'

'Thank you, goddess.'

Smiling, she helped him to his feet. The Korinthians moved forward, gathering around the captain, mystified and amazed by his recovery.

Derae looked at the newcomer. 'Do you mean harm to the child?' she asked.

'No, lady,' came the metallic voice, 'but I need him.'

'For what purpose?'

'To free me from the curse of this helm.'

'How do you know that he can do this?'

'I was told to seek him.'

'By whom?'

'I do not know,' he answered wearily. 'I know so little.'

Derae reached into the man's mind and saw that he spoke the truth. There were no memories before waking upon the slab in the graveyard, no hint as to his identity.

241

The priestess withdrew, then called Alexander forward. 'Can you help him?' she asked.

For a moment the boy was silent. 'This is not the time,' he whispered.

*

Ektalis wrapped his white cloak around the shoulders of the naked goddess while two of the other Korinthians stripped a dead Makedones of his armour, pulling clear his tunic and offering it to Derae. The men were silent, awestruck. They had seen a goddess rise from the sea, and watched as their dead captain was brought back to life. And they had stood by as an enchanted warrior had slain the Makedones. Nothing would ever be the same for them again, and they waited for Ektalis to speak to them.

He drew them apart from the warrior, the goddess and the child, leading his men to a cluster of rocks some fifty paces to the west.

'You have all seen the miracle,' he said. 'I felt the sword pierce my belly. Yet there is now no wound. You saw Poseidon's daughter ride the dolphin. But where does that leave us, my brothers?'

No one answered. No one knew. Ektalis nodded, understanding their fears. The Makedones leader, Canus, had said it all. Their treachery was already known, their lives forfeit.

'The Spartans still stand against the Tyrant,' said Ektalis. 'What choice do we have, save to join with them? Either that or ride to the nearest port and seek a ship to Aegyptus, there to sign as mercenary soldiers?'

'What of our families?' a young soldier asked.

'What indeed?' answered Ektalis sadly. 'We have no hope of seeing them unless the Tyrant is overthrown.'

'But the Spartans cannot win,' said the lean, bearded warrior who had first stood by Ektalis.

'Yesterday I might have agreed with you, Samis. But today? Today I have seen the power of the gods – and they are not with Philippos. I was killed today – yet I live. I am a new man, Samis. I will never bow the knee to evil again.'

242

'What of the others?' asked Samis. 'They didn't see the miracles. When they arrive, how will we persuade them to follow us? What if they turn against us, or deliver us to the Tyrant?'

Ektalis nodded. 'You are right. We must hide the bodies and send the others back to camp. No one else must know.'

Samis suddenly smiled. 'This is madness,' he said, 'but I'll stand by you. I hate the cursed Makedones – always have. If I have to die in battle I'd sooner it was while killing those scum.'

'Are we all agreed?' asked Ektalis.

'Aye,' chorused the other seven Korinthians.

'Then let us hide the bodies and return to the cliff-top.'

*

Parmenion hauled himself clear of the breakers and collapsed on the beach. A wave broke over him, dragging him back, but he dug his fingers into the sand, fighting the undertow. Pushing himself upright he staggered towards the shelter of a shallow cave in the cliff-face. The rain lashed at his tired body and the wind howled around him. The cave was not deep, but the wind was less here and it was dry.

Slumping to the ground he looked back over the storm-lashed sea, but there was no sign of Attalus.

The rain began to ease, the clouds breaking. A thin shaft of sunlight broke through to the east, and a rainbow appeared like a huge bridge across the Gulf. It seemed then that the grey storm-clouds were fleeing from the light, and the sky shone clear blue. Within a few heartbeats the storm was but a memory, the sea clear and calm, the beach and cliffs bathed in sunlight. Parmenion stood and walked out towards the shoreline, his keen eyes scanning the shimmering water. Several bodies lay on the beach and one floated face-down in a shallow pool. They were all sailors from the Makedones trireme.

What now, *strategos*, he asked himself? What wonderful plan can you conceive?

Hearing a sound behind him he reached for his sword, but the scabbard was empty. Fists clenched he swung round – to see the giant Gorgon standing with hands on hips, watching him.

'You were to give me my dream,' said the monster softly. 'So tell me, where is Iskander?'

'I am alive,' answered Parmenion, gazing into the glowing eyes. 'You are alive. If Iskander lives, then so too does the dream. If not, then it is finished.'

'I should not have listened to you,' said Gorgon. 'I should have killed you as I first planned. Perhaps I will even now. That would give me at least some small pleasure.'

'No, it would not,' said Parmenion swiftly. 'For then you would truly have nothing. You have made your decision. You have set yourself against Philippos for good or ill. There is no turning back for you. Now swallow your anger and let us search for the others.'

'You want me to search the seabed? Even now the crabs are feasting on the child. He was not Iskander.' Lifting his serpent-framed head, Gorgon let out a deafening roar of anger and frustration. Parmenion tensed, waiting for the beast to turn on him.

'Now you see his true soul,' said the voice of Brontes, and Gorgon turned to see the minotaur sitting upon a boulder. Gone was the man. Once more he was the creature of Enchantment, horned and colossal.

'I should have known you would return to haunt me, brother,' muttered Gorgon. 'What words of comfort do you offer?'

'I have nothing to say to you. But the Human is right. Until we know Iskander is dead we must continue. And I shall – even if it means continuing in your foul company.'

Gorgon laughed, his good humour curiously restored. 'I shall stay the course. But know this, Human,' he said, turning to Parmenion. 'If the child is dead, you will follow him to Hades.'

Parmenion said nothing, for in that moment the sweet voice of Thena flowed into his mind:

We are safe, Alexander and I. We are less than an hour's walk to the east of you. Attalus is asleep exhausted in the bay just to your west. I cannot locate the centaur.

'Thank you,' said Parmenion, aloud.

'You thank me for threatening your death?' said Gorgon. 'You are a strange man.'

'The child is alive,' said Parmenion. 'The quest goes on.'

'How do you know this?' Brontes asked.

Parmenion ignored the question. 'I am very weary. But if you are still strong, Brontes, I would be grateful if you could walk to the next bay and bring Attalus to us. He is resting there.'

'It is the witch woman,' said Gorgon. 'She is alive, is she not?'

'Yes,' said Parmenion, with a wide smile. 'Alive.'

'Is she your lover?' enquired the Forest King.

'No.'

'But you would like her to be.'

Parmenion walked away, but the words stayed with him. His heart had leapt when her voice whispered into his mind, and the weight of his emotion surprised him. Put such thoughts from your head, he told himself. She is not a priestess of Aphrodite selling her services for silver.

He lay down in the cave, allowing himself to drift into a healing sleep, but her face stayed in his mind and his thoughts were far from battles and enchantments, plans and strategies.

He dreamt he lay in a grove of oak trees back in Arkadia, where the sun was setting behind the mountains. Beside him lay Thena, her head on his shoulder, and he was at peace. He stroked her hair and kissed her, but as he gazed lovingly at her face it shimmered and changed, becoming Derae.

Guilt touched him then, and the dreams faded.

*

Unaware of his torment, Derae also experienced the surge of joy when her questing spirit found Parmenion alive, and now her soul flew high above the war-torn land of Achaea, tracing the course of the Gulf as it ran east towards the white-walled city of Korinthos.

Far below her she saw the armies of the Tyrant, the

phalanxes and cavalry of the Makedones, mercenary archers from the islands to the south, warriors from Illyria and Thrace; a host geared for slaughter.

She flew to the south, seeking the Sparta of this strange world. But before she reached it she saw another army marching to face the Makedones. Though fewer in number they marched proudly and her Talent reached out to them. They were the warriors of Kadmos, their city destroyed but their courage remaining. With them were soldiers from Argolis and Messenia, and rebels from Athens and Euboea. She sought out the Spartan force, and found to her surprise that only 300 were from the city.

Mystified, she moved on, flying further south until she hovered over the twin of the city of her birth. So much was the same – the Cattle Price Palace was still there, and the statue of Zeus at the top of the acropolis – but many of the streets were subtly different. The Avenue of Leaving did not boast a statue of Athena, the temple of Aphrodite was nowhere in sight; instead a barracks was built near the sacred lake. Yet, though it was not her home, still it was close enough to bring a touch of sorrow to her soul.

Sensing a presence close by she garbed her spirit in armour of white light, a blazing shield upon her arm. A figure hooded and robed in white appeared, the face in shadow.

'Who are you?' came a familiar voice.

'Tamis?' whispered Derae. 'Is it you?'

'Who else would it be to guard Sparta in this hour?' responded the woman. 'But I asked for your name.'

'I am called Thena. I am not an enemy.'

'I know that, child. Come to my home.'

The hooded figure became a glowing sphere that sank towards the city. Derae followed it to a small house nestling in a grove of cypress trees close to the sacred lake. There were only two rooms here, with little furniture and no rugs. The floors were baked earth, the chairs simply made and unadorned. In the tiny bedroom upon a pallet bed lay an old woman, her blind eyes open, her wasted frame covered by a single thin blanket.

'I can feel your presence,' she said aloud, her voice faint like a breeze whispering through dead leaves. 'I have been waiting for you.'

Derae could find no words. This was not the Tamis she had known, the woman whose meddling had caused the birth of the Dark God, yet even so the sight of this twin caused a mixture of emotions Derae found hard to contain.

'Speak to me, child,' said Tamis. 'I have waited so long for you that I often wondered if the visions had been false.'

'Why have you waited? What can I do for you?'

The old woman smiled. 'Only the Source could answer that, and I am but the least of His followers. But I have seen the Chaos Spirit abroad in the land, listened to the screams of the dying, heard the cries of the dispossessed and widowed. These have been hard years, Thena. Hard, lonely years. Even now, with your coming, the darkness moves towards my city.'

'What would you have me do?'

'Is he with you?'

'Of whom do you speak?'

'The One who is to be. The *strategos*.'

'Yes, he is here.'

Tamis sighed and closed her opal eyes. 'The Spartan King is riding to his death. Nothing will change that. He is a noble man, a good man. I have helped him through these desperate years. But even now the Fates have worked against me. This is the time of the Festival of Apollo, when the priests say no Spartan army can march, so the King is leading the forces of Light with only his personal bodyguard. And he will die.'

Derae said nothing. Even in her own world Sparta had suffered through such stupidities. When the Persian King Xerxes led his army into Greece, the Spartans had refused to march against him because of a religious festival. And then, as now it seemed, the King had led his personal bodyguard of 300 men to block the pass of Thermopylae. Three hundred against a quarter of a million! Their courage and valour had held against the Persian horde for several days, but at the last they were slain to a man.

'What was your vision?' Derae asked.

'I saw the *strategos* and the Golden Child, and a warrior with a face of bronze. And with that vision was a rainbow and the fleeing of a storm. I hoped it meant the Dark God was vanquished. But perhaps it did not. Perhaps my hopes have been in vain.'

'Did you try to prevent the birth of the Dark God?' asked Derae, remembering the dark deeds of Tamis in the world of Greece.

'I considered it, but it seemed folly. Was I wrong?'

'No,' said Derae. 'You were wise, very wise. I will bring the *strategos* here. But I do not know what he can achieve.'

'You will understand very soon, child. Very soon. May the Source bless you.'

'He has, in many ways,' said Derae, but there was no response from the blind seeress.

*

Parmenion awoke from an uneasy sleep, his mind whirling with the many problems he faced. His head ached as he sat up and he sucked in a deep breath. Alexander was alive, and that in itself was a victory; but the *strategos* knew that, in battle as in life, only the final victory counted. And all the odds favoured Philippos.

One step at a time, he cautioned himself. Brontes had not yet returned with Attalus and Gorgon was sitting nearby staring out over the Gulf. Parmenion leaned his back to the cliff-face, calming his thoughts.

Through most of his life he had been forced to battle against the odds. In Sparta, as a despised mix-blood, he had fought alone against the hatred of his fellows. In Thebes he had engineered a victory against the Spartan overlords, inflicting the first major defeat on a full Spartan army. In Persia he had led the forces of minor satraps and governors, always finding the path to conquest. And in Macedonia he had helped a young King, beset by enemies, to build a nation feared across the world.

But here, in this enchanted realm, he was not a *strategos* or a general. He was a weaponless stranger in a world he scarcely understood. There were some similarities. Philippos was King of Makedon and had built an army to crush all opposition. Sparta was still the city of heroes. But here magic ruled; creatures like Gorgon, Brontes and Camiron were accepted as a normal part of life. Winged beasts patrolled the skies and the Demon King could read the hearts and minds of his enemies.

How then can I defeat him, Parmenion wondered?

Chiron had said the King was invulnerable to all weapons of war, his body immune to poisons. 'I only ever saw him hurt once,' the *magus* had told him. 'He was a child and playing with a sharp dagger. It cut his finger and blood flowed. It healed very swiftly. His mother scolded him in my presence, then turned to me, offering me the blade. "Cut him," she told me. At first I refused, but she insisted. So I took the dagger and gently ran the edge over the skin of his arm, but could make no impression.'

'Then why did it cut him?' Parmenion had asked.

'The sorcery protects him from his enemies, but he is *within* the spell. Should he choose, he could no doubt kill himself.'

Parmenion smiled at the memory. All he had to do was find a way to defeat the greatest army of this strange world, outthinking a King who could reach his mind and ultimately forcing that King to take his own life.

'Why do you smile?' asked Gorgon.

'Why should I not? The sun is shining.'

'You are a curious man, Parmenion,' observed the Forest King, turning his great head to stare out over the waves. Parmenion sat quietly, watching the creature. The skin of Gorgon's huge shoulders seemed lighter here in the sunlight, the mottled colours of the forest, dark green and rust brown, giving way to the paler hues of summer grass and polished pine. The snakes hung lank and lifeless from his head and his eyes had lost their demonic glow.

'What are you looking for?' asked the Spartan.

'I am not looking. I am remembering. It is more than a century since I last gazed upon the sea. I had a house once, with Persephone, on the island of Andros. We often came to the beach, to swim and to laze. The memories have been buried too long. Ah, but she was a beauty, her skin pale as marble, even in summer, her eyes like *turkis*, yet not cold and blue but warm and enchanting as the midsummer sky.' Gorgon sighed, then a low growl rumbled from his misshapen mouth. 'Why do I talk like this? My mind is failing.'

'You have spent too long in the forest,' said Parmenion softly.

'Aye, that is true. Persephone used to sing. We would sit under an awning watching the sunset over the waves, and she would sing. Yet I can remember no words. All that fills me is the memory of peace and joy. But I was a man then, and arrogant in the ways of youth. I could not begin to imagine a time when she would not be beside me, sending the sun to sleep with a song.'

'No one can take that from you, my friend. Not ever.'

'I have no friends, Human,' snapped Gorgon, surging to his feet and walking away. Parmenion watched the giant for a few moments and then followed him to the shore-line.

'I do not pretend to know your pain,' said the Spartan, 'and it would be trite to point out that we all carry scars. But I will do all that I can to fulfil my promise to you. Iskander tells me he is the chosen one. I believe that, and I will risk my life to see that he has the chance to prove it. But that is the greater quest, Gorgon, and for another day. Today we are a small group, battling for survival, and friendship is not to be spurned – not even by a child of the Titans.'

'You seek to lecture me?' hissed Gorgon.

'Perhaps I do. Perhaps your years in the slime of the dark forest have affected your perceptions.'

Gorgon nodded. 'Perhaps they have,' he conceded, his voice carrying no conviction. Then he smiled. 'Or perhaps I am now what I always was, a distorted monstrosity.'

'If that were true, would Persephone have loved you?'

'You do not understand, Human. How could you? The war was terrible and we all committed acts which would turn your soul to ashes. There is no escape from those memories. My brother Brontes is correct – you do not know

250

what I have done, what colossal evils are stamped upon the pages of history in my name.'

'Nor do I need to,' answered Parmenion, 'for you are right that they would change my thoughts of you. But that was yesterday and whatever is hidden in the past can remain there. Today you stand on the side of the just, and seek to save the people of the Enchantment. And yes, if you succeed it will not wash away the evil of the past, but it will give at least some hope for a future.'

'How can we succeed,' asked Gorgon, 'when all the forces of Philippos are ranged against us?'

'We are not talking of defeating Philippos in a battle. We are speaking of opening the Giant's Gateway. If the Spartans can hold the Demon King for a little while, we can bring Iskander to his destiny.'

Gorgon sighed. 'I will not travel on with you, Human. Now that you are – for the moment – safe, I will return to the forest to gather what followers remain and bring them to the Gateway.'

'How will you bring them all across the Gulf?'

'We will not cross the Gulf. We will travel the old paths, between Achaea and Hades. No Human may pass them and keep his sanity. But my . . . people . . . can walk them. I have played my part, Human. I have brought you across the sea. Now it is for you to bring Iskander to the Gateway.'

'We will succeed or die, my lord. It is all we can do. But let us, at least, part as friends.'

'Why is that important to you?'

'It is important to both of us,' answered Parmenion, extending his hand.

Gorgon glanced down at it, then looked into Parmenion's eyes. 'I have said it before, but you are a strange man, and I do not remember the last time I talked of friendship.' His arm came up, his fingers gripping Parmenion's hand, and they stood for a moment in silence.

Then the Forest King waded out into the sea and began to swim.

It was late afternoon before Brontes returned with Attalus. The swordsman's face was bruised, his right eye swollen where a wave had dashed him against the rocks, but he did not complain as he sank down beside Parmenion.

'It was difficult to rouse him,' said Brontes, 'but he refused my offer to carry him.'

'I am glad to see you alive,' said Parmenion, gripping the Macedonian's shoulder.

Attalus smiled. 'You saved my life. I shall not forget it. The breastplate would have killed me. What now?'

'We will find the others and make our way south.'

'And after that?'

'I do not know.'

Attalus nodded. 'No, of course not. It is just . . . well, I am used to you, *strategos*. And my faith in your talents grows day by day.'

'I cannot see why. After all, I failed to get the trees to uproot and march with us.'

Attalus chuckled. 'Forgive me for that, Spartan, but that cursed forest seeped into my soul. By all the gods, I swear it is good to be back in the sunlight. Brontes tells me Alexander is safe?'

'Yes,' answered Parmenion. 'And now it is time to find him. But first I must speak with Brontes.' The Spartan rose and walked to where the minotaur sat on a boulder overlooking the sea.

'Where is my brother?' Brontes asked.

'Gone.'

Brontes nodded. 'I thought he might stay the course. But what can you expect from such a creature?'

'He told me he was returning to gather his forces, and that he would bring them to the Giant's Gateway. I think that he will.'

The minotaur lifted his head and laughed. 'You cannot trust him, Parmenion. He is a creature of darkness.'

'We shall see. But we must proceed as if we do believe him.'

'Why?'

'Because if Gorgon does lead his beasts towards the south it is likely the people of the Enchantment will think he is attacking them.'

'As he probably will,' Brontes muttered.

'Listen to me: put aside your hate. I need you to travel alone to the woods around the Gateway. I want you to prepare the way for Gorgon.'

'Never! He is a traitor and a killer.'

'Then I shall see Iskander does not fulfil his destiny.'

The minotaur stormed to his feet. 'You dare to threaten me, Human?' he raged.

'Yes,' answered Parmenion. 'What is wrong with you? The war is over – and he is your brother. Without his aid none of us would be alive.'

'For his own purposes he helped us. Do not forget that!'

'And are you any different? Did you not threaten to kill me? You are only here because of Iskander.'

'You don't understand! Gorgon killed my children and raped my . . . our . . . mother. There is no good in him. He was born in darkness and he thrives on it. And you want me to prepare the way? Better for the Enchantment to die than for a creature like him to benefit from its return.'

'You do not believe that,' whispered Parmenion. 'That is the voice of your hatred. We are not talking here about your grief, or your bitterness. We are considering the future of all the people of the Enchantment. You have no right to make decisions concerning them. You are a dying race with one hope of survival: Iskander. Now go to the woods and do what must be done.'

'You will deny us Iskander if I refuse?'

'No,' admitted Parmenion. 'I will not deny you. That was the voice of my anger. Will you do as I ask?'

'I will think on it,' promised Brontes, but he looked away as he spoke, avoiding Parmenion's eyes.

The Plain of Mantinea

Helm was the first to see the two men emerge from the tree-line and walk towards the waiting group. He studied them as they approached, his hand resting lightly on his sword-hilt. The nine Korinthians all stood, but the golden-haired child shouted a name and began to run towards the newcomers.

The first of the men leaned forward to sweep the child into his arms. He had no sword, Helm noticed, but he moved like a warrior, smoothly and always in balance. The second man was pale-eyed, his movements cat-like and sure. The lion and the wolf, thought Helm.

The taller man lowered the child to the ground, ruffling his hair, then swung his gaze over the waiting warriors, coming at last to Helm. There was no expression in his blue eyes as he saw the face of bronze.

The Korinthians were waiting, but the newcomer strolled directly to Helm. 'Who are you?' he asked, the tone easy, the question spoken without a sign of arrogance yet with quiet authority. Here, thought Helm, is a man used to command.

'I wish I could tell you. But I know nothing of my past, save that I was told to find the child.'

'For what purpose?'

'I do not know that either – but it was not to do him harm.'

'My name is Parmenion. If you ride with me, you follow my orders. If that should not suit you, then you can leave now.'

'It suits me,' answered Helm easily.

The man smiled and nodded, then turned to the Korinthians, singling out Ektalis. 'My thanks to you, sir, for helping the boy. You and your men have risked much, and I applaud your courage. I see there are enough horses for all of us, and I think it wise we move south before continuing our conversation. The enemy is closing in on us even as we speak.'

Ektalis nodded and gave the order to mount. Parmenion walked to the woman, laying his hand on her shoulder, but Helm could not hear the words that passed between them and moved on to the horses. The mounts of the Makedones were smaller than the horses of the Korinthians, but they were deep-chested and powerful, reared for stamina rather than speed; Helm chose a roan gelding, taking hold of the mane and smoothly vaulting to its back.

'You know your horses,' said Parmenion. 'He is one I would have chosen.'

For two hours the group rode in silence, angling south and east through rolling hills, skirting small villages and towns and holding to the tree-line.

At last, as the sun began to set, they made camp in a sheltered hollow.

Parmenion called Ektalis to him. 'We will need sentries,' he said, 'one on that hillside, a second in the trees to the north.'

As Ektalis saluted and moved away, Helm grinned. The salute had seemed natural, Parmenion accepting it as his due.

'I think you are used to larger armies than this,' offered Helm.

'I am indeed,' the man answered, his hand resting on the hilt of a Makedones sword now belted at his side, 'but this is all we have. May I see your sword?'

'Of course,' answered Helm, sliding the blade from its scabbard, reversing it and passing it hilt first to the general.

'It is a fine weapon. How did you come by it?'

'When I awoke it was close by, along with the armour and the helm.'

'What made you think it was yours?'

'I cannot answer that. I was naked and alone . . . and it fitted me well. Especially the helm which, as you can see, has melted over my face.'

Parmenion was silent for a moment. 'You concern me, warrior,' he said, and Helm became acutely aware that the man before him was now holding his sword. 'How do I know you were not sent by Philippos?'

'You don't,' answered Helm. 'But then neither do I.'

'You fight well. That is good. Your slaying of the Makedones supplied Attalus and myself with weapons, and for that I am grateful. Such a deed makes it unlikely you are an enemy. Unlikely but not impossible.'

'I accept that, Parmenion. And where does that leave us?'

'In mortal peril either way,' the general answered, returning Helm's sword and turning away.

*

By the afternoon of the following day the riders had reached the high ground overlooking the Plain of Mantinea – a wide, flat area between the mountains, bordering on the kingdom of Argolis. In the distance they could see two mighty armies facing one another. Thena dismounted and sat on a cliff-ledge, closing her eyes, her spirit soaring out over the waiting forces.

What she saw sent a shiver through her and she fled back to her body, crying out as she woke.

'What is it?' asked Parmenion, dismounting and kneeling beside her, gripping her shoulder.

'Send the others south,' she whispered. 'Tell them we will join them later.'

'Why?'

'Trust me! You are about to walk a different path and you must send them on. Swiftly now, for there is little time.'

Parmenion called Attalus to him. 'You must travel on without me for a while, my friend. Take Alexander south – to the Gateway, if necessary. I will meet you when I can.'

'We should stay together,' argued Attalus.

'There is no time for debate. You must protect Alexander. Brontes has gone to prepare the way, and you will be safe in the south. I can tell you no more, for I know no more.'

Attalus cursed softly, then vaulted to his mount. 'Look after yourself, Spartan,' he called, as he led the company away to the south.

Parmenion returned to the priestess. 'Tell me all,' he said.

'Wait,' she advised. 'The battle is beginning.'

The *strategos* turned his attention to the two armies. At this distance they were just like the tiny carved models with which he had won his first encounter with his rival, Leonidas, thirty-three years ago in another world. They appeared as toys, glittering and bright, moving across the dusty plain. But they were not toys. Within moments living, breathing men would be cut down, swords and spears slashing and cleaving through flesh and bone. The army of Makedon, black cloaks and black banners swirling in the breeze, marched forward confidently, the cavalry on the left sweeping out to envelop the enemy flanks.

But then they were met by a counter-charge, warriors in blue cloaks and shining helms emerging from their hiding-places among the boulders at the foot of the slopes. Parmenion smiled. This was good strategy from the Spartan King. Straining his eyes, he could just make out the monarch standing at the centre of the Spartan phalanx, 300 men in tight formation six ranks deep, fifty shields wide. It was a defensive formation and had been placed at the centre of the field, with mercenary divisions around it. 'He seeks to hold the centre steady,' said Parmenion. 'See how they gather around the Spartans?' More allied cavalry rode from the right, but the Makedones swung their lines to meet the charge. It seemed to Parmenion that the Makedones' defence was moving into action even before the charge, and he recalled with sinking heart that Philippos could read the mind of his enemy.

Even so the charge carried through, pushing back the

enemy. The Spartan centre surged forward and Parmenion watched as the King mounted a fine grey stallion and rode back to join the reserve cavalry on the left. The battle was fully joined now, a great heaving mass of men vying for control of the field.

'Now!' whispered Parmenion. 'Now lead the charge!' As if the Spartan King had heard him Parmenion saw the great grey horse thunder into the gallop, riders streaming behind with the sun glittering on their lance-points.

But on the far side of the battle the allied cavalry suddenly gave way, panic sweeping their ranks. Swinging their mounts they fled the field. The Makedones poured into the breach, moving out to surround the allied centre. Two mercenary divisions broke and ran, leaving a gap on the Spartan right.

'Sweet Zeus, no!' shouted Parmenion. 'He had it won!'

The Spartan King disengaged his cavalry from the attack and led his men in a desperate ride across the battlefield, trying to close the gap, but Parmenion knew the attempt was doomed. Panic swept through the allied army like a grass fire, and all but the Spartans threw down their shields and ran.

The Spartan phalanx closed, becoming a fighting square, moving back from the centre towards a narrow pass in the mountains. But the King led one last desperate charge against the enemy centre, almost reaching Philippos. Now Parmenion saw the Demon King riding forward on a giant black stallion, hacking and cutting his way towards his enemy. A spear slashed into the grey stallion and it bolted, carrying the Spartan King clear of the action as he fought to control the pain-maddened beast.

Now the King was riding towards Parmenion and Thena, pursued by a score of black-cloaked riders. Glancing back, he saw them and swung the horse up on to a scree slope, the beast scrambling on to a ledge. There was nowhere else to go and the Spartan King leapt from his mount as the first Makedones reached the top. The man's horse reared as the King ran at it, toppling his rider, but then the others arrived, leaping from their horses and advancing on the lone warrior.

Parmenion's heart ached for the man. He had come so close, only to be betrayed by cowards and men of little heart. He longed to gallop down to fight alongside the King, but a gorge separated them and the King was but moments from death – before him a score of enemies, behind him a chasm. He fought bravely and with great skill, but at the last a sword gashed his throat and he fell back, teetering on the edge of the abyss. Parmenion cried out in anguish as the Spartan King toppled from the ledge, his bronze-clad body cartwheeling through the air to crash against the mountainside before pitching once more into space to be dashed against the rocks below. Parmenion groaned and looked away. 'So close – so near to victory,' he whispered.

'I know,' said Thena. 'Now we must wait.'

'For what? I have seen enough.'

'There is more, my dear,' she told him.

The enemy soldiers pulled back from the ledge, seeking a way to recover the body. But the cliff was too steep and they remounted their horses and vanished from sight.

'Now,' said Thena. 'Before they can circle round from the north, we must get to the body.'

'Why?'

'There is no time to explain. Trust me.' Remounting, Thena urged her horse over the crest of the hill and down the gentle slope to the valley floor. Parmenion had no wish to gaze upon the ruined body of so great a warrior, but he followed the priestess on the long ride, coming at last to the blood-spattered corpse. Thena climbed down from her mount and moved to the body, gently rolling it to its back. The red-plumed helm lay close by, scarcely dented, but the breastplate was split at the shoulder, where a white bone could be seen jutting from dead flesh.

The man's face was remarkably untouched, his blue eyes open and staring at the sky. Parmenion moved to the body and stopped, heart hammering and legs unsteady.

'I am sorry,' whispered Thena, 'but you stand before the body of Parmenion, the King of Sparta.'

*

259

Parmenion could find no words as he gazed down at his own corpse. He had observed Thena's magic back in the forest when she had created the illusion of the group still sleeping around the camp-fire. Though in its way that had been almost amusing, causing a lifting of tension and fear. But this was real. The dead man at his feet was his twin, and Parmenion felt the anguish of bereavement. Worse than this, the tragedy brought him a sickening sense of his own mortality. The Parmenion lying here had been a man with dreams, hopes, ambitions. Yet he had been cut down in his prime, his body smashed, broken.

The Spartan took a deep, shuddering breath.

'We must move him,' said Thena, 'before the Makedones arrive.'

'Why?' responded Parmenion, unwilling to touch his *alter ego*.

'Because they must not know he is dead. Come now! Lift him across your horse.'

Parmenion's hands were trembling as he pulled the corpse upright, draping the body over his shoulder, transferring it to the Makedones gelding, then vaulting to the beast's back. The horse was strong, but even so could not bear the double weight for long. Parmenion turned to see Thena sitting upon a boulder.

'Take my horse to the woods,' she commanded. 'I will be there by dusk.'

'You cannot stay here. They will kill you.'

'No, they will not see me. When you reach the woods strip the body and bury it. Then put on his armour. Go now!' Parmenion tugged the reins and the gelding began to walk away to the west. 'Wait!' called Thena. Gathering up the King's fallen sword and helm, she passed them to Parmenion. 'Now ride – for time is short.'

The ground was rock-strewn and hard-packed, the gelding's hooves leaving little sign as the Spartan rode away. Now and again he glanced back to see Thena sitting quietly, awaiting the Makedones. He tried not to look at the body, but his eyes were drawn to it. It was no longer leaking blood, but the bowels had opened and the stench was strong. There is no dignity in death, thought Parmenion as he angled the horse up to the tree-line and into the woods.

Once there he followed Thena's instructions, stripping the body, digging out a shallow grave in the loam and rolling the corpse into it. The body fell to its back – dead eyes staring up at the Spartan, dead mouth sagging open.

'I have no coin for the ferryman,' Parmenion told the dead King. 'But you were a man of courage and I believe you will find the Elysian Fields without it.'

Swiftly he pushed the dark earth over the body, then sat back trembling.

After a while he picked up the King's sword, and was not surprised to find it the same blade he himself had won more than thirty years ago in another Sparta. It was the legendary blade of Leonidas, the Sword King, beautifully crafted and wondrously sharp.

Leonidas! A glorious name from the past yet also the name of Parmenion's first enemy, the brother of Derae, in whose name Parmenion had suffered taunts and beatings, hatred and dark violence.

That era had come to an end at Leuctra when Parmenion's battle plan had smashed the Spartan line, killing their King and freeing the city of Thebes from Spartan dictatorship. When the battle ended, so too had Spartan power in Greece.

Parmenion remembered well the day he had won the sword. It was the final of the General's Games where the young men of Sparta, using carved model armies, engaged in battles of tactics and strategy. The final was contested at the house of Xenophon, the renegade Athenian general who had become a close friend of the Spartan King Agisaleus.

Agisaleus, believing his nephew Leonidas would win the final, had offered the legendary blade as a prize. But Leonidas had not won. He had been crushed by the hated mix-blood, humiliated in front of his peers and his King.

And the sword came to Parmenion.

Yet at Leuctra, with Sparta crushed, it had been Leonidas who had come to discuss the recovery from the battlefield of the Spartan dead, and it was Parmenion to whom he had come.

Leonidas had been dignified in defeat, strong and proud, and – in a moment he had never quite understood – Parmenion had given him the sword, ending for ever their enmity.

Yet now he sat in an alien forest with the twin of the blade in his hand.

What now, he asked himself? But the answer was inescapable. Parmenion the King had been slain, leaving his enemy triumphant and the Spartan army leaderless.

The Demon King had won.

*

Derae watched until Parmenion was no longer in sight, then she relaxed, calming her mind, honing her powers, reaching out to seek the Makedones riders who were coming to claim the body of their enemy.

They were still half a mile distant and she focused on the leader, Theoparlis – a stocky, dark-eyed man, strong and fearless, his heart darkened by bitter memories of slavery and torture in the early years of his life. Derae floated within his subconscious, silently preparing him. Then she moved on to the others, one by one.

When at last she opened her eyes they were riding towards the rocks, fanning out, their eyes scanning the boulders. Drawing rein they dismounted and began to search.

Derae took a deep breath. Not a man had noticed her. Now she stood.

'He is not here,' she said softly. The nearest man gasped and staggered back. He did not see a tall, bony woman in an ill-fitting *chiton*. His eyes widened in awe as he drank in the sight of a regal warrior woman, a doric helm pushed back on her head, a golden breastplate adorning her torso. An owl sat upon her shoulder, its bright eyes blinking in the sunlight.

The twenty warriors stood silently before Athena, Goddess of Wisdom and War. In her hand was a golden spear, and this she raised to point at Theoparlis. 'Return to your King,' she said, her voice ringing with authority, 'and tell him that Parmenion lives.'

'He will kill us all, lady, and brand us liars,' Theoparlis protested.

'Draw your swords,' she said softly. They did so. 'Now gaze upon them.'

The blades writhed in their hands, becoming serpents. With cries of shock and horror the men flung the weapons aside . . . all but Theoparlis. 'It is still a sword,' he said, his face white, his hand trembling.

The serpent blade stiffened, the snake disappearing. 'Indeed it is, Theoparlis; you are a strong man,' said Derae. 'But then the magic was not wrought to harm you but to allow you to go to your King and convince him. Has he not the Eye to read a man's mind? He will know you do not lie.'

'How could the Spartan have survived such a fall?' he asked.

Derae pointed to the man beside Theoparlis. 'Take up your sword,' she ordered. The man obeyed. 'Draw the blade across your palm.'

'No!' shouted the man, but the sword rose of its own accord, his left hand opening to receive it. 'No!' he screamed again, but the sharp iron cut into his flesh and blood welled from the wound.

'Hold up the hand so that all may see,' Derae ordered. 'This is no illusion. Theoparlis, touch the blood.' The Makedones obeyed. 'Is it real?'

'Yes, lady.'

'Now watch . . . and learn.'

Derae closed her eyes. The cut was shallow and even and it was a matter of moments to accelerate the tissue bond, producing ten days of healing in as many heartbeats. When she opened her eyes the men had gathered around the injured warrior and were staring at his blood-covered hand. 'Wipe clear the blood,' said Derae. Using the edge of his black cloak the man did so. Only a faint scar remained.

'Now you know how the King survived,' she told them. 'I healed him. And I tell you this, he is beloved of the gods. The next time you see him will be on the day of your deaths – if he should so choose.'

'His army is destroyed,' said Theoparlis.

'You have yet to face the might of Sparta.'

'Five thousand men cannot stand against the forces of Makedon.'

'We shall see. Go now. Report what I have said to Philippos. And tell him the words of Athena – if he marches against Sparta he will die.'

Theoparlis bowed and backed away to his horse, his men following.

Derae let fall the illusion, and it seemed to the warriors as if the goddess had suddenly disappeared from view. Unnoticed, the priestess walked away to the west and the distant woods.

She found Parmenion sitting by the freshly-covered grave. 'You will take his place?' she asked.

'I don't know, Thena,' he answered. 'We were heading for Sparta because we thought it would be safe and Aristotle could meet us there. But now? Now the Spartans have no war leader and the Makedones could march all the way to the city.'

'What choices are there?'

He shrugged. 'We could make for the Gateway and allow Alexander his destiny – if such it be . . . and hope Aristotle is there to bring us home before the Makedones arrive.'

'And the Demon King?'

'He is not my problem, Thena. This is not my world.' His words lacked conviction and his gaze strayed to the grave. He sighed and stood. 'Tell me what is right,' he said.

'Are you asking me – or him? He was you, Parmenion. Ask yourself what you would wish for if the roles were reversed. Would you prefer to see your city conquered, your people enslaved? Or would you hope that your twin could achieve what you could not?'

'You know the answer to that. But there is Alexander to consider.'

'Yet the situation is the same as before,' she said. 'We need Sparta to hold back the Makedones, to give Alexander time at the Gateway. Who better to ensure the Spartans can do just that than their own Battle King?'

'But I am not him. It feels wrong, Thena. He may have a

family – a wife, sons, daughters. They will know him. And even if they do not, surely it is an insult to his memory?'

'Would you consider it an insult to yours if it was he who fought for you?'

'No,' he admitted. 'Yet still it does not sit well with me. And what of Attalus and the Korinthians? They know I am not the Spartan King.'

'Attalus knows what he must do. But you and I must ride to Sparta. There is much to be done, and little time, for Philippos will march upon the city within a few days.'

Suddenly Parmenion cursed. 'Why me?' he shouted. 'I came here to rescue my son, not to become embroiled in a war in which I have no interest.'

Derae said nothing for a while, then came close to the Spartan and laid her hand on his arm. 'You know the answer to that, my dear. Why you? Because you are here. Simply that. Now time is short.'

Parmenion moved to the graveside. 'I never knew you,' he said softly, 'but men spoke well of you. I will do what I can for your city and your people.'

Swiftly he donned the dented armour of the dead monarch, strapping the sword of Leonidas to his side. Turning to Derae, he smiled.

'There is much to do,' she told him.

'Then let us begin,' he said.

For two hours they rode south, then cut towards the east over rolling hills, stopping at dusk in a ruined and deserted settlement. Parmenion built a fire against the stones of a fallen wall and sat in silence staring at the flames. Derae did not intrude on his thoughts. At last he spoke.

'The King's bodyguard were engaged in a fighting retreat,' he said suddenly. 'Did they escape?'

'I will find out,' she said. Moments later she nodded. 'They lost more than a third of their number, but they are defending a narrow pass and still holding the Makedones.'

'We must be with them by dawn. If I can convince the King's captain that there is a chance, I can carry this through.'

'Even then,' she whispered, 'can you win against the Demon King?'

'I have fought in many wars, lady, and I have never lost. I do not say this with arrogance, but I am the *strategos*. If there is a way to defeat Philippos I will find it. Or be buried like . . . like my brother in an unmarked grave. I can do no more.'

'You know that you need not fight this war? It is not your world, not your city. You could ride to the Giant's Gateway and wait for Aristotle.'

'No, I could not do that.'

'Why?'

He shrugged. 'Ever since I came here I have heard nothing but good of the Spartan King. Even the creatures of Enchantment speak well of him, saying he gave them lands for their own where they would not be hunted. He was everything I would wish to be. But our lives took different paths. I became a wandering mercenary, filled with bitterness and hatred, with war my only talent. He became a King – and a better man.'

'That is not so. You also are kind, noble and generous of spirit.'

'I am the Death of Nations, Thena, not the father of one.'

'The woman who gave you that title was wrong – wrong in all that she did. She manipulated your life, causing you grief and fuelling your hatred. But you rose above that.'

'You knew her?' he asked, surprised.

'I was . . . a disciple. It was part of a plan she had – a dream. You were to be the warrior who would stand against the Dark God. But it was a futile, self-defeating vision, and she died knowing it. But here there was no bitterness and hatred. You understand? He was no different from you. He was a man of courage and nobility, intelligent and caring. But then so is the Parmenion I know.' Her breathing was ragged, her colour high, and she turned away from him, lying down and covering herself with her cloak.

He moved to her, his hand touching her shoulder. 'You are angry with me,' he said, his voice soft, his touch gentle.

'No,' she told him, 'there is no anger. Let me sleep now, for I am very tired.'

She heard him move back to the fire and closed her eyes.

266

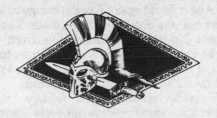

The Pass of Tegaea

Leonidas shouted an order and stepped back from the line. The warriors on either side of him closed ranks and waited, shields held high, short stabbing swords extended. Leonidas ran several paces, then climbed to a high boulder and gazed back down the pass.

The Makedones were dragging aside the corpses, preparing the way for yet another charge. Leonidas strained his eyes to see the new troops massing. The golden sunbursts on their black breastplates proclaimed them to be the King's Guards. So at last they send the best, he thought. But then the Spartans had held against the Illyrians, the Thracians and other mercenary units. How many attacks had they faced? Twenty? Thirty? Leonidas had lost count. It was enough that the battleground was slick with enemy blood. Hundreds of the Tyrant's troops had fallen. Hundreds more would fall.

The pass was narrow here, less than seventy paces, and the three Spartan lines were holding their ground. Barely . . . Leonidas cursed softly. The moon was high, the skies clear, and there was no opportunity to withdraw in battle order. Yet holding this pass was a doomed enterprise, for even now the Makedones cavalry would be riding the high ridges to cut them off. By morning the Spartans would be trapped.

Leonidas was weary, weighed down with the muscle-numbing tiredness that follows defeat. The battle had been won – and then the cursed Kadmians had broken. Gutless bastards! Anger flared again, feeding energy to his muscles. Yet it was not the fickle courage of the Kadmians that enraged him. No, the main thrust of his anger was against the Spartan Priest of Apollo, Soteridas, who had declared the timing of the battle inauspicious. And the Spartan army could not march without the god's blessing.

Now Soteridas would appear to have been proved correct. Yet Leonidas knew, as did every Spartan fighting man here, that had the whole army been present they would have cut the Makedones to pieces. Instead the allied army had been crushed, the King slain.

Leonidas closed his eyes. Slain . . . He could hardly believe it.

The enemy drums beat out the signal to advance and Leonidas jumped from the boulder, running to take his place in the front line alongside the giant, Nestus. Blood was flowing from a wound in the warrior's cheek and his breastplate had been gashed.

'Here they come,' muttered Nestus, with a smile. 'They must like dying.'

Leonidas said nothing.

The black-garbed Makedones bore down on the Spartans, the sound of their war-cries echoing in the pass.

At that moment a low rumble, like distant thunder, echoed through the mountains. Leonidas glanced up at the steep rock-face to the left. Several stones clattered down, followed by fist-sized rocks. At the top of the pass, above the Makedones, Leonidas saw a figure in golden armour pushing against a boulder that hung precariously on a narrow ledge. The huge rock slid clear of the ledge, almost dislodging the warrior, then it fell some sixty feet to explode against a second ledge which tore itself from the cliff-face.

'Avalanche!' screamed a Makedones warrior and the cry was taken up. The enemy charge faltered and stopped, the leading warriors turning, trying to get back from the pass. A massive slab of limestone thundered into the Makedones and Leonidas saw men disappear from sight, their bodies crushed beyond recognition. Panic swept through the enemy ranks as they fought to escape the rain of death. Another huge section of rock yawed out above them . . . and fell, killing a score of warriors.

A choking dust-cloud billowed up, the wind sweeping it to the north – into the faces of the Makedones still waiting at the mouth of the pass.

Leonidas gazed up through the dust. At the crest of the cliff he caught a glimpse of the warrior in the golden breastplate – and his spirits soared.

'The King!' he shouted. 'The King lives!'

The figure on the cliff-top waved, pointing to the south, and Leonidas understood instantly. The Makedones were in disarray, hundreds of them slain by the rock fall. Now was the time to move back.

'By rank,' bellowed Leonidas, 'file six!'

Smoothly the Spartans fell back into columns and marched in close order from the pass. His lieutenant, Learchus, moved alongside him.

'Was that truly the King?'

'I believe so. He started the avalanche.'

'Zeus be praised! Then we do have a chance.'

Leonidas did not reply. A chance? All that was left to face the Tyrant was the Spartan army – 5,000 fighting men, with no cavalry, archers or javeliners. Ranged against them would be more than 20,000 Makedones infantry and 10,000 cavalry. The only hope would be a defensive battle, holding a ridge or a pass. And between Tegaea and Sparta there were only ragged hills and plains. The land was open to the conqueror.

Parmenion will find a way, he thought. He will! That was love and loyalty speaking, he knew, and his mood darkened.

As children they had been enemies, but always he had held the young mix-blood in high esteem, and as the years passed that esteem had given way to a kind of awe. Now they were closer than brothers. Yet what plan could even such a general as Parmenion produce to counter the demonic skills of Philippos?

The pass widened and as the soldiers filed out on to the plain two riders came galloping towards them.

'The King!' someone shouted and the Spartans drew their blades, crashing them against their bronze shields in salute. Leonidas ran forward as the riders approached.

'Welcome, sire!' he called out. The King sat silently for a moment, expressionless, then he smiled.

'It is good to see you, Leonidas.'

The voice was cool and there was a tension about him that Leonidas could not understand. But then these last two days had been hard, and the King had suffered a bitter reverse.

'What are your orders, sire?'

'South to Sparta,' said Parmenion. 'Battle speed, for the enemy cavalry is close.' Leonidas bowed and then looked to the woman. She was stern of countenance but her eyes were locked to him. The King made no effort to introduce her, which surprised Leonidas, but he said nothing and returned to the head of the column.

The men marched until two hours after dawn; then the King commanded a halt, signalling Leonidas to make camp in a small wood on the slopes of a range of gentle hills. The Spartan soldiers moved into the shelter of the trees and then gratefully sank to the ground, stretching tired bodies to the grass.

Leonidas ordered sentries to watch for signs of the enemy, then made his way to where the King sat with the woman. 'I had thought you dead, sire,' he said, sitting opposite Parmenion.

'It was close,' replied the King. 'You fought well in the pass. What were our losses?'

'Eighty-two died in the battle on the plain, a further thirty in the pass itself. Epulis, Karas and Ondomenus are dead.' The King nodded, but no expression of regret showed. Leonidas could barely contain his surprise, for Ondomenus had been one of the King's closest companions.

'The Makedones cavalry,' said the King, 'has reached the pass but not followed in pursuit. We will rest here for two hours, then continue south.'

'How do you know this, sire?'

The King smiled. 'I am sorry, my friend. My mind is occupied and it has affected my manners. Let me introduce you to the seeress, Thena. She has many talents – and saved my life during the battle.'

Leonidas bowed his head. 'For that you have my gratitude, my lady. Without the King all would be lost. Where are you from?'

'Asia,' Thena answered. Parmenion stretched out on the ground, closing his eyes. 'The King is weary,' she continued. 'May we walk for a while and talk?' she asked Leonidas.

'Of course,' he answered, perplexed. The King's behaviour was beginning to unsettle him. Taking Thena's arm, he strolled with her to the edge of the woods and they sat upon a fallen log looking back over the plains.

'The King,' said Thena, 'fell from a ledge, suffering a severe blow to his head.'

'I saw the dent in his helm, lady. I am surprised he survived.'

'He is a strong man.'

'He is the best of men, lady.'

'Yes, I am sure that he is. I have known him but a little time. Tell me of him.'

'Surely even in Asia you have heard of Parmenion?'

'I meant tell me of the man. It is said he is a mix-blood. How did he become King?'

'He was the First General of Sparta. When Agisaleus was slain in the Great Athenian War three years ago, the ephors elected Parmenion.'

'But he has no links to the royal houses,' said Thena.

'That is not true, lady. He married well.' Leonidas chuckled.

'Married?'

'My own house is of the noble line, and I could have had the throne. But in the dark days of a seemingly lost war I knew we needed a better man than I. And Parmenion was that man. Therefore we brought him into my family. He married my sister, Derae.'

271

*

The shock was terrifying. Derae felt her heartbeat quicken, her hands tremble. She knew that her face was betraying her, for Leonidas leaned forward.

'Are you well, lady?' he asked, his voice full of concern.

But she could say nothing. An alternate world in which Philippos ruled and Parmenion was King of Sparta! You fool, she told herself. How could you have not known there would be a twin for you?

'Please leave me, Leonidas,' she said, forcing a smile. 'I have much to think about.' Bewildered the warrior rose, bowed and moved away.

Alone, she felt the full weight of grief descend.

'Why are you unhappy?' asked Tamis, and Derae jerked to awareness as the old woman's spirit hovered before her.

'I cannot talk,' whispered Derae, 'but I give you permission to share my memories. All answers lie there.'

'I would not wish to intrude on them,' said Tamis softly.

'You would not be intruding,' Derae assured her. 'Indeed, I would value your counsel.'

'Very well,' Tamis replied, and Derae felt a flicker of warmth as Tamis merged into her mind, flowing through the thoughts of the past. At last the old woman withdrew. 'What would you have me say to you?' she asked.

Derae shrugged. 'I love him. It seems that all my life I have loved him. Yet all we had was five days together. And the time here . . . where he does not know me. I cannot bear to see them together, I *cannot*.'

'Yet it is different here,' said Tamis gently. 'Here there was no rescue, no five days of passion. In this world Derae loved a man called Nestus, but was forced to put him aside in order to marry Parmenion. They live together now in cold comfort . . . without love.'

'She does not love him? I cannot believe it.'

'As I said, here he did not rescue her; they had few meetings before the wedding. And she was betrothed to Nestus, whom she adored. I believe she still does.'

'Then what has it all been for?' whispered Derae. 'Why

272

did this have to be? Why did the Tamis I knew have to interfere?'

'She did you both great harm, and I do not excuse it. But had she not done so then my vision could not have been realized. The *strategos* would not have come to the aid of my world.'

'What are you saying?'

'Let us assume that your Parmenion had never become the Death of Nations. How then could he help the Sparta of this world? He would never have come here, for there would have been no Alexander to follow, to rescue. Do you understand?'

Derae's mind reeled and she shook her head. 'Then you are saying the Tamis of my world did right? I cannot believe that!'

The older woman shrugged. 'You misunderstand me. In the context of your world she was wrong, for her actions led to the birth of the Chaos Spirit and destroyed your dreams of love. But here? Here the child may be Iskander and the hope of the Enchantment.'

'This is beyond me, Tamis.'

'It comes down to this, my dear. Every action we take has many consequences, some for good, some for evil. Consider your own life as an example. When you were kidnapped as a young girl it brought you and Parmenion together. An evil action, but the outcome was good. And though my namesake was wrong to take you from Sparta, you became a Healer. We none of us know where our actions will lead. That is why the followers of the Source must not use the weapons of evil. Everything we do must be governed by love.'

'You think that love cannot lead to evil?'

'Of course it can. For love creates jealousy, and jealousy hate. But love also conquers, and deeds inspired by love bring harmony far more often than discord.'

'And do we deal with Philippos with love?' countered Derae.

'I do not hate him,' answered Tamis. 'I feel great pity for him. But I did not bring Parmenion here – though I could

273

have done. Nor have I used my powers to see Philippos slain – though this also I could have done. For I do not know the will of the Source in this.'

'That sounds like evasion,' said Derae, 'for you cannot escape the simple point that my Parmenion is here, and he is a warrior. He will attempt to fight Philippos, and in that battle thousands will be slain. Surely that involves using the weapons of evil?'

The other woman nodded. 'Perhaps. But I cannot, of my will, change the world. All I can do is to maintain my own principles in the face of the world's evil. When a cancer is spreading through the body and the surgeon cuts it out, is he acting on behalf of evil? He is hurting the body and causing pain. Is that evil? All principles can be made to look foolish in the eyes of the world's wisdom. Once there was a city under siege. The enemy King said that he would spare the city if the inhabitants took a single babe and sacrificed it to him on the battlements. Now the city could not hold against him and surely, it was argued, the slaying of a single babe would be better than seeing all the babes of the city killed when the attacker breached the walls.'

'What did they do?'

'They refused.'

'And then?'

'They were slaughtered. No one survived.'

'What is your point, Tamis?'

'That is a question for you to answer, my dear. You think them wrong?'

'I cannot say. But the babe they might have sacrificed died anyway.'

'Yes.'

'Then why did they refuse?'

Tamis sighed. 'They understood that you do not turn aside a great evil by allowing a small one to be committed. Evil grows, Derae. Give way once and you will give way again . . . and again. Would you have killed the babe?'

'No, of course not.'

'Not even to save the city?'

'No.'

274

'Then why do you ask why they also refused?'

'Because I am used to the evil of Man and I understand the nature of selfishness and compromise. I am amazed that an entire city should exhibit such nobility of spirit.'

'They had a great leader, my dear. His name was Epaminondas and he was King Parmenion's closest friend. The people loved him for his virtue. They died for him.'

'What became of the enemy King?'

'He marches on Sparta, Derae. For the man was Philippos.'

'I will not stay to see it,' said Derae. 'I will travel south to the Giant's Gateway. I will not watch Parmenion with . . . with his wife. Nor will I wait to see him die.'

'You think he will fail?'

'How can he succeed, Tamis?'

The old woman had no answer.

*

Parmenion lay awake, deeply unhappy about the subterfuge. He knew himself to be an imposter, and it irked him. Yet what choices were there? Could he say to Leonidas, 'I am not your king, but a warrior from another world'? And if he did, would he still command the Spartan army? He sat up and gazed around at the camp.

He could see Nestus, the swordsman he had slain for ordering Derae's death. And Learchus, the boy he had killed in Sparta on the night of the attack on Hermias. Here and there were other men whose faces he recalled but whose names were lost to him, vanished in some dim corridor of memory.

He stood. 'Officers to me,' he called. They rose and moved to sit in a circle around him, all of them bowing save the giant Nestus. Parmenion met the man's eyes, sensing the hostility there. Leonidas appeared from the woods and joined him. Parmenion looked at his handsome face, the tightly curled hair of red-gold, the clear blue eyes. My enemy and my friend, he thought.

'We learned a great deal,' said Parmenion, 'even though the battle was lost. Philippos is not a good general.'

'How can you say that?' asked Nestus. '*He* has never lost.' There was an edge in the man's voice which was almost a sneer.

'The golden eye gives him a power to read the thoughts of his adversary. Then he reacts. Do you understand? He has no need of a battle plan. He merely thwarts the plans of others until they are overcommitted. Then he strikes.'

'How does that help us?' queried Leonidas.

'By telling us that strength merely disguises a weakness. If we can find a way to nullify his power, we can destroy him,' Parmenion told him.

'How do we do that?' asked the slender Learchus.

'I will find a way,' Parmenion promised, with a confidence he did not feel. 'Now tell me, Leonidas, how many men can we gather?'

'Men, sire? There is only the army. Five thousand.'

Parmenion fell silent. Back in the Sparta he knew there were the Sciritai, warriors from the mountains to the north-west of the city. But did they exist here?

'If we had to assemble a force that was not purely Spartan,' he said carefully, 'where would you look to find men?'

'There are none, sire. The Messenians have sided with Philippos. If we had time we could enlist the aid of the Cretans – but there is no time. We stand alone.'

'If every man in the city was given a sword, how many warriors would we count?'

'You mean if we armed the slaves?'

'Exactly.'

'Fifteen thousand . . . twenty. But they are not warriors, they would have no discipline. And afterwards – even if we won – how would we dispossess them of those weapons?'

'One step at a time, my friend. First we must win.'

'You think the Spartan army cannot win alone?' asked Nestus, his dark eyes angry.

'Given the right terrain, there is no force in all the world to equal us,' said Parmenion. 'But tell me, Nestus, where is such a terrain between here and Sparta? On open ground Philippos will surround us, his cavalry perhaps passing us by and raiding the city itself. And we cannot defend the city. We must bring Philippos to the battlefield and hold his entire army. We cannot do that with five thousand men.'

'Then what do we do?' Learchus demanded.

'As soon as we arrive back in Sparta you will gather all the slaves, and every Spartan man under the age of sixty-five and above the age of fifteen. Those slaves who agree to fight alongside us will be offered their freedom. Then it will be up to you to give them cursory training. We will have maybe five days, perhaps less.'

'Children, old men and slaves?' sneered Nestus. 'Perhaps we should surrender now.'

'If you are afraid,' said Parmenion softly, 'I will give you permission to remain at home with the women.'

All colour drained from the giant's face. 'You dare suggest. . . ?'

'I dare,' Parmenion told him. 'And I will have no faint-hearted man serve me.'

Nestus lurched to his feet, his sword snaking clear of its scabbard.

'No!' shouted Leonidas.

'Leave him be,' said Parmenion, rising smoothly but leaving his own sword sheathed.

'This is madness,' Learchus shouted. 'For Hera's sake, Nestus, put up your blade!'

'He called me a coward! I'll take that from no man.'

'Wrong, you arrogant whoreson!' snarled Parmenion. 'You will take it from me. Now you have two choices. The first is to use that sword; the second is to kneel and ask my forgiveness. Which will it be?'

Nestus stood still, aware that all eyes were upon him. In that awful moment he realized what he had done and the fate that awaited him. If he slew Parmenion – as he dearly wanted to – the others would fall upon him. But to kneel to the mix-blood!

'You brought it on yourself!' he shouted. 'You insulted me!'

'Two choices,' snapped Parmenion. 'Choose, or I'll kill you where you stand.'

For a moment Nestus hesitated, then he dropped the sword. 'On your knees!' roared Parmenion. The giant fell forward with head bowed. Parmenion ignored him, his gaze sweeping over the watching men. 'Is there another here who wishes to dispute my right to lead?'

'There is no one, sire,' said Leonidas softly. 'We are yours, heart and soul.'

Parmenion swung back to the kneeling Nestus. 'Get out of my sight!' he said. 'From this moment you will fight in the front rank. You have no command. Never open your mouth in my presence again.'

Nestus rose, stumbling back from the group of officers.

'That is all,' said Parmenion. 'Prepare to march in one hour.' Turning his back on them, he walked away into the wood.

Leonidas followed him. 'That should have been done three years ago,' he said. 'Your patience amazes me. But tell me, Parmenion, why now?'

'It was time. I am glad you are here, I need to talk with you. Look at me, Leonidas, and tell me what you see.'

'My King and my friend,' he answered, nonplussed.

'Look closely. Do I seem older, younger?'

'You are the same – maybe a little tired.'

Thena approached them and Parmenion turned to her. 'Deceit is not my way, Thena. I cannot do this.'

'You must,' she said.

'I want Leonidas to know the truth.'

She met his gaze and knew, without recourse to reading his mind, that argument would be futile. 'Then let me show him,' she pleaded. 'Then he will see it all.'

'As you wish.'

'What is happening here?' asked Leonidas. 'What is it that I do not know?'

'Sit down by that tree and close your eyes,' Thena commanded. 'All will be made known to you.'

Perplexed, Leonidas did as he was bid, sitting on the grass with his back to a slender cypress tree. Thena knelt before him and closed her eyes. Warmth like a hot summer breeze flowed through his mind and he found himself

278

gazing down on the city of Sparta from a great height. Yet it was not Sparta, he realized. There were subtle differences.

'What is this place?' he asked.

'Watch and learn,' Thena answered.

He saw the young Parmenion, hated and hunted, saw himself and his family. But nothing was right. The years fled on and he saw a duel between Parmenion and Nestus, watched the freeing of a city, experienced the defeat of a Spartan army and the death of a King.

Leonidas was entranced.

Then he saw Philippos and anger flared within him. Yet even here there were small changes. Philippos was called Philip and was possessed of no golden eye, no witchcraft to protect him. Events flowed by beneath his gaze – great battles, victories, defeats – until at last he saw the kidnap of the King's son and the journey of Parmenion to rescue him.

Derae's voice whispered into his mind. 'Prepare yourself, for what you are about to see will be painful.'

Once more the battle lines were assembled, the Kadmians on the right panicking and fleeing the field. He saw the King's horse bolt towards the western ridges.

'No,' he groaned as Parmenion fell, his throat slashed, his dead body crashing to the rocks. 'Oh, no!'

The man he served and loved was being buried now, his twin donning his armour and helm.

His vision swam and his eyes opened. At first he could not speak, then he shook his head. 'You are not my King,' he said softly.

'No,' admitted Parmenion.

'But he is the *strategos*,' Thena pointed out, laying her hand on Leonidas' arm.

He stood, drawing in several deep breaths. 'I knew something was wrong,' he whispered.

'I am sorry, Leonidas,' Parmenion told him. 'I did not wish this.'

'I know. I saw.'

'If you desire me to leave, I will do so,' said Parmenion. 'I do not relish the role of imposter.'

'Were the roles reversed my King would say the same.

He was a great man, kind and yet strong. That is why he tolerated Nestus. He felt he had done him harm and owed him a debt. What can I say? I do not know how to proceed.'

Thena stepped forward. 'You have lost a friend – a dear friend. Ask yourself what he would choose. Your Parmenion is dead, may the Source guide his soul. But this Parmenion is also a *strategos*. What would the King do?'

For a time Leonidas was silent, swinging away from them to stare through the trees. Then he spoke. 'You have been honest with me, Parmenion. For that I thank you. We will go to Sparta and raise the army. I do not see how we can win, but I will fight alongside you. But if we do survive you must leave us. You are not my . . . brother. It would be wrong for you to stay.'

'You have my word on it,' said Parmenion. 'Is there an oath you wish me to swear?'

'No oaths,' Leonidas told him. 'Your word – like my brother's – is promise enough.'

'Then we will continue with this . . . drama,' said Parmenion. 'I will need your help. There is much I do not know about this world and you must advise me, especially when we reach the city. Who are the ephors I can trust? Where are my enemies? Time is short.'

'You believe we can defeat Philippos?'

'I know I can nullify his sorcery. You and I will discuss the strategy. But it will still depend on the numbers we can raise.'

'I will do all that you ask of me. And you will remain King until the battle is decided.'

Leonidas offered his hand and Parmenion took it. 'Victory or death,' said the young Spartan.

'Victory is preferable,' Parmenion answered.

*

The Spartan smiled and moved away and Parmenion turned to Thena. 'You think I was wrong to tell him?'

She shook her head. 'No, you will need a friend in the city.'

'I have you.'

'No,' she said sadly, 'I will not come to Sparta. I shall ride south-west to the Giant's Gateway.'

'But I thought . . .'

'As did I. It was not to be.'

'I will . . . miss you, lady.'

'And I you. Is there a message for Attalus?'

'Yes. And for Brontes. Will you and I still be able to commune from such a distance?'

Thena nodded and stepped forward, taking his hand. 'Across worlds,' she promised.

They sat together for almost an hour as Parmenion outlined his plans. Then Leonidas returned. 'The men are ready,' he told them.

'As am I,' answered Parmenion.

The City of Sparta

Word of the defeat had reached the city, and there were no crowds to greet the returning soldiers as they marched in formation along Leaving Street to the marble-pillared palace.

'Stay close to me,' whispered Parmenion as the warriors returned to the nearby barracks and he and Leonidas entered the great gates, 'for I have never seen the inside of this place and it would not help our cause if I were to wander off and get lost.'

Leonidas grinned. 'There are six *androns* on the ground floor and the kitchens are ahead of you. Your quarters are up the first flight of stairs and to the right.'

Parmenion nodded and glanced at the luridly painted walls leading to the marble stairs. Battle-scenes were everywhere, filling the hall, and even the mosaic on the floor showed Spartan warriors in battle array. He smiled. 'Sparta does not change,' he said, 'even in another world.'

An elderly servant moved forward and bowed. 'Priastes,' whispered Leonidas.

'Welcome home, sire,' said Priastes. 'I have prepared you a bath and some refreshment.' The old man bowed once more and turned to the stairs, Parmenion and Leonidas following. The stairs were lined with statues of spear-carrying Spartan heroes from the past, none of whom Parmenion recognized. Priastes reached the top of the flight

282

and turned right into a wide corridor, opening a door to a series of east-facing rooms. Parmenion stepped inside, following the servant through to a small chamber where a bronze-plated hip-bath had been filled with hot, scented water. The servant unbuckled Parmenion's breastplate and the Spartan swiftly undressed.

The bath was a delight, the heat easing his tired muscles. Priastes poured watered wine into a golden wine-cup, first sipping it before passing it to his King.

'Thank you, Priastes, that will be all,' said Parmenion, lounging down into the bath. The man bowed and left. The new King scrubbed the dust of his travels from his skin and then rose from the bath. Leonidas handed him a towel which Parmenion wrapped around his waist before strolling out to the balcony beyond the main windows. A cool breeze whispered across his wet frame and he shivered. 'That feels good,' he told the Spartan warrior.

'It is always wise to remove the smell of stale sweat and horses before greeting your wife,' said Leonidas carefully.

'Wife? What wife?'

Leonidas took a deep breath. When the seeress Thena allowed him to see Parmenion's life in the other world of Greece, he had observed with sorrow the loss of his love. 'This will not be easy for you, Parmenion. In this world you married my sister, Derae.'

'She is here? In the palace?'

'Of course. But know this: she does not love you. She was to have wed Nestus, but duty came first and she married you to give you a link to the throne.'

Parmenion looked down at his hands; they were trembling. 'I don't think I can do this,' he whispered. 'You cannot know . . .'

'I know,' whispered Leonidas. 'Believe me, I know. But we have embarked on a course from which there is no turning back. Be strong, my friend. She will not wish to spend time with you. You will be able to avoid her. Tell yourself that she is not the woman you loved. This is a different world. Now,' he said gently, changing the subject, 'what are your battle plans?'

Parmenion shook his head, trying unsuccessfully to force thoughts of Derae from his mind. 'We will not discuss them in detail. Without Thena here I cannot know whether we are being observed.'

'We have our own seeress, Tamis. She is old, but once her powers were very strong. Shall I order her here?'

'Not yet. If she is gifted, she will know of my . . . deception. No. First summon the ephors. I will see them today. Bring her here in the morning. Now tell me, which of the ephors spoke against the battle with Philippos?'

'Chirisophus and Soteridas. They are very much the leaders of the council. Chirisophus is rich and many men live under his patronage, but Soteridas is also the chief priest at the Temple of Apollo, and it was his reading of the omens that prevented the full army from marching with us.'

'Can you find ten men with open minds and closed mouths?'

'Of course,' answered Leonidas. 'But why?'

'During the meeting I want you to have the houses of Chirisophus and Soteridas searched.'

'What do you expect them to find?'

'I hope to find nothing. But we must consider the possibility that one – or both – may be in the pay of Philippos. You and your men must seek links with the Makedones – letters, Makedones gold . . . anything.'

'It shall be as you say.'

'And send out riders to watch for the Makedones army.'

'Yes . . . sire.' The handsome Spartan bowed and backed away.

'Leonidas!'

'Sire?'

'I will do my utmost to be worthy of . . . him.'

'I do not doubt that, my friend. And I will be beside you.'

After Leonidas had gone Parmenion refilled his wine-cup and stood staring out over the eastern quarters of the city. From here he could see the market-place, where the food-sellers were just setting up their stalls. Several messengers were running along the narrow streets, carrying news of trade convoys or shipments to the merchants. Beyond the palace street cleaners were sweeping away the debris of yesterday, the sewage that flowed to the streets from the open clay pipes in every house; while high above the city, on the acropolis hill, the statue of Zeus gazed out over the mountains – stern, proud and forbidding.

Just under 40,000 people dwelt here, Leonidas had said, more than half of them slaves or servants. Parmenion's spirits were not high as he considered the coming battle.

It was not enough, he knew, to match the Makedones manpower. His twin had almost done that. No. Quality was the key . . . and surprise. But how do you surprise a man who knows what you intend? Was Philippos even now reading his mind?

The thought was not comforting.

The Makedones were coming, but how long before they reached the city? They had fought one battle a few days ago. It was likely that Philippos would let his troops rest, to enjoy the fruits of victory, the spoils and the plunder. Five days? Three?

He would not consider the Spartans a major threat – not with only 5,000 men. And the addition of a slave army would concern him not at all.

The door behind him opened and the scent of sweet perfume filled the air. He knew instantly who had entered and turned slowly, his heart palpitating, his mouth suddenly dry.

Derae stood before him, dressed in a gown of white bordered with gold. Her red hair was long, drawn back from her face in intricate braids. Her eyes were green, her skin burnished gold. His breath caught in his throat as she approached him. After all these years he was once more face to face with the woman he had loved and lost.

'Derae!' he whispered.

'You shamed Nestus,' she said, her eyes showing her fury, 'and I will hate you for as long as you live!'

*

Parmenion could not speak, the shock was too great. He felt his legs trembling and backed away from the balcony. For more than thirty years he had loved this woman. No, he tried to tell himself, not *this* Derae. But logic was useless against the vision before him. Her face and form had lived in his memory for three decades and the sight of her now unmanned him.

'Well, speak!' she demanded.

He shook his head and lifted the wine-cup, pulling his gaze from her, trying to break the spell.

'Have you nothing to say?'

Anger touched him then, flaring swiftly. 'Nestus is fortunate to be among the living,' he told her. 'And as for your hatred, lady, it will be shortlived. It is likely that we all have but five days to live. If you wish to spend those days with Nestus, go to him; you have my blessing.'

'Your blessing? That is something I have never had. I served your purpose: you wed me to become King, you stole my happiness – and now you give me your blessing. Well, a curse upon it! I do not need it.'

'Tell me what you need,' he said, 'and, if it is within my power, you shall have it.'

'There is nothing you can give me,' she answered, spinning on her heel and striding towards the door.

'Derae!' he called and she stopped, but did not turn. 'I have always loved you,' he said. 'Always.'

She faced him then, cheeks crimson and eyes blazing, but her anger died as she saw his expression. Without replying she backed away and fled the room.

Parmenion moved to a couch and sat, his thoughts sombre.

Soon the old servant, Priastes, returned to the King's quarters and bowed.

'What will you wear today, sire?' he asked.

'I will be garbed for battle,' answered Parmenion.

'Which breastplate do you desire?'

'I do not care,' he snapped. 'You choose, Priastes. Just bring it.'

'Yes, sire. Are you well?' the old man asked.

'Fine.'

'Ah,' said Priastes knowingly, 'but the Queen is angry.

The world is falling apart, but the Queen is angry. She is always so – why do you not take another wife, boy? Many kings have several wives . . . and she has given you no sons.' The old man obviously had a warm relationship with the King and Parmenion found the open friendliness comforting. He answered without thinking.

'I love the woman,' he said.

'You do?' responded Priastes, astonished. 'Since when? And why? I'll grant she has a fine body and good child-bearing hips. But, by Zeus, she has the foulest temper.'

'How long have you been with me, Priastes?'

'Sire?'

'How long? Exactly?'

'Exactly? You gave me my freedom after the battle at Orchomenus. When was that . . . the year of the Griffyn? The time has sped by since.'

'Yes, it has,' agreed Parmenion, none the wiser. 'Have I changed much in that time?'

'No,' said the old man, chuckling, 'you are still the same – shy and yet arrogant, both a poet and a warrior. This war has been hard on you, boy, you look older. Tired. Defeat does that to a man.'

'I'll try to see that it doesn't happen again.'

'And you'll succeed,' said Priastes, chuckling. 'All the oracles said you'd die in that battle, but I didn't believe them. That's my Parmenion, I said. There's no-one alive who can beat him. And I know you would have won but for those Kadmians. I hear you dealt with Nestus. About time. How long have I been telling you to do just that? Hmm?'

'Too long. Now fetch my armour – and then let me know when the ephors arrive.'

Priastes wandered away into a back room, emerging with a cuirass of baked black leather, edged with gold, and a kilt of bronze-reinforced leather strips. 'Will these suffice?'

'Yes. Bring me some food while I dress.'

'May I ask a favour, boy?'

'Of course.'

'Leonidas says you are asking every able-bodied man – including slaves – to take up swords in defence of the city.

287

Well, what about me? I'm only seventy-three and I am still strong. I'll stand beside you.'

'No,' answered Parmenion. 'The older men will be left to defend the city.'

Priastes stood his ground, his expression hardening. 'I would like to be with you . . . on the last day.'

Parmenion looked into the old man's grey eyes. 'You think I will die?' he asked softly.

'No, no,' answered Priastes, but he would not meet the King's gaze. 'I would just like to be there to share the glory of victory. I never had a son, Parmenion, but I've looked after you for nearly fifteen years. And I love you, boy. You know that?'

'I know. Then it will be as you say: you will come with me.'

'Thank you. Now I'll find some food for you. Cakes and honey? Or would you prefer some salted meat?'

*

While Priastes fetched the food Parmenion dressed, then wandered to the balcony. The Parmenion of this world had been a good man, he realized, caring and patient. Why else would he allow his servants to address him so informally? Why else would he have tolerated the insubordination of Nestus? Now an old man wanted nothing more than to die beside the man he loved. Parmenion sighed. 'You were a better man than I,' he whispered, staring up at the cloud-streaked sky.

Below the balcony and beyond the palace walls Sparta was beginning to stir. Slaves were moving towards the market-place and shops were opening, merchants displaying their wares on trestle-tables.

So like his own city, he thought. But here there was no Xenophon and no Hermias, he realized suddenly. His only friend in the Sparta of his own world, Hermias, had stood by him when all others felt only hatred and contempt for the mix-blood. Hermias, who had died at Leuctra, fighting on the opposite side.

'The ephors are ready, sire,' said Leonidas.

'Let him eat first,' snapped Priastes, moving in behind the Spartan officer.

Leonidas grinned. 'Like a she-wolf with her young,' he commented.

'Watch your tongue, boy, lest this old man cut it out for you,' retorted Priastes, setting a silver tray down before the King. Parmenion ate swiftly, washing down the honey-cakes with heavily-watered wine. Dismissing Priastes, he turned to Leonidas.

'I will not know the ephors,' he said, 'so I want you to greet them by name.'

'I will. And the men I have chosen are already on their way to the homes of Chirisophus and Soteridas. I will join them once the meeting is under way.'

'If you find anything incriminating, return to the palace and the discussions. Do not say anything, merely point at the guilty.'

'It will be as you say.'

'Good. Now lead me to the meeting.'

The two men walked from the King's quarters and down the statue-lined staircase to a long corridor. Servants bowed as they passed, and the sentries in the royal gardens stood to attention as the two men strolled across the grounds. They came at last to a set of double doors before which stood two soldiers, armed with spear and shield. Both warriors saluted, then laid aside their spears and pushed open the doors.

Parmenion stepped through into a huge *andron*. Couches were set around the walls and the floor was decorated with a magnificent mosaic showing the god, Apollo, riding an enormous leopard. The god's eyes were sapphires, the leopard's orbs fashioned from emeralds. Twelve columns on each side supported the roof, and the furniture was inlaid with gold. The six ephors rose as Parmenion entered. Leonidas moved among them and Parmenion listened as he spoke their names.

'Dexipus, I swear you are getting fatter day by day. How long since you attended the training ground, eh? . . . Ah, Cleander, any news yet of the shipment? I am relying on it to pay my gambling debts ... What's that, Lycon? Nonsense, I was just unlucky with the dice. I will win it back.'

Parmenion said nothing but moved to the large couch at the northern wall, stretching himself out and listening intently to the conversation. A man approached him – tall and broad-shouldered, wearing a simple blue tunic and a belt of black leather edged with silver thread. His hair was iron-grey, his eyes astonishingly blue.

'I am pleased to see you alive, sire,' he said, his voice deep and cold.

Leonidas moved alongside the man. 'We were also more than thankful, Soteridas,' he said. 'For had the King not caused the avalanche none of us would be here.'

'I heard of it,' said Soteridas, 'but it was such a small victory to set against so vast a defeat.'

'Indeed it was,' agreed Parmenion softly, locking his gaze to the man's eyes. 'But then defeat was assured, was it not, Soteridas?'

'What do you mean, sire?'

'Did you not predict it? Did you not claim the omens were against us? Now, enough idle talk, let us begin!'

Parmenion looked around the room and Soteridas moved back to sit alongside Chirisophus, a dark-haired man with a powerful, jutting jaw. He wore robes of shimmering green, and a golden torc gleamed at his throat.

'Today,' said Parmenion, 'we have only one question to answer: What now for Sparta?'

Leonidas bowed and backed away, the doors swinging shut behind him.

'Surely,' said Chirisophus, spreading his hands, 'there is only one response? We seek terms with Philippos. We cannot now stand against him.'

'I agree,' put in Soteridas. 'The Makedones King is unbeatable – as even our own *strategos* has now found.'

'It irks me to vote for such a course,' said Dexipus, a short swarthy warrior, balding and bearded, 'but I do not see how we can stand against him. On numbers alone he could envelop our flanks, forcing us in to a fighting square and winning merely by using his javeliners and archers.'

'I say we fight him anyway,' roared Cleander. Parmenion was surprised that a voice of such power could emanate from so skeletal a frame; Cleander was thin to the point of emaciation, his skin yellow and his eyes rheumy. 'What else can we do, my brothers? We are not dealing with an enemy King but with a demonic force. Surrender will not save us from the horrors of such a man. Better to die in battle.'

'With respect, Cleander,' said Chirisophus, 'you are dying anyway. All of us regret that, but you have less to lose than others in the city – the women and the children, for example.'

'Yes, I am dying, but that is not why I say we must fight. Our children will be no more safe than the children of Kadmos. We face the full force of evil here; there can be no compromise.'

'There is a great deal of exaggeration in any war,' said Chirisophus. 'Always the enemy is depicted as a beast. Philippos is a warrior King – unbeaten, invincible – but he is a man, no more than that.'

'I would disagree,' said another voice and Parmenion swung to see the speaker. He was Lycon, the youngest of the ephors, a good-looking youth in his mid-twenties, dark-haired and dark-eyed. 'I have met the Makedones King and I saw what he did at Methone and Plataea. I agree with Cleander: we must fight him.'

An argument began. 'Enough!' roared Parmenion. A tall thick-set man with a heavy black beard was sitting at the far end of the room and the King turned to him. 'You have not spoken yet, Timasion. Do you have nothing to offer?'

Timasion shrugged. 'I am undecided, sire. My heart says fight, my head says hold. Might I ask what the omens predict?'

Soteridas rose, bowing first to the King and then to the other ephors. 'Today,' he said, 'we sacrificed a goat to All-father Zeus. Its liver was spotted, its belly cancerous. Death and destruction will follow any attempt to make war on Philippos. The gods are against us.'

'As they were at Mantinea?' ventured Parmenion.

'Indeed, sire,' the chief priest agreed.

'It was an interesting battle,' said Parmenion. 'We broke their attack and almost took their centre. But even three hundred Spartans could not carry the victory. Of course, it is even more interesting to speculate what might have happened had we pushed ahead with five thousand Spartans.'

'The gods spoke against such a plan,' Soteridas pointed out.

'So you informed us. I find it curious that the gods of . . . Achaea . . . should choose to side with the Demon King. But then I am not a seer, and it is not for me to question the wisdom of Zeus. Tell me, Chirisophus, how you would appease the Makedones King and save Sparta?'

'You cannot consider this!' Cleander stormed.

'Silence!' thundered Parmenion. 'I wish to hear Chirisophus. Your turn will come again, Cleander.'

Chirisophus rose and began to speak, his voice smooth, his words comforting. There would be, he said, an ambassadorial delegation to Philippos offering fraternal friendship and lasting peace. Gifts could be taken. Philippos was known as a great horseman and Chirisophus himself would donate his prize Thracian stallions. War would thus be avoided and Sparta would be allied to the strongest nation in the world. He spoke for some time, finally pointing out that Philippos – being a warrior King – would inevitably lead his armies north and west, seeking to conquer the Etruscans and the Achaean cities of Italia. Further west even than this were the fabled lands of the Gauls, where buildings were constructed of gold and gems, and their Kings were said to be immortal. 'By suing for peace now,' Chirisophus ventured, 'we will in fact rid Achaea of Philippos all the sooner. I will naturally offer myself to lead the delegation,' he added, settling himself down on his couch.

'Naturally!' snorted Cleander.

At that moment Leonidas entered the room. Parmenion, the only man facing the doors, waited for his signal. When he pointed to Chirisophus and Soteridas, Parmenion nodded. Armed men moved into the room, walking slowly to stand behind the couches on which lay the traitors. Chirisophus swallowed hard, his face reddening.

'What is happening here, sire?' Cleander asked.

'Be patient,' the King told him. 'We stand at the edge of the abyss. A great evil stalks the land. We had an opportunity to rid the world of this evil, but we were thwarted, for the agents of Philippos are everywhere.' He paused, allowing his gaze to rest on the two traitors. Parmenion felt rage mounting within him. These men had caused the death of the Spartan King, and thousands of others on the field of Mantinea. He wanted nothing more than to walk across the room and cleave his sword through their foul hearts. Calming himself, he spoke again. 'It is the nature of Darkness to corrupt, and men of weak will, or men of lust and greed, will always be susceptible. Chirisophus and Soteridas have betrayed their city, their people and their King. They entered into secret negotiation with Philippos and they conspired to see the Demon King victorious at Mantinea. I do not know what they were offered for this treachery. I do not care. They have tried to doom us all and their crimes are written in blood.'

Chirisophus pushed himself to his feet, while Soteridas sat, all colour draining from his face.

'What I did was for Sparta!' Chirisophus insisted. 'There is no question of treachery. Philippos was always the ultimate victor; only a fool would try to deny him. But that is the past and it is foolish to dwell on it. I am the only man who can save the city. Philippos trusts me and will deal with me fairly. Without me you cannot survive. Think on that!'

'I have thought on it,' said Parmenion. 'Sparta will fight – and Sparta will win. But you – and your lickspittle priest – will not live to see it. Leonidas!'

'Sire?'

'Remove these . . . creatures. Take them to a place of execution. Do it at once and see their bodies are left in unmarked graves.'

Chirisophus backed away from the guards behind him and moved out into the mosaic floor. 'Do not be fools!' he shouted. 'I can save you!'

Suddenly he drew a dagger from his robe and rushed at Parmenion. The King rolled to his feet, his sword snaking from its scabbard and plunging through the shimmering green robe. Chirisophus grunted and fell back. Parmenion tore his sword clear of the dying man, and bright arterial blood soaked through the green silk. Chirisophus fell to his knees, hands clenched to his belly, then his eyes glazed and he toppled to his side. Several soldiers dragged the body back across the mosaic, leaving a trail of blood. Soteridas remained where he was, his face void of expression, until two soldiers took him by the arms and led him away.

'By the gods, sire!' whispered Cleander. 'I cannot believe it. His was a true Spartiate family. A noble house . . . a line of heroes.'

'To judge a man purely by his blood-line is folly,' said Parmenion. 'I have known the sons of cowards to be valorous, and sons of thieves who could be trusted with the treasure of nations. Such treachery is not of the blood, Cleander, but of the soul.'

'What now, lord?' asked Leonidas.

'Now? We prepare for war.'

*

Two days ride to the south-west of the city Attalus raised his arm to halt the company, then gazed around at the forbidding landscape – rockstrewn and jagged, thinly wooded and laced with streams. During their travels they had passed few villages in this inhospitable land, but had stopped at several lonely farms where they had been given food and grain for the horses.

Attalus was uneasy: the hunters were closing in. Helm had been the first to spot the pursuers, late the day before, when the setting sun had glinted from the lance-points of a large cavalry unit, perhaps an hour behind them. Through the heat haze Attalus had been unable to make out individual riders, but there were at least fifty.

Ektalis rode alongside the Macedonian, pointing at a dust-cloud to the west. 'Riders,' said the Korinthian. 'Probably Messenians. They serve the Tyrant.'

The company veered east and south, riding long into the night. But the horses were tired, and when the moonlight was lost behind unseasonal clouds Attalus was forced to call a halt. They made cold camp in a cluster of boulders on a hillside, where Ektalis set sentries and most of the company slept. But not Attalus.

Helm found him sitting alone, watching the trail to the north.

'You should rest,' the warrior advised.

'I cannot. Thoughts, plans, fears – they fly around my mind like angry wasps.'

'How far to the woods of the Enchantment?' asked Helm, moonlight gleaming eerily from his metal face.

'Another day – so Brontes told us.'

'Well, we have two chances,' said Helm, rising. 'Succeed or die.'

'Very comforting,' snapped Attalus.

'I find it so,' answered Helm, smiling and moving back amongst the boulders to sleep.

Silence surrounded the Macedonian, and a cool wind whispered across his face. For an hour he sat alone, miserable and dejected. Then the sound of a walking horse jerked him from his reverie. Rising smoothly, he drew his sword. Why had the sentries not warned them? The horse moved into the boulders and Thena dismounted.

Attalus sheathed his blade and moved to her side. 'Where is Parmenion?' he asked.

'In Sparta, raising an army.'

'Why? He should be here with us. Let the Spartan King fight his own battles.'

'Parmenion *is* the Spartan King.'

'What madness is this?'

'I am thirsty. Fetch me some water and then we will talk,' Thena told him, moving away to sit on the hillside. He did as she asked, then sat beside her as she drank. Slowly she explained the events leading to Parmenion's decision, and the problems he faced.

'But there is no hope of victory,' said Attalus. 'I am no *strategos*, Thena, but even I know that the first object of battle is to contain the enemy flanks. If you cannot do that, then you will be encircled and destroyed. Five thousand men cannot contain the army we saw on the plain.'

'I know that,' she answered wearily.

'Are you saying he will die there? Why? In the name of Hecate, why?'

'He is a man of honour.'

'Honour? What has honour to do with it? He owes these people nothing. His duty is to Alexander, and to his King.'

'But Alexander is in your care – and Parmenion trusts you.'

'Well, a curse on him! Does he think he is a god that he can conquer any who stand in his way? Philippos will destroy him.'

Thena rubbed at her tired eyes. 'Parmenion wants you to take Alexander on to the woods and locate Brontes. Once there, we will discuss a plan he has.'

'If this plan involves Alexander and me returning to Macedonia, I will support it – but do not expect me to ride to the city or take part in any ill-fated battle against the Demon King.'

A cold wind brushed against Attalus' back and a sibilant voice made his skin crawl. 'How wise of you,' it hissed. Attalus spun, his sword flashing into his hand. Before him hovered a pale form, seemingly shaped from mist. Slowly it hardened to become a broad-shouldered man, bearded and powerful, whose right eye shone like gold. Thena sat silently, saying nothing. 'Ah, Attalus,' whispered Philippos, 'how curious to find you set against me. Everything in your heart and soul tells me you are mine. You should be marching with me. I can offer you riches, women, lands, empires. And why do you oppose me? For a child who will one day kill you. Give him to me, and his threat to you will be at an end.'

'I do not serve you,' answered Attalus, his voice hoarse.

'No, you serve a lesser version of me. You follow a man. Here you can follow a god. The idea pleases you, does it not? Yes, I can read it in your heart. Palaces, Attalus, nations under your sway. You can be a king.'

'His promises are worth nothing,' said Thena, but her words sounded shrill and empty.

'He knows,' said Philippos. 'He knows I speak the truth; he knows that warriors with his talents will always earn the hatred and envy of lesser men. Even Philip will turn on him one day. But here – with me – he can have his soul's desire. Is that not so, Attalus?'

'Yes,' answered the swordsman. 'I could serve you.'

'Then do so. Bring the child to me. Or wait until my riders arrive. Either way I will reward you.'

The Demon King shimmered, his form fading. Attalus turned to Thena. 'We cannot defeat him. We cannot.'

'What will you do?'

'Leave me alone, Thena. I need to think.'

'No,' she said, 'that is what you do *not* need. You need to feel. He called Philip a lesser man. Do you agree with that?'

'It does not matter whether I agree or disagree. In life there is only winning and losing. Philippos is a winner.'

'Winning and losing? Life is not a race,' she told him. 'A man who never loses a battle but ends his life alone and unloved has not won. Whatever you may say to the contrary, that is something you understand. If you did not, you would not have served Philip so faithfully. Be honest, Attalus, you love the man.'

'Yes, I do,' he shouted, 'and that makes me as big a fool as Parmenion. But here I could be a king!'

'Indeed you could. All you have to do is betray Philip and see his son murdered.'

Attalus fell silent for a moment, his head bowing. 'I have betrayed men before,' he said softly. 'It is not so hard.'

'Ah, but have you ever betrayed a friend?' asked Helm, moving from the shadows.

'I never had any friends,' answered Attalus.

'What about this . . . Philip?'

Attalus sighed. 'He trusts me. He knows what I am and what I have done, yet he trusts me. He even calls me his friend.' Suddenly he laughed, the sound full of bitterness. 'And I am. I would die for the man . . . and I probably will.'

'Well,' said Helm, 'if the discussion is over I would like to get back to sleep.'

Attalus turned to Thena. 'I will not betray the boy.'

She rose, moving to stand before him. 'You are a better man than you know,' she told him.

*

Derae looked into the man's pale eyes. He shook his head. 'I am what I am,' he told her. She watched as he walked back into the boulders to lie alone. Briefly she reached out, soothing his fears and bringing him the sanctuary of sleep.

Her spirits were curiously lifted. Philippos had been wrong. He had read Attalus, and read him right, yet still he had made a mistake. It was the first small gap in the Demon King's armour of invincibility. The Tyrant had failed.

Derae could scarce believe it. Of all the men who could be swayed, the bitter hate-filled Attalus should have been the simplest of victims. Yet he had resisted the promises, even though the dark side of his character cried out to accept.

The priestess sat down, resting her back against a boulder. In the moment that Philippos had appeared she had linked with Attalus, intending to strengthen him, to help him. But there had been no need. There was in the Macedonian one tiny shimmering thread, glowing in the darkness of his soul: his love for Philip.

From where did it come, Derae wondered? Attalus was capable of almost any evil, yet he had proved himself incorruptible. She smiled.

'It is a fine night,' said Helm, seating himself beside her.

'I thought you needed sleep.'

He nodded. 'Sleep without dreams is akin to death, lady.'

'Have you remembered anything of your life?'

'No.'

'You seem very calm. I would not like to be robbed of my past.'

He smiled, the metallic skin stretching, showing teeth of bronze. 'But I do not know what that past is, or was. There is a kind of tranquillity in the lack of knowledge. Perhaps I

298

was an evil man. Perhaps there are deeds in my past that would shame me.'

'I sense no evil in you, Helm.'

'But then the world shapes us, Thena, evil begetting evil. If a man grows with hatred in his heart, then his actions will be governed by that hatred. Like Attalus, perhaps. I have no memories. I am unshaped.'

'The core of you is unchanged,' she said. 'You rescued Iskander, risking your life. And you understand friendship and loyalty.'

'But then the boy can free me from this . . . spell. That gives me a selfish reason to fight for him.'

'My life has been long,' said Derae, 'longer than this youthful body shows. It is my experience that evil thrives when men and women are weak. You are not weak. Trust me. I do not say you were a good man, or a holy one – your skill with the sword belies that. But you are not evil.'

'We shall see,' he answered.

*

Parmenion stood with Leonidas and Learchus at the north entrance to the training grounds, watching dispassionately as the slaves, servants and old men filed past them. Officers moved among the men, greeting old comrades and directing veterans to the west of the area where hundreds of swords, shields and spears had been piled against the walls.

In the distance Parmenion could hear the pounding of hammers as the city's armourers worked feverishly to produce more weapons, arrowheads and blades, spearpoints and helms.

'How many men so far?' asked the King.

'Four thousand,' answered Leonidas, 'but the training grounds will not take too many more. Those here this morning are from the south and east of the city. We have asked the . . . volunteers . . . from the north and west to assemble this afternoon.'

'How can we judge so many?' Learchus enquired. 'And how do we instill discipline into them in less than two days?'

'I wish to see only two skills imparted to the slaves,'

Parmenion told him. 'Those we choose must learn to stand in wide line battle order, and to move into close formation for an attack.'

'But that will be of little use,' pointed out Leonidas. 'No matter how good their formation at the onset, once the order to advance is given the lines will break. They will become what they are – a rabble.'

'I know that. But drill them in the two formations. When the order is given I want them to move as smoothly into place as the finest of Spartan warriors. Also find five hundred men who can use bows; we will need them to turn back the Makedones cavalry.'

'It will be as you order, sire,' said Leonidas.

'Good. I will return around mid-morning to supervise the training.'

'Do you want me with you, sire, when you see Tamis?' asked Leonidas.

'No,' he answered, with a wry smile. 'If she is good she will understand all. If she does not, then she can be of little use to us.'

The palace was all but deserted when Parmenion rode in through the main gates. All the male servants – bar Priastes – were at the training ground. Dismounting by the stables Parmenion led the grey mare into a paddock and pulled clear the leopardskin chabraque, which he hung over a rail. The mare whinnied and galloped around the paddock fence, tossing her head and rearing, announcing her presence to the stallions in the small meadow beyond.

Parmenion strolled into the palace, shouting for Priastes, and the old man came running from the upper rooms.

'The seeress, Tamis, is expected. Bring her to my quarters.'

'Yes, sire, but would it not be better to see her in the western gardens?'

'You think my quarters unfit for a seeress?'

'No, sire,' answered Priastes reproachfully, 'but the lady is very old and the stairs very steep. The garden will be cool and I will bring you wine and fruit.'

Parmenion smiled assent and walked down the long, cool

corridor to the western gardens. They were well laid out, with winding paths and small fountains built around four willows, their branches trailing in man-made streams. Several marble seats had been set in the shade and here Parmenion stretched out his frame, easing the muscles of his neck and back. He was tired and on edge. The night before had been spent in meetings – first with Leonidas, then the dying Cleander and the other ephors. At dawn he was still awake, discussing strategies with the Barracks Masters whose youngsters he had called upon. There were 2,000 boys over the age of fifteen, and for them he had a special purpose.

Now the sun was two hours short of noon and Parmenion's eyes were gritty and sore, his back aching with the weight of the breastplate.

Priastes brought embroidered cushions which he scattered on the bench, then returned with a stone pitcher of cooled wine and a bowl of fruit – oranges, pomegranates and apples – which he set down before the King.

'You should sleep for a while,' said the old man.

'I will . . . soon.'

It was restful here and he leaned back against the soft cushions and closed his eyes to think. So many plans to be laid, so many stratagems to consider, so many. . . .

He awoke in a moonlit meadow, refreshed and alert. He was without armour and the night breeze was pleasantly cool upon his body.

'Welcome, Parmenion,' said a voice. He sat up and saw an old woman sitting beneath a spreading oak.

'Where are we?' he asked.

'In a neutral place, far from wars and the threat of war. How are you feeling?'

'Rested. Are you the Tamis I knew, back in my own Sparta?'

'No. But then you are not the Parmenion I have known. What can I do to aid you? I must tell you that I will not kill, nor will I help you to kill.'

'Can you shield me from the golden eye?'

'If that is what you wish.'

301

'I must know also when we are being observed. That is vital.'

'Your meeting with the ephors, and the deaths of Chirisophus and Soteridas, were seen. As was the training this morning.'

'Last night with Cleander?'

'I do not know. But you must assume that Philippos is aware of your plans.'

'Can he see us now?'

'No,' answered Tamis. 'This is but a dream. Everything you say here is known only to me, and you, and the Source of All Creation.'

'Good. Where is the boy?'

'He and his companions are close to the Lands of the Enchantment. But they are in great danger. More than a hundred Messenian riders are waiting for them, and more follow.'

'Can we do anything to aid them?'

'No.'

Parmenion took a deep breath and pushed his fears for Alexander from his mind, concentrating only on the defence of Sparta. 'It is vital that we are not observed leaving the city. All our hopes rest on that. Yet I do not want Philippos to be aware that his . . . view . . . has been restricted. You understand?'

'No,' Tamis admitted.

'My strategy must needs be simple, for I will be leading a fledgling force. I am obliged to depend on Philippos for the victory. He will know that I have an army of slaves, children and old men, built around the power of the Spartan phalanx. His strategy will be based on that knowledge. My only hope . . . *our* only hope . . . is to fool him.'

'In what way?'

'I require him to attack my strongest point.'

'What has this to do with the army leaving Sparta?'

'I would sooner not say at this time, lady. I mean no offence.'

'I understand,' she said softly. 'You do not know me, Parmenion, and therefore you hold back your trust. That is

302

wise. I have a gift for you that will help; you will find it upon your return to the world of the flesh. When it glows warm you will know you are being observed, and all the time that you wear it no evil force can enter your mind, nor know of your thoughts.'

He awoke feeling rested, his body free of aches and pains. Sitting up, he looked around and saw the sun was still well short of noon. Filling his wine-cup, he sipped the drink which was still cool. Priastes moved into the garden, stopping and bowing before him.

'Sad news, lord,' he said. 'Tamis will not be coming. She died last night.'

Parmenion cursed softly and was about to speak when he felt a warm glow at his throat. His hand came up, his fingers touching the necklet he now wore.

'Thank you, Priastes, that will be all.'

'Can we win without her aid?' the old man asked.

'No,' answered the King. Standing, he strode from the gardens, returning to his apartments. A shining mirror of bronze was set into the wall and he halted before it. The necklet was of gold strands, interwoven around a fragment of golden stone laced with black veins.

It was still warm. Parmenion saw a movement in the mirror, a misty figure that hovered below the painted ceiling, but even as he looked upon it the figure shimmered and disappeared.

The warmth of the necklet faded.

'Thank you, Tamis,' he whispered.

*

'It is very dispiriting,' said Leonidas as he and Learchus moved into the small *andron* where Parmenion awaited them. There were only five couches here, set around a raised mosaic floor bearing the image of the goddess Artemis turning the hunter Actaeon into a stag. Leonidas sat down. 'So many men with so little talent,' he observed. Removing his helm, he laid it on the floor at his feet and swung up his legs to stretch out on the couch. Priastes filled two wine-cups, passing them to the young officers.

'It would take months,' put in Learchus, with a sigh. 'And even then . . .'

Parmenion looked at the two men and forced a smile. 'You expect too much,' he told them. 'This was only the first day. For myself I am pleased with the progress. The bowmen look promising and I am impressed with the officer responsible for their training . . . Daricles? A good man. Tomorrow it will be better.'

'It will need to be,' said Cleander, from the doorway. 'Our scouts report that Philippos is preparing to march.'

Parmenion rose, ushering the ephor into the room. Cleander's face was drenched in sweat, his eyes glowing with the brightness of fever.

'Sit down, my friend,' said Parmenion gently, leading him to a couch. 'I see that you are suffering.'

'The end is near,' Cleander whispered. 'My surgeon tells me I will not live to see the battle. I will prove him wrong.'

'Yes, you will,' agreed Parmenion. 'You *must*. For you will be in charge of the city's defence. The older veterans and the youngsters will be under your command. I want most of the streets barricaded, except for Leaving Street and the Avenue of Athena.'

'But they lead to the *agora*,' Learchus pointed out. 'The enemy cavalry will simply ride to the centre of the city.'

'Which is where I want them,' said Parmenion, his expression cold. 'That is where they will die in their hundreds.'

The planning went on deep into the night, until at last Cleander fell asleep and the two Spartan officers made their way to the Royal Barracks. Priastes covered the sleeping Cleander with a woollen blanket and Parmenion left the room and climbed to his quarters.

The moon was high, but despite his weariness the Spartan could not sleep. His thoughts were with Attalus and Alexander, and he was concerned that Thena had not made contact. Fear rose in him, but he pushed it away. One problem at a time, he warned himself.

Priastes had left a pitcher of cool water and some fruit by the bedside. Parmenion swung his legs from the bed and drank. The night air was cool on his naked skin as he walked to the balcony to stare out over the sleeping city.

He thought of Philip and Macedonia, of Phaedra and his sons. So far away . . . so impossibly far away.

You cannot win, said the voice of his thoughts.

He saw again the slaves crashing into one another as they tried to follow the shouted orders. Three men had been seriously injured during the afternoon. One had tripped and fallen on a sword; a second had moved the wrong way, colliding with another man and falling badly, breaking his leg; a third had been hit in the shoulder by a carelessly loosed arrow. Not an auspicious beginning for the new army of Sparta.

He thought of the men he had trained back in Macedonia – Theoparlis, Coenus, Nicanor . . . and imagined them leading their divisions through the gateways to stand alongside him against the Tyrant. 'I'd give ten years of my life to see that,' he whispered.

But this thought he also forced from his mind. Concentrate on what you have, he ordered himself. Five thousand of the finest warriors. Spartans. No battle could be called lost while such men stood ready.

Do not try to fool yourself.

He heard the door of his room open and smelt Derae's sweet perfume.

'I have neither the time nor the energy to fight with you, lady,' he said as she entered. Her hair was unbraided, hanging loose to her shoulders, and she wore only a long linen robe embroidered with gold.

'I do not wish to fight,' she told him. 'How goes the training?'

He shrugged. 'We will see,' he answered. Having spent the day motivating his officers, he was not surprised to find he had little strength left to lie.

'Why did you say you loved me?' she asked, moving to stand before him on the balcony.

'Because it was true,' he said simply.

'Then why have you never said it before?'

He could not reply. He merely stood gazing down at her

face in the moonlight, drinking in the living beauty, scanning every contour. She was older than the Derae of his dreams and memories, yet still youthful, her lips full, her skin soft. He was almost unaware of his hands moving up to rest gently on her shoulders, his fingers sliding under the robe, stroking her skin and feeling the warmth of her body.

'No,' she whispered, pulling back from him. 'That is no answer.'

'I know,' he told her, letting fall his arms and walking past her into the room.

'In two years you have never called for me, never asked me to share your bed. Now – with Sparta facing ruin – you tell me you love me. There is no sense in it.'

He smiled then. 'We are in agreement on that,' he admitted. 'Would you like some wine?' She nodded and he filled two golden cups, not bothering to add water. Silently he handed her a wine-cup, then lay down on the long sofa by the balcony wall. Derae sat in a chair opposite him.

For a time they remained in silence, sipping their drinks. 'Do you truly love Nestus?' he asked.

She shook her head and smiled. 'Once I thought I did, when my father first arranged the marriage. But the more time we spent together, the more I saw how boorish and arrogant he was.'

'Then why did you defend him so fiercely?'

'He was what you took from me,' she answered. 'You understand?'

'I think so. A marriage to Nestus would at least have been consummated, and you would have had a role to play. Instead you were used by a cold-hearted general who sought to be King. What a fool I have been!'

'Why did you never ask me to share your bed? Was the thought so painful?'

'Let us not talk of past bitterness, nor past stupidity. The man I was died at Mantinea; the man I am may be dead within a few days. This is the present, Derae. This is all there ever is in life. This is now.' Swinging his legs from the couch he stood, holding out his hand to her. She took it and he drew her towards him, then leaned down and gently kissed her cheek. Suppressed passion made him tremble and he longed to tear the robe from her body and carry her to the bed. Yet he did not. He stroked the skin of her neck and shoulders, then pushed his fingers through her red-gold hair. She moved into him and he felt the warmth of her body through the robe. His hands slid down her back to rest on her hips and her head came up. Tenderly he kissed her lips.

Her arms moved around him, fingers tracing the lines of tired muscle on his back. As she touched him warmth flowed into his frame, relaxing him. 'You have healing hands,' he whispered.

'Don't speak,' she replied, rising on tiptoe to kiss him again. He parted the robe, pushing it from her shoulders to fall to the floor, then felt her breasts against his chest, the nipples hard against his skin.

He carried her to the bed, then lay beside her – his right hand stroking her flank, tracing an invisible line along the outside of her thigh. Slowly he reversed the movement, this time along the inside, his hand coming to rest against soft, silken hair. She moaned as his finger slid gently inside her. Parmenion was almost beyond conscious thought. Desire was everything. Not the crazed, lustful desire that had seen him bed Olympias on that terrible night, but the desire born of a lifetime of suppressed feelings and empty dreams. She was here. Not dead, not white bleached bones at the bottom of the sea, but here! The love he had lost a lifetime ago was his again.

Images from the past kaleidoscoped through his brain as he rose above her, feeling her legs slide over his hips. The five glorious days in Olympia when the sun shone in glory, the sky was brilliant turquoise and two young lovers ignored the world and its laws. He saw again the smile of the young Derae, heard her laughter echoing in the mountains.

Together again! His passion mounted and he was suddenly, blissfully, oblivious to his surroundings. There was no Demon King, no army of terror. There were no Gateways between worlds, no sorcerers, no futures.

The *now* was everything.

Derae's back arched and she cried out again and again. But he did not stop . . . could not stop. And when the passion was too great to contain, and he felt as if his soul were flowing from him, he lost consciousness –falling into a darkness so sweet and so fulfilling that, in his last moment of conscious thought, he never wanted to wake.

The Hills of Gytheum

Attalus plunged his sword into an attacker's chest, wrenching it clear and pushing the body back over the boulders. A second man climbed into sight, hurling a short javelin at the Macedonian. Attalus threw himself aside and the missile tore into the back of a Korinthian warrior fighting alongside Helm.

Recovering his balance Attalus rushed at the javeliner, but the man ducked from sight.

'Come on, you sons of dogs!' Attalus yelled. 'Where are you?'

But the Messenians pulled back from the fort of boulders, dragging their wounded with them. Attalus spun round, scanning the defenders. Three Korinthians were dead, four others badly wounded. The seeress was helping to heal the more serious injuries, while Alexander sat calmly by, his young face expressionless.

Attalus wiped away the blood from a shallow cut in his forehead and moved alongside Helm. 'How many?' he asked.

'Twelve we have killed, with maybe six others unable to fight again.'

'Not enough,' Attalus muttered.

'We'll kill some more soon,' said Helm.

Attalus chuckled. 'I am beginning to like you. It is a shame we are to die here.'

'We're not dead yet,' the warrior pointed out.

Ektalis joined them. 'We won't be able to hold this position for much longer. Already we are stretched.'

'I can see that!' snapped Attalus. 'Are you suggesting surrender?'

'No, I am merely stating the obvious. One more concerted attack and they will breach the circle. Once inside we cannot hold them.'

'You have a plan?'

'We could make a run for it. Once in the woods they would find it hard to track us.'

Attalus climbed to the nearest boulder, his gaze resting on the woods less than a mile distant. So close – and yet the trees might as well be growing across the ocean, for more than thirty warriors were waiting below and their mounts were Attic stock – several hands taller than the Makedonian and Korinthian horses, and much faster. 'We would not make half the distance,' he told Ektalis, 'and once on the plain they would take us singly.'

'Then we must fight and die,' said the Korinthian.

Attalus bit back an angry response and merely nodded. They had escaped the first of the riders but been cut off by this second group. Helm had spotted the circle of boulders and here they had made their stand.

But to fail in sight of the woods! Attalus felt his fury rise. This was all Parmenion's fault. Had he remained with them none of this would have happened. But no: he had to play his hero's game.

'There are more coming,' said Helm and Attalus looked to the north. A dust-cloud heralded at least fifty more Messenian riders.

The swordsman swore. 'Let them all come. What difference does it make? Thirty was too many anyway. It might as well be eighty – or a hundred and eighty.' He swore again.

Below them the Messenians waited for their comrades and Attalus watched as the two enemy officers moved away from the men to discuss strategy. The sun was beginning to set, the sky turning flame-red over the distant mountains.

Thena approached Attalus. 'I shall take Alexander to the woods,' she said, keeping her voice low.

'They will capture you,' he argued.

'They will not see us,' she told him wearily. 'I cannot do the same for you and the others. My powers have been drained, but even at their height they would not have veiled such a large group.'

Attalus turned away, his emotions boiling with a murderous rage. 'Take him!' he said. 'Take him and be damned!'

For a moment only the priestess stood her ground, then she backed away and led Alexander to the horses, lifting the prince into place and mounting behind him. The Korinthians watched her in silence and Helm strolled to stand beside the mount.

'Where are you going?' he asked softly.

'To the woods. No one will stop me.'

'The boy is important to me. If he is lost, I will die without a past.'

'I know. Yet his destiny is greater than your desire.'

'Not to me, lady.'

'Then you must make a choice, Helm,' she told him, her voice neutral, her expression serene. 'You can draw your sword and stop me. But then the Demon King will have the child. For you cannot hold this hill against the warriors who surround it.'

'That is true enough,' he admitted. 'Ah well, go in peace, lady.' He lifted his hand and patted Alexander's leg. 'I hope you succeed in your quest, boy. I'd hate to die for nothing.'

Alexander nodded, but spoke no word.

Thena tugged on the reins and the horse moved out between the boulders, walking slowly down the hillside. Attalus, Helm and the Korinthians watched her as she rode in plain sight towards the Messenians. No one moved to stop her, nor showed any sign that they could see her, and the Makedonian mare walked through the enemy camp and on towards the trees.

Attalus pulled a whetstone from his hip pouch and began to sharpen his sword.

'Well, at least the enemy have been thwarted,' said Helm.

'That is great consolation to me,' hissed Attalus.

'Are you always this disagreeable?' the warrior responded.

'Only when I am about to die.'

'I see. You don't think we can win, then?'

Attalus swung to face the man, his fury close to madness. Then he saw the wide smile on the metallic face, the mocking look in the bronze eyes. All tension fled from the Macedonian and he smiled with genuine humour. 'How about a wager?' he offered.

'On what?' asked Helm.

'That I slay the most.'

'With what shall we wager? I have no coin.'

'Neither have I. So let's say a thousand gold pieces?'

'You have already killed three to my two,' Helm pointed out. 'I think we should start even, and count them only from the next attack.'

'It is agreed, then?'

'Absolutely,' said Helm.

'They are coming!' yelled Ektalis.

*

The priestess rode into the shadows of the trees and halted her mount. Alexander was silent, stiff-backed, his body rigid with tension. Gently her Talent reached out to him.

'Leave me!' came the command, with a burst of spiritual energy so powerful that the priestess swayed in the saddle and cried out. The sound of hoofbeats came from all around them as centaurs moved clear of the undergrowth with bows in their hands, arrows notched to the strings.

'Welcome, Iskander,' said one who was tall, white-bearded and maned, his golden skin merged into palomino flanks, his tail long and whiter than fleece clouds. 'My name is Estipan. Follow me and I will take you to the Giant's Gateway.'

'No,' answered Alexander. 'You think I will restore the Enchantment while my friends and those who serve me are

312

dying within my sight? You have watched the battle on the hill. I know this, for my power is great. You, Estipan, were asked whether it was proper to intervene. You told your brother, Orases, that if I were Iskander I would ride clear. Well, I have. Now it is for you to do my bidding.'

Estipan reared up, his front hooves drumming back into the earth, his face crimson. 'You give no orders here!' he shouted. 'You are here to fulfil your destiny.'

'Not so!' responded Alexander. 'I am here to fulfil *your* destiny. But first you must earn my friendship. You understand that? Deeds, not words. Now order your followers to attack the Messenians. If you do not I shall ride back to die with my friends. And I shall not come again, Estipan, though the Enchantment dies and all her creatures wither away.'

The palomino centaur hesitated, while the others looked to him for guidance. 'If your power is so great,' he said at last, 'why have you not rescued your friends?'

'Because I am testing you,' hissed Alexander. 'Enough of this! Thena, take me back. My quest is at an end.'

'No! If necessary I will take you by force,' roared Estipan.

'Think you so? Come then, coward, and feel the touch of Death!'

'I am no coward!'

'Deeds, not words, Estipan. Do not tell me – show me!'

Estipan reared again. 'Follow me!' he bellowed, and galloped out onto the plain. More than sixty centaurs armed with bows and knives rode after him. Alexander relaxed and sagged back into Thena's arms.

'I am so tired,' he whispered, and she dismounted, lifting him to the ground. There the boy lay down, his head resting on his arm. Within seconds he was asleep. Thena gazed back to the hill. Warriors were swarming up it, looking like ants at this distance. But the centaurs were closing fast.

Reaching out, she linked with Attalus. But she did not speak for he was fighting desperately against several attackers, and she could not risk distracting him. Sitting down on the grass, she allowed her spirit to fly free and sped to the hillside. Only three men were still alive – Helm,

Ektalis and the Macedonian – and they had been pushed back to the western wall of boulders.

She saw Helm block a thrust, then send a reverse cut through a warrior's throat. 'Seven!' he shouted. 'You'll never catch me now, Swordsman!'

The words mystified Thena, but she noticed Attalus smile.

Floating higher she watched as the centaurs reached the foot of the hill, their arrows hissing into the Messenians as they scaled the boulders. Panic-stricken, the enemy on the hillside fled to their mounts. But inside the circle of boulders the fight went on. Helm was cut on both arms, and blood was also seeping from a gash in his right thigh. Attalus had suffered no new wounds, the cut to his forehead having sealed in a jagged red line. Ektalis was unhurt, but tiring fast. Attalus blocked a wild slashing cut and shoulder-charged the attacker. The man went down, but Attalus slipped on the blood-smeared rocks and fell with him. Two warriors ran in to make the kill. Ektalis hurled himself into their path, despatching the first with a powerful thrust through the belly, but the second man's sword hacked down through the back of Ektalis' neck, killing him instantly.

Attalus rolled to his feet and, back to back with Helm, fought on.

A warrior rushed at Attalus, but an arrow-point punched through his temple and he staggered and fell. More shafts hissed through the air and the surviving Messenians scrambled back, hurling aside their swords and retreating. Helm staggered, but Attalus caught his arm, hauling him upright.

'How many?' Attalus asked.

'Nine. You?'

'Six. I owe you a thousand gold pieces.'

'I'd settle for a drink of rich red wine and a soft, soft woman.'

A white-maned centaur trotted across the clearing, stepping carefully over the bodies. 'Iskander sent us,' he said.

Attalus gazed down at the dead Ektalis. 'You were a little late,' he answered sombrely.

The City of Sparta

Parmenion awoke just before dawn. The room was dark save for a silver shaft of moonlight from the balcony window. He was alone . . . and cold. Sitting up, he rubbed the skin of his shoulders. It was like winter and he cast his eyes around the room, seeking a blanket or a cloak. The only warmth he could feel was from the necklet at his throat.

Beyond the shaft of moonlight something stirred and Parmenion rolled from the bed, snatching his sword from its scabbard.

'Show yourself!' he commanded.

A spectral figure moved through the moonlight. The shock was immense. Apart from the golden eye the man was Philip – hair and beard shining like a panther's pelt, movements sure and confident. But it was not Philip, and Parmenion recoiled from the spirit of the Demon King.

'You fear me? That is wise,' the man said. 'But you stand against me, and that is foolish. I know all your actions, I know your thoughts. Your plans lie before me. Why then do you persist in this meaningless struggle?'

'What do you want here?' countered Parmenion.

'There is a child with golden hair. Have him brought to me and I will spare you and your city. He means nothing to you; he is not even of this world. He is a demon, and carries within him a seed of evil that must be destroyed.'

'A demon, you say? Then surely he should be a friend to you, Philippos?'

'I am a man, Parmenion,' answered Philippos, his voice smooth and friendly, his golden eye gleaming in the pale light. 'My deeds are my own. You should understand that. You are a warrior, and a fine general; you came the closest to defeating me. But that is all I am, Parmenion, a warrior king building an empire. Thus has it been since the dawn of time. Great men will always seek power. Look at me! Do you see a demon?'

'I see a man who butchered his own children to try to become a god. I see a man possessed. Do not seek to sway me, Philippos. I am not to be bought.'

'One child for a whole city? And that child not even Spartan! Are you insane or merely stupid?'

'Your insults mean nothing to me,' said Parmenion. 'And you are wrong, I do not fear you. I learnt much during the battle at Mantinea. I learnt that you are a poor general, with no strategic skills. You rely always on your sorcerous eye to feed you victory, but without it you would be nothing. Within a few days you will face the might of Sparta. And you will know defeat and death. For I know how to kill you, Philippos.'

'Now I know that you are insane. I am invulnerable and invincible. No blade, no poison known to man can kill me. Bring on your five thousand, and your army of slaves and old men. We shall see how they fare against the power of Makedon! And no false goddess will save you this time. I will order you taken alive, and I will see the skin flayed from your body.'

Parmenion laughed then. 'Do I see fear, demon? How does it taste?'

The King shimmered, his form expanding, features twisting and stretching until his eyes were crimson slits in a mottled grey face, his mouth a huge, lipless gash rimmed by fangs. Curved ram's horns of black pushed through the dark hair, curling to rest against the misshapen skull. The beast advanced, but Parmenion held his ground with sword extended.

316

'Fear, Human?' came a chilling voice. 'You ask me if I know fear?' Parmenion's mouth was dry, but his sword was steady. The beast halted before him, towering over the slender swordsman.

'I am the Lord of this World. It is mine. It has always been mine, for all that exists is born of Chaos. Everything. From the smallest seed to the largest star. Before there were men I walked upon this world, when the ground below my feet boiled and the air was fire. I will walk upon it when it is barren and there are no mewling sounds of humans upon the face of it. For it will be ash and dust, dark and cold. I will be here when the stars burn out. And you think to teach me fear?'

'Not you,' admitted Parmenion. 'But *he* felt fear, else you would not have shown yourself.'

'You are clever, Human. And do not think that I do not know you are an imposter. I watched you in the forest, and in the sea when the death Ship sank. You will fail, even as your twin failed. You cannot prevail. What is more, you know it.'

'What I know is that you must be opposed. And you can be beaten. For your power is finite, it depends upon the men who serve you. They can die – and you can lose.'

'As I said, you are a clever man, Parmenion. But you are doomed. The Spartan army will avail you nothing, and the slaves will scatter and flee at the first charge. Your Spartans will be surrounded and destroyed. What purpose then will your defiance serve?'

Parmenion did not answer, could not answer, but he gazed into the demon's eyes and raised his sword. The demon shimmered and faded, but his voice whispered one last time: 'I will see that you live to watch every man, woman and child in this city put to death. You will be the last to die. Think on it, mortal, for that is your future!'

Parmenion sank back to the bed, letting the sword drop from his hand. Despair washed over him, choking his emotions and clouding his judgement. How could he have dreamt of defeating such a creature? 'I am with you,' said a voice in his mind.

317

'Thena?'

'Yes.'

'Did you see?'

'I did, and I am proud of the way you stood against him. Alexander is safe; we are at the Gateway, and there are many creatures here with great powers. Philippos would need his army to capture Alexander now.'

Relief swept through the Spartan. 'That at least is good news. Did you give Brontes my message?'

'I did. But he could not convince them to come to your aid: they are fearful of the ways of Man – and rightly so. For centuries they have been hunted and slain, betrayed and deceived. All they want now is for the Enchantment to be restored. But Brontes, Helm and Attalus are riding to join you. No others.'

'I half expected that, but even so it is more than a disappointment.'

'Consider something else for a moment,' she advised. 'Philippos could not read your mind, so at least your plans are safe from him.'

He smiled then. 'I have only one plan, lady. One giant gamble. If it fails, we fail.'

'Only one?'

'There is no time for great subtlety, Thena. One throw of the dice is all we have.'

'Then you must make it work . . . and you can. For you are the *strategos* and the hope of the world.'

Parmenion took a deep, calming breath. 'Philippos may not be able to read *my* thoughts, but others will know of my plan on the day of battle. I will need help then. The Demon King must be distracted. If he should learn of my strategy then all will truly be lost. Is there anything you can do?'

For a moment there was silence. 'I will think on it,' she promised at last.

'It is good to hear you again,' he told her suddenly.

'May the Source of All Life be with you, my . . . friend.'

'I would sooner have five thousand cavalry, lady.'

*

The day was long, hot and endlessly frustrating. The slaves, in their new breastplates and leather kilts, drove the officers training them to distraction. Scores were dismissed from service, many were injured in combat training – spraining limbs, sustaining cuts.

Parmenion moved among the toiling groups, offering words of encouragement to the officers and men, suggesting small changes in the training methods, urging the officers to have patience with their recruits. And so the day ground on.

By the afternoon Parmenion was helping the barracks youngsters to block the streets – carrying furniture from homes, filling sacks with earth and stones and hoisting them to the barricades.

'I want javelins left on every roof along Leaving Street and the Avenue of Kings,' he told Cleander. 'And men with strong arms to hurl them. I want several hundred bowmen stationed at the *agora*, behind barricades.'

'It will be done, sire,' the dying man promised.

Returning to the palace at dusk, Parmenion spent two hours with Leonidas, Timasion, Cleander and a group of officers, listening to their reports on the progress of the training.

'Within two days we will have a core of men with potential,' said Leonidas. 'But no more than five thousand. The rest would be useless in any major combat. I would suggest leaving them with Cleander to defend the city.'

'Agreed,' said Parmenion. 'But the men not selected must not be made to feel useless. Split them into groups of twenty, each with their own leader; then have the leaders report to Cleander. In this battle morale must take the place of discipline – let us all understand that. Do not criticize a man for lack of ability with a sword, or for clumsiness. Neither should you point out to them that Spartan skill comes only with years of training. You must coax the best from them, encourage them always. If you cannot commend their skill, then commend their courage. Treat them like brothers. Any officer who finds such methods disagreeable must be returned to his regiment. I saw several men today shouting and screaming at the recruits; that must stop.'

Black-bearded Timasion leaned forward. 'I appreciate what you are saying, my lord, but the truth is that no matter how hard we train the slaves they will not stand against the Makedones phalanx. Because it does take years of training for men to instantly follow a shouted command, to move smoothly into place, to change ranks. You cannot expect the slaves to learn it in a week or less.'

'Timasion is right,' said Lycon. 'An army is only as strong as its weakest part. We will have no cavalry and the wings will be slaves and veterans. The veterans we can trust, but they are too old to withstand a charge – and the slaves will break.'

'I will not argue with you, my friends,' Parmenion told them, 'but let me say this: To speak of defeat, or breaking, is to herald it. Once we believe that we are lost, then we *are* lost. The recruits are men; they will do their part. Trust me on this – and if you do not trust me, then pretend to. I want no talk of defeat or weakness. We are all warriors here, and we all understand the nature of war. Everything you say is true . . . but it must not be said. Ultimately battles are won or lost on the actions of a single man. One man panics and it spreads like the plague. One man holds and others hold with him. I do not want the slaves to march out with defeat in their hearts. I want them marching like men, full of belief and hope. I want them to be proud, filled with the knowledge that their Spartan overlords hold them in high esteem. I do not care if it is not true . . . but it must appear to be true. And then, when they have done their part and the victory is ours, it *will* be true.'

'You honestly believe we can win?' asked Leonidas.

'I don't believe it – I know it! We are Spartans. They will not break us. No. They will break upon us. Their cavalry will skirt us. They will ride for the city, for they will know that every man in the ranks will see them and fear for the lives of his wife and children, his mother, his sisters. Then their infantry will attack, outnumbering us by perhaps three to one. The battle will be won or lost in the next hour.'

'How can you be sure that the cavalry will pass us by?' asked Lycon.

320

'I saw his methods at Mantinea. Philippos is not a cavalryman; he uses his infantry for all major thrusts. And he wants the city taken. He wants it all, and he has no patience. But more important than this, he would not wish to push us back in a fighting retreat only to have us defending Sparta. He will want us isolated, the city destroyed behind us.'

'And if you are wrong?' put in Timasion. 'How then can we survive?'

Parmenion forced a smile. 'I am not wrong, but if his cavalry do not attack the city, then Cleander will march out with all his men and join us on the field of battle. One other matter. The slaves must not be issued with red cloaks; only the Spartans must wear them.'

'But why?' Cleander asked. 'Surely the object is to make the recruits feel like Spartans?'

'I want the Spartan regiments to stand out. I want the enemy to see them clearly.'

'It will be a day long remembered,' muttered Timasion. 'Five thousand Spartans against forty thousand barbarians!'

'It will be a day the Makedones will never forget,' promised Parmenion.

*

Nestus lay awake in the narrow pallet bed listening to the snoring of the other soldiers. Forty men slept in this long room, forty non-ranking Spartan soldiers, none of whom would speak to the giant. He was a man alone, and bitterness swamped him.

His own father had refused to receive him, and word of his shame had swept through the city. Friends shunned him in the streets, turning their faces away and pretending not to see him.

His mouth was dry and he rose from the bed and padded through to the empty dining area, where he poured himself a goblet of water. A cold breeze touched his bare back and he shivered.

Life had been so full of promise a mere two years before.

321

He had loved Derae and a splendid wedding had been planned. His father had been so proud. A link with the royal house – brother-in-law to the future King. Everyone knew that Leonidas was the heir apparent, and Nestus was his closest friend. Oh, how bright the future, how golden! It even outshone his frustration at having to serve the mix-blood who had become Sparta's First General.

Parmenion . . .

Now more than ever the mere thought of the name made bile rise in his throat, left his heart hammering.

The day had been burned into his memory, never to be erased: Agisaleus dead, Leonidas to be King. Summoned to see his friend at the Cattle Price Palace, he had joyed in the options before him. Was he to be promoted? Which regiment would he command in the new order? But no. He had learned that the wedding was cancelled and that his bride – his love – was to wed Parmenion, in order that the half-breed could become Sparta's King.

'I should have killed him then,' whispered Nestus. He pictured his sword-blade sliding through Parmenion's ribs, the light of life fading from the bastard's eyes.

Slumping down at a long table, Nestus poured another goblet of water.

And what is there now, he asked himself? Death to follow his dishonour. The destruction of Sparta, the massacre of its people. His thoughts swung to Derae and he pictured her being dragged from the palace, raped and then butchered by the barbarians.

The curse of the gods was upon the city for allowing a half-breed to sit upon the throne!

The room grew colder, but Nestus scarcely noticed it.

Why should you stay? The thought leapt unbidden to his mind, shocking him with its clarity. 'Where else could I go?'

Creta. You have friends on the island . . . and you have coin.

'I couldn't desert my friends, my family.'

They have deserted you. They shun you in the street.

'I did wrong. I drew a sword upon the King.'

The half-blood? A man who used dark sorcery to win his throne and steal your woman?

322

Sorcery? The thought had not occurred to him before. Of course, that was it. Leonidas had been bewitched. What other reason could there be for a noble-born Spartan to relinquish his rights to the throne?

Kill him.

'No. No, I couldn't.'

Like the heroes of old, kill the man who stole your bride. Take back what is rightfully yours. Derae loves you. Save her. Take her from the city – to safety in Creta.

'To safety, yes! I could rescue her. She loves me; she would come. We could be happy there. A short ride to Gytheum, then a ship. Yes! Kill the half-blood and reclaim what is mine! Yes!'

The cold disappeared and the room became clammy and hot. The sudden change made Nestus shiver and he rose, making his way back to his bed. Silently he dressed in a grey *chiton* tunic and calf-length sandals. Then, taking up his cloak and sword, he walked from the barracks.

His father's house was dark and quiet and he climbed through a ground-floor window, moving stealthily through the rooms until he came to his father's study. Here, hidden behind a carved oak chest, was a niche in the stone of the wall; in it were five large leather pouches, heavy with gold. Taking two he left the house, making his way to the stables. A groom sleeping in a bed of hay by the door awoke as Nestus entered. The giant's fist crashed into the man's face, splintering his cheekbone; the groom sagged back unconscious.

Nestus put bridles and reins on two of the fastest horses, then bound their hooves with cloth before leading them out into the moonlit street and on to the Cattle Price Palace. There were only two sentries at the main doors, and both men were known to him. Leaving the horses tethered out of sight beyond the main wall, Nestus strode through the great gates and approached the men.

'What do you want here?' hissed the first. Nestus' fist cracked against the man's jaw, spinning him unconscious to the ground. Then he leapt at the second, seizing him by the throat and savagely wrenching the soldier from his feet.

The man's neck snapped with a loud crack. Nestus had not meant to kill him and he dropped the body, stepping back horrified.

Kill the other, came the thought. Nestus drew his sword and, without hesitation, plunged it through the helpless warrior's throat.

Pushing open the doors of the palace he ran inside and up the long stairs to the third floor, making his way along the cold corridor to the Queen's apartments. His heart was beating fast now and his mouth was dry. The door to the Queen's rooms was ajar and he opened it just enough to slip inside. The moon shone brightly through the balcony window and the first thing he saw was a shimmering green robe tossed carelessly to a couch. Moving to it he lifted it to his face, smelling the perfume upon it. Arousal flared within him and he padded to the bedroom where Derae lay on top of the sheets. Nestus stood in the doorway gazing at her moonlit form. The Queen was naked and lying upon her side, her legs drawn up and her head resting on her left arm. Sweat broke out on Nestus' brow. Her golden skin seemed whiter than ivory in the moonlight, yet soft and warm, glowing with health. He swallowed hard and moved to the bedside, laying his blood-covered sword on the sheet. His hand moved to her arm, sliding over the skin, then down to her waist and up over the curve of her hips. She moaned in her sleep and rolled to her back.

Nestus smiled, thoughts of future joy flashing through his mind: a home by the sea, servants, children . . .

She awoke and screamed, scrambling to get away. Instinctively he grabbed for her, his fingers curling into her hair and dragging her back.

'Stop it! It is I, Nestus. I have come for you. To rescue you!'

She ceased her struggles, green eyes focusing on his face. 'What do you mean, rescue me? Are you mad? If you are found here you will die.'

'I don't care. I have killed two men tonight and I'll kill any others who try to stop me. I have a plan, Derae. We'll go to Creta. I have friends there and we will be happy. But

324

first you must dress. There is little time. I will explain all when we are on our way.'

'You are insane!'

'No! Listen to me. The city is doomed – nothing will save it. It is our only chance at happiness. Don't you see? We will be together.'

Glancing down, she saw the bloodied sword. 'What have you done?'

'What I had to do,' he answered, his hand reaching up, his fingers stroking her breast.

She pulled away from him. 'Parmenion will kill you for this,' she whispered.

'He is alone here. And he has never seen the day when he could defeat me in combat. No one has. I am the best.'

Suddenly she rolled from the bed. He lunged at her, but she was clear and running for the door. Seizing his sword he ran after her, but she had reached the corridor and was shouting at the top of her voice: 'Parmenion! Parmenion!'

He sprinted after her, catching her at the top of the stairs and hauling her back by her hair. 'You slut! You said you loved me and now you betray me!'

'I never loved you!' she answered him, her hand snaking out and cracking against his cheek. Flinging her from him, he raised his sword.

'I'll kill you!' he shouted. Ducking away from him she fled for the stairs, taking them two at a time. He ran after her but tripped and fell headlong, his sword clattering away from him. Dazed, he rose and gathered it from where it had fallen on an embroidered rug at the foot of the stairs. He swung round, seeking Derae.

'You have your sword,' said Parmenion softly. 'Now use it!'

The King was standing naked in the corridor, Derae behind him. 'You will die now, mix-blood,' Nestus told him.

Parmenion smiled and raised his own blade. Nestus ran forward, sword drawn back for the belly thrust, but Parmenion stepped aside –parrying the blade and hooking his foot round the charging man's leg. Nestus hit the floor hard, but rose swiftly. 'Be more cautious,' advised Parmenion, his voice cold. 'Anger makes a man careless.' Again Nestus charged, this time slashing his blade in a sweeping cut towards Parmenion's throat. The King dropped to one knee, the sword slicing the air above his head, his own blade ramming into Nestus' groin. The giant screamed. Parmenion tore his sword clear and rose. Nestus stumbled forward several steps and then slumped to his knees with blood gushing from the severed artery. The warrior struggled to rise, but all strength was seeping from him and he fell forward, his face against the cold stone of the corridor floor.

His fury seemed to flow from him with his lifeblood.

What am I doing here, he thought?

He heard the sound of running footsteps and a voice shouting: 'Someone tried to kill the King!'

That must be it, he thought. I was here to save the King from his enemies.

Yes. Relieved, he closed his eyes. Father will be so proud of me, he thought.

*

Parmenion stepped back from the body and ushered the naked Derae into his rooms, pushing shut the door and letting the sword fall to the floor.

'He was possessed,' said Derae, moving forward with her arms opening to him. He held her gently, his hands in the small of her back, and neither of them heard the door open nor saw Leonidas enter. The Spartan warrior said nothing for a moment, then cleared his throat.

Parmenion turned, but did not release his hold on Derae. 'What is it, Leonidas?'

'I wanted to see that you were unhurt . . . sire.'

'Oh, Leon, it was awful,' said Derae. 'You should have seen his eyes. I have never known Nestus to be like that.'

'He killed two sentries,' Leonidas told her, his voice cool. 'But I see that you are well, sire. I shall leave you . . . both. We will be ready to march in the morning. Five days, if you recall.' He bowed and left the room.

326

'His mood was strange,' whispered Derae, moving in close to her husband. Parmenion felt the warmth of her skin against his breast. Not strange, he thought; Leonidas has just seen his sister being embraced by an imposter.

'I love you,' said Derae. 'Promise me you will come back.'

'How can I make such a promise?' he answered huskily.

'You just say the words. I do not believe that you will be defeated. You are Parmenion, the King of Sparta. You are my Parmenion.'

He smiled and held her tightly. 'A wise man once told me to plan as if you were going to live for ever, but to live as if this were your last day on earth. Let us do that, lady. Let us treat tonight as if it were the last.'

He led her to his bedroom and lay down beside her, drawing her to him. They made love gently, slowly, for he felt no passion – only a desperate need to feel her skin against his, to be inside her, part of her. He felt himself building to a climax, but slowed and withdrew.

'Why are you stopping?' she asked him, reaching out to stroke the skin of his cheek.

'I don't want it to end. Not now, not tonight . . . not ever.'

'You said that so sadly, my dear. There should be no sadness. Not tonight . . . not for us.'

Her fingers slid along the surface of his chest, over the ridged muscle of his belly and down to his still erect penis, circling it. He groaned.

'Does that hurt?' she asked him, her tone serious but her eyes mocking.

'You are a wanton,' he told her, pushing her to her back and rolling on top of her. 'And I shall treat you like one.'

Sliding down the bed, he bit lightly at the inside of her thigh. She cried out, opening her leg to escape him, but he turned his head – his mouth brushing across her soft pubic hair, his tongue slipping into her. She cried out again, but he ignored her. She struggled under him, but his hands held her firm. Then suddenly she relaxed and began to moan, her body arching violently, her legs tensing. This

327

time her cries were not of pain nor outrage, but arose from the shuddering, violent release of tension that only orgasm can bring. Finally she slumped back to the bed, her arms outstretched.

Parmenion moved up alongside her. 'Does it feel good to be a wanton?' he asked.

'Wonderful,' she admitted. 'But promise never to tell me how you learned that skill.'

'I promise.'

'I've changed my mind. Tell me.'

'I swear upon my soul that I have never in this world done it before.'

'That cannot be true.'

'I swear it. You are the first woman in all Achaea to be so abused by me.'

Raising herself on one elbow she looked down at his face. Then she smiled. 'I believe you,' she said slowly, 'but there is something you are not telling me.'

'Are you a seeress then?' he asked, forcing a smile to hide his sudden discomfort.

'Tamis told me I had Talent, but it was undeveloped. What are you hiding?'

'At this moment,' he answered, gazing down at his naked body, 'I would appear to be hiding nothing.'

'I shall look,' she announced. Rolling to her knees she kissed his belly, her head moving down.

'Oh, no!' he said, reaching for her. 'You can't! It's not seemly.'

Her laughter echoed around the room. 'Not seemly? A kiss that is fit for a Queen should not be spurned by a King!'

He was willing to argue – but only for the one moment before her lips touched him, her mouth sliding over him. Then his arguments died.

Later, as they sat on a couch sipping watered wine, they heard footsteps in the corridor beyond the main room. Derae rose and walked back into the bedroom, while Parmenion gathered his sword and opened the door. Two sentries stood outside, Leonidas with them.

'What is going on?' Parmenion asked.

'Philippos is marching through the night. He seeks to surprise us. Two of our scouts have just come in: the Makedones will be within sight of the city by noon tomorrow.'

'We will be ready for him,' promised Parmenion.

'Yes. Is my sister still with you?'

'She is.'

'May I come in?'

'No, my friend. This . . . last night . . . is for us. You understand?'

'I think I do. But the wisdom of it may seem less sure in the morning.'

'My life is full of many regrets, but even if I die tomorrow this night will not be one of them.'

'I was not thinking of you,' said Leonidas.

The truth of the soldier's words struck Parmenion like a blow. Had he not made love to Derae then her memories of him would have been of a cold-natured King who felt nothing for her, her sorrow at his passing minimal.

Whether he enjoyed the glory of victory or death and defeat Parmenion would vanish from her life, for he had made his promise to Leonidas. For five days he would be King – or until the battle was resolved.

Then he would lose Derae again . . .

Leonidas saw the look of despair on the King's face and reached out. 'I am sorry, my friend,' he whispered. Parmenion said nothing. Stepping back, he pushed shut the door and stood in the darkness of his rooms.

'Who was it?' called Derae. He walked into the bedroom and lay down beside her.

'It was Leonidas. The Makedones will be here to-morrow.'

'You will defeat them,' she said sleepily. He stroked her hair and drew the sheet across them both.

He was still awake with the dawn when he heard Priastes enter the outer room. Parmenion rose silently and walked from the bedroom, softly closing the door behind him. Priastes, in breastplate, helm and greaves, bowed as the King made his entrance and Parmenion smiled.

'You look ferocious,' he said.

Priastes chuckled. 'Once I was a man to be feared. There is still something left of that man – as the Makedones will find. Now what armour shall you wear?'

'A simple cuirass with greaves and wrist-guards. I will be fighting on foot. And find me an unadorned helm.'

'You do not wish to stand out in the battle?' asked Priastes, surprised.

Parmenion paused. The old man was right. Always before, Parmenion had been a general serving either a monarch or a satrap, or a city. Yet here he was the King, and men were preparing to fight and die for him. It was their right to see their lord in action and, more than that, it was Parmenion's duty. Morale was a fragile creature, and on many occasions the Spartan had seen Philip turn the course of a battle merely by his presence in golden armour and high-plumed helm. Men watched him ride into danger, and their hearts swelled with pride.

'You are quite correct, Priastes,' he said at last. 'Fetch the brightest, gaudiest armour I possess.'

The old man laughed. 'That would be the golden helm with the white horsehair plume and the ivory-embossed cheek-guards. It is a work of great beauty, yet still strongly made. You will shine like the sun and fill Apollo with jealousy.'

'It is never wise to make the gods jealous.'

'Ah, but then Apollo is better-looking than you. He will not mind that your armour is bright.'

Within the hour, as the sun cleared the mountains, Parmenion – after meeting with Cleander and the city's defence council – strode out through the palace gates to be greeted by Leonidas, Timasion, Learchus and the officers. All bowed as he approached and Parmenion felt his cheeks reddening. The helm was everything Priastes had described and the armour was blinding in the sunlight, beaten gold overlaying iron and bronze. Even the wrist-guards and greaves were embossed with ivory and silver, and the white cloak he wore was interwoven with silver strands which made it glitter in the dawn light.

The army saw him and drew their swords, clattering the blades against their shields in an incredible cacophony of sound. Lifting his hand he returned their salute, his gaze sweeping over the massed ranks filling Leaving Street.

Leonidas approached him, a wide smile on his face. 'Is now the time to outline your plans?' he asked.

Parmenion nodded and called the officers to him. The necklet of Tamis was cool against his throat and he spoke quietly, watching their reactions. They listened in silence, but it was Leonidas who tried to ask the first question.

'What if. . . ?'

Parmenion raised his hand. 'No, my friend. No "what ifs". What if the sun turns to fire? What if the oceans rise from their bowls? There is no time now for such thoughts. I have seen the Demon King in action, and we have only one chance of victory. It is vital therefore that his infantry attack the Spartans, leaving the slaves – at first – alone. If we can make him do that we have a chance. Without it there is none. Now prepare your regiments and let us march.'

He glanced at the faces of the men around him. None of them was content with his strategy yet, even here in this other Greece, Spartan discipline was paramount. They saluted and moved away.

Parmenion strode out to the head of the columns with Leonidas beside him. 'I pray to the gods you are right, Parmenion,' the warrior whispered.

'Let us hope they hear you,' he answered.

The vanguard was clear of the city when the three horsemen came galloping from the south. Attalus and Helm rode side by side with the minotaur Brontes just behind them, sitting awkwardly on his mount.

Attalus reined in alongside Parmenion and leapt to the ground. 'There will be no aid from the south,' said the swordsman, his eyes drawn to the splendid armour.

'I expected none. Walk beside me.'

Brontes and Helm both dismounted, letting the horses walk free. Man and minotaur joined the King. 'Welcome, my friends,' said Parmenion, holding out his hand first to Brontes.

'I am sorry that my brothers of the Enchantment would not ride with you, Parmenion,' Brontes told him, 'but they will have no part in what they see as the wars of men. It might have been that I could have persuaded them, but when I told them you had offered the new Enchantment to Gorgon their minds were further set against you. Had you not befriended that demon, you might even now have had a second army.'

'Without Gorgon, Alexander would not have reached the Gateway,' pointed out Parmenion. 'But that is no longer important. We stand alone – and there is sometimes strength in that.' The Spartan turned to Helm. 'I thought you would have stayed with Iskander. Is he not the key to your memories?'

'He told me to come,' answered the bronze-faced warrior. 'He said my answer lies with you.'

'And what of you, Attalus?' asked Parmenion. 'You have no need to be here.'

'I have grown used to your company . . . sire. And I have no wish to miss the coming battle. The Demon King has hunted me across this world. Now I will hunt him.'

Parmenion smiled. 'We will hunt him together.'

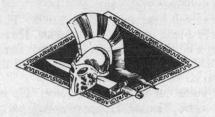

The Field of Blood

Philippos sat upon his battle stallion and thought of his enemy, directing the gaze of his Golden Eye towards the distant figure of the garishly armoured Spartan King.

It galled him that the man had a protective amulet, not because he feared his pitiful strategies but merely because he always enjoyed the fear and rising panic that swelled from the emotions of an enemy facing defeat.

He remembered his last meeting with Parmenion, felt again the wave of anger as the Spartan had spoken of his skills with such contempt. A poor general indeed! He was Philippos, the greatest Battle King the world would ever know!

'I do not need the Eye to defeat the likes of you,' he whispered aloud. And yet . . . why rob oneself of the small pleasures, he wondered? What dread despairs were felt by Parmenion's generals?

His concentration deepened as he sought out Leonidas . . .

'Are you contemplating your death?' whispered a voice in his mind, and Philippos jerked as if struck. It was the witch-woman who had pretended to be the goddess Athena. Closing his human eye, he sought out her spirit form; she was floating in the air some twenty paces from him.

'You cannot harm me, witch,' he told her.

'Nor will I need so to do,' she answered. 'Evil has a way of defeating itself. That will happen today.'

'Begone, woman! I have neither the time nor the inclination to debate with you!'

'Of course you have not,' she sneered. 'The Coward-King must first read his enemy's thoughts. He is incapable of planning a battle for himself. Go ahead. Do not let me disturb you. I would imagine the sight of all those farm-workers and slaves has unmanned you.'

Another voice cut in, a child's voice. 'He is not very impressive, is he, Thena?' Philippos swung his head to see the slim golden-headed boy he had hunted so long.

'I will find you, child. There is nowhere you can hide from me.'

The boy looked at him, his expression sombre. 'I do not think you shall,' he said softly, 'but if you do I will kill you.'

Philippos laughed then, though the sound faded as he stared at the solemn face of the child. 'Nothing can kill me! You hear me? Nothing!'

'I can,' whispered the boy, 'with one touch. But we are detaining you, coward. Shall we ask Parmenion to remove his necklet of power? Would that make it easier for you to destroy the slave army?'

The contempt in the child's voice stung the King with whips of fire and he started to reply, but the spirits vanished. Furious now, Philippos rode along his battle-lines, summoning his generals and priests. The soldiers stood silently as he passed, spears held vertically, eyes on the enemy some 800 paces ahead.

The Makedones King hauled on the reins and turned his horse to stand facing south. The enemy battle-line was as he expected: the Spartans, in their full-faced bronze helms and red cloaks, holding the low ground between two hills; the slaves split into two groups flanking them on the hillsides. Behind the centre of the main force he could see bowmen and javeliners, awaiting orders.

'How many?' Philippos asked.

An officer moved his horse alongside the King. 'Five thousand Spartans, sire, and around the same number of slaves. It is hard to see how many archers, perhaps a thousand.'

Philippos did not need to glance back to know the numbers of the Makedones. Directly behind him were the royal guards, 6,000 strong, standing in battle order twenty ranks deep and 300 shields wide, a vast black-garbed fighting square. They were the Bringers of the Storm, for when they marched their battle-cries rolled out like thunder and their swords were deadlier than the lightning bolts of Zeus. Flanking them were the 10,000 Regulars, powerful fighting men, highly trained, their helms and breastplates of polished iron gleaming like silver. On the right were the 5,000 mercenaries from Thessalia, Thracia and Illyria. Cloaks of many colours were worn by these warriors and, though they had little discipline, still they were ferocious in battle, having a lust for blood and death which delighted the Makedones King. Beyond them, on the right flank, were the cavalry – mainly Korinthian, numbering 7,000. Twenty-eight thousand battle-hardened men were ranged against 5,000 Spartans and a motley mob of hastily-armed slaves and old men.

'His strategy is pitiful,' sneered Philippos. 'You can see through it like a gossamer veil. He invites us to attack his centre; that is why the Spartans are defending the easy way, the low ground.'

'But if we thrust them aside, lord, the slaves will break and run and the day will be ours,' put in the officer. 'Surely we must attack the Spartans?'

'You saw them at Mantinea. To attack them head-on is like hurling water against a wall. They are fine soldiers and they do not break easily. No. That is what he wants – to withstand the full force of an infantry charge, to break the spirit of the Makedones. Once morale is gone the difference in numbers counts for little.'

'What are his thoughts, sire?'

'I neither know nor care. Order the Korinthians to ride wide of the enemy and strike at Sparta itself. Let us see how their morale is affected when they see that their battle is futile. Then order the Regulars and the mercenary units forward, as if to attack the Spartan centre. When they are within fifty paces, sound the charge. Have the mercenaries veer to the left, two regiments of the Regulars to the right. Storm the hillsides and scatter the slaves. The Regulars will then move on and turn to attack the Spartans from behind, while the mercenaries will assail them from the hillside. At that point I will order the Guards forward and we will have them encircled. But remember I want Parmenion alive.'

'Yes, sire. Alive.'

The King turned to his chief priest, a bald hook-nosed man with deep-set dark eyes. 'How are the omens for today, Pharin?'

'There will be a duel of Kings, sire, and Philippos will stand triumphant with his enemy dead at his feet.'

'But I want him alive!'

'That will not be the way of it, sire. You will meet your enemy, blade to blade, and you will kill him.'

Pharin's talent was beyond question but even so the King turned his head, the golden eye gleaming. 'You would not lie to me?'

'I speak the truth, sire: this is the way it will be. A sea of blood, a mountain of corpses, but Philippos victorious.'

'You have never been wrong, Pharin. Not once.'

'Nor am I now, sire.'

*

The Makedones battle-drums began to beat, the sound drifting across the battlefield like the heartbeat of some mythic beast of terror. Parmenion felt the fear of the slaves around him, saw them glance at one another, watched them wiping sweat from their eyes or licking dry lips with dryer tongues.

'You are men of courage,' said Parmenion suddenly, his voice carrying over the shifting ranks, 'and I am proud to stand here with you.' The slaves closest to him smiled nervously. 'Do not let the noise concern you. Padded sticks against stretched cowhide, that is all it is. And those men waiting to march against you are only men like yourselves. There is nothing special about them; they will die, as all men die.'

He fell silent; there was little else he could say. He was no Philip, no Battle King with amazing powers of oratory. Xenophon had called it heroic leadership, the ability of a single man to turn fear into courage the way an armourer fashioned sword-blades from base metal. 'There is within an army,' the Athenian had once said, 'a single, invisible spirit, easily swayed from cowardice to heroism, from savagery to discipline. The right general, or King, understands this. He comes to know the nature of this spirit; he knows that it both feeds from and gives sustenance to the men of the army. This spirit is the seed of panic, yet also the source of greatness. Some coax the best from it, others fill it with passion. But those who ignore it fail.'

Parmenion had always fed it before the battles, on training grounds and during manoeuvres – coming to know the men under him, filling them with confidence both in themselves and their general. It was a time-consuming process, and in this new world there had been not enough days for him to work his quiet magic.

The enemy began to move, mercenary units and Regulars marching out to the sound of the drums, linking shields and advancing across the flat plain towards the Spartan centre.

'Gods, but I could do with a piss,' said Helm, his deep metallic voice breaking the sudden silence. Nervous laughter swelled up around him and the release of tension was almost palpable. Parmenion chuckled. In that moment Helm had expressed the one condition known to all fighting men: a dry mouth and a seemingly full bladder.

His timing had been impeccable and Parmenion glanced at the enchanted warrior beside him. Helm looked up and smiled, one bronze eye winking. 'Thank you,' mouthed the King.

Parmenion cast his expert gaze over the approaching enemy. Five regiments were advancing, some 15,000 men. A dust-cloud rose up on the extreme left and the Spartan swung his head to see the Makedones cavalry outflanking them. 'Daricles!' he yelled and a tall, young bowman raised his hand. 'Fan your archers out in case the cavalry cut back to attack the rear.' The man saluted and Parmenion returned his attention to the infantry.

So far it was all going exactly as he had predicted, the cavalry swinging wide – hopefully to attack the city – while the infantry had been left with the task of clearing the way.

Suddenly the enemy force split, veering left and right, breaking ranks to charge the flanks. War-cries erupted in a terrifying wall of sound, and the pounding of feet upon the dry plain drowned out the incessant beat of the drums.

*

Philippos watched the battle from his place at the head of the Guards. He had observed with disgust the Spartan slaves moving into formation – men bumping into one another, shields being dropped – and he felt a lessening of excitement. Battles were usually full of savage joy and surging emotions, but this one left him dulled, almost bored. The chances were more than good that the slaves would break and run even before the Regulars struck.

What followed would be slaughter . . .

Transferring his gaze to the red-cloaked Spartans, he saw them move smoothly from offensive formation – a solid phalanx 250 shields wide and twenty ranks deep – to the wider 500-shields line. Their raised spears dropped in a perfect line that sent a shiver of appreciation through the Makedones King. Now these were warriors!

The Makedones broke into a run, the force splitting and angling across the field to left and right. Philippos smiled and peered through the rising dust to watch the dismay in the ranks of slaves. Arrows and javelins soared from the Spartan flanks, plunging home into the charging Makedones. Scores fell, many more tripped over the tumbling bodies. But the charge was now unstoppable.

Excitement rose again in the Makedones King and his hands began to tremble. The slave line on the right was breaking, even before the Makedones reached them.

No, not breaking!

Changing!

At first the King could not believe what he was seeing.

The slaves had expertly linked shields in the classic Spartan attack phalanx and were advancing down the hillside. In their haste to crush the enemy the Makedones had broken ranks, intent only on sweeping aside these pretend warriors. There were no battle formations now, only a dark horde racing towards the hills on either side. Philippos jerked his gaze to the right. Here also the slaves were advancing, in perfect formation, to meet the charge.

Madness, he thought. But a tiny sliver of icy fear began to grow in his mind.

Something here was wrong. Yet could it matter? How could slaves withstand a frontal assault?

The dust rose now, thick and blinding. The golden eye gleamed as the Demon King's spirit soared out over the battle-lines. The first Makedones warriors reached the slaves – only to be cut down with consummate ease as swords clove into their flesh, the enemy shields locking like a dam against the surging Makedones tide.

Philippos looked to the main Spartan force. Still they stood their ground, making no effort to come to the aid of the slaves on either flank.

Now the charge was faltering, the field littered with Makedones dead. The slaves continued their advance, hacking and cutting, their swords dripping blood. Desperately the Makedones tried to re-form their lines, but the slaves gave them no opportunity.

Philippos watched the slaughter and confusion tore through him.

You fool! came the voice in his mind. *Can you not see what is happening?*

'Leave me be!' he screamed.

Parmenion has outwitted you. The slaves are the Spartans. They have exchanged cloaks and helms. You have attacked, in broken formation, the greatest warriors in the world!

'What can I do?'

All is not yet lost. Send in the Guards against the Spartan centre.

'How will that aid us?'

The Spartans will have to break off their attack and it will give our troops time to re-form. Do it now, or all will be lost!

Philippos jerked to awareness and drew his sword. 'Forward!' he shouted.

And 6,000 elite warriors, the pride of Makedon, grim-faced and cold-eyed, hefted their swords and shields and marched against the slaves who surrounded the Spartan King.

The City of Sparta

Much to his disgust, Cleander needed to be carried to the roof-top by two young servants as news reached the city that the enemy cavalry had been sighted. Cleander's ruined lungs had all but given out on him, and he had been forced to discard even his simple leather breastplate and helm, the weight being too much for him. His breathing was ragged as the servants reached the top of the stairs, lifting him to the roof.

A deep shuddering breath was followed by a racking cough which spattered crimson drops of blood to the white-washed stone. Cleander heaved himself upright and moved slowly to the low parapet around the building. From here he could look down on Leaving Street. To the left was the barricaded *agora*, the market stalls overturned and blocking all exits. To the right he could see the open plains and the distant dust-cloud that heralded the enemy.

Lifting his hand he summoned his manservant, Dorian, a young Kadmian born into his service. The youth carried a curved oxhorn which he lifted to his mouth, blowing a single clear note that echoed across the city. Cleander's gaze raked along the roof-tops as the hidden javeliners and bowmen showed themselves, raising their hands to acknowledge the signal; then they dropped again from sight.

Sweat dripped into Cleander's eyes and his face was ashen below the deep tan.

'Lie down for a moment, sir,' whispered Dorian, taking his master's arm.

'If . . . I . . . lie down . . . I shall die,' he answered. Instead he knelt by the parapet. Pain racked his weary oxygen-starved body, but he willed himself to go on: the King had entrusted to him the defence of the city, and Cleander would be true to his duty. Once more he ran through the strategy, wondering if any flaws remained to be discovered by the enemy. He had closed off all streets, bar the Avenue of Kings and the parallel Leaving Street. Both led to the open market-place, with its scores of alleys and side turnings; but these too had been blocked with stalls and furniture from surrounding homes. He pictured the unit leaders he had selected. Some concerned him, others worried him. But then the best of the warriors had marched with Parmenion, and it was pointless now to fret about the quality of those left behind.

The enemy were closing fast and Cleander could see sunlight glistening on helms and lances. There were thousands of horsemen galloping towards the city and fear leapt in the Spartan's heart. Could they hold off so many?

'Father Zeus, give me strength,' he prayed. He glanced up at Dorian. 'Get down, boy, and be ready at my signal.' Three men now joined them on the roof-top. Two carried bows and several quivers of longshafted arrows; the third placed himself beside the twenty iron-pointed javelins resting against the parapet. The javeliner hefted the first weapon, testing it for weight and balance. 'Not . . . until . . . the signal,' warned Cleander and the man nodded and smiled.

I was a warrior once, thought Cleander. With helm and sword I would have been standing alongside my King, cutting down his enemies and glorying in my strength and power. Another spasm of coughing tore at his skeletal frame. Bright lights danced before his eyes and he felt himself slipping sideways. Dorian seized him, holding him upright. Cleander's vision was blurring, darkness closing in on him. With a supreme effort of will he fought it back, concentrating on the galloping cavalry. He saw the force separate and watched half of the riders thunder towards Leaving Street.

In the distant past Sparta had boasted a strong wall but Lycurgus, the legendary founder of the warrior creed, had told them that a wall of men was stronger than a wall of stone, and the city's defences had been torn down. Such was the pride of Sparta, such was the strength of their army that at no time in their history had an enemy ever come close enough to threaten the city.

Until now . . .

As the cavalry swept along Leaving Street Dorian looked to Cleander, but the dying man shook his head. On they came, their white cloaks streaming out behind them. Many of the cavalry were Korinthians and wore little armour, carrying only lance or sword, their protection lying in the speed of their mounts and the small buckler shields strapped to their left forearms. Cleander waited until they were almost to the end of Leaving Street, the column strung out below him. 'Now!' he whispered.

A long blast blew from the horn and men rose up on every roof-top, javelins slashing through the air in a dark rain of death that ripped into the invaders' ranks. Horses went down in their hundreds, spilling riders to the cobbled street. Then bowmen began to rake the survivors, who had nowhere to run. White cloaks and tunics blossomed with crimson stains and the screams of dying men echoed through the city. Cleander watched the slaughter dispassionately, then turned to see the vanguard of the column riding into the *agora*. Here they were met with a storm of missiles.

Armed slaves clambered over the barricades and charged into the demoralized invaders, dragging them from their mounts, sharp knives and hatchets ripping and cleaving into flesh and bone.

The routed cavalry fought to escape, but the only route was back the way they had come and the streets were choked with dead horses and men.

And the slaughter continued.

Cleander sagged back to the roof-top.

His vision darkened, the men around him fading and becoming shadows. Then a bright figure stepped into view, seeming to emerge from a glistening mist. Cleander rose, all pain vanishing, and looked into the eyes of the shining man before him.

'I did not let you down, sire. The city is safe.'

'You did well, cousin,' said Parmenion, King of Sparta. Cleander gazed down upon his own frail body, lying forgotten as the fighting raged on. So thin and wretched . . . it was such a pleasure to be free of it. Then despair touched him. If the King was here, then . . .

'Did we lose, sire?'

'Not yet. The battle continues. Come, follow me.'

'I always have, sire. I always will. But where are we going?'

'To the Field of Blood, my friend. For there are many Spartans there who will need a guide before this day is over.'

The Field of Blood

Despite the carnage on either side Parmenion felt detached from the battle, his mind focused entirely on the *feel* of the conflict. The Makedones had suffered a terrible reverse; their mercenaries, cut down in their hundreds, were on the verge of panic. Some were already running back, fleeing the combat. The Regulars were still fighting hard despite appalling losses, but they were being forced back by the savage skills of the disguised Spartans.

The battle was not yet won or lost, but balancing on a knife-edge. He looked to his right, where Leonidas and Timasion were leading the assault. The Spartans had formed a fighting line 200 shields wide, and they were gradually turning the enemy back towards the centre of the field. On the left Learchus was no longer making headway, the ground beneath his warriors covered with the bodies of the fallen.

Dust was billowing across the battlefield as Parmenion transferred his gaze to the enemy reserves, the elite Makedones Guards. He blinked and narrowed his eyes.

They were advancing.

Cold fear swept through him. Next to the Spartans these were the most disciplined fighting men of Achaea, victors of a score of major battles. On they came, a solid phalanx of fighting men in tight formation, twenty ranks at least. The

345

combined weight of their charge would carry them deep into any stationary enemy line.

Parmenion silently swore. Had his troops been truly Spartan he would now sound the advance, moving out to meet the enemy head-on, matching their formation and relying on the strength of his soldiers to withstand the charge. But they were not Spartans: they were houseslaves, messengers, gardeners and servants, with no experience of war.

In that dread moment a sudden realization struck him: he had no choice. If they stood still they would be swept aside. Spartans or no, the *strategos* was left with only one option.

Attack.

Curiously this thought swept away all his fears, and from some deep well of his being rose a savage lust for battle he had never before experienced.

'Attack formation!' he yelled.

The slaves had learned only two manoeuvres during their few days of training and this had been one, moving smoothly from a wide defensive line into a compact attacking unit.

'Drummers sound the beat!' shouted the King. 'By the step three!'

Behind the battle-lines the ten drummers began to mark the time with a steady, rhythmic pounding.

Parmenion eased himself into the third rank as the men began to march forward to meet the enemy. The first rank carried shield and sword, the men in the second wielding long iron-pointed spears. Once close to the enemy these weapons would be lowered, the men in the front line sheathing their swords and helping to guide the spears home while the wielders, gripping the hafts with both hands, rammed them into the opposing ranks.

Against an ill-disciplined force, or troops without formation, such a tactic was often decisive. But, in the main, close-order troops would block the spears with their shields and the initial stages of combat would be down to the strength and weight of the two phalanxes as they clashed, like two huge bulls coming together head to head.

'Level spears!' bellowed Parmenion and the weapons came down in a ragged line, but the billowing dust prevented the enemy from seeing clearly how inexpertly the spears were brought into position. 'Drummers by the step four!' The beat quickened, like the thudding of an angry heart.

'Now we will show them,' said Priastes, moving alongside his King. But Parmenion had no time to answer, for the enemy were close.

The Makedones were not moving as fast as he had expected. In fact they seemed hesitant, their line curving – wider at the flanks, concave at the centre. For a moment Parmenion was nonplussed, then realization came to him.

They were frightened! The Guards had seen what they thought to be slaves smashing their fighting lines, and now they believed themselves to be facing the finest warriors in the world. The men at the centre in the first rank were holding back, fearful of the clash. This had the effect of compressing the Makedones phalanx, rank after rank closing and eliminating the vital fighting space between the lines.

'Drummers by the step five!' shouted Parmenion. The drumbeat quickened, the advance gathering speed. 'Ready spears!'

The Makedones were hardly moving when the Spartans struck them. The second rank spear-carriers threw themselves forward, the iron points of their weapons hammering into the enemy. Tightly compressed as they were, the Makedones could not block them all and the points plunged home between their shields. 'Withdraw spears!' shouted Parmenion and back came the blood-covered weapons, only to stab forward once more.

The Makedones line buckled as hundreds of warriors went down. But the formation did not break.

Again and again the spears clove home, but now the Makedones reformed and began to fight back. The slaves in the front rank drew their swords and the fighting became hand-to-hand. The Spartan advance slowed.

Gaps began to appear in the front line.

Helm leapt into one breach, slashing his sword across the face of an advancing Makedones warrior. 'Keep close, brothers!' he shouted. His voice carried along the line and the effect was instant. The slaves gathered themselves, closing the gaps and fighting back.

All forward movement had ceased now and the two forces stood toe to toe, shield to shield.

Parmenion looked around him. Everywhere the slaves were holding their ground, and his pride in them soared. Cold reality touched the *strategos*. The Makedones were still hesitant, but soon they would become aware of the lack of skill and advance again.

And in that moment he knew how his twin had felt at Mantinea, the sweet taste of victory so close to his tongue.

Another gap opened before him. Just as he was about to leap forward the giant form of Brontes stepped into the breach, a huge axe in his hand. The blade slashed down, cleaving through helm and breastplate to smash a Makedones from his feet.

Turning, Parmenion raised his arm. 'Rear six ranks wide formation!' he called. No one moved, men glancing one to the other, for this was not something they had practised. Parmenion stifled a curse. 'Rear six ranks follow me!' he called again, pointing to the right. The lines began to move. 'Re-form and attack from the right!'

The men began to run, following the King in his golden armour as he moved across the battle-lines. 'Re-form in wide defensive,' he ordered. This the men understood, and swiftly they grouped themselves in three ranks 200 shields wide. In the first rank Parmenion drew his sword, hefted his shield and led them towards the Makedones flank. There were no drummers now, and the dust was thick and choking.

At the last moment the Makedones saw them and tried to turn.

Parmenion knew the slaves could not break through, but he hoped that the sudden switch of attack would slow the enemy as warriors were forced to defend both front and flank.

To his left he could see the minotaur still cleaving and hacking with his axe, the Makedones falling back before him – and Helm, fighting now alongside Attalus in the front line.

A sword slashed for his face. Parmenion deflected it with his shield and stabbed out his own blade in response, but this too was blocked. Dropping to one knee, the Spartan thrust his sword under the Makedones shield. The blade tore through the man's leather kilt, slicing into his groin. Wrenching the weapon clear, Parmenion rose to block another attack.

All around him the slaves pushed forward.

But the Makedones held them off.

And the enemy line began to move inexorably forward.

★

Leonidas eased himself back from the front line and ran swiftly up the hillside, turning to look down on the battle. Parmenion's plan had worked beautifully, but the weight of numbers was still against them. The Thracian mercenaries had fled the field, but the Spartan could see their officers desperately trying to regroup the survivors. Given time they would return to the battle.

Squinting through the dust, Leonidas saw that Parmenion was leading his disguised slaves against the Guards, while on the far left Learchus, hard-pressed by the Makedonian Regulars, was making little headway. As with all battles the first to fall were the less skilful, the weak, the slow, the inept. Now only the real fighting men remained, and there was no question of the bravery of the Makedones. Stunned and demoralized by the early charge, they were now showing their discipline and the battle was slowly beginning to turn in their favour.

The field was littered with corpses, the vast majority being the Makedones or their mercenaries, but Spartans had fallen too and Leonidas ran an expert eye over his fighting lines. He had begun with 2,500 men under his command; just over 2,000 remained in a phalanx 200 shields wide, ten ranks deep.

Against them were ranged some 4,000 Illyrian irregulars in their red breastplates and horned helms. Tough, seasoned fighters, but ill-disciplined. Leonidas' regiment was pushing them back, but the enemy were far from either panic or retreat.

Leonidas was racked by indecision. The slaves could not withstand the might of the Guards, and Learchus on the left needed support. Yet if Leonidas was to send any troops to their aid, his own force would not be able to withstand the Illyrians.

Nevertheless a decision had to be made.

Then he saw Parmenion leading the flank attack against the Guards. It was a courageous move, but doomed to failure unless supported. His decision made, Leonidas ran back to the battle.

'Rear five fighting wedge left!' he shouted. 'Formation Ten!' The rear five ranks of his regiment moved smoothly to the left, re-forming ten ranks deep, fifty shields across, Leonidas at the centre with two officers on either side of him. 'The King!' he bellowed.

The men in the first rank hefted their shields and began to march, angling to the left. The Illyrians, screaming their battle-cries, hurled themselves against the weaker right flank of the phalanx. This was the danger Leonidas had braved. Shields were always carried on the left arm, and when a regiment swung to the left the right side of the phalanx was open to attack, for the shields faced inwards. But he had no choice. To order a switch to the more standard fighting square would make forward movement almost impossible. The men on the right had only their swords to fend off their attackers, yet still they were Spartans and the Illyrians suffered heavy losses as they tried to crash through the phalanx.

Worse was to come, Leonidas knew, for as they fought their way forward the Illyrians would move in behind them. He could only hope that Timasion, with the troops left under his command, would see the danger and launch a counter-attack to defend the rear.

'At the slow run!' shouted Leonidas. There were no

drummers to sound the beat, but the Spartans responded instantly, the front line swinging further left. Leonidas glanced back. Timasion had ordered his men to advance into the breach created by Leonidas, and the harrying Illyrians were now caught between two forces.

A gap opened before the fighting wedge and Leonidas could see Parmenion and his warriors battling to contain the Guards. The huge minotaur and the warrior with the metal face were now surrounded by the enemy, but giving no ground. 'The King!' yelled Leonidas again.

'The King!' came the thundrous response from the Spartans.

He saw Parmenion glance back. Immediately the King ordered his men to pull aside, creating room for the charging Spartans to hammer home against the Guards' left. The enemy flank crumpled under the sudden assault, the Spartans pushing deep into the Makedones square.

For the first time Leonidas saw the Demon King at the centre of his regiment, a bright sword in his hand.

All was chaos now, the battle no longer the standard parallel lines of opposing forces. By breaking the Spartan right Leonidas had gambled everything on crushing the enemy centre.

But here stood the Demon King. And he was invulnerable.

*

Even in the thick of the fighting, his sword-arm weary, Parmenion knew that the pivotal point in the battle had been reached. He could feel it, in the same way that a runner senses the presence of an unheard rival closing behind him. The Makedones were fighting furiously, but there was an edge of panic in them. For years they had fought and won, and this battle was to have been their easiest victory. That expectation had been cruelly crushed, and their morale was now brittle and ready to crack.

Parmenion blocked a savage thrust, slashing his own blade through his attacker's neck in a deadly riposte. The man fell back, and for a moment Parmenion was clear of the action. He swung, looking to the left where Learchus and his regiment were once more making headway against the Regulars. To the right and rear Timasion was urging his men forward into the Illyrians in a bid to reach the centre of the field.

All around the King the slaves were standing firm, though their losses were great, and Parmenion felt afresh the surging determination not to lose. These men deserved a victory.

But there was no place for strategy now. Amid the carnage of the battleground there was room only for strength of arm, allied to the courage of the human spirit. The Makedones fought only for conquest and plunder, while the slaves were fighting for their freedom and the Spartans battling for city, home and honour. The difference was significant as the two armies, their formations broken, fought man to man on the blood-soaked field.

A movement on the hilltops to the south-west caught Parmenion's eye. The swirling dust made identification difficult at first, then the King saw the giant form of Gorgon moving down the slope. Behind him came hundreds of beasts from the forest, some reptilean and scaled, others covered in matted fur. Many were armed with crude clubs of knotted oak, but most needed no weapon save fang and claw. Vores circled above them and, at a signal from Gorgon, swooped down over the Makedones ranks to hurl their poison-tipped darts.

The Makedones at the rear saw the monsters approaching – and panicked. Throwing aside their weapons they fled the battlefield. Others, with more courage, tried to link shields against this new enemy.

The forest creatures fell upon the Makedones with terrible force, their talons slicing through armour and chain-mail, ripping flesh and snapping bones like rotten wood. Nothing could withstand them.

The Guards' defences collapsed.

One moment they were an army, the next a seething, frightened horde desperate to escape.

Gorgon, wielding two iron clubs, clove into their ranks,

smashing men from their feet. His pale eyes glowed. Warriors in his path screamed and froze, their bodies stiffening, shrinking, crumbling to the earth, dry and withered.

Seeing the panic among the Guards, the Illyrians facing Timasion's regiment turned and fled.

Now only a tight-knit fighting square surrounded the Demon King. Philippos drew his sword and waited, secure in his invincibility. Gorgon broke through the shield-wall, one huge club hammering down on the King's shoulder. But the weapon bounced clear and Philippos leapt forward, his sword cleaving into Gorgon's chest. The Forest Lord staggered back with dark blood gushing from the wound. Philippos advanced but Brontes hurled himself forward, dropping his axe and curling his huge arms around the King's frame. The King struggled in his grip, trying to turn his sword on this new attacker, but Brontes pinned the King's arms to his side, lifting him from his feet. Philippos screamed but could not free himself.

The last Makedones resistance crumpled, men throwing down their swords and falling to their knees begging for mercy. At first they were cut down despite their pleas, but Parmenion's voice rose above the battle.

'Enough! Let them live!'

A strange, unnatural quiet fell over the battlefield. To the south the once invincible army of Makedon was fleeing in disorder. Here at the centre the remaining Makedones laid down their weapons.

Brontes threw the Demon King to the ground, dragging back the defeated monarch's arms and calling for thongs to bind him. An archer offered his spare bowstring. Brontes tied the King's thumbs together and then stood, watching Philippos struggle to his knees.

Helm stepped forward and stood before Philippos, staring down into the King's face. Then he staggered and seemed about to fall. Attalus leapt to his side, catching him.

'Are you all right?' the Macedonian asked. Helm did not answer and Attalus saw the bronze face stiffen and swell, becoming solid once more. The enchanted warrior lifted his hand to the helm he now wore; it was no longer part of his face.

Yet he did not remove it.

Parmenion moved swiftly to where Gorgon lay, his lifeblood draining to the churned ground. Kneeling beside the monster Parmenion took his hand, but could find no words for the dying Titan.

Gorgon's eyes opened. 'Surprised to see me?' asked the Forest King.

'Yes. But you were more than welcome, my friend. I think you saved us.'

'No. They were ready to crack.' Gorgon struggled to rise, but fresh blood gushed from the awful wound in his chest. 'I cannot feel my legs. Am I dying?'

'Yes,' whispered Parmenion.

Gorgon smiled. 'Curious . . . there is no pain. Will you promise me that my people will have their chance at the Gateway?'

'Of course.'

'Your friendship . . . carries . . . a high price. But . . .' The Forest Lord's head lolled back and his body began to tremble. The skin of his face seemed to shimmer, the snakes receded. Parmenion remained where he was as the body slowly changed, becoming at the point of death the handsome dark-haired man Gorgon had once been in life.

Weary and full of sorrow, Parmenion rose.

Brontes stumbled forward, kneeling by his brother. 'Why?' he shouted. 'Why did you do this?' Taking hold of Gorgon's shoulders, he began to shake the body.

'He cannot hear you,' said Parmenion softly.

The minotaur looked up, his huge brown eyes streaming with tears. 'Tell me, Parmenion, why he came?'

'For friendship,' answered the Spartan simply.

'He did not understand the meaning of the word.'

'I think that he did. Why else would he and his people have risked their lives? They had nothing to gain here.'

'But . . . my own people refused to help you. And yet this . . . creature . . . died for you. I do not understand.'

Lifting his horned head, the minotaur screamed his torment to the skies.

The laughter of Philippos pealed out. 'That's it!' he called, 'Wail, you pitiful monstrosity. I killed him. Release me and I'll kill you. I'll kill all of you!'

Brontes lurched to his feet, gathering up his axe. Philippos laughed again. The axe-blade hammered into the King's face, but the skin was not even marked.

Helm stepped forward, approaching Parmenion. 'Let him loose,' said the warrior. The Spartan turned to Helm. The voice was no longer metallic, the helmet now separated from the skin.

'Your memory has returned?' Parmenion asked him, knowing the answer.

'It has. Let him loose. I will fight him.'

'He cannot be killed.'

'We shall see.'

'Wait!' whispered Parmenion. Swiftly he unclasped the necklet, stepping forward to fasten it around Helm's neck. 'Now he will not be able to read your mind.' The warrior nodded and moved away from the Spartan, drawing his sword. Brontes looked to Parmenion. 'Release him.' Brontes slashed the axe-blade through the bindings. Philippos staggered, then righted himself and swung to see Helm approaching him with sword extended.

The Demon King laughed. 'The first to die,' he said, gathering his blade from where it had fallen during the struggle with Brontes. 'Come, let me arrange your journey to Hades.'

Helm said nothing but his advance continued. Philippos leapt to meet him, blade stabbing forward in a disembowelling thrust. Helm parried it, sending a reverse cut that sliced through the skin of the Demon King's bicep. Philippos jumped back, gazing down in horror at the blood oozing from the wound.

'I cannot be hurt!' he screamed. 'I cannot!'

Helm paused and, lifting his left hand, removed his helmet. Philippos reeled back, the light fading from his golden eye.

355

Warriors of both armies stood transfixed – for facing the Demon King was his twin, save that his eye was not gold but the colour of opal.

'Who are you?' whispered Philippos.

'Philip of Macedon,' the warrior answered.

The Demon King tried a desperate attack, but it was easily parried and Philip's blade plunged into his enemy's throat. Blood bubbled from Philippos' mouth. 'That,' hissed Philip, 'is for threatening my son! And this is for me!' The sword slashed in a glittering arc, decapitating the Demon King. The head fell to the left, bouncing on the hard-packed earth. The body, spouting blood, pitched to the right.

'Is that dead enough for you?' asked Philip.

*

The aftermath of the battle proved long and mind-numbingly complex. The disarmed Makedones were herded together and Parmenion called their officers to him. They were, he told them, free to return to Makedon, there to elect a new King. But first they were obliged to swear sacred oaths that they would help to rebuild the ruined city of Kadmos. This they did. The baggage-train of the Makedones was captured, and with it the enormous wealth accrued by Philippos. This was taken by the Spartans, but Parmenion promised one-half of it to the victims of Makedones aggression, including twenty gold pieces for every slave who had fought alongside him.

The surviving slaves and half the Spartan army were sent back to the city, while Brontes agreed to lead Gorgon's followers to the Giant's Gateway, there to await Parmenion's arrival.

Emissaries arrived from the scattered Illyrians and Thracians, begging for peace terms. These were granted, on the understanding that the warriors returned immediately to their homelands.

During all of these negotiations Makedones and Spartan surgeons moved among the wounded of both sides, performing operations under torchlight.

By the end of the day more than 11,000 enemy corpses had been counted on the battlefield, another 4,000 slain in the attack on Sparta. The Makedones dead were stripped of their armour, while their living comrades dug several mass graves. The 870 Spartan dead would be returned to the city for honourable funerals. Of the slaves more than 2,000 were dead. The Spartans dug a special grave for them, and Leonidas promised that a monument would be raised above it.

Long after midnight Parmenion finally retired to the tent of Philippos, and was there joined by Philip, Attalus and Leonidas.

'I do not understand,' said Attalus, as the three men relaxed, 'how the Demon King was slain. He was said to be invulnerable.'

'Except to self-inflicted wounds,' Parmenion told him wearily. 'Philip was . . . is . . . Philippos: the same men in different worlds. I would imagine that the spell protecting him could not differentiate between the two.'

Leonidas rose. 'I will leave you friends alone together,' he said. 'But first may I speak with you privately, sire?' Parmenion nodded and followed the young Spartan from the tent.

'I think I know what you are going to say,' whispered Parmenion, 'and I have not forgotten my promise. Will you allow me to ride to Sparta one last time to say farewell to Derae?'

Leonidas shook his head. 'You are wrong, my friend. I am asking you to stay. There is so much to be done now. Who else would be King? Timasion? He will want to go to war with Korinthos and Messenia. He would seek to punish our enemies, creating new hatreds. Lycon is too young and headstrong. There are no others.'

'You do yourself an injustice. You would make a fine King.'

Leonidas smiled. 'Not so, Parmenion. I am a warrior, that is enough for me. Think about what I have said. We need you here.'

The officer walked away into the night, past the glittering

torches that lit the battlefield. Parmenion stood silently staring out over the plain, then a hand touched his shoulder. 'There is much to what he says.'

Parmenion nodded. Philip took his arm and the two men strolled out, avoiding the camp-fires around which the Spartan soldiers slept.

'This would be a good life for you, Parmenion. Here you are revered as a saviour. You could build an empire.'

'I have no wish for empires, sire. And I have never desired to be a King.' The Spartan sighed. 'This is not my world.'

'You know how much I need you, and it would hurt like Hades to lose you. But think carefully about this,' Philip advised.

'I shall. But tell me, how did you become Helm?'

Philip swore, then laughed. 'The day after you left a man came to see me, saying he had news of Alexander. Since he insisted on seeing me alone, he was brought to my chambers. Naturally he was searched, but he carried no weapons. In fact, apart from his clothes he had only a small leather pouch containing a stone veined with gold. A lucky charm, he said. He entered the room – and that is the last I remember. I awoke in a graveyard. Can you believe that? How he spirited me here I do not know. Nor do I know why he took away my memory and turned my face to metal.'

'I would guess that the man was Aristotle,' said Parmenion, 'and I cannot say why he left you with no knowledge of your identity, but the metal face was a great protection. Had you been recognized as Philippos your life would have been short indeed.'

'Philippos,' whispered the Macedonian, letting the name hang in the air. 'Was he truly me? Do you think I could be like him? A destroyer, a demon?'

'No, sire. He was possessed. Driven by a spirit of Darkness.'

'Even so, his army swept across the world much as mine has in the past. It is not a good feeling to see such savagery from the side of the victims.'

'Perhaps it is,' argued Parmenion.

Philip chuckled. 'Maybe,' he agreed. 'When we get home I shall rethink my plans. Diplomacy shall be the key. I shall convince the Athenians, the Spartans and the Thebans to make me the leader of Greece. Only then will I carry the war into Persia. I shall never be a Philippos, Parmenion. *Never.*'

'I do not doubt that, sire. It would never occur to me that you would.'

'Stop calling me sire. Here you are the King and I am the soldier.'

'Old habits die hard . . . Philip.'

The Macedonian looked into Parmenion's eyes. 'I will not forget what you have done for me, and for my son. You are a good friend, Parmenion; the best a man could have.' Unfastening the necklet which had protected his thoughts from the Demon King he clasped it around Parmenion's neck once more.

Suddenly uncomfortable, Parmenion said nothing and the King laughed, clapping him hard upon the shoulder. 'You always were uneasy with compliments, Spartan. Come, let us celebrate your victory and get drunk together.'

But when they returned to the tent Attalus was asleep upon a couch and, after only a single goblet of wine each, consumed in comfortable silence, Philip also declared himself weary and settled down on the floor to sleep.

For a while Parmenion lay awake, his thoughts jumbled, a series of almost kaleidoscopic images tumbling through his mind. Derae, Phaedra, Thena, Alexander, Leonidas . . . Two worlds and a choice of lives. A king or a general. Derae or Phaedra? The latter he did not love, but she had borne his children and duty demanded he return.

To the pit with duty, he thought! Have I no right to happiness?

But then he thought of Alexander and the beast within him. Another Philippos waiting to wreak his evil on the world. 'I cannot stay,' he whispered.

And a deep sorrow flowed through him.

The Giant's Gateway

Alexander sat alone at the edge of a small tree-lined lake, gazing up at the hilltop to his left. Upon it, silhouetted in the moonlight, stood the twin pillars of the Giant's Gateway, and upon them was a marble lintel stone deeply etched with writings of a form and language Alexander had never seen.

Three times that day the boy had been drawn to the stones, walking around and between the pillars trying to make sense of their hidden messages. The columns themselves were ornately carved and, save for the most subtle differences, identical. There was a sunburst surrounded by eighteen spheres on the left column; on the right there were nineteen spheres. At the base of each was a curious carving of what appeared to be the footprint of a beast with four talons, and higher above it the outline of a crab, or spider, or even a three-headed monster. It was hard to tell what had been intended by the sculptor.

Alexander picked up a stone and skimmed it across the surface of the lake. The Gateway haunted his thinking and he lay back on the soft grass seeking the clue he needed. On each pillar, facing inward, was a jutting stone – like fingers pointing at one another. According to legend the giant who created the Gateway had reached out from between the pillars, taking hold of both stones. Then he had vanished.

But Alexander could not copy such an action. As he held the first stone and stretched out his arm, he was still some six feet from touching the second stone.

Doubt crept into his mind. Are you truly Iskander? He had believed he would need only to see the Gateway in order for its secrets to be revealed.

'What am I to do?' he asked the night.

'Whatever you can,' came a familiar voice, and Alexander swung to see Chiron walking down the hillside.

'You are alive!' shouted Alexander, pushing himself to his feet and running to meet the *magus*. Chiron knelt to greet him, taking the boy in his arms.

'Yes, I am alive. And glad to be human once more.'

'But you – Camiron – fell overboard during the storm. I could not locate you. I feared you dead.'

'Camiron managed to reach the shore-line and from there, lost and confused, headed south, coming at last to the woods. Here there were those who knew him – me – and had the power to reverse the Change. I shall never again be tempted into shape-changing.'

'Why did you risk it at all so near to Gorgon's Forest?'

The *magus* looked away, then smiled ruefully. 'I had not intended the Change. But I was frightened, Alexander. Simply that. The Makedones were coming. Parmenion had decided to walk into the demon-haunted depths of the most evil place in Achaea.' He shrugged. 'I fell asleep, but my dreams were all born of terror. Camiron at least could outrun his enemies – but what I could not have guessed was that the centaur would discard the stone of power . . . leaving me trapped. I think in some way he knew that this was his only chance of true life.'

'Poor Camiron. He was so happy to wake every morning with his memories intact.'

Chiron smiled and sat down beside the boy. 'He could not have lived, Alexander. Centaurs cannot absorb food while their bodies are merged. He did not know it, but he was starving to death when at last he came here. He had no real hope of independent life.'

'I shall miss him,' said Alexander.

'And I shall not,' the *magus* told him. 'But let us return to your problem. What have you discovered about the Gateway?'

'Little or nothing. The carvings upon the pillars are not quite identical, but that could be considered human error – though somehow I doubt it. The jutting stones are handles of some kind but, as with the myth, it would take a giant to grip them together.'

'Yet that is the secret,' said Chiron. 'The writings inscribed on the lintel are Akkadian, derived from an ancient Atlantean alphabet of forty-two characters. The Akkadians reduced the alphabet to twenty-nine.'

'You can read it?'

'Of course.'

'What does it say?'

'Nothing now of interest. It tells how the pillars were first brought here, lists the names of the Senior Magus, and the current King in whose name it was erected, and says that the Gateway was built in the thousandth year of the Akkadian Empire. That is all.'

'I had expected more,' said Alexander, disappointed.

Chiron laughed. 'Like a list of instructions? I don't believe that instructions were needed in those days. The Gateway was always open.'

'Then how did it radiate Enchantment?'

'I do not believe it ever did.'

'What? You mean I cannot restore the magic to this realm?'

'I fear not.'

'Then what can I do?'

'The Gateways – and there are many of them – allowed travel between nations, worlds, times. In the far east they are called *lung mei*, the Dragon Paths. In the west they are known as the Dream Gates, and in the cold, bitter north they are named the Paths of the Gods.'

'How does that help me, if I cannot use them to return the Enchantment?'

'If a horse is too weak to travel to water, then what does the rider do?'

'He brings water to the horse,' Alexander replied.

'Exactly. You cannot bring the Enchantment to Achaea. You must then allow the people of the woods to pass through the Gateway to a world where Enchantment is still strong.'

'Then I must open the Gate?'

'I believe that is your destiny.'

'How will I know where to send them?'

Chiron shrugged. 'I cannot answer that.'

Alexander rose and began the slow walk up the hillside. Chiron followed him and together they examined the pillars anew.

'This section here, what is it?' asked Alexander, running his fingers over the curving lines that made up the bestial footprint.

'That is a map of Achaea. See, here is Sparta and here the Gulf of Korinthos.'

'I do see! The crab then is the Chalcidice, what you call the lands of the Trident.' Moving to the right-hand pillar, he traced the second map. 'And this is the same – except that the Gulf is more narrow. And look, here the lands of the Trident are changed also, the prongs linked.'

Returning to the first pillar, he looked in amazement at the map. 'Wait! Now there is no Gulf of Korinthos. What is happening here, Chiron?'

'As you touch them they change,' whispered the *magus*. 'Now the one on the right is not Achaea at all. All the islands have linked to the mainland.'

As they watched the maps began to writhe and change faster and faster, in a bewildering series, as if an invisible hand was drawing charcoal lines across the stone.

Alexander moved closer to the left-hand pillar, reaching out and touching his finger to a small indentation at the centre of the lower map. The movement of lines stopped immediately. Slowly the shifting maps on the right-hand pillar also slowed and froze.

Chiron leaned back, hands on hips. 'That is at least an answer in part,' he said. 'This was how they set up the Gateway. One map must be of this world, the second sets up the destination point. I do not believe it is a time portal. I have seen those and they are much larger, full circles of stone. Yet it is more complex than other Akkadian Gateways used to travel the length of the empire. This must be one of the legendary Six Gateways to alternate worlds.'

'Where are the others?'

'One you have already travelled: Philippos drew you through it. There is another I know of in the east, but the pillars were smashed by superstitious tribesmen. The others? I don't know. Below the sea, perhaps, with lost Atlantis. Or under the new ice at the far edges of the world?'

'How can I open the Gateway?' Alexander asked.

'I don't know,' admitted Chiron, moving between the pillars and examining the stone handles. 'The Guardians of the Gates possessed stones of Sipstrassi, nuggets of power. I too have several, but my store of them is far away and therefore of no use to us. But one thing is certain – this Gateway was once aligned to other portals. At some point in time these alignments were severed.'

They examined the Gateway for another hour, but weariness overtook Alexander and he lay down between the pillars to sleep. He dreamt of Pella and his father's palace, and of Parmenion. The dream was full of anxiety and fear, for a dark mist hovered at the edge of his vision and always he refused to turn his head and look at it. It hung there, never moving, black and forbidding.

At last Alexander could bear it no more and he spun . . . to find himself gazing on a mirror within a frame of smoke. His own reflection gazed back at him.

'You are not me,' he said.

'You are not me,' the mirror replied, then the image laughed and horns erupted from its temples to curl back over its ears. 'You cannot open the Gateway without me,' said the Chaos Spirit. 'You know that, don't you?'

'Yes,' Alexander admitted.

'What will you offer me to help you?'

'Nothing,' said the boy.

'Nothing? The people of the Enchantment will tear you to pieces if you fail them.'

'Exactly,' said Alexander, his voice growing in confidence. 'Only you can prevent it.'

'Why should I?'

'Come, you do not need me to answer that. Where are you without me?'

'It would not kill me,' the Spirit told him. 'It would merely mean more waiting until another vessel is ready.'

'But you are impatient,' the boy pointed out.

'That is true,' admitted the Spirit. 'But I ask again, what will you give me?'

'We will strike no bargains,' said Alexander. 'It is enough that we return to our own world, there to continue whatever battles await.'

'I will have you, you know,' the Spirit whispered. 'Just as my brother in this realm had Philippos. Ah, what joys await, Alexander. And you will share them. You should not hate me; I am here to bring you your heart's desire.'

'At the moment my desire is to be rid of this place.'

'Then it shall be so. You have seen the pillars and the maps upon them. But look to the uppermost carvings. They are star maps. You must align these, as well as those of the earth below. When the original settings are duplicated, the Gate will glow into life. Think of it like a man standing between two mirrors, each facing away from him. As they turn there will come a point where he is perfectly reflected in both. When this happens, the Gateways will draw together and become one. Then the second world will be open to the creatures here.'

'But that might send them to our world. I don't want that. They would suffer there as they suffer here. Indeed it would be worse, for at least the people here have known of them always. In Greece they would be feared, hated and slaughtered.'

'Once they existed – even in Greece. How else did you come by your fables? And as for despair – that is a feeling they will know wherever they are,' the Chaos Spirit explained. 'It is their nature, for they are incomplete. The old gods used them – created them – for their own pleasures. They are like left-over toys, Alexander. The war was everything to them. Winning it was the death of them. However, we shall help them, brother, you and I. We will find them a world where they can fight anew.'

'You can do this?' Alexander asked.

'We can do it,' answered the Spirit. 'Together we can do anything. Never forget that. Now let us begin.'

Alexander awoke. Chiron lay beside him, asleep and snoring. The prince rose and gazed up at the left-hand pillar. 'Climb it,' ordered the Chaos Spirit.

It was not difficult, for the carvings made good hand- and foot-holds. Alexander scaled the pillar, traversing to the front. Just above his head was a carved sphere surrounded by smaller globes. 'Touch your hand to the central stone,' said the Spirit. Alexander did so and, like the maps earlier, the stones began to shimmer and move. 'It is realigning itself,' said the Spirit. 'Now climb the second pillar.'

Alexander did so, but did not reach out when ordered. 'What is the matter, brother?' the Spirit asked.

'How can I trust you? For all I know you will send these creatures to a world of doom and dread.'

'Indeed I would,' admitted the Spirit. 'But you are Iskander, the promised one. You will not send them there.'

'I do not understand you.'

'Your coming was foretold, young prince. The Gateway has been waiting for you. The alignments are already set, awaiting you. Can you not see? In this you are merely an instrument of destiny. The last man to pass these Gates deliberately misaligned them. Only your hand can make the magic flow.'

Yet still Alexander did not move. 'What more can I say to you?' asked the Spirit. 'Tell me how I can convince you.'

The prince did not reply. Slowly his hand reached out to touch the stone globe. The pillar began to vibrate, almost shaking Alexander loose. Swiftly he climbed down, stepping back from the Gateway. The grey stone began to shine, and a strange smell like burning leaves filled the air, acrid and unpleasant.

Chiron awoke and scrambled to his feet, moving back to join Alexander. 'You solved the mystery?'

'I believe so.'

The stones shone more brilliantly now, silver in the moonlight, the maps and carved script glowing with flames that licked out from the cuts in the stone. The globes were also aflame, like miniature suns, and the hillside was bathed in light.

The Gateway itself began to shimmer, and through it could be seen a plain between mountains and a distant forest lit by glorious sunshine. Alexander stepped forward, intending to pass through the Gateway, but Chiron's hand gripped his shoulder. 'No,' whispered the *magus*. 'It is not yet open.'

The creatures of the Enchantment moved out from the tree-line. Alexander turned to look at them. They were moving slowly, their eyes gazing in awe upon the gleaming portal. This moment, he knew, had been in their dreams for centuries. For them, this was the culmination of all their hopes. In a great half-circle they spread out at the foot of the hill: centaurs, dryads, nymphs, tall men with huge wings growing from their shoulders, dark-skinned Vores, reptiles, minotaurs; a seething, silent mass, edging forward.

The sunlight of another world bathed the scene in gold, shining upon the faces of the host. And no one spoke. Not a sound came from the creatures of the Enchantment.

Alexander's mouth was dry, and he felt the weight of their expectation like a boulder upon his heart.

Closing his eyes, he sought out Thena; she was sitting alone at the centre of the woods. Alexander felt her sorrow, but then it was as if an iron mask had fallen into place, shielding her.

'What do you require of me?' she asked him.

'I need you to make a journey,' he told her. Her spirit flowed from her. Keeping his eyes closed, his concentration total, he watched with his spirit as the seeress passed through the shimmering Gateway. She returned within moments.

'It is a world of savagery and pain,' she told him.

Once more Alexander climbed the right-hand pillar, touching his fingers to the stones.

Now the Gateway changed colour again, this time shining like polished gold. The view between the pillars altered, becoming a pale blue ocean lapping against a beach of white-gold sand. 'Travel there,' Alexander told Thena.

'There is no need,' her spirit told him. 'I can feel the Enchantment. It is pure and born of joy.'

*

The woods were silent as Parmenion, Philip and Attalus rode between the trees. The moon was high, her silver light bathing the woods and glistening from stream and rock. But there was no sign of life as the trio rode ever deeper.

Thena's voice echoed in Parmenion's mind. 'Keep moving south until you reach a waterfall, then turn west.'

They rode for just under an hour, emerging at last into a wide clearing filled with creatures of the Enchantment: centaurs, cyclopes, winged men and women, dryads and fauns. Parmenion dismounted and bowed as the white-haired goddess approached him. Her naked body gleamed in the moonlight, but there was nothing about her that aroused the Spartan. Ethereal and exquisite she seemed, far beyond the lusts of a mortal man.

'Welcome, Parmenion,' she said. 'Your road has been long and perilous.'

'Yet we are here, Lady,' he answered. 'Where is the boy?'

'He is examining the Gateway. Tell me how my son died.'

'Among friends,' Parmenion told her.

She nodded and smiled. 'That is good to know. At least a spark of nobility remained in him.'

'More than that, I think.'

'In a thousand years he befriended no one. What special quality do you possess?'

'None that I know of.'

The goddess moved away from him, facing Philip. 'Little did I expect ever to speak to one with your face, sir. Even now I can scarce bring myself to look upon you.'

'I am not Philippos.'

'I know that. You fought well.'

'It was not hard to kill him. All his life he had been

368

invincible, and therefore had no need to learn basic defence.'

'You are a King in your own land?'

'I am.'

'And do you also bring despair and terror to your neighbours?'

'I do,' he admitted. 'It is the nature of Greece, Lady. We are always at war. But soon we will be as one nation; then we will cease to kill each other.'

'Under your rule, of course?'

'Of course,' he agreed.

'Nothing changes,' she said sadly, moving on to Attalus. 'And you, sir, what have you learned from your visit to this realm?'

The swordsman shrugged. 'Little I did not know.'

'Is that really true? Have you not at least seen yourself in a different light?'

Attalus smiled. 'I know who I am, what I am. I have no illusions.'

'But you faced the Demon King and did not buckle. Did that not make you proud?'

'No. I came too close to giving in. There is no pride in that.'

'You are wrong, Attalus. You came here with hatred and bitterness, and you will leave much of it behind when you depart. Is that not so?'

'Yes,' he admitted.

The goddess moved back to Parmenion, taking his arm and leading him away into the trees. 'You found love here, Human,' she said. 'Will you leave it behind you?'

'I will, for I must,' the Spartan told her.

'Your guilt still haunts you, then?'

'It does. I must see that Alexander lives. The demon is still within him, as it was with Philippos. He will need a true friend – someone who cares, someone who loves him.'

'Indeed he will.' She stopped then and turned to look up into Parmenion's face. 'You know that he will one day kill you?'

'All men die, and no future is written in stone.'

'Not so. Not for you. Alexander will kill you, Parmenion. It is written in the stars, it is carried in whispers upon the wind, it is carved in the stone eternal. You cannot escape it.'

'We shall see,' he told her, his mouth suddenly dry.

'You are a good man,' she said, after a while, 'and you will carry my blessing with you. There is little power in it any more, but a blessing is always better than a curse.'

'Indeed it is,' the Spartan replied. 'Are all our futures set in this stone eternal?'

'No. Only yours and Alexander's. And now it is time to seek the Gateway, to leave this tortured realm. Come – and bid us farewell.'

*

Parmenion stood alongside Philip at the centre of the vast, silent throng waiting before the Gateway. High above them the moon shone clear and bright, the stars gleaming like gems on sable. But beyond the Gateway all was sunshine which lit the hillside with golden light.

'The *magus*!' said Philip suddenly, pointing to Chiron. 'That's the sorcerer who cast the spell upon me!'

'I think not, sire,' Parmenion told him. 'That is Chiron. He is of this world.'

'If I see any more twins I shall go insane,' muttered Philip.

Alexander walked back to the pillars, taking hold of the jutting stone on the right and stretching out his hand towards the other stone. For a moment only he stood, then his head fell back, dark smoke oozing from his nostrils and mouth to flow down over his chest and along his arm. The smoke took shape, becoming another Alexander – horned and yellow-eyed, a bizarre and deformed mirror image. Holding to Alexander's hand, the Chaos Spirit reached out and took hold of the second stone.

In that instant lightning forked between the pillars. Alexander was flung forward to the ground, the Chaos Spirit hurled into the air.

The voice of Tamis echoed in Parmenion's mind. 'The necklet! Put it on the boy!'

Parmenion ran forward, kneeling by the unconscious prince. Glancing up, he saw the smoke form of the Chaos Spirit floating down towards them. Unclipping the necklet he fastened it around Alexander's neck. The smoke covered the child but then a cool breeze blew, dispersing it.

Alexander opened his eyes. 'Is the Gate open?' he asked.

Parmenion looked up. 'Yes,' he answered. The first of the centaurs was moving between the pillars.

Alexander struggled to rise. 'I cannot sense the Dark God,' he whispered.

'He is not within you,' Parmenion told him. 'You are wearing now a necklet of great power. No evil can enter your mind as long as it remains in place.'

Philip moved alongside them to kneel by his son. 'You did well, boy,' said the Macedonian King, reaching out. Alexander embraced his father and Philip rose, holding the boy to his chest.

Parmenion sighed and stood. The creatures of the Enchantment were slowing filing through the Gateway into a new world.

The white-haired goddess approached him. 'Whatever else the future holds, Parmenion, be proud of this day.'

'I shall, Lady.'

With a smile she turned and walked through the Gate. At last only Chiron and Brontes were left and the *magus* walked to Parmenion, extending his hand. 'Sadly I missed most of your journey,' he said, 'and was of little help to you.'

'You did enough,' Parmenion assured him. 'You rescued us from the Vores on that first day and, as Camiron, you carried Alexander to safety in the Forest of Gorgon. What will you do now?'

'I shall pass the Gateway and see what the new world offers. But there are many gates, Parmenion, and I feel we will meet again.'

'I will look forward to it.'

Chiron bade farewell to Alexander and Philip while the minotaur approached Parmenion.

'I shall not forget you, Human,' said Brontes.

'Nor I you.'

'You gave my brother a chance of redemption; I believe that he took it. For that alone I will always be grateful. May the gods walk with you, Parmenion.'

'And with you,' said the Spartan, as Brontes moved away between the pillars.

As Brontes passed through the Gate the pillars shimmered once more, darkening to the grey of cold stone . . . and the world beyond flickered and was gone.

Attalus approached Parmenion. 'What now, *strategos*?' he asked.

The Spartan shrugged, all energy leaving him. Moving to a nearby tree, he sat with his back to the trunk. In a few short days he had travelled half-way across a strange land, fought a major battle and known, albeit briefly, the life of a King. Now his body was numb with fatigue, his mind confused and weary.

He heard Thena's soft footfalls and smiled as she sat beside him. 'What now?' he asked, echoing Attalus' enquiry.

'We wait for Aristotle,' she said. 'Did you enjoy being King?'

'Yes,' he admitted. 'I found my love there. Derae.' He sighed and tears began to well in his eyes. Clearing his throat, he looked away for a moment.

'You could stay,' Thena whispered.

'No. My destiny is beyond this world. I must remain with Alexander. What will you do?'

'Return to my Temple. I am a Healer and there are those who need my skills.'

'You sound sad, lady. You should not be,' he told her, reaching out to take her hand.

'Life is full of sorrow,' she replied, 'and yet it is still life. You are a good man. I hope you find happiness.' She rose and walked away down the hillside and into the trees.

Aristotle's voice whispered into her mind, echoing as if from a vast distance: 'Have the creatures passed the Gateway?'

'Yes.'

'All of them? Every one?'

'Yes, all of them. Including your twin.'

'Then help me come through to where you are.'

'How?'

'Hold to my voice. Picture me. The Sipstrassi will do the rest.'

Derae felt a pull on her spirit and was almost torn from her body. Crying out she resisted the force, but pain ripped through her and she cried out again. As suddenly as it had come it vanished and a misty figure formed before her, slowly becoming Aristotle. The *magus* staggered and fell to his knees, his fingers convulsively digging into the solid earth beneath him.

'That was a hard journey,' he said. 'You did well, Derae.'

'Send me back,' she said softly, 'and in my own form.'

'But you wish to keep your youth, surely?' he asked, rising.

'No,' answered Thena-Derae, 'I wish to be as I was.'

He shook his head in disbelief but raised his hand in which a golden stone shone brightly. Her dark hair became again silver, shot with fading red, the skin of her face sagging into middle age, her eyes clouded and once more blind. 'How could you want this?' whispered Aristotle.

'It is who I am,' she answered. 'Now send me back.'

'You have said your farewells?'

'I have said all that can be said.'

Aristotle lifted his hand. The golden stone gleamed and soft light covered the priestess. When it faded, she was gone.

He made his way up the hillside to where the others waited.

'Chiron!' shouted Alexander. 'You came back!'

'Yes, I did,' answered the *magus*. 'I have come to take you home.'

'Which one is this?' asked Philip stonily.

'This, I believe, is Aristotle,' said Parmenion with a grin.

'Are you sure?'

'What do you think, Attalus?'

'I agree. This is Aristotle, sire.'

'Good,' said Philip. He took a deep breath. 'You whoreson!' he roared, advancing on the *magus*.

Aristotle leapt back in sudden surprise and fear. 'It had to be done, sire!' he said.

'Why did you take my memory?'

'That is hard to explain but, if you will give me the chance, I will tell all.'

'I for one would like to hear it,' said Parmenion softly.

Philip folded his hands across his chest. 'Come then, *magus*, for I like a good tale,' he hissed, his eyes still angry.

Aristotle settled himself down with the others before him in a semi-circle. 'I am called Aristotle . . .' he began.

'We know that, damn you! Get on with it,' stormed Philip and the *magus* raised a hand for silence.

'In my own way, my lord, if you please. I am now Aristotle – but once I was Chiron and I lived here with the people of the Enchantment. This is where I first met Parmenion, and Helm, the warrior with no memory, and Attalus the swordsman. Here in this world I also saw, for the first time, the Golden Child Iskander. And – as you have just seen – I passed through this Gateway with the exodus of the children of the Titans. For you it is but moments. But for me it is four centuries since I left this realm.'

'What happened to you then?' asked Parmenion.

'I explored many lands, through many centuries. I found other gates, paths between worlds. I journeyed far. But I longed for human company and so, at last, I came to Asia and then Greece – and heard once more of Parmenion. And I realized I had travelled a great circle in Time: I had arrived at a point *before* he passed through to Achaea. This was a great problem for me. Could I interfere? Had I already interfered? Of course I had, for when Parmenion first came to Achaea he told Chiron that a sorcerer in another world had sent him. That man, he said, looked just like me. And I realized too that I was caught in a dangerous web. I had to recreate everything as it was, or else risk changing the past – and perhaps destroying myself. Such a paradox, my friends. I sent Parmenion and Attalus through; then I sought you out, sire. I could not know what adventures would befall you all, for my memories of this time were blurred by my existence as Camiron. You see my dilemma?

374

I could tell you nothing – for you knew nothing when first I met you. I longed to come with you, to help you, but I could not. Some laws are immutable. It is not possible to pass through a Gateway into a time, or a place, where you already exist. No man can meet himself. So all I could do was wait, and hope and pray that events would fashion themselves as they had before.'

'For a while there,' said Philip, 'I almost had a grip on what you were saying. But understanding you is like trying to catch a trout with your fingers.'

'I appreciate your difficulty,' Aristotle told him. 'For you these adventures were new, but for me they were part of my history. They had already happened. I had to rely on what I knew as Chiron. All he knew was that a warrior called Helm appeared on the battlefield and killed Philippos, and that this man was the King of Makedon in another world. Chiron . . . I . . . also knew that this King had been robbed of his memory. So when faced with the problem from the other end of Time, I merely recreated the circumstances.'

'That's what I mean!' snorted Philip. 'Just as I begin to understand, it all slips away. But answer me this, whose idea was it – originally – to take away my memories and abduct me?'

'It is a circle, sire. Therefore it has no beginning and no end. There is no one to blame.'

'No one to . . . Listen to me, *magus*, I am a King, and there is always someone for a King to blame. That is the way of the world. You came into my palace and – without a by-your-leave, sire – abducted me. Give me one good reason why I should not strike your head from your shoulders.'

Aristotle spread his hands and smiled. 'The only answer I can think of, sire, is that were you to try it I would turn you into a lizard and tread on you.'

Philip was silent for a moment, then he turned to Parmenion. 'I'd say that sounds like a good reason.'

'I agree, sire.'

'I like you, *magus*,' said the King, 'but you owe me a debt. How will you pay it?'

'How would you like it paid, sire?'

'Come with us to Pella, as tutor to my son.'

Aristotle laughed. 'I would have asked for that as a gift,' he said, 'and willingly accept it as a penance.'

'Good! Now take us home.'

'Parmenion has not yet said farewell to his Queen,' pointed out Aristotle, his smile fading. 'And she is waiting at the foot of the hill.'

Parmenion sighed, pushed himself to his feet and walked down towards the trees. He found Derae sitting on a fallen tree and she stood as he approached.

'You would have left without seeing me, without saying goodbye?'

'Yes. It was the coward's way, I know, but I felt I could not bear to say the words. You have spoken with Leonidas?'

'He told me everything. Am I like her?'

He nodded. 'In every way.'

'So it was not me you loved,' she said sadly.

'It was you,' he assured her. 'At first it was an image, a memory. But the woman I made love to was you. The woman I love *is* you.'

'Yet you cannot stay?'

'No. I must look after Alexander. It is my duty and my life. Will you forgive me?'

She nodded and stepped into his embrace. Kissing him once on the cheek, she pushed him gently from her. 'Go then,' she said. 'Go now – and swiftly. I know that you will return one day. I know of your secret, Parmenion. I know the reason why you must travel with Alexander. But your destiny is here and one day you will come back. And I shall be waiting here, just as you see me. I shall be here.'

'I cannot promise that,' he said, 'though I desire it with all my heart.'

'You do not have to. Last night I had a dream. A grey-bearded sorcerer appeared to me and told me to be here tonight. He said you would leave, returning to your own world. But he also said that he would do his best to send you back to me. I will wait.'

Parmenion said nothing. Backing away several steps, he spun on his heel and strode up the hill.

Aristotle was waiting, and as the Spartan came alongside him the *magus* lifted his arm.

The Gateway shimmered once more . . .

Book Four

The City of Mieza, 337 BC

The man called Aristotle sat alone in the deserted gardens of the school building, gazing towards the north, watching the storm-clouds loom above the rearing Bora Mountains. A cold breeze blew and he shivered, drawing his grey woollen cloak more tightly about his frame.

Glancing back towards the house he saw his wife, Pythias, gathering herbs in the small cultivated patch of earth by the kitchen. It would soon be time to leave, putting behind him the last fourteen years –saying farewell to Mieza, to Macedonia, to Greece.

He sighed. Immortality was a burden and yet, like the narcotics of Egypt, wholly addictive. To be relieved of the prospect of death only heightened the fear of dying. The longer he lived the more bored he became, the more he longed for the peace of the grave, the more terrified he became at the thought of it.

And the memories . . .

So many . . . Three thousand years ago he had almost gone mad with them. But Pendarric had saved him, teaching him to use the Stones more wisely. Each life of his past had been reduced to a single key word, locked in his mind. The Makedones years had become Iskander. Merely by summoning the word to conscious thought he could see again the Golden Child and the shining Gateway, and all the years that preceded it. But now he was reaching the point where even the keys shone in his mind like stars, thousands upon thousands.

What is there that is new, he wondered?

The answer came swift as a stab in the heart.

There is nothing that is new under the sun. All is vanity.

He smiled and unlocked the key to the life he had shared with the Philosopher. Golden days. A time when there were still discoveries to be made, surprises to be enjoyed.

Why are you so melancholy, he asked himself? Around the bench where he sat were a dozen seats, empty now, but not long ago they were occupied by the sons of Macedonian nobles – young men full of hope, nurturing dreams. And – always at their centre, a bright shining sun in their lives – there was Alexander.

Now you have it, he realized.

Alexander.

Aristotle rose and wandered to the northern gate, pushing it open and walking out into the foothills of Mount Bermion. Throughout the ages he had seen men, great men, men of wisdom, men of war, secure in their arrogance, dismissive of the past. Yet the past held all the answers to life's mysteries and each successive generation unknowingly locked them away. Then searched for them in the unborn futures.

I had high hopes for you, Alexander, he thought. You have a fine mind, perhaps the most brilliant since the Philosopher ruled in Jerusalem. Certainly you rival Pendarric in the days when he reigned over Atlantis.

Yet what is it that calls you? Wisdom? The pursuit of knowledge? No. You hear the trumpets of war, you seek the Whore of Conquest. Even with the Chaos Spirit locked outside you, still you are a man, and men will always lust for glory.

And the others will follow you. He pictured them, their young faces bright with longing for a future they knew to be rich with promise: Ptolemy, Nearchos, Philotas, Nicci, Derdas and the others. Like all young men, they revelled in their strength and were scornful of the deeds of their fathers.

382

Aristotle stopped by a trickling stream, sitting with his back to a boulder out of the wind. A hawk swooped out of the sky, dropping like a stone, his talons ripping into a young rabbit just emerging from its burrow into the dusk. The captured beast did not struggle as the bird swept back into the air, it hung limply in the hawk's grip. Aristotle's spirit reached out to touch the creature. It was dead.

'A curse on all hawks,' he said aloud.

'He has mouths to feed,' said a voice. Aristotle looked up and smiled at the tall figure moving through the shadows of the trees to sit beside him. The man settled himself, wincing as his arthritic knee refused to bend.

'I thought I'd find you here,' said Parmenion, removing his helm and running his hand through his sweat-soaked iron-grey hair. 'Philip wants you to come to Pella for the wedding.'

Aristotle shook his head. 'I shall not be there, Parmenion.'

'Philip will not be best pleased.'

'His anger is immaterial to me. I shall be walking the Dragon Paths to other worlds.'

'And Pythias?'

'I will leave her money. She will not mourn my passing; she kept my bed warm, but there is little love between us.' He looked deeply into Parmenion's face, seeing the sharply chiselled lines, the dark smudges below the bright blue eyes. 'You look tired, my friend.'

Parmenion shrugged. 'I am sixty-three years old. I expect to be tired after a long campaign.'

'Surely you can rest now? Since Philip crushed the Athenians and Thebans at Chaironeia he has become, in all but name, the Lord of Greece. Where now are his enemies?'

'Everywhere,' replied Parmenion, with a wry smile.

'I accept that,' said Aristotle, returning the smile, 'but I meant where are the enemies that can cause him harm? There are no armies left for him to conquer. He rules from Thrace to Epirus, from Paionia to Thessaly. Everyone pays him homage – even Athens. I hear they erected a statue to him after Chaironeia. Unbelievable!'

'Not really. The Athenians expected us to march on their city and ransack it. Instead Philip returned their dead with full military honours and sued for peace. Their relief was immense.'

'Why did he spare them? Athens has been a thorn in his side for years.'

Parmenion shrugged. 'Philip has always remembered the deeds of his twin in Makedon. He was determined never to repeat such evils. But also he has a greater dream: he looks to extend his realm to the east.'

'Where else can he go? He cannot take on the might of Persia.'

'He has no choice. Macedonia now has a huge army – cavalry, siege-engineers, mercenaries. All need feeding, payment. Where else can he go? The Great King rules over a hundred nations, all rich.'

'And that is your answer,' said the *magus*. 'One hundred nations, all with armies. The Great King could put a million men in the field against you.'

'I know,' said Parmenion wearily.

Aristotle pushed himself to his feet, extending his hand to haul Parmenion upright. The Spartan's knee cracked painfully and he stretched his leg. 'I am better from the back of a horse these days,' he said.

'Come, let us go home. You and I shall have a farewell drink.'

Long into the night the two men sat talking in the small *andron* at the rear of the schoolhouse. A brazier of coals burned at the centre of the room, and several lanterns flickered on the walls. The room was warm, the night wind rattling the shutters on the single window.

'Are you content?' asked Aristotle suddenly. Parmenion smiled, but did not answer. 'Do you wish you had remained in Achaea?'

'Of course. But it is foolish to dwell on past mistakes.'

Aristotle nodded. 'You are wise in that. How is Philotas?'

Parmenion's face darkened. 'The same. We rarely speak now. His arrogance is all-consuming and yet he fawns on Alexander like a table slave. I try not to allow myself to become angry. It is not easy for the son of a general; he feels the need to prove himself better than his father.'

'He has great ambition,' said Aristotle softly.

'His mother fed him thoughts of glory from his birth. I should have stopped it long ago.'

'His ambition may bring you down one day,' Aristotle warned. 'He dreams of becoming King.'

'It will never happen. He has neither the wit nor the strength.'

'I know. I taught him for thirteen years. He will be an able captain, though. He might yet distinguish himself.'

'He did well in the Triballian campaign, but the glory was Alexander's. Philotas must have found that hard to bear.'

'He was not the only one.'

Parmenion shook his head. 'Do not believe all you hear, *magus*. Philip is not jealous of his son. He loves him and is proud of his achievements. So am I.'

'It is said that Philip's new bride is already pregnant – and that she will bear him a son. That will be hard for Alexander to take.'

'Why so?' queried Parmenion. 'Alexander is eighteen and the heir to the throne. Nothing will change that.'

'Come now, *strategos*, do not let your allegiance blind you. Use your mind. He is marrying Cleopatra, a high-born Macedonian. All his other wives are foreigners. She is the ward of Attalus. You do not think that many of the Macedonian nobles will see the child as the first true-born heir? You yourself are a mix-blood. Alexander's mother is an Epirote, which makes him a half-breed.'

'I do not wish to talk of this!' snapped Parmenion.

Aristotle sighed and lay back on his couch. 'Then we shall not. We will finish our wine and say our farewells.'

In the darkness just before dawn Aristotle, dressed for travel in a long tunic and heavy cloak, moved silently into the room where Parmenion slept. The Spartan was deeply asleep and the *magus* moved to the bedside. From the pouch at his hip Aristotle took a small golden stone, touching it to Parmenion's right knee. The Spartan stirred and groaned softly, but did not wake. The power of the Stone flowed into the sleeping man, the iron grey of his hair darkening slightly, the chiselled lines of his face becoming more shallow.

'One gift, my friend,' whispered Aristotle, 'but not the last. One day I will return.'

He backed away to the door and walked from his house, returning to the stream in the foothills and a shallow cave partly hidden by thick bushes. The new sun rose in glory and Aristotle paused to drink in the beauty of its light upon the verdant countryside.

'Why are you leaving now?' he asked himself. The answer leapt to his mind, sharp and bitter. The days of blood were coming and the Dark God was reasserting himself. He could feel the Spirit's presence hanging over the land like an unseen mist, swirling in the hearts of men, flowing into their minds, whispering in their ears.

Did Parmenion think the necklet could protect the boy for long? It was but metal, enhanced with the power of Sipstrassi Stone. It could be removed, torn from his neck with a single tug. And then?

The Dark God would return.

Will return, he corrected himself. Nothing will stop him.

You are running away, he realized: hiding from the great battle to come.

'I want to live,' he said aloud. 'I have done my part. Better to be a live dog than a dead lion.' But he was not convinced.

With a last glance over the Macedonian countryside he stepped inside the cave.

And was seen no more in the land of Greece.

Pella, Summer 337 BC

Alexander sat back, occasionally touching his lips to his wine-cup but swallowing little as he listened to his Companions discussing the forthcoming Persian campaign. As always, it was Philotas who had the most to say. Alexander found it bizarre that a son could look so much like his father, yet enjoy so few of his sire's talents. Philotas was tall and slender, a fine runner and a good cavalry officer, but his grasp on the subtleties of strategy was tenuous at best. Yet, like so many men of limited talent, his main ability was in mastering the art of hindsight, always seeing where others had made mistakes.

'As at Chaironeia,' Philo was telling the others, 'my father should never have allowed the left to swing so wide. Had it not been for Alexander's charge, Philip would have been slain.'

Alexander smiled and said nothing. It did no harm whatever to have his comrades see him as a young god of war, but the truth – as always – was not as simple.

'We will each be kings,' Ptolemy declared. 'I shall have a golden throne and a thousand concubines.'

'You wouldn't know what to do with them,' said Nearchos, chuckling. Alexander laughed with the rest at Ptolemy's discomfort. The youngest of the Companions, Ptolemy's good nature was legendary.

'I would have great pleasure in finding out,' put in Ptolemy, grinning.

'If you are all to be kings,' said Alexander, 'what will be left for me?'

'You will be the King of Kings, naturally,' Ptolemy told him. 'You will rule the world and we will be your satraps.'

'And kill all your enemies,' Philotas added.

'An interesting thought. What happens when I have no more enemies?'

'A great man always has enemies,' said Ptolemy. 'What would be the point of being great if that were not so? How dull it would be.'

'I take it,' asked Nearchos, 'that you are already building up a stock of enemies?'

'Yes. I've started with you, you low-born dolt!'

Nearchos' laughter rippled out, swift and infectious. 'Me? Is that wise? Do you no longer wish me to speak well of you to my sister?'

'A good point,' said Ptolemy, rubbing his chin. 'You are correct. It is not an opportune time to have you for an enemy. It will have to be Philo then: he'll be my first enemy.'

'Enough of this talk,' put in Alexander. 'You are all a little drunk. Get off home with you! I intend to be riding at dawn. It is said there is a lioness raiding the cattle and goatherds at a small village north of the city. It should be a fine hunt.'

'I shall kill the beast with my bare hands,' said Nearchos, rising and flexing his muscles. Like his father, Theoparlis, he had enormous breadth of shoulder and a barrel chest.

'If that doesn't work, you could try breathing on him,' pointed out Ptolemy. 'Put all those onions to good use.'

Nearchos leapt at the slender youngster, but tripped and fell over a small table laden with sweetmeats. As he scrambled to his feet, chasing the younger man out into the royal gardens, Philotas turned to Alexander and bowed.

'Until tomorrow, sire,' he said softly.

'It is not fitting to call me sire. I am not a King,' said Alexander, his tone mild.

'Not yet,' said Parmenion's eldest son, bowing once more before striding from the room.

At last only Craterus was left. Older than the others, almost twenty, he was a quiet, introverted man, but he seemed at ease in the ribald meetings of the Companions.

'Something troubling you?' asked Alexander.

'Your ankle is still swollen from the fall and you are limping badly. Is this the right time to hunt lions?'

Alexander clapped the taller man on the shoulder. 'It will be better by morning, and I shall strap it well. But that is not the reason you have waited to see me.'

Craterus shrugged and smiled. 'No. I am uneasy, my lord. There is a lot of talk at court about the King's marriage and the child Cleopatra carries.'

The smile left Alexander's face. 'This should not concern you. It does not concern me. My father already has six wives.'

'Not like this one.'

'Do not take this any further, Craterus,' warned the prince. 'There are some things that should not be said.'

'Very well. As always I shall obey you. But know this – if you need me I will be beside you.'

'All the royal pages give oaths to serve the King. The King is Philip,' Alexander pointed out.

'That is as maybe. But I serve Alexander.'

The prince moved close to his friend, looking up into the man's deep-set dark eyes. 'It is comments like that which lead to the death of princes. You understand me? I will never lead a rebellion against Philip. Never! If I wished him dead I would have let him be slain at Chaironeia, when his horse was killed under him. Now say no more of this. There is nothing to fear, Craterus. Nothing.'

The Companion bowed and departed, pulling shut the door behind him. Alexander wandered back to the centre of the room, lifting his wine-cup and sipping the contents. He had made the one cup last all evening, disliking the effect of alcohol on his system.

'You should listen to him, my son,' said Olympias, moving into the room from the shadows of the outer corridor.

'It is normally considered courteous, Mother, to announce your presence.'

'Are you angry with me?'

He shook his head and smiled. Stepping in close Olympias kissed his cheek. Her red-gold hair was touched with silver now, but her face was still youthful and her body slender. 'Why is everyone seeing danger in the shadows?' asked Alexander. 'It is only a wedding.'

'She is the ward of Attalus . . . and Attalus hates you.'

'He risked his life to save me once. I shall not forget that.'

'That was *then*!' she said, her eyes flashing. 'Now he poisons Philip's mind against you. Why can you not see it?'

'I choose not to. Philip built this realm from nothing. Beset on all sides, he alone made Macedonia feared and respected. What have I done? I took an army into the north and subdued the Triballians. How does that compare with the King who conquered Thrace, Illyria, the Chalcidice, Thessaly, Paionia – and crushed the combined armies of Athens and Thebes?' He laughed and gently took hold of his mother's shoulders. 'Do you understand what I am saying? He owes me nothing. If he chooses to make his new son the heir, what right have I to oppose him?'

'Right?' she stormed, pulling away from him. 'You are the heir – the first-born son. It is your destiny to rule. But think on this, Alexander: if you are dispossessed there will be those who will seek your death. You will not be fighting for a crown alone, but for your life.'

'No,' he told her. 'Philip would never order my death – any more than I would countenance killing him. But all this talk is dangerous. The words fall like sparks on dry grass and I will not have them spoken around me.'

'You are altogether too trusting,' she told him. 'But there is someone coming to Pella who may be able to convince you.'

'Who?'

'The Lady of Samothrace. Her name is Aida and she is a seeress of great power. She can tell you of your destiny.'

Alexander said nothing, but he turned away from his mother and strode towards the door. 'You will see her?' called Olympias.

'No, I will not,' answered Alexander, his voice cold. 'Can none of you see what you are doing? When Philotas calls me *sire*, when Craterus says he puts me above my father, when you seek to turn me against Philip –you are all only increasing any danger there might be. You keep this Aida away from me.'

'But it is all for you – because we care!' Olympias shouted. Alexander did not reply, but walked out into the moonlit gardens and away from the palace.

★

The grass was growing crimson, dripping blood to the parched earth beneath it. The sky was the colour of ash, grey and lifeless. Not a bird flew, no breath of wind disturbed the plain. Philip knelt and touched his hand to the crimson stems and blood smeared across his skin. He rose, trembling, noticing for the first time the bodies that lay all about him. Thousands upon thousands of corpses, the grass growing around them, from them, through them. He shuddered. A man was lying on his back with weeds growing from beneath his eyelids.

'What is this place?' shouted Philip. The sound died even as it left his lips.

'You are not comfortable here?'

He spun on his heel, sword snaking into his hand. Before him, dressed in armour of black and gold, stood Philippos, the Demon King.

'You are dead!' screamed Philip, backing away.

'Yes,' the Makedones King agreed.

'Get away from me!'

'Is that any way to treat a brother?' asked Philippos, drawing his own sword and advancing. Philip leapt to meet him, their blades clashing together, and his sword slashed across his opponent's neck to open a jagged wound that spouted blood. Philippos was hurled to the right, twisting to fall face-down on the ground. Slowly he rose to his knees with his back to his enemy. Philip waited. The Demon King stood and slowly turned. Philip cried out. Gone was the bearded face that mirrored his own. Now Philippos had golden hair, sea-green eyes and a face of surpassing beauty.

391

'Alexander?'

'Yes, Father, Alexander,' said the Demon King, smiling and advancing with sword extended.

'Do not make me kill you! Please!'

'You could not kill me, Father. No. But I shall slay you.'

Dark horns sprouted from Alexander's temples, circling back over his ears. His eyes changed colour from sea-green to yellow, the pupils slitted. Philip gripped his sword and waited as the demon before him moved slowly to the attack; he tried a swift lunge to the throat, but his arm was heavy, his movements slow, and he watched in sick horror as Alexander's sword parried his own and rose up gleaming and sharp, the blade slicing into his throat and up through his mouth, stabbing into his brain like a tongue of fire . . .

Philip awoke and cried out. The woman beside him stirred but did not wake as the King sat up. His head was pounding, his body drenched in sweat. The old wound in his leg throbbed painfully, but he pushed himself from the bed and limped across to the nearest couch. The wine pitcher upon the small table was empty. Philip cursed and slumped down upon the couch, holding the pitcher in his lap.

The dream was always the same. He could never defeat Alexander.

'I should have killed him at birth,' he thought. A cold breeze whispered across the room and Philip shivered and returned to his bed. Beside him Cleopatra slept on. Tenderly he stroked her hair. So beautiful, so young. His hand moved down to rest upon her belly – still flat and taut, despite the three months of the pregnancy. In her was a son. Not demon-possessed, not born of darkness and sorcery, but a true son – one who would grow to love his father, not plan his murder.

How could you do this to me, Alexander? I loved you. I would have risked anything for you.

At first Philip had ignored the reports that Attalus drew to his attention – the fawning remarks of Alexander's Companions, the criticisms levelled at the King and his generals. But as the months passed Philip became more and more convinced that Alexander would not be content until he sat upon the throne.

The Triballian campaign showed that. Does he think I am a fool? Oh yes, he crushed the enemy, forcing them to pay tribute. But in whose name did he demand it? Not for Philip. Not for Macedon. No, in the name of Alexander.

Arrogant whelp! Of course you beat the Triballians, for you had my army behind you. *My* army!

But is it mine? How they cheered the golden prince at Chaironeia, carrying him shoulder-high around the camp. And after the Triballian victory, when he awarded every warrior ten gold pieces, they gave him the salute of kings, swords beating against shields.

Is it still mine?

Of course it is, for I have Parmenion. Yes, the Spartan will always be loyal.

Philip smiled and lay back, resting his head upon the soft, satin-covered cushion. The Lion of Macedon is with me, he thought, and drifted once more into sleep.

The grass was growing crimson, dripping blood to the parched earth beneath it. The sky was the colour of ash, grey and lifeless. Not a bird flew, no breath of wind disturbed the plain . . .

*

The bath had been designed and built by Philip, using only the finest marble. It took six slaves more than an hour to fill it with heated, perfumed water, and a dozen men could sit on the sunken seats or swim across the centre. The King had constructed it after the second Thracian campaign, when his right leg had been smashed and the bones had knitted badly, leaving him with an exaggerated limp and constant pain. Only immersed in warm water did the limb cease to throb, and Philip had taken to holding meetings in the bath with his officers around him.

Today only Parmenion was present and the two men sat side by side as slaves added boiling water, keeping the temperature high. Crimson flowers floated on the surface, their scent strong, and Parmenion felt the tension and weariness of his long ride ebbing away.

'He is gone then,' said the King. 'I shall miss him.'

'He sent you his best regards, my lord.'

Philip chuckled. 'You remember when he threatened to turn me into a lizard?'

'Yes. You took it well, as I recall.'

'Fine days, Parmenion. Days of strength. I miss them.'

The Spartan glanced at his King. Philip was beginning to show signs of age – his black hair and beard speckled with silver, the skin pouching below his eyes. But his grin was still infectious and his power alarming.

'Have we made contact with the Asian cities?' asked Philip.

'Yes. Mothac is receiving reports. We will be welcomed in all the Greek cities of Asia Minor, but the supply lines will be stretched. Thirty thousand men need a great deal of feeding.'

'The Athenian fleet will supply us,' said Philip dismissively. 'What do you hear about the new Persian King?'

'He is a diplomat and a warrior. I knew him years ago; it was through him that I lost my commission and came to Macedonia. He is arrogant but not unintelligent. He will not rush at us; he will send his satraps against us at first and try to foment rebellion behind us. Already he has made contact with Sparta and Thebes, and his agents are in Athens and Corinth.'

Philip leaned forward, splashing his face and beard with perfumed water. 'This time it will avail them nothing. There is no army to tackle us – not even Sparta. No one could act alone.'

'Attacking Persia is a major enterprise,' said Parmenion. 'I hope you are not taking it too lightly?'

'Do not concern yourself with that fear, Parmenion. I have dreamt about this for nearly twenty years, but always I knew the dangers. Almost half a century ago Agisaleus of Sparta invaded Persia. What happened? He scored military successes but was summoned home when Thebes rose against him. It is the Persian way. With their limitless gold and our greed, they have kept us at each other's throats for centuries. That's why I waited so long, ensuring that

Greece would be safe behind us. Now the Persians have no leverage here.'

'What command will you give Alexander?' asked the Spartan.

Philip's expression hardened. 'None. He will stay behind.'

'To rule in your absence?'

'No. Antipater shall be my Regent.'

'I do not understand, sire. Alexander has proved his competence.'

'It is not his competence that concerns me – it is his loyalty. He plots against me, Parmenion. Before long he will seek to overthrow me – led no doubt in his treachery by his Epirote whore of a mother. They must think me foolish, or perhaps blind in both eyes. Happily I still have friends who report to me.'

'I have never seen any sign of treachery,' said Parmenion.

'Truly? And would you tell me if you did?'

'How could you doubt that I would?'

Philip rose from the bath and limped across the marble floor. Two servants brought him warmed towels; throwing one around his waist, the King used the other to rub dry his hair and beard. Parmenion followed him. 'What is happening to you, Philip? How can you doubt your son's devotion? Twice he has saved your life, and never once have I heard him speak against you. What poison has Attalus been speaking –for I feel his presence in this?'

'You think I have no other spies than Attalus?' retorted the King. 'I have many. Alexander gave a banquet for his friends last month where he made a speech. You know what he said? "What will my father leave me to conquer?" He wishes me dead!'

'That depends on how you read the sentiment. I take it he was speaking of his pride in your achievements.'

'And what of your own son, Philotas? He is constantly speaking about your and – by implication – my failures: the sieges of Perinthos and Byzantion. He used the word stupidity. About me!'

'Stupid people are always the first to use such words. He

is not bright, sire, but Alexander always rebukes him. And as for the sieges, well, we hardly covered ourselves with glory. We took neither city. Perhaps we were . . . less than brilliant.'

'Why do you always speak up for Alexander?' roared Philip. 'Have I no right to expect your loyalty?'

'Every right,' responded Parmenion. 'And should I ever see a single shred of evidence that you are betrayed I will report it to you. More than that, I will kill any man – any man – who seeks to bring you down.'

Philip took a deep breath and slowly let it out. Then he smiled and relaxed. 'I know. But you are too trusting, Spartan. You still think of the Golden Child. Well, he's a man now, with his own ambitions. But enough of that – what do you think of my new bride?'

'She is very beautiful, sire.'

'Yes – and sweet-natured. You know, once I thought I loved Olympias, but I am convinced now that I was bewitched. I see her as she truly is – a vile harridan, foul of temper and viper-tongued. But Cleopatra is everything I could have wished for. She has given me true happiness. And soon I will have another son, one born of love.'

'Yes, sire,' said Parmenion, trying to hold the sadness from his voice.

*

The wedding festivities were scheduled to last for eight days and no one in Pella could remember any festival like it. Free wine was distributed to every household, while all men over the age of fifteen received a specially struck gold coin bearing the head of Philip, with Cleopatra's portrait on the reverse. The coin represented half a year's wages to the poorer servants and land workers, and the celebrations were loud, raucous and unforgettable.

An athletics competition had been under way for twelve days, its size and scope rivalling the Games of Olympia, and the city was packed to overflowing as citizens from surrounding areas and guests from all over the country arrived for the wedding. All the champions of Greece were

396

present at the Games and the King presented to each winner a crown of laurel leaves made from finest gold. There were only two Macedonian victors: Philotas won the middle-distance race, and Alexander rode Bucephalus to victory against horsemen from Thrace, Athens, Sparta, Thessaly and Corinth.

The 10,000 crowd sent up a thunderous roar as Alexander crossed the line on the giant black stallion, his nearest competitor some twenty lengths back. The prince cantered Bucephalus in a long circuit of the stadium, acknowledging the cheers, finally halting before the royal dais where Philip sat with Cleopatra beside him, flanked by his generals Parmenion, Antipater, Attalus and Cleitus.

'A fine victory,' said Cleitus, gazing admiringly at the young rider.

'Anyone would have won on that horse,' muttered Philip, pushing himself to his feet. Lifting the golden laurel crown from the table beside him, he handed it to Parmenion. 'Go,' he said, 'present the winner with his prize.'

The crowd fell silent as the general walked out to the prince. Everyone knew the King should have presented the prize and a confused murmuring began in the stands. Alexander lifted his leg and leapt from Bucephalus' back, bowing his head to receive the laurel crown. As it was placed upon his head he gave a wide grin and waved to the crowd, earning another ovation.

With the smile still in place he whispered to Parmenion: 'What is wrong with my father? Have I done something to displease him?'

'We will talk later,' Parmenion replied.

'I shall come to your home.'

'No, that would not be wise. Mothac has a small house in the western quarter, near the Temple of Healing. Be at the rear of the Temple at midnight. I will see you there. Be sure you are not followed.'

Still smiling, Alexander took hold of Bucephalus' mane and vaulted to the beast's back. Parmenion returned to the dais and, as he mounted the steps, caught sight of Attalus watching the prince riding towards the exit gates.

The years had not been kind to the swordsman. His hair was white and thinning, his face lean and skeletal, with deep lines carved into his cheeks, the skin of his throat loose and wrinkled. Yet he was barely sixty. Attalus saw Parmenion watching him and smiled. The Spartan nodded in reply, then took his place at the King's side as the boxing bouts began.

Parmenion waited for another hour, then he asked leave of the King and walked back from the dais, moving to the huge tents erected outside the stadium where food and drink was being served. Everything was free and many of the city's poor were congregating here, drinking themselves into a stupor. The Spartan moved slowly through the crowds towards the Officers' Tent.

He saw Philotas talking with the youngster Ptolemy and the sombre Craterus. The youths spotted him and Philotas broke away from them.

'I ran well,' said Philo. 'Did you see me?'

'I did. Your timing was impeccable.'

'Am I as fast as you were?'

'I would say faster,' Parmenion admitted. 'I never had a finishing burst of speed. I thought for a moment the Spartan would take you, but you destroyed him from the final bend.'

For a moment Philo stood as if shocked by the compliment, then his face softened. 'Thank you, Father. I . . . thank you. Will you join us for a drink?'

'No, I am tired. I think I will go home.'

The young man's disappointment was sincere, but it was replaced almost instantly by the guarded, cynical look Parmenion had come to know so well. 'Yes, of course,' said Philo. 'I should have known better than to ask you to spend time with me. It is not possible to break the habits built up during a lifetime.' And he swung away, returning to his companions.

Parmenion cursed softly and moved on. He should have stayed, and guilt touched him. Philo was right: he had never had time for the boy, nor for any of his sons save one. Alexander.

At the rear of the Officers' Tent was the paddock where the horses were tethered. A servant brought him his mount and he rode slowly back through the city to his town house. Phaedra was not due until tomorrow, which gave him at least a few more hours of relative contentment.

He found Mothac in the small study to the rear of the house. The old Theban was poring over reports from Asia, and there were papers and scrolls scattered across the wide desk.

'Anything new?' asked Parmenion, removing his ceremonial helmet and laying it carefully on the bench beside him.

'New? It is all new,' answered Mothac. 'And yet as old as the balls of Zeus. Treachery, double-dealing, compromise. New names, ancient vices. But I must say, I do love diplomacy.' He lifted a scroll and grinned. 'I have a letter here from a man named Dupias, assuring me that he is an ardent supporter of Philip. Through his good offices we can be assured of a fine reception in Tyre, should the Persian army be overcome by the "valiant Macedonians".'

'It sounds promising,' said Parmenion.

'True, and yet I have a report from another source that Dupias is in the pay of the Persians.'

'Even better. We can use him to feed Darius false information.'

'Yes. Life is wonderfully complex. I can remember the boring old days when all that counted was the strength of a man's sword-arm and the justice of his cause.'

'No, you can't,' Parmenion told him. 'It just seems that way. The past is all bright colours. The shades of grey have vanished. This is how it has always been. If you walk from here to the Guards Barracks and talk to those earnest young men, they will tell you of the justice of their cause and boast of the strength of their sword-arms. Their eyes will shine with glory. It is the way of young men.'

Mothac sighed. 'I know that. I was trying to be light-hearted. What is the matter with you?'

Parmenion shrugged. 'It is all going sour, Mothac. I think Philip is preparing to assassinate Alexander.'

'What? I can't believe that!'

'He told me yesterday that he does not intend to take the prince with him on the Persian expedition. He will have a role in Macedonia. What does that suggest?'

The old Theban ran his fingers over his bald dome, scratching the skin of his crown. 'Philip is too canny to leave a potential enemy behind him – but to kill his own son? Are you sure?'

'I am sure.'

'What will you do?'

'I have no idea. I am meeting the prince tonight; I will advise him to leave Pella.'

'What is wrong with Philip?' asked Mothac. 'The boy loves him, there is no question of that. You know how many spies report to me, but none has ever suggested that Alexander would betray his father.'

'Unfortunately that is not true of his followers,' put in Parmenion. 'I have seen the reports of comments by Philo and Nearchos, Ptolemy and Cassander. The young men worship Alexander. And then there is Pausanius – an ugly business.'

'He brought it on himself,' muttered Mothac. 'Pausanius is a fool. Philip has always enjoyed the attention of young men, but none of them last in his affections. The boy was too pushy.'

'That may be true,' Parmenion admitted, 'but he is still a high-born Macedonian, and his punishment was cruel and ill-advised.'

Mothac said nothing. How could he argue? Pausanius had enjoyed the King's devotion and while the favourite had made an enemy of Attalus – making him the butt of many jokes and jibes. Attalus had waited for the youngster to fall from favour, and had then ordered Pausanius to be soundly thrashed and abused by soldiers from his personal guard.

The humiliation was intense, for the young noble had been left, naked and tied, on a stall in the market-place. The incident had many repercussions. The young men who followed Alexander were all friendly to Pausanius, and saw his treatment as unjust. The older nobles at court were cheered by his humiliation, seeing it as a timely and salutary lesson for a youth they considered a loud-mouthed braggart.

It was also well known that Pausanius was a close friend to Alexander. Soon after his ordeal the noble approached the prince, asking for justice against Attalus; Alexander took his plea to the King in open court, but Philip dismissed it, calling the incident a 'prank' that should be forgotten.

But in the months that followed few forgot it, for it highlighted the extent to which Attalus' star had risen in the Macedonian court, and many men now walked warily, or openly courted the company of the one-time assassin.

'Cruel it may have been,' said Mothac at last, 'but it should not concern you. Attalus no longer fears you. You are not on his list of enemies – and that is how it should stay. You may be the foremost general of Macedonia, Parmenion, but Attalus is stronger now than he has ever been. Enmity between you will leave you dead.'

'We will not become enemies,' said Parmenion, 'unless he plans harm to Alexander.'

'If he does, it will be on the King's order,' warned Mothac, his voice a whisper.

'I know,' the Spartan answered.

The Temple, Asia Minor

The Temple grounds were overgrown; most of the roses were long since dead, strangled by wide-leafed ivy, or masked from the sun by the overhanging branches of the many trees. Grass was growing between the paving stones, pushing up with the slow strength of nature, distorting the paths and making the footing treacherous.

The fountains were silent now, the water stagnant. But Derae did not care. She no longer had the strength to walk the gardens and rarely left the room behind the altar. Only two servants remained, both women she had healed long ago before her powers had faded.

No longer were there ragged tents beyond the Temple, filled to overflowing with the diseased, the lame and the crippled. No one needed tokens now to see the Healer.

Shallow cuts she could seal, minor infections would still vanish at her touch. But no longer could she bring sight to the blind, nor draw the cancers from the lungs and bellies of the dying.

Now it was she who suffered, her limbs racked with arthritic pain, her joints swollen. If she moved slowly, supporting herself on two sticks, she could just reach the Temple doorway, there to sit in the afternoon sunshine. But she needed help to return to her room when dusk and the cool breeze of evening stiffened her limbs.

Derae sat on the marble bench with deep cushions around her, the afternoon sun warm on her face, and recalled the days when her power was at its height, when the blind saw again and the crippled were made strong.

She was lost in her memories when Camfitha came to her.

'There is a carriage coming, mistress. It is black, but adorned with gold. It must be some great lady. Soldiers ride before and behind and the carriage is drawn by six black stallions. It could be the Queen.'

'Let us hope she has but a chill,' answered Derae sleepily.

Camfitha settled her plump form alongside the slender old woman. 'Shall I help you into the altar room?'

'No, dear. I shall wait here. Bring some fresh water from the well, and some fruit. The travellers will be thirsty and in need of refreshment.'

'It will be dusk soon. I will fetch you a shawl.'

Derae listened as Camfitha hurried away, her heavy steps echoing in the hallway. She remembered the lithe child Camfitha had been – slim and beautiful, but with a twisted leg and a crippled foot. Derae had healed the limb, and Camfitha had sworn to serve her always.

'Do not be foolish, child. Go from here. Find a good man and bear him strong sons.'

But Camfitha had refused. And oh, how grateful Derae had been.

The sound of horses' hooves on the flagstones jerked her mind to the present. She was too tired now to use what remained of her Talent to look upon the newcomers. But there seemed to be at least a dozen horsemen; she could smell the lather on the mounts, mixed with the sweet, smoky aroma of worn leather.

The carriage had halted before the narrow gate and she heard the door being opened, the steps pulled out and thudding against the ground.

Suddenly a cold touch of fear swept through her, as if an icy wind had whispered across the ruined garden; she shivered. She heard the soldiers move away, but there followed a soft rustling, like a snake moving through dry grass and dead leaves. A sweet perfume filled the air and the rustling drew closer. Derae identified it then as the swishing of a woman's gown.

'Who are you?' she asked.

'An old enemy,' said a cold voice.

Derae's mind swept back to her first meeting with the Dark Lady and their clash of souls, the spears of lightning and the cries of the Undead. Then she saw again her journey to Samothrace and her efforts to prevent the conception of the Chaos Spirit.

'Aida?'

'The very same. And I do mean the same. My body is still young, Derae – not old and withered, not rotting on my bones.'

'I dare say the same cannot be said for your soul.'

Aida laughed, the sound full of humour. 'The dying dog can still bite, I see. Will you not ask me why I came?'

'To kill me?'

'Kill you? No, no, Derae. You will die soon without my help. I have watched you for these last years, revelling in your fading powers. But kill you? Why would I do that? Without you my precious boy could never have been born.'

'Your precious boy was defeated, cast out,' said Derae. 'Alexander is now a strong, fine young man.'

'Of course he is,' Aida agreed. 'He is as I need him to be. I am a patient woman. The time was not right for the Dark God to become flesh. But now? Now is his time.'

'Empty words cannot frighten me,' Derae told her.

'Nor should they. But I am on my way to Pella, for the wedding of Philip to Cleopatra. And once I am there my words will seem less empty. You think a golden necklet will protect Alexander? A trifling ornament? It could have been removed at any time during these thirteen years, but it was necessary for the boy to become a man, to build his friendships, to prepare the way for the One to come.' Aida laughed again, and this time the sound was cruel. 'You will see him in his glory, Derae. And you will know the ultimate despair.'

'It will not be,' said Derae, her words sounding hollow and unconvincing. 'Parmenion will stop you.'

'He too grows old. His day is past. And Aristotle has run away to distant worlds and other times. There is no one left to stop me.'

'Why did you come here?'

'To torment you,' said Aida brightly. 'To bring you pain. To let you know that the Day of the Dark God is dawning. Nothing will stop him.'

'Even if you are right, it will only be for a short time. Alexander is not immortal. One day he will die.'

'Perhaps. Perhaps not. But what will it matter? Once his flesh has been devoured by carrion birds, or eaten by worms, or consumed by fire, the Chaos Spirit will be free once more and his disciples will find another suitable vessel for him. He is immortal.'

'Why do you serve him, Aida? He brings only pain and suffering, hatred and despair.'

'Why? How can you ask that? You sit there decaying even as I watch, while I am still youthful, thanks to his blessing. I am rich, with many slaves and soldiers. My body enjoys all the pleasures known – and many that are not known. What other master could give me all this?'

Now it was Derae's turn to smile. 'Such worthless treasures. You are welcome to them.'

'Worthless? I concede you have more experience of worthlessness than I,' hissed Aida. 'You only ever knew one lover. I have known thousands, both men and women – yes, and demons. I have been pleasured in ways you could not dream of.'

'Nor would I wish to. And you are wrong, Aida: you have never known a lover, for you are incapable of love. You have no conception of its meaning. You came to torment me? You failed. For once I hated you, and now I feel only pity. You have brought me a gift . . . and I thank you for it.'

'Then here is another,' whispered Aida, rising. 'Parmenion will be slain by his son, Alexander. Cold iron will be thrust into his flesh. Everything you ever dreamed of will come to nothing. Ponder on that, you blind hag!'

Derae said nothing, but sat very still as the Dark Lady walked away. She heard the carriage door open, listened as the steps were withdrawn and heard the whip crack, the horses whinnying.

'Have they gone then?' asked Camfitha, laying the silver tray on the marble bench.

'Yes, they have gone.'

'Was it the Queen?'

'No. It was just a woman I once knew.'

*

Lightning speared the sky as Alexander walked from the palace, heading west along the wide, deserted avenue towards the market-place. There were few people on the streets as midnight approached, but he was sure he was being followed. Twice he thought he caught glimpses of a tall man wearing a black cloak, but when he turned there was no one in sight.

Two prostitutes hailed him as he crossed the *agora* square, but he smiled and shook his head. 'A special price for you, handsome one,' called the younger of the two, but he spread his hands.

'No coin,' he answered and they turned from him, walking away arm in arm.

A flicker of movement came from his left and he spun with dagger in hand. There was no one there. Lightning flashed, black shadows danced from the giant pillars of the Temple of Zeus. Alexander shook his head.

Shadows. You are jumping at shadows. Slipping the dagger back into its sheath he walked on. Once he would have used his Talent to search those shadows, but ever since Parmenion had clipped the golden necklet to his throat his powers had vanished. A small price to pay for the peace he had enjoyed since the Dark God was banished from his body.

No one who had not endured his sense of solitude as a child could possibly understand the joy he had known since his return from the world of Achaea. To touch and not to kill, to embrace without fear and feel the warmth of another body against his own. So many simple pleasures. To sit, no longer alone, at the centre of a group of children, to ride, and to laugh, and to share.

Reaching up, he touched the cold gold of the necklet.

He moved on, cutting across the Street of Tanners and on to the wider Avenue of the Stallion, keeping close to the shadows and listening for sounds of pursuit.

How could it have come to this, he wondered? Slinking through the midnight streets for a secret meeting. The return from Achaea had been full of joy. Philip's good-humour had lasted for months, and even when away on his constant campaigns in Thrace or the Chalcidice the King had continued to send messages to his son at Mieza. Where had it gone wrong?

Could it have been the horse?

He remembered the day, five years before, when Parmenion had first brought Bucephalus to the King. The Festival of Artemis had been celebrated for the previous four days, and Philip was relaxed and mildly drunk when the Thessalian handler walked the huge black stallion on to the parade ground. Alexander's breath had caught in his throat. Seventeen hands high, the stallion was the most wondrous sight, powerful of shoulder and proud of eye. The King had sobered instantly. He was not lame then and he had leapt from the dais to approach the beast.

'Never,' said Philip, 'have I seen such a horse.'

'His sire was Titan,' Parmenion told him. 'I rode him only once and have never forgotten it.'

'I will give you five talents of silver for him,' the King announced.

'He is not for sale, sire, not even to you. He is a gift for Alexander.'

'This is no horse for a child. This is a war-horse.' Philip reached up to stroke the sleek black neck, his hand trembling. 'Ten talents, Parmenion. He can have another horse.'

The fifteen-year-old Alexander gazed up at the Spartan, saw his cheeks redden, his mouth tightening. 'You cannot buy another man's gift, my lord. I have several other war-horses I would be pleased to offer you.'

'I want this one!' declared the King, his voice deepening as his anger rose.

'No,' said Parmenion. The word was spoken softly, but there was no doubting the strength of feeling behind it.

Philip took a deep breath and swung to see Alexander watching him. 'If he can ride the stallion, he may have him,' said Philip, striding back to the dais.

'Thank you, Parmenion,' whispered Alexander, moving forward to stand alongside the stallion. 'But how will I mount such a beast? I would need to carry steps.'

'Stroke his nose and blow gently into his nostril, then step back,' advised the Spartan. Alexander obeyed the instruction and was both amazed and delighted when Bucephalus knelt before him. Taking hold of the black mane, he vaulted to the horse's back. Instantly Bucephalus rose.

'Aia!' shouted Alexander, touching heels to the stallion's flanks. Bucephalus broke into a run, and the prince had never forgotten the intense exhilaration of that first ride – the incredible speed, the awesome power.

But his father's fury had lasted for days, and even when it faded an edge remained.

Alexander was not unduly troubled by it, for he knew the King was concerned with the coming war against Thebes and Athens, two enemies of fierce reputation. It was the Athenians who two hundred years before had destroyed a massive Persian army at the Battle of Marathon, and the Thebans who three decades ago had ended Spartan domination at the Battle of Leuctra. Now united against Philip, they posed the greatest threat ever faced by the Macedonian King.

Stopping at a public fountain Alexander drank a little water, taking time to cast furtive glances at the buildings around him. There was no sign of the man in the black cloak . . . if ever there was such a man, thought the prince with a wry smile. A low rumble of thunder sounded in the distance, followed closely by a trident of lightning. The wind began to blow harder, but as yet there was no rain.

There had been lightning the night before Chaironeia, he remembered.

He had stood with Parmenion on the high ground

overlooking the enemy camp. Almost 30,000 men: the battle-hardened warriors of the Sacred Band, Corinthian cavalry, Athenian *hoplites*, peltasts, javeliners.

'Does this make you sad?' whispered Alexander. 'I mean, did you not help to form the Sacred Band?'

'Yes, I did,' Parmenion answered, 'and down there will be some of the men I trained, and the sons of others I knew. It makes my heart sick. But I have chosen to serve your father and they have chosen to become his enemies.' The Spartan shrugged and walked away.

The battle had been fierce, the Sacred Band holding the Macedonian phalanxes, but at last Philip had led a successful cavalry charge against the enemy left, scattering the Corinthians and splitting the enemy force.

Alexander saw again the javelin that speared the heart of the King's horse and watched, with his mind's eye, his father being thrown to the ground. Enemy soldiers rushed towards him. Alexander had kicked Bucephalus into a run and led a wild charge to the King's aid. Philip was wounded in both arms, but Alexander had reached him in time, stretching out his hand and pulling his father up behind him. Bucephalus had carried them both to safety.

It was the last time Alexander could remember his father embracing him . . .

The prince sighed. He was almost at the meeting place, and just crossing the Street of Potters, when three men appeared from the shadows. Alexander paused in his stride, eyes narrowing.

The men, all dressed in dark tunics, spread out, knives gleaming in their hands. Alexander backed away, drawing his own blade as he did so.

'We just want the necklet, young prince,' said the leader, a burly man with a silver-streaked black beard. 'We mean you no harm.'

'Then come and take it,' Alexander told him.

'Is a piece of gold worth your life?' asked another man, this one leaner and wolf-like.

'It's certainly worth more than yours,' Alexander retorted.

'Don't make us kill you!' pleaded the leader. Alexander took several steps back, then his shoulders touched the wall of the building behind him. His mouth was dry, and he knew he could not kill all three without suffering serious injury. For a moment only he was tempted to give them the necklet, then he remembered the touch of death and the terrible loneliness of his childhood. No, it would be better to die. His gaze flickered to the lean man; he would be the deadly one, swift as a striking snake. They moved in closer, coming from left, right and centre. Alexander tensed, ready to leap to his right.

'Put up the blades,' said a deep voice. The men froze, the leader turning his head to see a tall man in a black cloak standing behind them with a glittering sword in his hand.

'What if we do?' the leader asked.

'Then you walk away,' said the newcomer reasonably.

'Very well,' muttered the robber, easing himself to the right, his men following him. Once clear of the action, the three attackers turned and disappeared into the shadows.

'My thanks to you,' said Alexander, but his knife remained in his hand.

The man chuckled. 'I am Hephaistion. The lord Parmenion asked me to watch over you. Come, I will take you to him.'

'Lead the way, my friend. I will be right behind you.'

*

Mothac's house was in the poorer quarter of Pella, where he could meet and hold interviews with his many agents. The building was two-storeyed and surrounded by high walls. There was no garden but to the rear of the property, facing east, was a small courtyard half-covered by a roof of vines. There was only one *andron*, windowless and unadorned, in which three couches and several small tables were set. It was in this room that Mothac spoke with his spies, for they could not be overheard from outside.

'What is happening to my father?' asked Alexander as Parmenion ushered the prince inside.

The general shook his head and shrugged. 'I cannot say

with certainty.' The Spartan stretched out his lean frame on a long couch, and Alexander saw the weariness in the older man. It surprised him for Parmenion had always been his hero, seemingly inexhaustible. Now he looked like any man in his sixties, grey-haired and lined, his pale blue eyes showing dark rings. It saddened the prince and he looked away. 'Sometimes,' continued the Spartan, 'a man will find that his dreams were more magical before they were realized. I think that might be one answer.'

'I don't understand you. He is the most powerful King in Greece. He has everything he ever desired.'

'Exactly my point.' The general sighed. 'When first I met him in Thebes he was but a child, facing with courage the prospect of assassination. He never wanted to be King. But then his brother was slain in battle and Macedonia faced ruin. Philip took the crown to save the nation. Soon after that he began to dream of greatness – not for himself but for the kingdom, and the future of his unborn son. He wanted nothing more than to build for you.'

'But he has done that,' said Alexander.

'I know. But along the way something happened to the man. He no longer builds for you but for himself. And the older he becomes the more he regards you, your youth and your talent, as a threat. I was with him in Thrace when news of the Triballian revolt came through. He was ready to march home, for he knew the strength of the tribesmen, their courage and their skills. Any campaign against them would take months of careful planning. Then came word of your stunning victory. You outflanked them, outthought them and won the war in eighteen days. That was magnificent. I was proud of you. So, I think, was he. But it only showed him how close you are to being ready to rule.'

Alexander shook his head. 'I cannot win, can I? I try to please him by excelling, but that makes him fear me. How should I act, Parmenion? Would it be better if I were retarded, like my half-brother Arridaeus? What can I do?'

'I think you should leave Pella,' advised the Spartan.

'Leave?' Alexander was silent for a moment. He looked into Parmenion's face, but for the first time in all the years he had known him the Spartan refused to meet his eyes. 'He means to kill me?' he whispered. 'Is that what you are saying?'

The general's face was grim as, at last, he looked into Alexander's eyes. 'I believe so. Day by day he convinces himself – or is convinced – of your imminent treachery. He gathers information about you, and the words of your friends. Someone within your group is reporting to him. I cannot find out who.'

'One of my friends?' asked Alexander, shocked.

'Yes – or rather, someone who professes to friendship.'

'Believe me, Parmenion, I have never spoken against my father or criticized a single action. Not even to my friends. Anyone who speaks against me is lying or twisting the truth.'

'I know that, boy! I know that better than anyone. But we must find a way to make Philip realize it. It would be safer for you to leave the city. Then I can do my best to convince the King.'

'I cannot do it,' said Alexander. 'I am the heir to the throne and I am innocent. I will not run.'

'You think only guilty men die?' Parmenion snapped. 'You believe innocence is a shield to turn away a blade? Where was the shield tonight when the assassins came? Had it not been for Hephaistion you would have been killed.'

'Perhaps,' agreed Alexander, 'but they were not assassins. They wanted the necklet.'

Parmenion said nothing, but his face lost its colour and he moved across the room to a table where a flagon of wine and two shallow cups had been left. He did not offer the prince a drink, but filled a cup and drained it swiftly. 'I should have guessed,' he said softly.

'What?'

'Aristotle leaving. It bothered me at the time. Now I know why. Many years ago – just before you were born – I went on a journey . . . a perilous journey. He accompanied me. But when it seemed that all was lost, he fled. As Chiron, he did much the same. You remember? When we came close to the Forest of Gorgon he became the centaur, returning to his own form only when the danger was past.'

'He told me of that; he said he was frightened.'

'Yes. There is to him an edge of cowardice he cannot resist. I have always seen it in him – and I do not blame him for it. It is his nature, and he tries hard to overcome it. But it is there nonetheless. Now he has run away again, and tonight someone tried to steal the necklet.'

'They could just have been robbers, surely?'

'Yes,' Parmenion admitted, 'they could. But I doubt it. Three men in a deserted street. What were they doing? Hoping some rich merchant would walk by after midnight? And the necklet is not readily visible, especially at night, nor does it look particularly valuable. No. Ever since we returned from Achaea I have lived in fear, waiting for the return of the Dark God.' The general refilled the wine-cup and moved back to the couch. 'I am no mystic, Alexander, but I can feel his presence.'

'He is gone from me,' argued the prince. 'We defeated him.'

'No, not gone . . . waiting. You were always to be his vessel. All that protects you is the necklet.'

'They did not get it,' Alexander pointed out.

'*This* time! But there will now be other attempts. They must feel the time is right.'

'Twice in the last year I have almost lost the necklet,' said Alexander. 'In the battle against the Triballians an arrow struck my breastplate, the shaft snapping and the head tearing two of the gold links. I had it repaired. The goldsmith could not understand why I refused to take it off while he soldered the gold; he burned me twice. Then, while hunting, a jackdaw swooped down upon me, its talons hooking into the links. I struck the bird with my hand and it lost its grip upon the gold. But as it flew away the clasp snapped open. I managed to hold it in place while I refastened it.'

'We must be on our guard, my boy,' said Parmenion. 'Now, if you will not leave Pella, will you at least allow me one request?'

'Of course. You have but to ask.'

'Keep Hephaistion with you. He is the best of my young

413

officers. He has a keen eye and a good brain; he will guard your back. Take him into your counsel, introduce him as a new Companion. Given time, he will find the traitor.'

Alexander smiled ruefully. 'You know, it is hardly accurate to describe a man who reports to the King as a traitor. Indeed, this could be seen as treason: the King's general and the King's son in a secret meeting.'

'There are those who would see it so,' agreed Parmenion. 'But you and I know it is not true.'

'Answer me this, Parmenion: Where will you stand if my father goes against me?'

'By his side,' answered the Spartan, 'for I am pledged to serve him and I will never betray him.'

'And if he should kill me?'

'Then I will leave his service and depart from Macedonia. But we must ensure that it does not come to that. He must be made to see that you are loyal.'

'I would not harm him – not even to save my own life.'

'I know,' said Parmenion, rising and embracing the younger man. 'It is time for you to go. Hephaistion is waiting by the front gate.'

The Summer Palace, Aigai

Olympias knelt before the Lady of Samothrace, bowing her head to receive the blessing.

Aida leaned forward. 'You are a Queen now. You should not kneel to me,' she said.

'A Queen?' responded Olympias bitterly. 'To a man with seven wives?'

'You are the mother of his son, the heir. Nothing can take that away from you.'

'You think not?' asked Olympias, rising and sitting beside the black-clad Aida on the satin-covered couch. 'Cleopatra will bear him a son. I know this, he brags of it constantly. And he has grown to hate Alexander. What am I to do?'

Aida put her arm around the Queen, drawing her close and kissing her brow. 'Your son will be King,' she told her, holding her voice to a whisper and flicking a glance at the open window. Who knew what spies lurked close by? Her spirit snaked out, but there was no one within hearing distance.

'I used to believe that, Aida. Truly. And I was so happy on Samothrace before the wedding. I thought that Philip was the greatest King in all the world. My happiness was complete. But there has always been something between us, an uneasy . . . I don't know how to describe it. Only on that first night did we ever achieve the union you taught me to expect. Now he can scarce look at me without his face darkening in anger. Did he never love me?'

Aida shrugged. 'Who can say what is in a man's mind? Their brains hang between their legs. What is important is what we do now. You know you were chosen to bear a special child, a king of kings, a god. You have fulfilled that part of your destiny. Rejoice in that, sister! And leave your fears in my care.'

'You can help Alexander?'

'I can do many things,' she answered. 'But tell me of your son. What kind of man has he become?' The Queen drew back, her face suddenly radiant, and she began to speak of Alexander's triumphs, his goodness, his strength and his pride.

Aida sat patiently, assuming an expression of rapt fascination, smiling occasionally, even clapping her hands in delight at various points. Her boredom was almost at the point of exasperation when Olympias' voice trailed away. 'I am talking too much,' said the Queen.

'Not at all,' put in Aida swiftly. 'He sounds wonderful – everything we ever dreamed of. I saw him today, walking with a group of young men. He is very handsome. But I noticed that he was wearing a necklet and it interested me. The workmanship is very old. Where did he come by it?'

'It was a gift, many years ago. He wears it always.'

'I would like to see it. Can you bring it to me?'

Olympias shook her head. 'I am sorry, I cannot. You see, there was a time when he seemed . . . possessed. The necklet protects him. He cannot remove it.'

'Nonsense! He was a gifted child with powers too strong to contain. But he is a man now.'

'No,' said Olympias. 'I will not risk that.'

'You do not trust me?' asked Aida, her face showing exactly the right amount of hurt.

'Oh no!' replied Olympias, taking Aida's hand, 'of course I trust you. It is just . . . I fear that the darkness that was once within him could return and destroy him.'

416

'Think on this, my dear. Without the necklet he will be so powerful no man will ever be able to kill him.'

'You think Philip would. . . ? No, I cannot believe that.'

'You have never heard of a King killing his son? Strange. It is not a rare occurrence in Persia.'

'Nor here,' Olympias agreed. 'But Philip is not that kind of man. When he became King, upon his brother's death in battle, he spared the life of his brother's son Amyntas. That surprised many, for Amyntas was the natural heir.'

'And where is he now?'

'Amyntas? He serves in the King's bodyguard. He is ferociously loyal to Philip; he has no desire to be King.'

'Not now, perhaps – but what if Philip were to die?'

'Alexander would be King.'

'And is Amyntas loyal to Alexander?'

Olympias frowned and looked away. 'No, they are not friends.'

'And Amyntas is a true-born Macedonian,' put in Aida softly. 'Is that not so?'

'Why are you trying to frighten me? Amyntas is no danger.'

'There is peril everywhere,' snapped Aida. 'I have been here but three days, and the whole court talks of nothing apart from the succession. The family of Attalus dream that Cleopatra's child will be King. Others swear allegiance to Amyntas. Still more talk of Arridaeus.'

'But he is retarded; he drools and cannot walk a straight line.'

'Yet he is Philip's son, and there are those who would seek to rule through him. Antipater, perhaps.'

'Stop this!' shouted Olympias. 'Do you see enemies everywhere?'

'Everywhere,' agreed Aida, her tone soft. 'I have lived for many, many years. Treachery, I find, is second nature to Man. Alexander has many friends and many enemies. But that is not important. The real secret is being able to tell which is which.'

'You understand the Mysteries, Aida, can you see where the peril lies?'

'There is one great enemy who must be slain,' answered the Dark Lady, her eyes holding to Olympias' gaze.

'Who?' whispered Olympias.

'You know the answer. I need not speak the name.' Aïda's slender hand dipped into a deep pocket in her dark gown, then came clear holding a round golden coin which she lifted between thumb and forefinger. 'It is a good likeness, don't you think?' asked the sorceress, flipping the coin into Olympias' lap.

The Queen stared down at the golden, silhouetted head of Philip of Macedon.

*

Hephaistion stretched out his long legs, lifting them over the carved foot-rest at the end of the couch. His head was aching with the noise from the revellers and he merely sipped at the heavily-watered wine in the golden Persian goblet. At the far end of the room Ptolemy was wrestling with Cassander and several tables had been upturned, throwing fruit and sweetmeats to the floor. The two men slipped and slithered on them, their clothes stained with fruit-juice. Hephaistion looked away. Philotas and Alexander were playing a Persian game involving dice and counters of gold and silver. Elsewhere other Companions of the prince were either gambling or lying in a drunken sleep on the many couches.

Hephaistion was bored. A soldier since the age of fifteen, he loved the wild, open country, sleeping beneath the stars, rising with the dawn, following the horns of war. But this? Soft cushions, sweet wines, mind-numbing games . . .

He sat up, his gaze drifting to where Philotas sat hunched over the table. So like his father in looks, he thought, yet so different. It was interesting to compare them. They even walked alike with shoulders back and eyes aware, the movements sure and catlike. But Parmenion merely showed confidence whereas Philo exuded arrogance. When the older man smiled men warmed to him, but with Philo it seemed he was mocking. Subtle differences, thought Hephaistion, but telling.

418

He stretched his back and stood. Approaching the table where Alexander sat, he bowed and asked for leave to depart.

Alexander looked up and grinned. 'Sleep well, my friend,' he said.

Hephaistion moved out into the torchlit corridor, nodding to the guards who stood to attention as he passed. The gardens were cool, the night breeze refreshing. He sucked in a deep breath and then, with a glance behind him, stepped into the shadows of the trees by the eastern gate. There was a marble bench here, hidden from the path by overhanging vegetation, and he sat down to wait.

An hour passed . . . then another. Finally a cloaked figure left by the rear door, moving swiftly down the path. But he did not pass through the gate; instead he cut across the garden to a second inner gateway. Hephaistion stood and, keeping to the shadows of the wall, followed the man. Hanging ivy grew thickly by the inner gate and the scent of roses came from beyond the wall. Hephaistion slowed his walk, moving with care through the undergrowth. He could hear low voices in the small garden beyond and he recognized them both.

'Is he talking treason yet?' Philip asked.

'Not as such, sire. But he grows more discontented day by day. I asked him tonight how he felt about the coming campaign and he outlined his plans for the taking of a walled city. He speaks like a general, and I think he sees himself leading the army.'

Hephaistion's eyes narrowed. That was not as it had been. He had listened to that conversation and Alexander had merely pointed out – when pushed – that patience was needed when besieging fortified towns.

'Attalus believes,' said Philip, 'that my life is in danger. Do you agree with him?'

'Hard to say with certainty, sire. But I detect a great jealousy over your recent marriage. All things are possible.'

'Thank you,' said the King. 'Your loyalty does you credit – I shall not forget it.'

Hephaistion slipped deeper into the shadows and knelt

behind a thick bush as the man reappeared. He waited there for some minutes then rose and walked out into the night, making his way past the Guards Barracks to Parmenion's house. There was a single lantern burning in the lower study, thin lines of golden light showing through the wooden shutters of the small window.

The soldier tapped at the wood and Parmenion pushed open the shutter, saw him and gestured him to the side door. Once inside the general offered him wine but Hephaistion refused, accepting instead a cup of water.

'Is it Philo?' Parmenion asked.

Hephaistion nodded. There was no expression on the general's face as he returned to the wide leather-covered chair behind the desk. 'I thought so. Tell me all.'

The soldier did so, reporting the twisted facts Philotas had relayed to the King. 'What does he gain, sir? The prince is his friend and the heir to the throne. Surely his future success would be assured under Alexander?'

'That is not how he views it. You have done well, Hephaistion. I am pleased with you.'

'I am sorry that the information I gained should bring you grief.'

Parmenion shook his head. 'I knew it anyway – deep in my heart.' The Spartan rubbed at his eyes, then lifted a full wine-cup to his lips, draining it at a single swallow.

'May I now return to my regiment, sir?' asked the soldier. 'I am not suited to palace life.'

'No, I am sorry. I think Alexander is in danger and I want you close to him for a little while longer. Will you do this for me?'

Hephaistion sighed. 'You know I will refuse you nothing, sir. But please let it not be too long.'

'No more than a month. Now you should get some rest. I understand Alexander rides on a hunt tomorrow . . . today . . . at dawn.'

Hephaistion chuckled. 'That will come as a welcome relief.' His smile faded. 'What will you do about Philotas?'

'What I must,' Parmenion answered.

*

Parmenion awoke soon after dawn, but he was not refreshed by his sleep. His dreams had been full of anxiety and despair, and on waking he felt no better.

Rising from the bed, he opened the shutters of his bedroom window and stared out over the city. When men looked at him they saw Macedonia's greatest general, a conqueror, a man of power. Yet today he felt old, weary and lost.

One son, Alexander, was being betrayed by another, Philotas, while the King Parmenion loved was fast convincing himself of the necessity of murdering his heir.

This was no battlefield where the *strategos* could work one of his many miracles. This was like a web of poisoned thread, weaving its way through the city and the kingdom, corrupting where it touched. But who was the spider?

Attalus?

The man was cold-hearted and ambitious, but Parmenion did not believe him capable of manipulating Philip. Yet who else stood to gain?

He summoned two of his manservants, ordering them to prepare him a bath. Only a few years before he would have first left the house for a morning run, loosening his muscles and refreshing his mind. But now his limbs were too stiff for such reckless release of energy. There was a tray of apples by the window and he bit into one. It was sweet and over-ripe and he threw the remainder from the window.

Who was the spider?

There were no easy answers. The King was middle-aged now and it was natural for young men to turn their eyes to a successor. There were many who favoured Alexander, but others would be happier with the half-wit Arridaeus, while still more remembered that Amyntas was the son of Perdiccas, the King before Philip.

But Parmenion pushed such thoughts from his mind. He knew Amyntas well; the boy had no desire for the crown, and less aptitude. He was easygoing and friendly, a capable officer, but with little imagination or initiative.

No, the answer lay with Philip and his increasing mistrust of Alexander. Philotas was feeding him lies and half-truths, but he had neither the wit nor the natural cunning to build such a web.

Parmenion lazed in the deep bath for an hour, wrestling with the problem, but was no nearer a solution when Mothac arrived to discuss the messages from agents in Asia Minor.

'The Great King has strengthened his forces in the west and sent troops to the Greek cities of the coast. But not many. Maybe three thousand. Curious,' said the old Theban.

'Persia is vast,' said Parmenion. 'He could gather an immense army in little more than a month. No, he is just letting us know that he knows. What news from Thebes?'

'There's been the usual unrest. No one likes having a foreign garrison in the Cadmea. You should remember that!'

'I do,' Parmenion agreed, remembering his days in the city, when a Spartan force occupied the fortress at the centre of Thebes.

'There is some talk in the city of Persian gold for the hiring of a mercenary army to retake the Cadmea.'

'I don't doubt the money is there,' said Parmenion. 'The Great King will be throwing gold in every direction: Sparta, Athens, Corinth, Pherae. But this time the Persians will fail. There will be no revolt behind us.'

'Do not be too sure,' muttered Mothac. 'Thebes has freed herself of conquerors before.'

'There was Epaminondas then, and Pelopidas. And Sparta was the enemy. The situation is different now. Sparta was forced to tread warily for fear of starting another war with Athens. Now Thebes would stand alone, and she is no match for even one-fifth of the Macedonian army.'

Mothac grunted and shook his head angrily. 'Spoken like a Macedonian! Well, I am Theban and I do not agree. The Sacred Band is being re-formed. The city will be free again.'

Parmenion rose from the bath, wrapping a thick towel around his waist. 'The old days are gone, Mothac; you know that. Thebes will be free – but only when Philip decides he can trust the Thebans.'

'Such arrogance,' hissed Mothac. 'You were the man who freed Thebes. Not Epaminondas. You! You helped us retake the Cadmea and then came up with the plan to crush the Spartan army. Don't you remember? Why is it so different now? How do you know there is not a young Parmenion even now in Thebes, plotting and planning?'

'I am sure that there is,' answered Parmenion with a sigh. 'But the Spartan army was never more than five thousand strong, and they were spread thin. Philip can call upon forty-five thousand Macedonians, and half again that number of mercenaries. He has a forest of siege-engines, catapults, moving towers. It is not the same.'

'I would expect you to take that view,' said Mothac, his face crimson.

'I am sorry, my friend, what else can I say?' asked Parmenion, approaching the old man and laying his hand on Mothac's broad shoulder. But the Theban shrugged it away.

'There are some matters better left undiscussed,' muttered Mothac. 'Let us continue with other problems.' He scooped up his papers and began to leaf through them. Then he stopped, his bald head sagging forward, and Parmenion saw there were tears in his eyes.

'What is it? What's wrong?' Parmenion asked, moving to sit alongside him.

'They are all going to die,' said Mothac, his voice shaking.

'Who? Who is going to die?'

'The young men of my city. They will rise, swords in their hands. And they will be cut down.'

Understanding flowed into Parmenion's mind. 'You have been helping them to organize?'

The old man nodded. 'It is my city.'

'You know when they plan to attack the Cadmea?'

'No, but it will be soon.'

'It need not end in bloodshed, Mothac. I will send another two regiments into Boeotia and that will give them pause. But promise me you will sever your connections with the rebels. Promise me!'

423

'I cannot promise that! You understand? Everything I do here makes me a traitor. Ever since Chaironeia, when you crushed the Theban army. I should have left you then. I should have gone home. Now I will!'

'No,' said Parmenion, 'don't leave. You are my oldest friend and I need you.'

'You don't need me,' said the old man sadly. 'You don't need anything. You are the *strategos*, the Death of Nations. I am getting old, Parmenion. I shall go home to Thebes. I will die in the city of my birth and be buried alongside my love.'

Mothac rose and walked, stiff-backed, from the room.

City of Aigai, Midwinter 337 BC

They had many names and many uses, but to Aida they were the *Whisperers*. The Persians had worshipped them as minor demons or daevas; the ancient peoples of Akkady and Atlantis believed them to be the souls of those who had died evil. Even the Greeks knew them, in a corrupted form, as Harpies.

Now they gathered around Aida like small wisps of mist, barely sentient but pulsing with dark emotions, exuding the detritus of evil, despair, melancholy, gloom, mistrust, jealousy and hatred.

The cellar was colder than the heart of a winter lake, but Aida steeled herself against it, sitting at the centre as the smoky forms hovered about her.

The house was set apart from the city, a former country home for a minor Macedonian noble who had died in the Thracian wars. Aida had purchased it from his widow, for it had a number of advantages. Not only was it secluded but there was a garden hidden behind a high wall where her acolytes could dispose of the bodies of the sacrifices – those unfortunates whose blood had been needed to keep the *Whisperers* strong.

She reached out her hand, summoning the first of the ghostly shapes. It flowed over her fingers and immediately images formed in her mind. She saw Philip slumped on his throne, his thoughts dark and melancholy, and she laughed aloud. How simple it was to twist the minds of men! Summoning a second form, she watched Attalus plotting and scheming.

One by one she received her image reports before sending the *Whisperers* back to their human hosts. Then, at last, the cold began to seep into her bones and she rose and left the room, climbing the dark stairs that led to the lower gardens.

All was well and Aida was deeply satisfied. Soon Philip would face his doom, and the Lady of Samothrace would be on hand to guide his son to the throne. Such a handsome boy! Oh, how she would aid him, supplying such joys and then, while he was asleep, she would remove the necklet and open the gates of his soul.

Aida shivered with exquisite pleasure. All her life she had dreamed of this coming day, as had her mother before her. Her mother's hopes –and worse, her spirit and her will to live – had been crushed by Tamis. But there is no one now to thwart me, she thought.

Soon Philip of Macedon would be dead, slain in his palace while he slept.

Arousal stirred in her and she summoned two of her guards. Mostly she found the touch of men distasteful, but on occasions such as this there was a satisfaction in using them that bordered on pleasure. It was always heightened when she knew her lovers were about to die. As their youth and strength was expended on her, she gloried in their coming demise.

The two men were handsome and tall, mercenaries from Asia Minor. They smiled as they approached her and began to remove their clothing.

The first reached her, arrogantly laying his hand on her breast, pulling clear the dark robe she wore.

Tomorrow, she thought, your soul will be shrieking on its way to Hades . . .

Pella, Midwinter

Philip was drunk and in high good humour. Around him were his friends and generals – twenty men who had served the King well over the last two decades – and they were celebrating the last night of the wedding festival. Philip leaned back in his chair, his gaze moving from man to man.

Parmenion, Antipater, Cleitus, Attalus, Theoparlis, Coenus . . . men to march the mountains with. Strong, loyal, fearless. A movement at the far end of the table caught his eye. Alexander was smiling at some jest made by the youngster, Ptolemy.

Philip's good humour evaporated. The joke was probably about him.

But he shrugged the thought away. Tonight was a celebration and nothing would be allowed to mar it.

Servants cleared away the last of the food plates and jugglers came forward to entertain the King. They were Medes, with curled beards and flowing clothes of silk and satin. Each of the three carried six swords which they began to hurl into the air, one by one, until it seemed that the blades were alive, spinning and gleaming like metal birds above the throwers. The Medes moved apart and now the swords sliced through the air between them, scarcely seeming to touch the hands of the throwers so fast did they move. Philip was fascinated by the skill and wondered, idly, if the men were as talented when it came to using the blades in battle. According to Mothac's reports the Persian king had 3,000 Medean warriors in his army.

At last the display finished and Philip led the cheers. Several of Alexander's companions clapped their hands, which made the King frown. It was becoming the custom to show appreciation by slapping the palms together, but for centuries such clapping had been considered an insult. It had originated in the theatre, used by the crowd to drown out bad actors and forcing them to leave the stage. Then the Athenians began to use clapping at the end of a performance to signify approbation. Philip did not like such changes.

The jugglers were replaced by a knife-thrower of exquisite skill. Seven targets were set up and the man, a slim Thessalian, found the centre of each while blind-folded. Philip rewarded him with a gold coin.

There followed four acrobats, slim Thracian boys, and a saga poet who sang of Heracles and his labours. Through it all Philip's cup was never empty.

Towards midnight several of the older officers, Parmenion among them, asked leave of the King and returned to their homes. But Philip, Attalus, Alexander and a dozen others remained, drinking and talking.

Most were drunk, Philip noted, especially Attalus who rarely consumed alcohol. His pale eyes were bleary, but he was smiling blissfully, which brought a chuckle from the King who clapped him on the shoulder.

'You should drink more often, my friend. You are altogether too solemn.'

'Indeed I should,' Attalus replied, enunciating the words with great care and total concentration. 'It is . . . an . . . extraordinarily . . . fine feeling,' he concluded, standing and performing an exaggerated bow.

Philip flicked a glance at Alexander. The boy was cold sober, nursing the same cup of wine he had ordered some two hours before. 'What's the matter with you?' he roared. 'The wine not to your liking?'

'It is very good, Father.'

'Then drink it!'

'I shall – in my own time,' responded the prince.

'Drink it now!' the King ordered. Alexander raised the goblet in a toast, then drained it at a single swallow. Philip summoned a servant. 'The prince has an empty cup. Stand by him and see that it does not become empty again.'

The man bowed and carried a pitcher to the end of the table, positioning himself behind Alexander. Satisfied with the young man's discomfiture Philip swung back to Attalus, but the swordsman had fallen asleep on the table with his head resting on his arms.

'What's this?' shouted Philip. 'Is the King to be left to celebrate alone?'

Attalus stirred. 'I am dying,' he whispered.

'You need some wine,' said Philip, hauling the drunken man to his feet. 'Give us a toast, Attalus!'

'A toast! A toast!' roared the revellers.

Attalus shook his head and lifted his wine-cup, slopping half the contents to the table. 'To Philip, my ward Cleopatra and to their unborn son.' The swordsman saw Alexander and smiled. 'Here's to a legitimate heir!' he said, raising his cup.

A stunned silence fell upon the revellers. Alexander's face lost all colour and he pushed himself to his feet. 'What does that make me?' he demanded.

Attalus blinked. He could not believe that he had used the words. They seemed to spring to his lips unbidden. But once said they could not be withdrawn. 'Do you hear me, you murderous whoreson?' Alexander shouted. 'Answer me!'

'Be silent!' bellowed Philip, surging to his feet. 'What right have you to interrupt a toast?'

'I will not be silent,' responded Alexander. 'I have taken your insults long enough. But this is not to be borne. I care nothing for the succession – you can leave your crown to a goat for all I care – but any man who questions the legitimacy of my birth will answer for it. I will not sit by and allow my mother to be called a whore by a man who clawed his way to eminence over the bodies of men he has poisoned or stabbed in the back.'

'You've said enough, boy!' Philip pushed back his chair and rushed at Alexander, but his foot cracked against a stool and he stumbled as he reached him. His crippled leg gave way beneath him and he began to fall. His left hand flashed out, reaching for Alexander, but his fingers only hooked into the necklet gleaming at the prince's throat. It tore clear instantly and Philip crashed into the table, striking his head on a chair as he fell.

Alexander staggered, then righted himself. There was no sound in the hall now, and the lamps flickered as a chill breeze swept through the open windows.

The prince looked down at the fallen man. 'There he lies,' he said, his voice deep and uncannily cold. 'The man who would stride across the world cannot even cross a room.'

Alexander backed away towards the door, Ptolemy and Craterus following him. The prince spun on his heel and strode from the hall.

*

Parmenion did not hear the hammering on the main doors, for the feast had left him exhausted and he had slumped into a deep, dreamless sleep. The past days had been full of gloom and heartache, with the departure of Mothac and the arrival of the shrill Phaedra.

A servant silently entered his room, gently shaking the general's shoulder. Parmenion awoke. 'What is it?' he mumbled, glancing through the open window at the still dark sky.

'The King sends for you, sir. It is urgent.'

Parmenion sat up, rubbing his eyes. Swinging his legs from the bed, he waited while the servant brought him a clean *chiton* and a fur-lined hooded coat. The winter was drawing in and now there was a chill to the night air.

Dressed at last, he walked downstairs and saw Philotas, cloaked and ready to accompany him.

'Do you know what's happening?' he asked his son.

'Alexander has fled the city,' answered Philo. 'There were heated words after you left.'

Parmenion cursed inwardly and strode from the house, Philo following him. The younger man increased his pace and came alongside Parmenion.

'There could be civil war,' said Philo. Parmenion glanced at his son, but said nothing. 'Craterus, Ptolemy and Cassander have all gone with Alexander,' the younger man continued. 'And that officer of yours, Hephaistion. I never trusted him. How much of the army do you think will desert to the prince?'

Parmenion paused and turned on his son. 'There will be no civil war,' he said, his voice colder than the night air. 'No matter how hard you may push for it, Philo.'

'What does that mean?'

'The words are not hard to understand,' snapped Parmenion. 'You have carried your lies and your twisted half-truths to the King, and you – and whoever you serve – are responsible for tonight's events. But there will be no war. Now get away from me!'

Parmenion swung away from his son and marched on towards the palace, but Philo ran alongside, grabbing his father's arm.

'How dare you treat me like a traitor!' stormed the youth, his eyes blazing with anger. 'I serve the King loyally.'

Parmenion looked into his son's face and took a deep breath. 'It is not your fault,' he said at last, his voice echoing his sorrow. 'Your mother was once a seeress, albeit not a good one. She became convinced you were to be a great King. And when you were too young to understand she filled your mind with thoughts of future glories. She was wrong. Listen to me now: she was wrong. Everything you strive for will only see you slain.'

Philo stepped back. 'You have always hated me,' he said. 'Nothing I have ever done has earned your praise. But Mother's vision was not wrong. I know it; I can feel it within me. I have a destiny that will dwarf all your achievements. Nothing will stop me!' The younger man backed away still further, then stalked off into the night.

Parmenion sighed, the weight of his years seeming suddenly intolerable. He shivered and walked on to the palace. Despite the lateness of the hour servants and slaves still moved through the halls and corridors and he was led to the throne-room where Philip waited with Attalus. The swordsman was sober now. He nodded to the Spartan, but said nothing as Philip outlined the events of the evening.

'You cast doubts on his legitimacy?' asked Parmenion, swinging to face Attalus. 'I can't believe it!'

'I don't know why I said it. I swear to Zeus the words just leapt from my mouth. I was drunk. But if I could take them back, I would.'

'This has all gone too far,' said Parmenion, turning back to the King.

'I know,' said Philip softly, sitting slumped on his throne. 'Suddenly I see everything differently: It is like the sun emerging following a storm. I cannot believe I have treated him so badly. He is my son! When I fell I struck my head and was dazed for a while. But when my senses returned it was as if I was looking through another man's eyes. All my fears were gone and I felt free. I went looking for him to apologize, to beg his forgiveness. But he was gone.'

'I will find him, sire,' Parmenion promised. 'All will be well again.'

'He saved my life. Twice,' whispered Philip. 'How could I think he wanted me dead?'

'I don't know, sire. But I am glad you now see him for what he is, a fine young man who worships you.'

'You must find him, Parmenion.' Philip pushed himself to his feet and limped towards the taller man. 'Return this to him, for I know it means much.' Extending his hand, he opened his fingers.

The Spartan looked down – and felt as if a knife had been thrust into him, cold iron to the heart. The necklet glistened in the lamp-light and Parmenion took it with a trembling hand.

'How . . . did you come by it?'

'As I fell, I reached out. My fingers hooked into it.'

In that moment Parmenion realized just why the King's paranoia had disappeared. The magic of the necklet prevented any evil from entering the heart or mind of the wearer.

But what had its loss meant to Alexander?

'I will ride at once, sire,' he said.

'Do you know where he has gone?'

'No, but I know where to look.'

'I will come with you,' said Attalus.

'I do not think that would be wise,' the Spartan told him.

'Wise or not, I will apologize to his face.'

'He may kill you – and I would not blame him.'

'Then I will die,' said Attalus. 'Come, let us go.'

The River Axios, Winter 337 BC

Sleet had begun to fall, icy needles that penetrated the thickest cloak, and the waters of the nearby river – swollen by incessant rain over the last few weeks – surged angrily against the bank. Hephaistion built a fire against a fallen log and the Companions gathered around it, huddled into their cloaks.

'Where shall we go?' asked Ptolemy, holding out his slender hands to the flickering flames. Alexander did not reply. He seemed lost in thought.

'West to Epirus,' said Craterus. 'We all have friends there.'

'Why not north-west into Pelagonia?' put in Cassander. 'The army there are the men we rewarded after the Triballian campaign. They would rise in Alexander's name.'

Hephaistion looked to the prince, but still Alexander gave no indication that he was listening. Hephaistion added fuel to the fire and leaned his back against a rock, closing his mind to the cold.

It had been a night like this when first he had met Parmenion ten years ago, with sleet turning to snow on the high ground. Only then there had been the sound of the hunting dogs howling in the night, the stamping of hooves as the hunters searched for the runaway boy. Hephaistion had been thirteen years old, living with his widowed mother on a small farm in the Kerkine Mountains. Early one morning Paionian tribesmen from the north had raided into Macedonia, sweeping down from the high passes, killing farmers and sacking two towns. Outriding scouts had come to their farm. They had tried to rape his mother, but she fought so hard that they had killed her, stabbing her through the heart. The young Hephaistion slew the killer with a hand-axe and then ran for his life into the woods. The scouts had war-dogs with them and these had raced after him. Despite the cold the boy had waded through swollen streams, throwing them off the scent for a while. But as midnight approached the dogs had closed in.

Hephaistion shivered as he recalled what had happened. He had picked up a sharp rock and was crouched waiting. The dogs, two huge beasts with slavering jaws, had bounded into the clearing, closely followed by the six scouts on their painted ponies.

On a shouted command from the leader – a slim, wiry man wearing a yellow cloak – the dogs halted before the boy. Hephaistion had backed away to a boulder, the rock in his hand.

'See the dogs, child,' said the leader, his voice guttural and cruel. 'In a few moments I will order them to rip you to pieces. See how they stand, as if leashed? They are well trained.' Hephaistion could not keep his eyes from the hounds. Their lips were drawn back over heavy muzzles, showing long, sharp, rending fangs. In his terror the boy's bladder had given way and the six riders had laughed aloud at his shame.

A tall man in bright armour stepped from behind the rocks, a short, stabbing sword in his hand. The dogs howled and charged but the warrior moved swiftly in front of the boy, his sword sweeping out and down, half decapitating the first hound and skewering the heart of the second.

The action had been so swift that the men had not moved. But the leader, seeing his war-dogs slain, dragged clear his sword and kicked his horse forward. Arrows sliced through the night air. The first shaft took the leader behind the ear, punching through to his brain. He toppled sideways from his mount. The other Paionians tried to escape, but the arrows came from all sides. Within a few heartbeats all six men and four of the horses were dead or dying.

Hephaistion dropped the rock and turned to the tall warrior, who was wiping blood from his blade.

'Thank you, sir,' he managed to say. The man sheathed his sword and knelt before him, his eyes seemingly grey in the moonlight.

'You did well, boy,' he said, reaching out to grip Hephaistion's shoulders. 'You stood your ground like a warrior.'

The boy shook his head, tears beginning to flow. 'I wet myself in fear.'

'And yet you neither ran, nor begged for your life. Do not be ashamed of a momentary weakness of the bladder. Come, let us go somewhere warm and find you some dry clothing.'

'Who are you, sir?'

'I am Parmenion,' answered the man, rising to his feet.

'The Lion of Macedon!'

'The very same.'

'You saved my life. I shall not forget it.'

The general had smiled and moved away into the centre of the clearing, where Macedonian archers were stripping the corpses. A young officer led Parmenion's horse forward and the general smoothly vaulted to its back. Then he held out a hand to Hephaistion. 'Come, ride with me!'

Hephaistion smiled at the memory.

'He is coming,' said Alexander suddenly.

'Who?' asked Ptolemy.

'Parmenion. Attalus is with him.'

The youngster stood, staring south through the sleet. 'I see no one, Alexander.'

'They will be here within the hour,' said Alexander, almost dreamily.

'How do you know?' asked Craterus.

'A vision from the gods,' the prince answered.

'If it is a true vision, how could Parmenion know where to find us?'

'How indeed?' responded Alexander, his sea-green eyes gleaming as they focused on Hephaistion.

'I left a message for him, telling him we had headed north,' said the officer.

'What?' roared Craterus. 'You are a traitor then!'

'Be quiet, my friend,' said Alexander, his voice soft and almost gentle. 'Let Hephaistion speak.'

'The general asked me to watch over the prince, to see that no harm befell him. I have done that. But Parmenion is Alexander's only true friend among the elders. I felt it vital that he should know where to look for us.'

'And yet he brings Attalus with him,' put in Ptolemy. 'How do you read that situation?'

Hephaistion slowly placed two thick branches on the guttering fire. 'I trust Parmenion,' he said at last.

'As do I,' said Alexander, moving across the fire to sit beside the officer. 'But can I trust you, soldier?'

'Yes,' Hephaistion told him, meeting his gaze.

Alexander smiled. 'Do you have dreams, Hephaistion? Ambitions?'

'Of course, sir.'

'My dreams will take us all across the world. Will you follow me to glory?' His voice was soothing, almost seductive, and Hephaistion felt himself drifting, visions filling his head of great armies marching, tall cities burning, rivers of gold flowing before his eyes, rivers of blood swirling around his feet. 'Will you follow me?' asked Alexander again.

'Yes, sire. To the ends of the earth.'

'And maybe beyond?' the prince whispered.

'Wherever you command.'

'Good,' said Alexander, clapping the young man on the shoulder. 'Now let us wait for our visitors.'

*

The sleet turned to snow, icy flakes that stung as they touched exposed skin. Craterus, Ptolemy and Cassander began to strip branches from surrounding trees, trying in vain to build a small shelter but being constantly thwarted by the gusting winds.

Alexander sat silently by the tiny fire, snow settling on his cloak and hair as his eyes gazed into the flickering flames. Hephaistion shivered, drawing his own woollen cloak more tightly about him. The prince's mood worried him: Alexander seemed in an eldritch state, uncaring of danger, seemingly comfortable even within this sudden blizzard.

The cold seeped into Hephaistion's bones and he rubbed his hands together, blowing hot air to his palms.

'This is more to your liking, is it not?' asked Alexander suddenly.

'My lord?'

'The cold, the naked sky, enemies at hand. You are a soldier – a warrior.'

'I like it a little warmer than this,' Hephaistion answered, forcing a smile.

'You prowled my rooms like a caged lion, never at ease.'

'I was doing as the lord Parmenion ordered.'

'Yes, of course. You worship him.'

'Not worship, my prince. I have much to thank him for. After my mother was killed I was forced to sell our farm at auction, in order to pay the fees at the military academy. When I came of age the deeds to the farm were returned to me. Parmenion had bought it.'

'He is a kindly man – and I understand he saved you from Paionian raiders?'

'Yes. How did you know of it? Did he tell you?'

'No,' said Alexander, 'but I like to know all about the men who follow me. Why do you think Attalus is with him?'

Hephaistion spread his hands. 'I am a soldier, not a *strategos*. How many men are with them? Did your vision show you?'

'They are alone.'

Hephaistion was truly surprised. 'That seems unlikely, sir. Attalus has many enemies and should rightly now judge you among them.'

Alexander leaned in close. 'Where will you stand if I go against Attalus?'

'By your side!'

'And against Philip?'

'The same answer. But do not ask me to fight Parmenion.'

'You would be with him?'

'No – that is why I do not want you to ask me.'

Alexander nodded, but said nothing. Swinging his head he saw his three Companions huddling under a rough-built shelter, but a sudden gust of wind toppled it over them. The prince's laughter rippled out. 'These are the men who would conquer the world for me,' he said.

They struggled clear of the wreckage and gathered around the fire. 'Do you not feel the cold?' Ptolemy asked Alexander. The prince grinned. 'It cannot touch me.'

The Companions began to joke about Alexander's new-found powers and Hephaistion leaned back against the rock, closing his ears to their banter, letting it wash over him like the background noise of the river, blending in with the shrieking of the wind.

He was both amazed and angry at his exchange with the prince: amazed because of the surprising way he had pledged himself to follow him, angry at himself for his easy betrayal of Parmenion. That he had grown to like and respect Alexander was understandable: the prince was a man of honour and courage. But Hephaistion had never guessed how deep this respect had become, and understood now that it bordered on love. Alexander was the sun and Hephaistion felt warm in his company. But do you not love Parmenion, he asked himself? The answer was swift in coming. Of course, but it was love born of debt, and debts can always be repaid.

The snow eased, the wind dying away. The fire crackled and grew, dancing tongues of flame licking at the wood. Hephaistion opened his cloak, allowing the warmth to bathe his upper body.

Alexander was looking at him. 'Our guests are almost upon us,' said the prince. 'I want you to ride out behind them and scout for any larger force that might be following.'

Hephaistion's mouth was suddenly dry as he stood and bowed. 'As you command,' he answered.

And here it was, the moment of betrayal. If the Companions slew Parmenion and Attalus, it would mean civil war. But Alexander had given Hephaistion a way out. He would not be present when the killing began. The officer felt nauseous as he strode to his mount.

But he rode away without a backward glance.

*

Parmenion saw the distant camp-fire and reined in his mount. The light appeared like a flickering candle and, at this distance, it was not possible to make out the men around it.

'You think that's them?' asked Attalus, riding alongside.

'It is likely,' the general answered. 'But it is possible they are a band of robbers.'

Attalus chuckled. 'Would they be a match for the two greatest swordsmen in Macedonia?'

Parmenion smiled. 'Once upon a time, my friend. I fear age has withered our skills a fraction.'

'Speak for yourself, Spartan. I am as fast now as ever.'

Parmenion glanced at the white-haired swordsman, surprised at the conviction in his voice. He actually believed the words he spoke. The Spartan offered no argument, but heeled his horse forward.

Closer they came to the camp-fire. The ears of Parmenion's stallion pricked up and he whinnied, the sound being answered from the trees beyond the fire.

'It is them,' said Parmenion. 'That was Bucephalus. He and Paxus were stable companions.'

'What if they come at us with swords?' Attalus asked.

'We die,' answered Parmenion, 'for I'll not fight Alexander.'

The clouds broke and the moon shone bright upon the snow-covered land, the nearby river glinting like polished iron. Parmenion rode to the camp-fire and dismounted.

Alexander sat cross-legged before the flames, but he rose as the general approached.

'A cold night,' remarked the prince, looking past Parmenion at Attalus.

'Yes, sir,' the swordsman agreed. 'A cold night following hot words.'

'What do you wish to say to me, Attalus?'

The swordsman cleared his throat. 'I have come . . . to . . .' he licked his lips. 'I have come to apologize,' he said, the words flowing out swiftly as if their taste was acid upon his tongue. 'I don't know why I made that toast. I was drunk. I was as shocked as you were, and I would do anything to withdraw the words.'

'My father sent you to say this?'

'No, it was my choice.'

Alexander nodded and turned to Parmenion. 'And you, my friend, what have you to tell me?'

'Philip is deeply sorry. He loves you, Alexander; he wants you home.'

'He loves me? There is a thought! I have not seen much evidence of such love in a long time. How do I know that I do not ride back to Pella in time for my own murder?'

'You have my word,' said Parmenion simply. 'Now, will you not ask your Companions to join us? They must be frozen stiff waiting in the woods.'

'They will remain where I order them,' said the prince, cloaking the refusal with a smile. 'Let us sit down by the fire and talk for a while.'

Alexander added more fuel and the three men sat while Parmenion outlined Philip's regret and sadness. Finally the Spartan opened the pouch at his side, producing the necklet. 'When the King touched this, all his thoughts and fears concerning you vanished. You understand why? The magic of the necklet cut through the spells that were weaving about him.'

Alexander gazed down at the necklet. 'You are saying he has been bewitched?'

'I believe so.'

'Then perhaps he should wear it?'

'You do not want it back?'

'I have no need of it; it served its purpose. Obviously the Dark God has chosen another vessel. I am free of him.'

'What harm would it do to wear it once more?' asked Parmenion softly.

'No harm at all – save that I do not wish to. Now, you say my father is anxious to welcome me home and that I should trust you. Therefore I shall. For you have always been my friend, Parmenion, and the man I most admire – save for Philip. Will you ride with me to the King?'

'Of course, sir.'

Attalus cleared his throat once more. 'Am I forgiven?' he asked.

'Why would I not forgive you, Attalus? Your actions have brought about a change I have been longing for through these many years. I am grateful to you.'

'What change is that?' asked Parmenion sharply.

'The return of my father's love,' answered Alexander smoothly. 'Now let us ride.'

The City of Aigai

Aida dismissed the *Whisperers*, for they had served their purpose and the Dark Lady was exultant. She had felt the moment when Philip ripped the necklet from Alexander, experiencing a surge of emotion wonderfully similar to a sexual climax.

Now she knelt in the darkened cellar beneath the house with the bodies of her two recent lovers stretched out on the cold floor, blood drying on their chests.

Aida smiled and, reaching out to the nearest body, traced a bloody line with her finger from the chest wound to the belly. Throughout history there had been many forms of payment – the Akkadians using crystal, the Hittites iron, the Persians gold. But for the demonic forces beyond the ken of mortals there was only one currency. Blood. The source of life.

Aida closed her eyes. 'Morpheus!' she called. 'Euclistes!'

Even now the assassins would be approaching Pella, and it was vital that the palace guards were removed from the fray.

She called again and the darkness in the room deepened, the cold increasing. Aida felt their presence and whispered the words of power. Then the demons vanished and with them went the bodies of the slain. Not even a single spot of blood remained on the marble floor.

Aida rose and trembled with excitement. Tonight the new era would be born. Tonight the King would die.

Pella, Winter 337 BC

Unable to sleep, Philip rolled from the bed, walking out on to the balcony. He shivered as the winter wind touched his naked body but remained where he was, enjoying its caress. I have been such a fool, he thought, recalling his treatment of his son. How could a man be so wise in the ways of the world, he wondered, yet so blinded to the values of his own flesh and blood?

For years Philip had schemed and plotted to rule Greece, organizing an army of agents and subversives in all the major cities, outwitting the likes of Demosthenes and Aischines in Athens and the most brilliant minds of Sparta, Thebes and Corinth. Yet here in Macedonia he had perhaps lost the love of his son by misreading the young man's intentions.

It was galling.

He shivered again and returned to his room, wrapping himself in a warm, hooded cloak of sheepskin before returning to the balcony.

His mind fled back over the years, seeing himself once more a hostage in Thebes, waiting for his own death. Unhappy days of solitude and introspection. And he remembered the sick sense of horror when he had heard of his brother's death in the battle against the Illyrians and had seen the shape of his own destiny. He had never wanted to be King. But what choice was there? His country was surrounded by enemies, the army crushed, the future dark with the promise of despair.

He gazed out over the sleeping city to the low hills beyond. In little more than twenty years he had made Macedonia great, putting the nation beyond the reach of any enemy.

Philip sighed. His leg was throbbing and he sat down on a narrow chair, rubbing at the scar above the old wound. His bones ached and the constant pain of his blind eye nagged at him. He needed a drink.

Rising, he swung to enter the royal bedroom and stared, surprised, at the thin white mist that was seeping under the bedroom door. At first he thought it was smoke, but it clung to the floor, rolling out to fill the room. Philip backed away to the edge of the balcony. The mist followed but, once outside, the night winds dispersed it.

But inside the room it flowed over the rugs and chairs and up over the bed in which Cleopatra lay sleeping. As he watched the mist slowly faded, becoming at first translucent and then almost transparent. Finally it disappeared altogether. Philip stepped back into the room, crossing swiftly to where Cleopatra lay. His fingers touched the pulse at her neck. She was sleeping deeply; he tried to rouse her, but could get no response.

Concerned now, he limped across the room, pulling open the door to summon the guards. Both men were slumped in the corridor with their spears beside them.

Fear swept into the King's heart as, throwing aside the cloak, he moved to the rear chambers. On a wooden frame hung his armour and shield and he swiftly buckled on breastplate and a bronze-reinforced leather kilt. Dragging his sword from its scabbard, he returned to the outer room.

All was silence. His mouth was dry as he stood in the doorway listening. How many assassins would there be?

Don't think of that, he cautioned himself, for there lies defeat and despair.

His thoughts turned to Cleopatra and the child she carried. Was she safe? Or also a target for the killers?

446

Crossing to the bed he lifted her clear and lowered her to the floor, covering her with a blanket and easing her body under the bed and out of sight.

You are alone, he realized. For the first time in twenty years you have no army to call upon. Anger touched him then, building to a cold fury.

Once more he moved to the doorway, listening. To his right was the stairway leading to the great hall and the lower *androns*, to his left the corridors of the women's quarters. Taking a deep breath, he stepped out over the sleeping guards. A curtain to his left flickered and a dark-robed assassin leapt from hiding. Philip spun, his sword plunging through the man's chest and ripping into his heart. Dragging the blade clear, he whirled round as a second swordsman, hooded and masked, ran at him from the left. Philip blocked a savage cut, then hammered his shoulder into the man, knocking him to the floor. From behind he could hear the padding of many feet upon the rugs. Philip leapt over the fallen man and ran for the staircase. A thrown knife thudded against his breastplate, ricocheting up and slicing the skin behind his ear.

Reaching the top of the stairs, he halted. Three more guards were down, stretched out in a drugged sleep. Snatching up a fallen spear, the King turned to see seven men racing towards him along the corridor. Philip waited. As they closed upon him his arm went back, the muscles bunching, then swept forward, the spear flashing into the chest of the first man and punching through to emerge by the spine. Blood gushed from the assassin's mouth and he stumbled. Philip did not wait for the others to reach him but ran down the stairs, taking them three at a time, trying to keep the weight on his good leg.

Half-way down he stumbled, pitching forward and losing his grip on his sword. He hit hard, rolling to the foot of the stairs and striking his head on the base of a statue. Half-stunned, he struggled to rise. His sword was ten steps above him, but there was no chance to recover it, for the six remaining assassins were almost upon him.

Glancing to his right, he saw the bodies of two sentries

and ran towards them. An assassin leapt to his back, a wiry arm encircling the King's throat, but Philip ducked his head, twisted on his heel and threw the man into the path of his fellows. His vision blurred, Philip staggered on towards the fallen guards, desperate to lay his hands upon a weapon. A thrown knife slashed into his leg, but he ignored the pain and threw himself full-length to fall across the body of a guard. He just had time to grab for a sword before the assassins were upon him. Rolling, he thrust the blade upwards, lancing it through a man's groin. A booted foot cracked against his temple and a knife plunged into his thigh. With a roaring battle-cry Philip came to his knees and launched himself at the killers. The sword was knocked from his right hand, but his left caught an assassin by the throat – the man stabbed out at the King, but the blade was blocked by Philip's breastplate. The King's fingers dug into the man's neck, closing like an iron trap around his windpipe; a sword lanced into his hip, just below the breastplate, and he cried out, releasing his hold on the assassin's throat. The man staggered back, gasping for breath. Philip's fist cracked against another man's chin and, for a moment only, he had space. Lurching to his left the King staggered towards an open doorway – the assassins sprang after him but he reached the empty room and slammed shut the door, dropping the narrow bar into place.

The assassins hurled themselves at the door, which creaked and tore at its hinges.

Knowing they would not be thwarted for long, Philip swung round, seeking a weapon. But the room was the lower, small *andron*. Windowless, it boasted only six satin-covered couches, a row of tables and an iron brazier filled with glowing coals. Earlier that evening he had sat here with Cleopatra calmly discussing their future.

A door panel cracked open and the King moved into the centre of the room, blood gushing from the wounds in his leg and hip. The entire door sundered and the five remaining assassins pushed inside. Philip ran to the brazier as they advanced. One assailant, bolder than the rest, charged at the King, but he swept up the brazier to hurl it into the man's face. Hot coals struck the assassin's mask, falling into his hood and down behind the neck of his dark tunic. He screamed as smoke and flames billowed up around him, and the smell of scorched flesh filled the air. The man fell, hair and beard alight, and writhed screaming as flames engulfed him.

The four remaining killers edged forward to encircle the King.

Weaponless and wounded, Philip waited for death.

But the assassins suddenly froze and the King saw their eyes widen in fear and shock. One by one they backed away from him, turning to flee from the room.

Philip could scarce believe his luck. Then a cold breeze whispered against the back of his neck and he turned.

The far wall shimmered, then darkened – a huge, bloated shape forming from floor to ceiling. A head emerged, gross and distorted, lidless eyes peering into the room. The mouth was rimmed with long fangs, curved like sabres. The King blinked, unable to believe what his eyes were seeing. It must be a nightmare, he thought, but the pain from the wounds in his leg and hip were all too real.

With a whispered curse Philip started to run towards the door – just in time to see it slam shut, bars of fire dancing across it. He swung back to the monster. The creature had no arms, but in their place huge snakes grew: heads the size of wine barrels, fangs as long as swords. A sibilant hissing came from the snakes and they writhed towards the King.

Backing away, Philip came to the corpse of the assassin he had struck with the brazier and, stooping, lifted the man's knife. It seemed but a tiny weapon against the monstrosity emerging from the wall.

The creature came clear at last and stood on its huge fur-covered legs, its head touching the high ceiling, its eyes focused on the man before it. The snake arms swept out.

Left without an avenue of retreat, the King advanced on the enemy.

*

Parmenion's mount, the grey Paxus, found itself hard

pressed to keep up with Bucephalus, who cantered on ahead tirelessly, and the Spartan did not push him. Paxus was a thoroughbred of the same blood-line as Titan, Bucephalus' sire, but there was no comparison between the stallions. Though fast, Paxus could not match the awesome speed of the black, nor his stamina.

Yet still Parmenion had to hold back on the reins, for Paxus dearly wanted to run, to take on his rival. The general's thoughts were sombre as he rode behind Alexander. The prince had dismissed his Companions, assuring them of his safety and – disgruntled and unsure – they had ridden away. But it was not their unease that bothered Parmenion. It was Hephaistion. The young officer had approached them from the south, spoken quietly to Alexander and then angled his mount away to the south-west. He did not speak to Parmenion and avoided the general's gaze.

Parmenion was hurt, though his face did not show it. He had been surprised when Hephaistion was not present at the camp-site, and now he knew that the young man's loyalty was no longer his for the asking. Youth will always call upon youth, he told himself, but the hurt remained.

The moon was high when the trio rode into Pella. The mounts of both Parmenion and Attalus were lathered and tired, but Bucephalus' black flanks merely gleamed. Alexander waited while the others came alongside and grinned at Parmenion. 'Never was a prince given a greater gift,' he said, patting the stallion's sleek, dark neck.

At the stables a sleepy groom, hearing hoofbeats on the flagstones, wandered out into the night, bowing as he saw the prince. 'Give him a good rub-down,' ordered Alexander as he dismounted. The prince seemed in good humour as he walked towards the palace – but then he stopped in mid-stride, his eyes narrowing.

'What is wrong?' Attalus asked.

Parmenion saw instantly what was troubling the prince. 'There are no sentries,' hissed the general. Drawing his sword, Parmenion ran towards the huge bronze-reinforced oak doors beneath the twin columns at the front of the palace. As he reached them he saw a fallen spear in the shadows and his heart began to hammer. 'The King!' he shouted, hurling himself at the door on the left. It slammed open and the Spartan ran inside.

Lamps flickered on the walls and by their dim light he saw the sentries lying flat upon the floor. A shadow moved to his right and four armed men emerged from the lower *andron*; they were clad in dark *chitons* and leggings, their faces hooded and masked. Seeing the Spartan they ran at him, long knives in their hands, and Parmenion leapt to meet them. Veering, three of the assassins tried to make a break for the doorway, but Alexander and Attalus moved into their path.

Parmenion swayed aside from a vicious thrust, sending his own blade slashing down into the outstretched arm. The iron edge bit deep, smashing bone and severing arteries. Screaming, the knifeman fell back. Parmenion stepped forward to plunge his sword into the man's chest.

Behind him Alexander despatched another assassin with a thrust to the belly, while Attalus grappled with a third. The fourth man ran out into the night. Attalus' sword was knocked from his hand, then a fist cracked against his chin and he sagged against the wall. Alexander moved in behind the attacker and, just as the man's knife rose above Attalus' throat, the prince's blade clove into the killer's back.

Attalus staggered as the man fell, then stooped to gather his sword.

Parmenion had started to climb the stairs when a weird, unearthly cry came from the lower *andron*. Alexander was first to the door, which seemed to be locked. The prince hurled himself against it, but it did not move despite the fact that the hinges were torn loose.

Nothing seemed to be holding the door in place, yet it stood as strong as iron.

Alexander stepped back and stared for a moment at the wood. Then he raised his sword.

'That will not cut . . .' began Parmenion.

The sword slashed down and the door seemed to explode inwards, shards and splinters flying into the room.

Alexander leapt inside, with the two officers following him. All three froze as they saw the huge demon at the far end of the *andron*, the King advancing upon it.

Snake arms slashed out to circle the King's waist and drag him from his feet. Alexander and Parmenion sprang forward. Attalus, horrorstruck, found he could not move. The King was slowly lifted towards the creature's cavernous maw, its fangs dripping saliva on his chest. Alexander ran forward but then stopped, his sword-arm swinging back like a javeliner. His hand flashed forward, the iron blade slicing through the air. Just as the fangs were about to close on Philip the sword punched home through the demon's eye. As its neck arched back, Philip thrust his dagger into the stretched, scaly skin of the throat. Black blood bubbled from the wound and the snake arms went into spasm, dropping the King to the mosaic floor where he landed heavily and lay winded. Parmenion ran in, hacking and cutting at the creature as Alexander moved to the King, pulling him back across the centre of the room.

Smoke billowed from the demon's wounds, filling the *andron* and choking the lungs of the warriors.

'Get back!' Parmenion shouted.

Attalus joined Alexander and together the two men lifted Philip, carrying him out into the corridor. Parmenion joined them and together the trio carried the wounded King out of the palace, laying him down between the twin pillars of the doorway.

'Fetch a surgeon,' ordered Parmenion, but Attalus knelt by the King, his face a mask of shock and disbelief.

'He must not die!' the swordsman whispered.

Parmenion shook him roughly. 'Nor will he! Now fetch a surgeon!'

'Yes . . . Yes,' muttered Attalus, pushing himself to his feet and running to the Guards Barracks.

'The wounds are deep,' said Alexander, 'but I do not think they are mortal. Already the gash in the thigh is clotting.'

'He is a tough man.' The moon emerged from behind the clouds, bright silver light bathing the palace entrance.

'Look at that!' whispered Parmenion, pointing to Philip's iron breastplate. The metal was twisted and bent where the snake arms had coiled around it. Swiftly the two men unbuckled the armour, pulling it clear; then with a dagger Alexander slit Philip's *chiton* tunic. The King's upper body was covered in bruises. Parmenion pressed a finger to Philip's ribs. 'One at least is cracked,' he announced.

The King stirred, his eyes opening. 'Alexander?' he whispered.

'I am here, Father.'

'Thank . . . the . . . gods. Will you forgive me?'

'There is nothing to forgive. Parmenion says you have suffered under a Dark Enchantment. All is well now. We are together.'

Philip struggled to rise, but Parmenion gently pushed him back. 'Wait for the surgeon.'

'A pox on all surgeons!' snorted Philip. Parmenion shook his head, but helped the King to a sitting position.

'What was that thing?'

'Euclistes,' answered Alexander. 'Once a Titan, but now a servant to all with the power to call upon him.'

'How do you know of him?' Parmenion asked.

The prince smiled. 'I had a fine teacher. Aristotle told us many tales of the damned.'

'You saved my life again, boy,' said Philip, reaching out and gripping his son's arm. 'Three times now.' Suddenly the King chuckled. 'You know, I think I might just live for ever. Gods, if eight assassins and a beast like that cannot kill me, then what can?'

Aigai, Summer 336 BC

Philip awoke to the brightness of the summer sunshine streaming through the open window. He stretched and rose from the bed, listening to the sounds of bird-song from the garden below his rooms. The scent of flowers filled the air and he felt almost young again.

He padded to a long bronze mirror, standing before it and gazing at his reflection. No longer was he overweight; the muscles of his belly stood out ridged and firm, and his black beard and tightly curled hair shone with health. The scars on his hip and thigh had faded now to faint white lines against his bronzed skin. 'I am in my prime,' he told his reflection. He had seldom felt better. The wound in his leg rarely troubled him now, and the pain from his blinded eye was but a memory.

Servants brought him his white tunic and ceremonial cloak and he dressed and dismissed them before wandering out to the balcony. The sky was wondrously blue, not a cloud in sight. High above the palace a golden eagle banked and glided on the warm air currents.

It was a good day to be alive!

Last evening Cleopatra had delivered him a son – a healthy, bawling babe with jet-black hair. Philip had raised him high, carrying him to the window and holding him up for the troops and crowds outside to see. Their cheers had almost made the palace tremble. Today they would celebrate his birth in true Macedonian style with marches, games, parades and performances from the finest actors in Greece. It would be a day to remember – and not just for the arrival of a new prince.

At midnight Philip had received word from Parmenion. The forward troops had crossed the Hellespont into Persia unopposed. Several of the Asian Greek cities, including Ephesus, had risen against the Persian overlords. Philip's dreams were all coming true.

Twenty years of planning, scheming, battling and plotting – and here it was: the culmination of all he had fought for. Athens had finally agreed to Philip becoming the Leader of Greece. All the city states had followed her lead, save Sparta; but Sparta no longer counted. The Greek army had invaded Persia and soon Philip would join them. Then they would free all the Greek cities of Asia and the Persian King, Darius, would pay a fortune in tribute to prevent Macedon's army from marching further into his empire.

Philip laughed aloud, the sound rippling out over the gardens.

In the five months since the demon almost slew him, the King had rediscovered the joys of living. Olympias' face appeared before his mind's eye and he scowled, but not even thoughts of her could dampen his mood.

A servant entered and announced that Alexander was waiting outside.

'Well, bring him in, man!' ordered Philip.

Alexander was dressed in the black and silver armour of the Royal Guard, a white-plumed helm on his head. He bowed and smiled. 'You look splendid, Father. White suits you.'

'I feel good. It will be a fine day.'

'Indeed it will. The crowds are already gathering and the procession is ready.'

'As am I,' Philip announced. Together the two men strode from the palace. Outside the great gates the marchers were preparing themselves. There were horsemen from all the provinces and troops from every district. There were actors and singers, poets, jugglers, tumblers.

Two white bulls garlanded with flowers were led out at the start, gifts for Zeus the Father of the Gods. They were followed by twenty carts bearing carved wooden statues of Artemis, Apollo, Ares, Aphrodite and all the gods of Greece.

A crown of golden oak leaves upon his head, Philip walked at the centre of the procession, flanked by the Royal Guard with Alexander at their head. Behind them came ambassadors from the city states of Athens, Corinth, Thebes and even Sparta, plus representatives from Boeotia, Pherae, Euboea, Thrace, Illyria and Paionia.

Philip glanced back over his right shoulder at the towering distant mountains, then forward again to the great sweep of the Emathian Plain. Macedonia. His land!

Unlike Pella, where the King's palace stood at the centre of the city, here in this ancient capital it was built on the top of a high hill, with the city spread out below white and glistening. In the distance Philip could see the amphitheatre where he would address his people, and from the foot of the hill to the entrance the crowds lining the route.

Handlers urged the white bulls forward and they began the long descent to the plain, passing on the left the disguised tombs of Macedonia's Kings, buried deep beneath the hillsides with tall trees growing above them. Lying here were Philip's ancestors, their riches hidden from the prying eyes of would-be thieves.

One day I will lie in such a place, he thought. And shivered, despite the sunshine.

The procession stretched for almost a quarter of a mile, and the crowds on either side of the avenue threw flowers under the feet of the walkers. Philip waved to his people, acknowledging their cheers, feeling the power of their love wash over him.

'Long live the King!' someone shouted, and the cry was taken up all along the route.

His leg began to ache, but they were close now to the amphitheatre where 2,000 Macedonians, and other dignitaries, waited to see their King and listen to his words of future glories. None of them yet knew of the success Parmenion and Attalus had enjoyed in the invasion of Persia, and Philip shivered with anticipation, his speech prepared.

'Fellow Macedonians, we stand at the gates of a new era. The power of the Persians is finished, the dawn of freedom awaits . . .'

The procession cut off to the left, ready to enter the arena from the wide gates. Philip and his Royal Guard moved to the right, to the low tunnel leading to the royal dais. In the shadows of the tunnel he paused, looking back at the armed men guarding him.

'I do not wish to enter here surrounded by swords,' he said. 'It will make me appear as a tyrant. I shall go in first; you follow me some thirty paces back.'

'As you wish, Father,' Alexander agreed.

Philip stepped into the shadows, his single eye fastened on the square of light ahead.

The Ruins of Troy, Winter 335 BC

Parmenion rode Paxus to the brow of the hill overlooking the broken columns of Troy. His aides came alongside him – six young men, sons of Macedon's noble families.

'That is where Achilles fought and fell,' whispered Perdiccas, his voice trembling.

'Yes,' said Parmenion, 'where Priam the King stood fast against the armies of Greece. Where Hector was slain and where the beautiful Helen lived with the adulterer Paris. That is all that remains of the glory that once was Troy.'

'May we ride down, sir?' Ptolemy asked.

'Of course. But be wary. There are many villages nearby and the inhabitants may be none too friendly.'

The nobles urged their mounts forward, galloping down the hillside towards the ruins. To the south Parmenion could see a white-walled temple and he touched heels to Paxus and cantered towards it.

There were no Persian troops within a day's ride, and his warning to the young men had been largely unnecessary. Yet he liked his officers to be constantly on their guard.

As he approached the Temple a short, plump woman opened a side gate and walked out to meet him. Parmenion reined in the stallion and halted before her.

'Would you be the Lion of Macedon, sir?' she asked.

Parmenion was surprised. Fifteen thousand Macedonian

soldiers were in the vicinity, and there were at least a dozen officers of his own age and height.

'I have been called that, lady. Why do you ask?'

'My mistress sent me to find you. She is dying.'

'I am no Healer; I am a soldier. What did she tell you?'

'She said I was to walk from the Temple and approach the warrior riding the grey stallion. That is all, sir. Will you come?'

Parmenion shivered, suddenly cold despite the sunshine. Something stirred in his subconscious, but he could not raise it to full awareness. He looked down at the woman. Could this be a trap? Were there soldiers or killers waiting within those white walls?

No, he decided. There was no tension in the woman before him; she was simply a servant following the orders of her mistress. Parmenion dismounted and led the stallion through the narrow gate, following a twisted path through an overgrown garden.

Still his thoughts were troubled.

What was it about this place?

It was tranquil here, harmonious and restful, but his senses were shrieking at him and he found himself growing more tense.

He halted before the main doors and tied the stallion's reins to an overhanging tree branch. 'Who is your mistress?' he asked.

'She was the Healer, sir,' the woman answered.

It was dark within the Temple and Parmenion was led to a small room where the single window was covered with a thick, woollen curtain. An old woman lay on a narrow bed; her face was emaciated, her eyes blind. Parmenion moved to the window, drawing back the curtain. Bright sunshine filled the room.

The Spartan looked down on the brightly-lit face of the old woman and his breath caught in his throat. He staggered back, gripping the curtain to stop himself from falling. And then the memory surged up from the darkest recesses of his mind. He saw again the garden at Olympia, where he and Derae had first embraced. And he saw her lying in his bed and heard again her soft, sweet voice.

'I dreamt I was in a temple, and all was darkness. And I said, "Where is the Lion of Macedon?" The sun shone then and I saw a general in a white-plumed helmet. He was tall and proud, and standing with the light at his back. He saw me. . . '

'Sweet Hera!' whispered Parmenion, falling to his knees. 'It cannot be you, Derae. It cannot!'

The old woman sighed. 'It is I,' she said. 'When they threw me from the ship I did not die. I reached the shore. I waited here for years, thinking you would come for me.'

With trembling fingers Parmenion reached out and took her hand. 'I thought you dead. I would have walked across Hades for you.'

'I know.'

'Why did you not get a message to me?'

'I couldn't. I became a Healer, a priestess. And when I found out where you were, I saw you living in Thebes with another woman.' There was nothing he could say and he felt incapable of forcing words through the lump in his throat. He merely sat, holding her swollen, arthritic hand as she told him of the years spent at the Temple, of the spirit journeys across the seas, of saving him and Thetis from the plague in Thebes and guiding him through the underworld to save the soul of Alexander, healing Parmenion of his brain tumour and returning to him a portion of his youth. Lastly she told him of her journey, disguised as Thena, into the world of the Enchantment. This time he groaned aloud.

'Why did you not show yourself to me?'

'I think I would have – but then you found the other . . . me.' His tears fell then and she felt a soft, warm droplet touch her hand. 'Oh, my dear, do not be sad. I have had a wonderful life, healing many. And I have watched you and watched over you. I feel no sorrow. I have treasured our days together, holding them warm and glowing in my memories.'

'Don't die!' he pleaded. 'Please don't die!'

She forced a weak smile. 'That is beyond my powers to grant,' she said. 'But I did not send Camfitha to find you so that you should suffer. I needed to warn you. The Lady of Samothrace . . . Aida, you remember?'

'Yes.'

'She is in Macedonia. She intends to rob Alexander of his necklet of power, but she must be stopped. Without the necklet the Dark God will win.'

'I know. Do not concern yourself. I will protect Alexander.'

'Her powers are very great. You must be on your guard at all times.'

'I will be,' he said wearily. 'But tell me: is there a way to defeat the Chaos Spirit? Can you kill the demon without harming Alexander?'

'No,' she answered, 'he cannot be killed. And even when Alexander dies he will live on – once the host body is destroyed, consumed by fire or devoured by worms or carrion birds, he will be free once more.'

'But if we hold him back will he not tire of trying to possess Alexander? Surely it would be simpler to find another human and capture his soul?'

'He cannot do that,' she answered. 'That night in Samothrace where you . . .' Pausing for a moment, she squeezed his hand and gave a gentle, almost apologetic smile, then went on, '. . . where Alexander was conceived was not chosen at random. It was a special, unholy time. Great spells were cast, the blood of innocence was spilt. The purpose of it all was to bond the conceived child to the evil of Kadmilos. The child became the Gateway through which the Beast could pass. As long as Alexander lives, he will be linked to Kadmilos. Equally the Dark God cannot leave Alexander; they are chained together for as long as the body survives.'

'Then there is no hope?'

'There is always hope, my dear,' she told him. 'Evil does not exist alone. There are balances.'

Her voice faded and, for a moment only, he thought she had died. All thoughts of the Dark God fled from his mind. Gripping her hand, he called her name. Her blind eyes opened and she gave a weak smile.

'Let us not talk of this any more,' he whispered. 'Tell me of your years here. Let me share them with you.'

461

He sat and listened as the sun faded from the sky, unaware that his officers had arrived and were standing silently by the doorway. They did not intrude on his obvious grief.

Finally, as the first stars of evening were appearing in the sky, Derae drew in a deep shuddering breath.

And was gone . . .

No goodbyes, no tearful farewell. One moment she was alive, the next her soul had departed.

As her breathing stopped Parmenion fell back, and there came over the room a sense of peace that none present would ever forget. It was warm and comforting, uplifting and filled with love, touching heart and mind and soul.

Ptolemy moved forward and embraced his general. The others followed.

And with great gentleness they led the weeping Spartan back to the gardens where his war-horse waited.

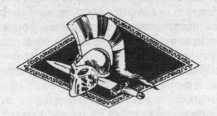

Greater Phrygia, 336 BC

In the weeks that followed Parmenion threw all his energies
into the planning of the campaign, working from before
dawn to after dusk and exhausting even his younger
officers. He checked the supplies, ordered cartographers to
map the countryside, organized food wagons, sent riders to
watch for the Athenian supply ships and arranged billets,
pushing himself to his limits.

Attalus tried to reason with him, begging him to slow
down, but the Spartan would not be opposed. Ignoring all
advice, he pressed on. In the past he had been aided by
Mothac, whose organizational skills had been breathtaking.
But now he felt he could trust no one. An army soon to
number 30,000 would be moving across the Hellespont.
Horses would require safe pasture, the men would need
meat, cereal and water. Battles, in the main, could almost
take care of themselves, but keeping men ready for war was
an art in itself. A four-ox cart could carry thirty barrels of
water across a desert, but the oxen needed to drink and after
ten days there would be only fifteen barrels left. Such were
the problems in which Parmenion immersed himself to
cloak his soul from the pain of Derae's death.

Then there were the squabbles and fights that flared
within an army made up of such ancient enemies as
Paionians, Illyrians, Macedonians, Athenians and

Thracians. Blood feuds were reported daily, and many men were slain in duels. Parmenion and Attalus were often called upon to judge the survivors of such combats and it irked the Spartan to sentence good fighters to death.

But even these considerations were better than the constant, acid thought that Derae had been alive all these years and now had been taken from him for good.

In the mid-afternoon of his fifth week in this outpost of the Persian Empire, scouts brought word of a group of Macedonian officers who had landed from an Athenian ship. There was no sign yet of Philip and Parmenion cursed inwardly.

The Persians had fled before the invading force, and many of the Greek cities had invited the Macedonians to liberate them. Yet Parmenion could not spread the advance army so thin that a counter-attack would crush it, and he was forced to wait for the arrival of the King and the rest of the army. This delay, he knew, would soon lead to a weakening of resolve in the cities, and many would withdraw their support.

The Spartan had commandeered a house in the captured city of Cabalia, and this he shared with Attalus. The swordsman had been in fine mood since the invasion and enjoyed sharing the command. In the main the two men got on well, Attalus leaving what he regarded as the minutiae to Parmenion, while he rode out every day hunting or scouting the land ahead.

The old warrior had even become popular with the troops, for he never hesitated to ride at the front of the battle-line and had distinguished himself in the first clashes with the Persian army.

Parmenion pushed the papers across the broad desk and stretched his back. He was tired. Bone-weary. It had not been hard to march into Asia, but a long campaign called for more stamina, nerve and sustained concentration than he had needed for longer than he cared to remember.

Three years was the timetable he had given Philip. Three years to control Asia Minor and make the land safe. Three years and 60,000 troops. This was no small undertaking and, at sixty-four, Parmenion wondered whether he would live out the campaign.

There were so many problems to overcome, foremost among which was food for the army. They had brought supplies for thirty days when they crossed the Hellespont, and two-thirds had already been consumed. Foraging parties were bringing in what could be found locally, but Parmenion was anxious for the supply ships to reach the designated – and defended – bays. Philip had a mere 160 ships. Should the Persian fleet move into the Aegean Sea, the Macedonian vessels would be outnumbered three to one, and the land-based army could be starved into submission or withdrawal.

But even with food supplies assured, there was still the problem of the Persian army. Given time the new King, Darius, could raise an army of almost a million. This was unlikely, Parmenion knew, but even if he chose only to conscript warriors from central Persia the Macedonians would face more than 120,000 well-armed, disciplined men. Among these were almost 40,000 trained slingers and archers. Even when Philip arrived with reinforcements, the Macedonians would have only around 1,000 bowmen.

Parmenion believed that despite his awesome skills Philip had never truly understood the Persian Empire and its composition.

The Great King ruled from Phrygia in the west to the distant lands of the Hindu Kush, from fertile farmland to arid desert, from ice-covered forests to impenetrable jungle. But it was the method of his rule that made conquest of the empire so difficult. Satraps and vassal kings were mostly autonomous, raising their own armies and setting local taxes. Even if Philip were to crush Darius he would still have a score of powerful enemies to face, each of them capable of bringing to the field an army greater than Macedon's.

Two million square miles of territory, one hundred different nations. All of Philip's past triumphs would count for nothing against such odds!

The sun was dipping into the west when the Spartan

strode through the camp, stopping to examine the picket-lines and the guards who patrolled the horse paddocks. He found one young sentry sitting quietly eating bread and cheese, his helmet and sword beside him. As the boy saw the general he scrambled to his feet.

'I am sorry, sir. I have not had an opportunity to eat today.'

'It is difficult to eat with your throat ripped open,' Parmenion told him. 'This is an enemy land and you have few friends here.'

'I know, sir. It won't happen again.'

'That is true. Next time I find you slacking I shall open your throat myself.'

'Thank you, sir . . . I mean . . .'

'I know what you mean,' grunted the Spartan, moving away.

They were all so young now, beardless children playing a game of war.

For an hour or more he wandered the camp outside the city, then returned to the house. It was white-walled, with beautiful statues lining the walks and gardens, and the rooms were large, the windows tall and wide. The floors were not crafted with mosaics but covered with rugs and carpets, deep and soft beneath the feet. Huge paintings adorned the inner walls, depicting the gods of the Persians, the mighty Ahura Mazda, the Wise Lord, and the minor daevas that served him.

A slave-girl brought the general a pitcher of mead wine made from honey. He accepted a goblet, then dismissed her. As dusk approached another girl moved in, lighting the copper lamps that hung on the walls. The room was soon bathed in a soft golden glow and the Spartan removed his breastplate and greaves, settling down with his mead on a wide couch.

Attalus found him there in the early evening. The swordsman was dressed in a long grey *chiton*, his white hair held in place by a black leather band edged with silver.

'A productive day?' asked Attalus.

The Spartan shrugged. 'Perhaps. I wish Philip were

here: many of the cities would receive us now with cheers and welcome banquets. If we leave it much longer, their backbones will start to melt. They will hear of the Great King's preparations for war and will bar their gates against us.'

'You are still in that dark mood, I see,' said Attalus. 'It comes from drinking that Persian goat's-piss. Good Greek wine is what you need,' he added, filling a golden wine-cup and draining half the contents at a single swallow.

'I am no longer in a dark mood,' said Parmenion slowly, 'but our spies report that the Great King is building an army the like of which has not been seen since Xerxes invaded Greece. Messengers are travelling all over the empire – Cappadocia, Pisidia, Syria, Pontica, Egypt, Mesopotamia . . . Can you imagine how many men will come against us?'

'We will defeat them,' said Attalus, settling down and stretching out his legs.

'Just like that?'

'Of course, *strategos*. You will think of a great plan for victory and we will all sleep soundly in our beds.'

Parmenion chuckled. 'You should have started drinking years ago. It agrees with you.'

'It is never too late to learn. However, I am in agreement with you. I can't wait to see Philip; it has been too long. The last I heard was six months ago when Cleopatra was waiting to give birth to her son and the King was planning the celebrations. It will be good to see him.'

Attalus laughed. 'There was a time, Spartan, when I wished you dead. Now I find you good company. Perhaps I'm getting old.'

Before Parmenion could reply, a servant announced the arrival of the messengers from Pella. Parmenion rose and walked out to the centre of the room to meet them.

The first to enter was Hephaistion, followed by Cassander and the cavalry general, Cleitus. Hephaistion bowed, but his face was set and tension showed in his eyes.

'A difficult journey?' ventured Parmenion.

'We have letters from the King,' answered Hephaistion stiffly, approaching Parmenion. Cassander and Cleitus advanced towards Attalus. Cleitus held a tightly rolled scroll of papyrus which he offered to the swordsman.

Parmenion had received such messages on hundreds of occasions. Yet there was a terrible tension in the air and the Spartan's senses were aroused. His gaze flickered to Cleitus; the cavalryman was proffering a sealed scroll to Attalus, but his right hand was inching towards the dagger at his hip. Cassander also was moving to Attalus' left, his right hand hidden beneath his cloak. In that one awful moment, Parmenion knew what was to come.

'Attalus!' he cried. Hephaistion leapt upon the Spartan, pinning his arms, and although Parmenion struggled the younger man was too strong. The two officers drew their swords and rushed at Attalus. The old man stood stock-still, too shocked to move. An iron blade clove into his belly and he cried out. A second sword slashed into his neck, opening a terrible wound. Attalus' knees buckled. Swords and knives slashed into his body even as he fell, and he was dead before he struck the floor.

Hephaistion loosened his grip on Parmenion who staggered back, his hand trembling as he drew his sword.

'Come then, you traitors!' he yelled. 'Finish your work!'

'It is finished, sir,' said Hephaistion, his face grey under the tan. 'That is what the King ordered.'

'I do not believe it! You have just killed Philip's best friend.'

'I know, sir. But Philip is dead.'

The words struck Parmenion like poisoned arrows and he reeled back. 'Dead? DEAD?'

'He was murdered as he entered the amphitheatre where he was to celebrate the birth of his son. The killer was hiding in the shadows and he stabbed Philip through the heart.'

'Who? Who did it?'

'Pausanius,' answered Hephaistion. 'He nursed his hatred, though he masked it well, but he never forgave Philip for refusing him justice against Attalus.'

'But why was the King not guarded?'

'He ordered the Royal Guard to walk some thirty paces

behind him, saying he did not wish to be seen as a tyrant who needed protection in his own realm. He died instantly.'

'Sweet Hera! I cannot believe it! Not sorcery, not assassins, not armies could stop Philip. And you tell me he was cut down by a spurned lover?'

'Yes, sir. Alexander is King now. He will be here as soon as the troubles in Greece are put behind him. But he ordered us to kill Attalus as soon as we arrived.'

Parmenion gazed down at the dead man, then dropped his sword and moved to a couch, slumping down with his head in his hands. 'What is happening in Macedonia?' he managed to ask.

Hephaistion sat beside him. 'There was almost civil war, but Alexander moved swiftly to eliminate his enemies. Amyntas was slain, as was Cleopatra and her new child, followed by some thirty nobles.'

'He began his reign by murdering a baby? I see.' Parmenion straightened, his eyes cold, his face a mask. He stood, gathered his sword and slammed it back into its sheath. 'See that the body is removed and the blood cleaned from the carpets. Then get out of my house!'

Hephaistion reddened. 'Alexander asked me to take Attalus' place. I had thought to use his rooms.'

'Then you thought wrong, boy!' said Parmenion. 'There was a time when I believed you had the seeds of greatness within you, but now I see you for what you are: a murderer for hire. You will go far, but you will not share my company – nor my friendship. Do we understand one another?'

'We do,' replied Hephaistion, tight-lipped.

'Good.' The Spartan swung towards the others, his gaze raking over them; then he glanced down at the body on the floor. 'He was a man,' said Parmenion. 'He had many dark sides to his nature, but he stood by his King loyally. Many years ago he risked his life to save Alexander. Well, you brought him his reward. Tomorrow we will have a funeral for him, with all honours. Do I hear an objection?'

'I have . . .' Cassander began.

'Shut your mouth!' roared Parmenion.

'We obeyed the orders of our King,' said Cleitus, his face red and his eyes angry.

'As did he,' Parmenion retorted, pointing to the corpse. 'Let us hope you do not enjoy the same benefits!'

Without another word Parmenion strode from the room. Several servants were standing grouped in the corridor outside. 'Do not be alarmed,' he told them. 'The killing is over. Remove the body and prepare it for burial.'

A young girl stepped forward, her head bowed. 'There is a man, lord; he came some while ago. He said he is a friend to you and that you would want to see him in private.'

'Did he give a name?'

'He said he was Mothac. He is an old man and I took him to your rooms. Did I do right?'

'You did. But tell no one he is here.'

*

Mothac sat quietly in the soft glow of the lamplight, his eyes staring at nothing, unfocused, his gaze turned inward. His emotions were exhausted now, and even the memory of the flames and the ruins could not stir fresh sadness within him.

What are you doing here? he asked himself. The answer was swift in coming: *Where else could I go?*

The old Theban heard footsteps in the corridor and rose from the couch, his mouth dry.

Parmenion entered but said nothing. The Spartan simply filled two goblets with watered wine and passed one to Mothac. The Theban drank it swiftly. 'Everything is destroyed,' he said, slumping back to his seat.

Parmenion sat beside him. 'Tell me.'

'Thebes is in ruins: every house, every hall, every statue. There is nothing left.'

Parmenion sat silently, his face expressionless. 'We rose against the invader,' continued Mothac, 'but we could not retake the Cadmea. The Macedonians closed the inner gates against us. Yet we had them trapped there, at the centre of the city, and for a while we thought we would be free. But Athens refused to acknowledge us and we could get no aid from the other cities. Even Sparta refused to send soldiers.

Then Alexander came, with an army. We realized we could not fight him and offered peace, but his soldiers stormed the city. The killing was terrible to see – men, women, children, cut down – for there was nowhere to run. Thousands died; the rest were taken into captivity to be sold as slaves. Alexander himself ordered the razing of the city, and the siege-engineers moved in. Every statue, every column was toppled and smashed to dust. There is no Thebes now . . . it is all gone.'

'How did you escape?'

'I hid in a cellar, but they found me. I was dragged out and hauled before an officer. Luckily it was Coenus and he recognized me. He gave me money and a fast horse, so I rode to Athens and booked passage on a ship to Asia. Why did Alexander do it? Why destroy the city?'

'I cannot answer that, my friend. But I am glad you are safe.'

'I am so tired,' whispered Mothac. 'I have not slept well since the . . . the destruction. I keep hearing the screams, seeing the blood. What was it all for, Parmenion?'

The Spartan put his arm around his friend's shoulder. 'Rest here. We will talk in the morning.' Taking Mothac's arm, he led the Theban to the wide bed. 'Sleep now.'

Obediently Mothac stretched out and his eyes closed. Within seconds he was fast asleep. But the dreams came again and he groaned, tears seeping from his closed eyelids.

*

Parmenion left the room and wandered down to the moonlit gardens, the words of Tamis echoing from the corridors of time. The old seeress had come to him in Thebes four decades ago, just before he led the attack on the Spartan-held Cadmea.

'*You stand, Parmenion, at a crossroads. There is a road leading to sunlight and laughter, and a road leading to pain and despair. The city of Thebes is in your hands, like a small toy. On the road to sunlight the city will grow, but on the other road it will be broken, crushed into dust and forgotten . . .*' She had advised him to travel to Troy, but he had ignored her, believing her to be a Spartan spy.

471

Yet had he followed her advice he would have found Derae and they would have lived their lives together in peace and harmony. There would have been no Macedonian army, and he would never have sired Alexander.

Parmenion found his mind reeling under the weight of all he had learned. Derae alive . . . but now dead, Philip gone, Attalus murdered, Thebes in ruins.

He could almost hear the Dark God's laughter.

'No,' he said aloud, 'do not even think of that!' He sat down on a wooden bench, his mind whirling with many overlapping images: Derae, young and vibrant – old and dying; Philip laughing and drinking; the Golden Child Alexander in the forests of the Enchantment; Attalus, tall and courageous, standing against the foe. And from deeper within his memory the slender, ascetic Epaminondas, sitting quietly in his study planning the liberation of Thebes.

So many faces, so many precious memories . . .

Gone now. He could not quite believe it.

How could Philip be dead?

Such vitality. Such power. One dagger-thrust and the world changed! Parmenion shivered. What now, Spartan, he asked himself? Do you serve the child as you served the man? And what if the Dark God has returned? Could you kill Alexander?

He drew his sword, staring down at the blade gleaming in the moonlight, picturing it cleaving into the new King. Shuddering, he threw the weapon from him. A cool breeze rustled the undergrowth and he stood, walking to where the sword had fallen. Stooping, he lifted it, brushing dirt from the blade.

He had seen the evils Philippos had visited upon his world. If Alexander had become such a man . . .

'I will kill him,' whispered Parmenion.

Ionia, Spring 334 BC

But Alexander did not come to Asia, for news arrived that the tribes of Paionia and Triballia had risen again in the north of Greece and a Macedonian expedition, led by the new King, was forced to move against them.

The campaign was brilliantly fought, leaving Alexander triumphant, but Persian gold was once more creating unrest in the southern cities led by Sparta, and the seeds of revolt flowered.

In Athens the orator Demosthenes spoke out against the Macedonians, and Alexander marched his army south, past the ruins of Thebes, using a massive show of strength to coerce the Greek cities to obedience. Though successful, it cost him time, and Parmenion was left in Asia for more than a year – short of manpower and supplies, playing a cat-and-mouse game with the Persian army.

Morale was low as Parmenion and Hephaistion marched the beleaguered army along the Ionian coast, making fortress camp in a bay close to the isle of Lesbos. Hastily-built ramparts were thrown up and the Macedonians settled down to a well-earned rest as the sun sank into the Aegean. Supplies were short and the men gathered around their camp-fires to eat their rations: one strip of jerked beef and a section of stale bread per man.

Hephaistion doffed his helm and ducked under the

canvas flap that formed the doorway to Parmenion's tent. The old general and his Theban friend, Mothac, were sitting on the ground poring over maps and scrolls.

Parmenion glanced up. 'Are the scouts out?' he asked.

'Yes,' answered Hephaistion.

Parmenion nodded and returned to the map. 'Tomorrow we strike through Mysia. There are several small cities there; they will buy us off with food and coin.'

'The men are getting tired of running,' Hephaistion snapped. 'Why can we not stand and show the Persians the strength of Macedonian spears?'

'Because we have not the power,' retorted Parmenion. 'Memnon now has close to fifty thousand warriors, highly trained and well armed. We would risk being crushed.'

'I do not believe that.'

'Believe what you will.'

Hephaistion crouched down beside the Spartan. 'Listen to me, sir, the men are becoming downhearted. We must have a victory.'

Parmenion's cold blue eyes locked to Hephaistion's gaze. 'You think I do not want a victory? Gods, man! I would give my right arm for one. But look at the terrain,' he said, gesturing at the goatskin map. 'Once we accept battle the Persians will envelop our flanks, cutting off any retreat. Then we would be lost. I know this is not easy for a young man like yourself to accept, but we have fewer than a thousand cavalry and only a few hundred bowmen. We could not hold them. But what we can do is keep the enemy on the march, allowing Alexander an unopposed crossing of the Dardanelles with the main army. Then we will have the battle you dream of.'

'So speaks the Lion of Macedon!' muttered Hephaistion with a sneer. 'There was a time when the very mention of your name would send the enemy into flight. But all men grow old.'

Parmenion smiled. 'If fortunate we grow wiser with age, child. And the yapping of puppies bothers us not at all.'

The Spartan returned his attention to the map and Hephaistion, swallowing his fury, left the tent. For an hour

474

or more he patrolled the camp, checking on sentries, talking to the men, then he climbed the winding path of the eastern cliff and stood in the moonlight gazing east over the fabled lands of the Persian Empire. Such wealth for the taking! Such glory to be won! Beyond Ionia was Phrygia, rich in metals, silver, gold and iron. Beyond that Cappadocia, Armenia, Mesopotamia. And then the heartlands of the Empire: Babylonia, Media and Persia itself.

The annual revenue of Macedonia was 800 talents of silver – a vast fortune. But, so it was said, in Babylon there was a minor treasury containing 240,000 talents of gold.

Hephaistion trembled at the thought of such riches. There were cities of gold and statues of purest silver. There were gems the size of a man's head. Persia! Even the fabled Midas, whose touch transformed all to gold, could not in a single lifetime have created Persia's wealth.

The moon was bright when Hephaistion saw the rider galloping his mount across the narrow plain. The man was wearing the wide-brimmed leather hat sported by the Paionian scouts and Hephaistion waved and shouted to attract his attention. The rider saw him and veered his pony to climb the hillside.

'What news?' Hephaistion asked the scout.

'The King is at Troy, sir,' answered the rider.

Hephaistion punched the air with delight. 'You are sure?' There had been many false reports of Alexander's arrival.

'I saw the army myself. He has with him more than thirty thousand men.'

'Then it has begun!' shouted Hephaistion exultantly.

The Ida Mountains, 334 BC

The two armies met on a plain in the shadows of the towering Ida Mountains. Hephaistion, riding alongside Parmenion, saw the tents of the Macedonians strung out like pearls upon a necklace, white against the green of the flatlands.

His soldier's eye scanned the regiments waiting ahead. He could see the six brigades of the Macedonian Foot Companions, 9,000 men standing to attention with spears held vertically. Alongside them were the 3,000 Shield Bearers, as Philip's Guards were now known. To the left were the Athenians and Corinthians, around 7,000 allied troops whose presence gave the expedition a united Greek appearance. To the right were the massed ranks of the savage Thracians. It was difficult to see how many there were, for they did not hold to formation but jostled and pushed in a heaving mass. But there must be, Hephaistion reckoned, more than 5,000 of them.

Alexander rode out from the centre of the army: his iron armour shining like polished silver, his helm beneath its white plume glinting with gold. Even Bucephalus was armoured now, with light chain-mail tied around his neck and over his chest, silver wires braided into his black mane and tail.

Hephaistion drew rein as Alexander approached, his

captains riding behind him; Cassander, Philotas, Cleitus, Coenus and Parmenion's second son, Nicci.

The King rode directly to Parmenion and dismounted. The older man followed suit and knelt before Alexander.

'No, no,' said the King, stepping forward to lift the Spartan to his feet. 'I'll never have you kneel to me. Well met, my friend.' Alexander embraced the taller man. 'I want to hear all your news. But first I'll address your men, and then we will talk in my tent.'

Parmenion bowed and the King turned back to Bucephalus. The horse knelt as he approached and he mounted and rode to the head of Parmenion's 12,000 troops. They sent up a great cheer as he approached them, and snapped to attention. Their armour and cloaks were dust-covered and the men looked tired and drained.

'Well, my lads,' cried Alexander, 'it is good to see you again! You have led the Persians a merry chase. But the running is over now; from this moment we run no longer. We take the battle to the enemy and we will crush the might of Darius beneath our Macedonian heels.' A feeble cheer went up, but it soon died away. Alexander removed his helm, running his fingers through his sweat-drenched golden hair. 'Each man among you will today receive a golden Philip, and I have brought a hundred barrels of Macedonian wine to remind you of home. Tonight we will celebrate your achievements with a grand feast in your honour.'

Hephaistion was stunned. 12,000 gold Philips – each one a year's pay for a common soldier . . . and given so casually! A tremendous roar went up from the soldiers which startled Bucephalus, and he reared on his hind legs. Alexander calmed the stallion and cantered back to where the officers waited.

'Now to serious matters,' he said softly and led them back to the main camp.

Throughout the afternoon Alexander listened intently to the reports of Parmenion and Hephaistion as to the nature and organization of the Persian army. Darius had given command of the warriors to a renegade Greek named

Memnon, and he, Parmenion pointed out, was a wily and skilful general. The Persians numbered some 50,000, half being cavalry from Cappadocia and Paphlagonia in the north.

'Brilliant horsemen,' said Hephaistion, 'and utterly fearless.'

'Have there been any major encounters?' Alexander asked.

'No,' answered Parmenion. 'Perhaps twenty skirmishes between outriders, but I avoided full confrontation.'

'No wonder your troops looked so weary,' put in Philotas. 'They have spent the last seven months running away from the enemy.'

'Parmenion was wise to do so,' said Alexander. 'Had we suffered a major defeat here, it is likely we would have lost support in Greece. That in turn would have made this current expedition almost impossible to mount.' He swung back to Parmenion. 'How much support can we expect from the Greek cities?'

'Very little, sire,' said Parmenion. 'At first they welcomed us, sending delegations to assure us of support. But as the months went by they lost heart. And Darius has now strengthened the garrisons in Mytilene and Ephesus.'

Hephaistion listened to the exchanges and watched Parmenion. The Spartan seemed stiff and ill-at-ease, his pale eyes never leaving Alexander's face. But if the King noticed his general's stare he gave no indication of it.

'Where is the enemy now?' Alexander asked.

'They are camped near the town of Zeleia,' Parmenion told him. 'Two days' march to the north-east.'

'Then we shall seek them out,' said Alexander brightly. Suddenly leaning forward, he gripped Parmenion's shoulder. 'Something is troubling you, my dear friend. Speak of it.'

'It is nothing, sire, I assure you. I am merely tired.'

'Then you shall rest, and we will meet again tomorrow morning,' said Alexander, rising.

Hephaistion remained behind when the others had gone and Alexander took him by the arm, leading him out into the moonlight to walk around the camp.

'What is wrong with Parmenion?' asked the King.

'As I wrote you, sire, he was angry at the slaying of Attalus and he spoke against the killing of Cleopatra and the babe. Also he was soon joined by the Theban, Mothac, who I understand witnessed the destruction of his city. Something changed in Parmenion then. He is not the same man. Perhaps it is just his age . . . I don't know. Except on matters of discipline or strategy, we rarely speak.'

'You think I can no longer trust Parmenion?'

'I do not think he is . . . yet . . . considering treachery,' answered Hephaistion carefully. 'But there is a great bitterness inside him.'

'I need him, Hephaistion – perhaps not for much longer. But I need him *now*. He knows the Persians and their methods. And whatever else he may – or may not – be, he is still the greatest general of this age.'

'He was once, sire. I am not sure about now; he is old and tired.'

'If that proves to be true,' whispered Alexander, 'then you shall see he joins Attalus for a very long rest.'

*

Parmenion drained his third goblet of mead wine and poured another. He knew he was drinking too much, but over the last few months only alcohol could dull the ache he felt, only wine could lift the weight from his soul. In his dreams he saw Philip and Attalus, young again and full of hope for the future. He saw the Sparta of the Enchantment, and held again the youthful Derae.

On waking he would groan and reach for the wine. So far his skills had not been affected – or had they? Could he have done more to thwart Memnon? Could he have defeated the Persian army?

'I don't know,' he said aloud. 'I don't care.' There was an iron brazier at the centre of the tent, glowing coals taking the chill from the night air and casting dark, dancing shadows on the canvas walls. Parmenion drew up a padded leather-topped stool and sat before the fire, staring into the tiny caverns within the flames.

'Do you wish to be alone?' asked Alexander, ducking under the tent-flap and approaching the seated man.

Parmenion did not rise. He shook his head. 'It does not matter. I am alone. Now and always,' he answered.

Alexander seated himself opposite the Spartan and sat silently for several minutes, scanning Parmenion's face. Then he reached out to take the general's hand. 'Talk to me,' he urged. 'There is something dark inside you. Let us shine a light on it.'

'Inside *me*?' responded Parmenion, shaking his head in disbelief. 'Have I slain any babies of late? Have I ordered the murder of a loyal general? Have I removed from the face of Greece a city rich in history and legend?'

'I see,' said the King softly. 'You are angry with me. But you judge me too harshly, Parmenion; I have only done what you taught me to do. All those quiet lessons in strategy in the sunshine at Mieza and on your estates. Well, what would you have done? Thebes rose against us. Athens sent messages of support, but sat back to wait and watch what the *boy*-king would do. Sparta sent an army north, five thousand men camped at Megara. Every southern city was ready to break their treaties with Macedonia, for they were treaties made with Philip – the *warrior*-king. Not with the *boy*, Alexander. Persian agents were everywhere, showering the Great King's gold upon any who would declare enmity to Macedon. Philip could have cowed them – but he would have had the weight of his reputation behind him. The *boy* had no reputation save for victories against "*crude tribesmen*".' Alexander shook his head, his expression sorrowful. 'I was negotiating with the Thebans, trying to find a peaceful way to end the deadlock. But there was an incident near a postern gate in the southern wall, when a group of young Thebans attacked a scouting party of Macedonians led by Perdiccas. The Theban army then issued out, storming our camp. We routed them swiftly and entered the city, at which point our besieged garrison in the Cadmea opened their gates and attacked from within. You have seen the fall of cities, Parmenion – warriors everywhere, small skirmishes, running battles. There is no order. And yes, the slaughter was great. It took hours to stop it, to restore discipline.

'The following day I ordered the destruction of the city and marched the army south. The Spartans retreated. The Athenians sent emissaries pledging their loyal support. The razing of Thebes was like an earth tremor, destroying the foundations of rebellion. But it hurt me, Parmenion. The glory that was Thebes, the home of Hector's tomb, the works and statues of Praxiteles. You think it did not hurt me?'

The general looked up, saw what appeared to be anguish on the young man's face and sighed. 'And Attalus? Did *that* hurt you?'

'No,' admitted Alexander, 'but you know I had no choice. He hated me and feared me. For years he tried to poison Philip's mind against me: he was my father's man, he would never be mine. But I tell you this, had he been living in retirement on his estates I would have let him live. But he was not. He was in Asia in joint command of an army – an army he might have tried to turn against me.'

Parmenion could not argue with the truth of that. Philip himself had come to power after having organized the murder of possible rivals. But there was one last, lingering boil to be lanced. 'What of the babe?' he asked.

'That was a terrible deed – and none of my doing. I am ashamed to tell you that I believe it was my mother, aided by a friend of hers from Samothrace – Aida. The night after my father's murder the two women went to Cleopatra, who was later found strangled with a length of braided silver wire. Olympias denied it – but who else could it have been? It was a ghastly way for my reign to begin – the murder of my infant brother.'

'You had no part in it?'

'Did you think that I would?' Alexander was genuinely shocked and the Spartan read the sincerity in his eyes.

Parmenion felt as if an awesome weight had slid from his shoulders. Reaching out, he embraced the younger man, and there were tears in his eyes. 'I cannot tell you how relieved I am,' he said. 'The killing of the child has haunted me. I thought . . .'

'You thought the Dark God had taken control of me?'

Parmenion nodded. Alexander reached down, drawing a slender dagger from his belt. Taking Parmenion's hand, he pressed the hilt of the dagger into his palm. The Spartan's fingers closed around the weapon and Alexander leaned his body forward so that the point of the dagger touched his chest.

'If you doubt me, then kill me,' he told Parmenion.

The Spartan looked into the young man's eyes, seeking any sign of the Beast from the Enchantment. But there was nothing. All he could see was the handsome young man his son had become. Letting slip the knife, he shook his head. 'I see only a King,' he said.

Alexander chuckled. 'By all the gods, it's good to see you again, Parmenion! Do you remember the day we sat in the palace at Pella, discussing your victory at the Crocus Field? I asked you then if you would one day be my general. You recall?'.

'Yes, you were about four years old. I said I might be a little old by the time you became King. And indeed I am.'

'Well, now I ask you again: Will the Lion of Macedon lead my army to victory?'

'If the gods are willing, sire, he will.'

The River Granicus, 334 BC

Bodies lay everywhere, and the mud-churned banks of the
Granicus were slippery with blood. Parmenion removed his
helm, passing it to Ptolemy who took it in trembling hands.
The Spartan looked into the youngster's unnaturally pale
face, saw the sheen of cold sweat upon his cheeks. 'Are you
enjoying the glory?' he asked.

Ptolemy swallowed hard. 'It was a great victory, sir,' he
answered.

'Follow me,' the general ordered. Parmenion and his six
aides walked slowly across the battlefield, stepping over the
bloated corpses of the Persian slain. Dark clouds of crows
and ravens rose from the bodies, their raucous cries harsh
upon the ears. Parmenion halted beside the mutilated
corpse of a young Persian noble, dressed in silk and satin.
The fingers of his left hand had been cut away, then
discarded once the gold rings had been stripped from them.
His face was grey, his eyes torn out by carrion birds. He
would have been no older than Ptolemy. In the midday heat
the body had swelled with the gases of death and the stench
was terrible. 'He dreamed of glory,' said Parmenion
harshly, turning on his officers. 'Yesterday he rode a fine
horse and sought to destroy the enemies of his King. He
probably has a young wife at home, perhaps a son.
Handsome, is he not?'

483

'Why are we here, sir?' asked Ptolemy, averting his eyes from the dead Persian.

Parmenion did not answer. Across the field some Macedonian and Thracian soldiers were still looting the dead, and above the battleground flocks of dark birds were circling, crying out in their hunger.

'How many lie here, do you think?' the Spartan asked.

'Thousands,' answered Perdiccas, a tall, slender young cavalryman who had arrived in Asia with Alexander.

'Somewhere near sixteen thousand,' Parmenion told him. To the far left Macedonian work parties were digging a mass grave for their fallen comrades. 'How many did we lose?' continued the general, looking at Ptolemy. The young man shrugged and spread his hands.

Parmenion's face darkened. 'You should know,' he told him. 'You should know exactly. When you ride into battle your life depends on your comrades. They must be confident that you care for them. Can you understand that? They will fight all the better for a caring commander. We lost eight hundred and seventeen Macedonians, four hundred and eleven Thracians, and two hundred and fifteen allied Greeks.'

The general walked on and, mystified, the officers followed. Here the bodies lay in groups, hundreds one upon another. 'The last stand of the Royal Infantry,' said Parmenion. 'With the army fleeing around them, they stood their guard . . . to the death. Brave men. Proud men. Do them honour in thought and word.'

'Why should we do the enemy honour?' asked Perdiccas. 'What purpose does it serve?'

'Who will rule this land now?' said Parmenion.

'We shall.'

'And in years to come the sons of these brave men will be your subjects. They will join your armies, march under your banners. But will they be loyal? Will you be able to trust them? It might be wise, Perdiccas, to honour their fathers now in order to win the love of their children later.'

Parmenion knew he had not convinced them, but the walk among the slain had become a ritual, a necessary ordeal – more, he realized, for himself than for the young men he forced to accompany him.

Silently he strode from the battlefield, back along the line of the river to where the horses were tethered, then he mounted and led his small company on to the former Persian camp.

The victory had been swift and terrifying.

The Persian army of around 45,000 men had fortified the far bank of the River Granicus, cavalry on left and right, mercenary infantry and Royal Guards – and the general Memnon – at the centre. By all the rules of engagement it should have produced a stalemate. But Parmenion had secretly sent men ahead to gauge the depths of the river. It had been a dry season and the water was only hip-deep, slow-moving and sluggish.

Alexander had led the Companion cavalry in a charge on the enemy's left flank. Parmenion ordered Philotas and his Thessalian horsemen to attack on the right. The shocked Persians were slow to react, and by the time Parmenion sounded the general advance their lines were already sundered. Only the mercenary infantry and the Royal Guard offered any stout resistance, the other units – and Memnon, the enemy leader – fleeing the field. It was a battle for less than an hour, a massacre for a further two.

Sixteen thousand Persians died before the sun reached its zenith.

The conquest of Persia was under way. Alexander's legend had begun.

That night, Alexander held his victory banquet in the tent of a dead Persian general. He had brought with him to Asia a Greek writer and poet named Callisthenes, a skeletal figure with a wispy black beard and an unnaturally large head which had long since outgrown the attempts of hair to cover it. Parmenion did not like the man but was forced to admit he had great skill as a saga poet, his voice rich and deep, his timing impeccable.

During the feast he performed an improvised work, after the style of Homer, in which he sang of Alexander's exploits. This was greeted by tremendous applause. The young King, it seemed, had personally slain 2,000 of the half-a-million Persians facing him, while Zeus, the Father of the Gods, stretched his mighty hand across the sky, opening the clouds to look down upon this mightiest of mortals.

Callisthenes sang of Athena, Goddess of War, appearing to Alexander and offering him immortality on the eve of the battle, and of the young King refusing the honour since he had not yet earned it.

Parmenion found the song stirring to the point of nausea, but the younger men clapped and cheered at each exaggerated point. Finally Callisthenes told of the moment when Alexander's generals had counselled against him crossing the 'swirling torrent of the Granicus', and gave the young King the answer that he 'would be ashamed if, after crossing the Hellespont, he allowed the petty stream of the Granicus to stand in his way'.

Hephaistion, who was sitting beside Parmenion, leaned in close. 'That is not the way it was,' he whispered.

'None of it is the way it was,' answered the general, 'but it sounds very fine to the young and foolish.'

The feast continued long into the night and, bored, Parmenion made his way back to his own tent. Mothac was still awake, sitting stretched out on a huge padded Persian chair. The Theban had been drinking.

'A wonderful day,' he said as Parmenion entered. 'Another nation ripe for conquest. More cities to be burnt and razed.' His face was flushed, his eyes bleary and red-rimmed.

Parmenion said nothing. Adding fuel to the brazier, he stripped himself of his ceremonial armour and stretched out on a long couch.

'Has the god-King grown tired of hearing stories about himself?' asked Mothac.

'Speak more quietly, my friend,' Parmenion advised.

'Why?' asked Mothac, sitting upright and spilling his wine. 'I have lived for more than seventy years. What can he do to me? Kill me? I wish I'd died ten years ago. You know, after the razing of Thebes I could not even find the grave of my Elea. My sweet Elea!'

'You will find her. She does not rest with the cloak of her body.'

Mothac wiped the back of his hand across his eyes. 'What are we doing here, Parmenion? Why don't we go home to Macedonia? Raise horses and leave this slaughter to the young men. What do we achieve here? More death, more destruction.'

'I am what I am,' replied the Spartan. 'It is all I have left.'

'You should not serve him. He is not like Philip, fighting to save his nation. He is a killer. He will build nothing, Parmenion; he will ride across the world as a destroyer.'

'I do not believe that. He is capable of greatness.'

'Why are your eyes so blind to his evil? What hold does he have on you?'

'Enough of this!' roared Parmenion. 'You are a drunken old man, full of bitterness and despair. I'll hear no more of it!'

'Drunk I may be, but I am not fooled by him.' Pushing himself to his feet, Mothac stumbled from the tent.

*

The old Theban sucked in great gulps of the cool night air and wandered away from the camp, out to a low range of hills to the south. He sat down against the hillside and lay back, trying to focus on the stars, but they swam around making him feel nauseous. Rolling to his side, he retched violently. His head began to pound and he sat up, the screwed-up parchment falling from his hand.

He picked it up, smoothing it out. Perhaps if he showed it to Parmenion? No, it would serve no purpose, he knew. The report would be disbelieved. Parmenion was truly blind to any criticism of the young King.

The moon was bright and Mothac read once more the report from his agent in Pella. Much of it concerned the new regent, Antipater, left in charge of the army at home, with Olympias ruling as Queen. It also spoke of unrest in the western regions. But the last section spoke of the murder of Cleopatra and her baby son.

A palace servant talked of the double killing and was then

murdered himself. All the slain man's friends, and the families of those friends, were removed from Pella and executed.

But the story survived, whispered among Alexander's enemies. It was surely too appalling to be true, wrote Mothac's agent. Alexander was said to have gone to Cleopatra's apartments and strangled her with a golden wire. Then he took the babe to the rooms of a foreign witch woman from Samothrace where, in order to ensure the success of his bid for the throne, he sacrificed the child to an unknown god – and then ate the babe's heart.

Sober now, Mothac stared at the parchment. A chill breeze blew at his back and he shivered.

'It is time to die,' hissed a cold voice. A searing pain clamped around Mothac's heart with fingers of fire. The old man struggled to rise, but the agony was too great and he sank back to the grass, the parchment fluttering from his fingers.

As it touched the ground the document burst into flames – writhing on the grass with dark smoke billowing from it.

Rolling to his belly Mothac tried to crawl, but a powerful hand grasped his shoulder and turned him to his back. He looked up and saw a pair of yellow, slitted eyes, and felt the long dagger slide under his breastbone.

Then all pain left him and the grass was cool against his neck. He remembered a day in a Thebes of long ago, when he had sat by a trickling stream with Elea beside him, her head resting on his shoulder.

The colours were bright, the greens of the cypress trees above him, the dazzling blue of the sky, the statues in the garden seemingly carved from virgin snow. Life had been beautiful that day and the future was brimming with the promise of further joy.

'Elea . . .' he whispered.

*

Alexander rose slowly from the depths of a dark dream and drifted up towards consciousness, becoming aware first of the silk sheet covering his naked frame. It was luxurious and soft, clinging to his skin, warm, and comforting. He rolled to his back and noticed that his hand seemed to be coated with mud, the fingers stuck together. Opening his eyes, he sat up. The dawn light was bathing the outer wall of the tent and he lifted his hand to rub sleep from his eyes. He stopped and his heart began to hammer. Hand and arm were covered with dried blood, as was the bed. He cried out and dragged back the sheet, searching his body for a wound.

Hephaistion ran into the tent, sword in hand. 'What is it, sire?'

'I have been stabbed,' replied Alexander, on the verge of panic, his hands probing the skin of his body. Hephaistion dropped his blade and moved to the bedside, eyes scanning the King's naked torso.

'There is no cut, sire.'

'There must be! Look at the blood!'

But there was no wound. By the doorway of the tent lay a dagger, the blade crusted with congealed blood. Hephaistion scooped it into his hand. 'It is your dagger,' he said, 'but the blood is not yours.'

Alexander padded across to the far wall where a pitcher of water had been left on a small table. Swiftly the King washed himself clean, still searching for a cut or gash. He swung on Hephaistion. 'What is happening to me?'

'I don't understand you, sire,' answered the young officer.

'Last night . . . the feast. When did I leave?'

'Just before dawn. You had drunk a great deal and were staggering. But you refused my offer of a helping hand.'

Alexander returned to the bed and sat with his head in his hands. 'The blood must have come from somewhere!'

'Yes, sire,' said Hephaistion softly.

'Am I going insane?'

'No! Of course not!' Hephaistion crossed the room, putting his arm around the King's shoulder. 'You are the King – the greatest King who ever lived. You are blessed by the gods. Do not voice such thoughts.'

'Blessed? Let us hope so.' Alexander took a deep breath.

'You said you would talk to me, sire, about Parmenion.'

'I did?'

'Yes. But now that he has won such a victory I doubt you'll want him to join Attalus.'

'What are you talking about? Is this a dream?'

'No, sire, you remember . . . several nights ago? We discussed Parmenion and you said it might be necessary to kill him.'

'I would never say such a thing. He is my oldest friend; he risked his life for me . . . many times. Why do you say this?'

'I must have misunderstood, sire. You were talking about allowing him a long rest, like Attalus. I thought . . .'

'You thought wrong! You hear me?'

'Yes, sire. I am sorry.'

Men began shouting outside the tent and Hephaistion turned, moving swiftly out into the sunshine. Alexander remained slumped on the bed, trying to remember what happened after the feast. He could picture the laughter and the jests and Cleitus, the old cavalryman, dancing on a table. But he could not recall leaving the feast, nor coming to his bed.

Hephaistion returned and walked slowly across the tent, his face grave.

'What is happening out there?' asked the King.

Hephaistion sat down but said nothing, his eyes not meeting Alexander's gaze.

'What is it, man?'

'Parmenion's friend, the Theban Mothac . . . he has been murdered.' Hephaistion glanced up. 'Stabbed, sire . . . many times.'

Alexander's mouth was dry. 'It wasn't me. I loved that old man. He taught me to ride; he used to lift me upon his shoulders. It wasn't me!'

'Of course it wasn't, sire. Someone must have come into the tent while you were sleeping, and smeared blood upon you.'

'Yes . . . yes. No one must know, Hephaistion. Otherwise stories will start to spread . . . you know, like in Pella about the child.'

'I know, sire. No one will hear of it, I promise you.'

'I must see Parmenion. He will be distraught. Mothac was with him back in Thebes when Parmenion freed them, destroying the power of the Spartans. My father was there . . . did you know that?'

'Yes, sire. I will call your servants and they will fetch you clothes.'

Picking up the blood-covered dagger Hephaistion dipped it into the murky red water of the pitcher, washing the weapon clean. Then he moved to the bed, dragging clear the blood-covered sheet and rolling it into a tight bundle.

'Why would anyone do this to me, Hephaistion?'

'I cannot answer that, sire. But I will double the guard around your tent.'

Carrying the blood-soaked sheet, the young officer backed away and Alexander sat silently staring down at his hands. Why can I not remember, he thought. Just like in Pella after he had seen the woman, Aida.

She had held his hand and told his fortune. Her perfume had been strong and she had talked of glory. Her skin was whiter than ivory. He remembered reaching out, as if in a daze, and cupping his palm to her breast. Her fingers had stroked his thigh and she had moved in to him, her lips upon his.

But after that. . . ? There was no memory. Aida later told him that she and Olympias had murdered Philip's widow and the child. It was necessary, she had assured him. Alexander had not believed her, but he had done nothing to punish the women.

For then, as now, he had woken in his bed with dried blood upon his hands and face.

*

It had seemed to Parmenion that there was no further room for pain in his heart and soul. The death of Derae and the murder of Philip had lashed his emotions with whips of fire, leaving him spent and numb. Yet now he knew he was wrong. The killing of Mothac opened another searing wound and the ageing Spartan was overcome with grief.

491

There were no tears, but the *strategos* was lost and desolate.

He sat in his tent with his sons Philotas, Nicci and Hector, the body of Mothac laid out on a narrow pallet bed. Parmenion sat beside the corpse, holding Mothac's still-warm dead hand.

'Come away for a while, Father,' said Nicci, moving to stand beside Parmenion. The Spartan looked up and nodded, but he did not move. Instead his gaze swung to his children: Philo tall and slender, the image of his father; Nicci shorter, dark-haired and stocky; and the youngest, Hector, so like his mother, fair of face and with wide, innocent eyes. They were men now, their childhood lost to him.

'I was your age, Hector,' said Parmenion, 'when first Mothac came to my service. He was a loyal friend. I pray you will all know such friendship in your lives.'

'He was a good man,' agreed Philo. Parmenion scanned his face for any sign of mockery, but there was nothing to see save regret.

'I have been a poor father to you all,' said Parmenion suddenly, the words surprising him. 'You deserved far more. Mothac never ceased to nag me for my shortcomings. I wish . . . I wish . . .' He stumbled to silence, then took a deep breath and sighed. 'But then there is nothing to gain by wishing to change the past. Let me say this: I am proud of you all.' He looked to Philo. 'We have had our . . . disagreements, but you have done well. I saw you at the Granicus, rallying your men and leading the charge along-side Alexander. And I still remember the race you won against the champions of Greece – a run of skill and heart. Whatever else there is between us, Philotas, I want you to know that my heart swelled when I saw that race.' He turned to Nicci and Hector. 'Both of you have needed to fight to overcome the handicap of being sons of the Lion of Macedon. Always, more was expected of you. But not once have I heard you complain, and I know that the men who serve under you respect you both. I am growing old now and I cannot turn back the years and live my life differently.

But here . . . now . . . let me say that I love you all. And I ask your forgiveness.'

'There is nothing to forgive, Father,' said Hector, stepping into his father's embrace. Nicci moved to Parmenion's left, putting his arm around his father's shoulder. Only Philo remained apart from them. Walking to Mothac's body, he laid his hand on the dead man's chest.

Philo said nothing and did not look at his father, but his face was trembling and he stood with head bowed. Then, without a word, he spun on his heel and strode from the tent.

'Do not think badly of him,' said Nicci. 'Most of his life, he has wanted nothing more than to win your love. Give him time.'

'I think our time has run out,' answered Parmenion sadly.

Mothac was buried in the shadows of the Ida Mountains, in a hollow surrounded by tall trees.

And the army moved on towards the south.

The Issus, Autumn 333 BC

With a boldness few of his enemies could have expected, Alexander marched the allied army along the southern coastline of Asia Minor, through Mysia, Lydia and Caria. Many of the Greek cities immediately opened their gates, welcoming the victorious Macedonians as liberators and friends, and Alexander accepted their tributes with a show of great humility . . .

It contrasted with the savagery he unleashed on those towns and cities who tried to oppose him.

The Ionian city of Miletus was stormed by the King's Thracian mercenaries, and appalling tales of murder, rape and slaughter swept east across the Persian empire and west to the cities of Greece. Even Alexander's enemies could scarcely believe the scale of the atrocities.

It was even whispered that the Macedonian King himself was present, dressed as a common soldier and urging the Thracian savages to even greater depths of depravity.

When Alexander heard of it he flew into a towering rage and an immediate inquiry was launched, headed by an Athenian general. Miletian survivors were questioned and brought to the Macedonian camp. The Thracians were ordered to stand in file while the survivors walked among them, pointing out soldiers alleged to have taken part in the atrocities. By dusk on the fifth day of the inquiry, some seventy Thracians had been executed.

The swiftness of Alexander's justice earned him credit among the allies, and the Macedonian army moved on.

By the spring of the following year Alexander had reached the southern satrap of Cilicia on the coastline of the sea of Cyprus. No Persian army had come against him and Darius' general, Memnon, had moved his offensive to the sea – sailing through the Aegean with a force of 300 warships, destroying Macedonian supply ships and raiding the coastal cities which had declared support for Alexander.

In the captured port of Aphrodesia Parmenion watched the unloading of three Greek ships which had broken through the Persian blockade. The first, an Athenian trireme, carried supplies of coin desperately needed to pay the troops. Alexander had decreed that there should be no plunder of the liberated lands. All goods would be paid for and any soldier found guilty of looting or theft would be instantly executed. This was good policy, for it meant that the King could continue to be seen as a liberator and not an invader. But it carried with it a serious problem. If soldiers had to pay for food or clothing or women, then they needed coin – and that was in short supply.

Three gold shipments so far had been intercepted by the Persian fleet, and no Macedonian had received pay for more than three months. Disquiet was growing, morale low.

Parmenion counted the chests as they were carried from the ship and loaded on ox-carts, then mounted his stallion and led the convoy to the city treasury. Here he watched the unloading of the carts and left Ptolemy and Hector to supervise the storing of the treasure in the vaults below the palace.

Alexander was waiting in the upper rooms, Hephaistion and Craterus with him. The King looked tired, thought Parmenion, as he entered the room and bowed. Alexander, in full armour of shining gold-embossed iron, was sitting on a high-backed chair by the wide window.

'The coin is safely stored, sire,' said Parmenion, untying the chinstrap and lifting his helm from his head. His grey hair was streaked with sweat and he moved to a nearby table where a pitcher of watered wine had been set, with six goblets around it.

'What news of Darius?' asked the King, standing and moving to where Parmenion stood.

The Spartan had reached for the pitcher but now he paused. 'The moment is coming,' he said. 'Last year the Greek King ordered a full conscription from all the satrapies. But he was persuaded that our invasion was merely a swift incursion into Asia Minor in order to plunder the Ionian cities. Now he has realized his error. Our reports are not as complete as I would like, but it seems he is amassing an army of great size.'

'Where?' asked the King, his eyes gleaming.

'That is difficult to say. The troops are moving from all over the Empire. One army is reported at Mazara, which is some three weeks to the north-east of us. Another is said to be at Tarsus, a week's march to the east. Yet another is gathering in Syria. There may be more.'

'How many will come against us?' asked Hephaistion.

The Spartan's mouth was dry and he found himself longing to lift the pitcher, to feel the strength of the wine flowing in his limbs. He shook his head. 'Who can say?' He reached for the wine.

'But you can guess?' Alexander insisted.

'Perhaps a quarter of a million,' Parmenion answered. Swiftly he filled a goblet and lifted it to his lips, intending only to sip at the wine, but the taste was almost overpowering and when he replaced the goblet on the table it was empty.

Alexander refilled it for him. 'A quarter of a million? Surely not!' argued the King.

The Spartan forced himself to ignore the wine and moved to a couch at the centre of the room. Rubbing his tired eyes he sat down, leaning back against the silk-covered cushions. 'Those who have never been in Asia,' he began, 'find it difficult to visualize the sheer size of the Empire. If a young man wanted to ride slowly around its outer borders he would arrive back at his starting point middle-aged.

Years and years of travel, through deserts and mountains, lush valleys, immense plains, jungles and areas of wilderness that stretch on a hundred times further than the eye can see, even from the tallest mountain.' He gazed around the room. 'Look at the wine pitcher,' he told them. 'If that is Greece, then this palace is the Persian Empire. It is so vast that you could not count the Great King's subjects: a hundred million . . . two hundred million? Even he does not know.'

'How then do we conquer such an Empire?' Craterus asked.

'By first choosing the battleground,' answered Parmenion, 'but more importantly by winning the support of its people. The Empire is too vast to defeat as an *invader*. We must become a part of it. Darius took the throne by poisoning his rivals. He has already faced his own civil wars and won them. But there are many who distrust him. Macedonia was once considered a part of the Empire and we must build on that. Alexander is here not only to liberate the Greek cities, he is here to liberate the Empire from the usurper.'

Hephaistion laughed. 'You jest, Parmenion! How many Persians will accept that an invading Greek is a liberator?'

'More than you would believe,' said Alexander suddenly. 'Think of it, my friend. In Greece we have many city states, but we are all Greeks. Here there are hundreds of different nations. What do the Cappadocians care if it is not a Persian sitting on the throne? Or the Phrygians, or the Syrians, or the Egyptians? All they know is that the Great King rules in Susa.' He turned to Parmenion. 'You are correct, *strategos*, as always. But this time you have surpassed yourself.' The King brought Parmenion a fresh goblet of wine, which the Spartan accepted gratefully.

'There is still the question of the Persian army,' pointed out Craterus. 'Who will lead it?'

'That is a problem,' Parmenion admitted. 'Memnon is a skilled general. We defeated him at the Granicus because he was not aware of the scale of reinforcements which had arrived with Alexander. He was marginally outnumbered.

But wherever this battle is fought, we will face a ten-to-one disadvantage.'

'Do not concern yourself with Memnon,' said Alexander, his voice curiously flat and emotionless. 'He died two nights ago.'

'I had not heard that,' said Parmenion.

'Nor should you,' said the King. 'I saw it in a vision: his heart burst like an over-ripe melon.'

Alexander walked to the window and stood staring out over the sea.

Hephaistion moved to his side, speaking so softly that Parmenion could not make out the words. But Alexander nodded.

'The King wishes now to be alone,' Hephaistion stated.

Parmenion rose and gathered his helm, but Alexander remained at the window. Baffled, the Spartan followed Craterus from the room.

'Is the King well?' he asked the younger man as they walked out into the sunlight.

Craterus paused before replying. 'Last night he told me he was about to become a god. He was not joking, Parmenion. But then later, when I asked him about it, he denied ever saying it. He has been so . . . fey of late. Visions, talks with the gods. You have great experience, sir, of men and battles and long campaigns. Do you understand what is happening to him?'

'Have you spoken of this to anyone?'

'No, sir. Of course not.'

'That is wise, my boy. Say nothing – not to Hephaistion, nor any of your friends. Even if others discuss it in your presence, stay silent.'

Craterus' eyes widened. 'You think he is going insane?'

'No!' replied Parmenion, more forcefully than he intended. 'He has genuine powers. He had them as a child: the ability to see events a great distance away, and other . . . Talents. Now they have returned. But they create in him terrible pressures.'

'What do you advise?'

'I have no more advice to offer. He is marked for

greatness. All we can do is support him and follow him. He is strong-willed and I hope this . . . malaise . . . will pass.'

'But you do not think it will?'

Parmenion did not reply. Patting the young man's shoulder the Spartan walked away, his thoughts sombre. For too long he had pushed away the doubts, turned his eyes from the truth. Mothac had been right, he had blinded himself to the obvious.

The *strategos* had allowed emotion to mask intellect, had even dulled his reason with wine. How many times had he warned his junior officers of just such stupidity? But now he was forced to face, head on, the fear he had lived with for so long.

The Chaos Spirit had returned.

Battle at the Issus, 333 BC

The morning was chill as Parmenion, in full battle armour, rode the grey, Paxus, towards the north, and steam billowed from the stallion's nostrils. The sky was the colour of iron and a sea-mist had crept in from the west, seeping across the camp-site, dulling the sounds as the Macedonian infantry moved into formation. Parmenion tied the chin-straps on his helm and swung to watch the gathering men.

For five days the Macedonians had marched south, apparently fleeing before Darius' vast army, but now – as the dawn light bathed the Mediterranean – the Greeks swung back to the north, marching through a narrow rock-strewn pass.

With the Persian camp less than four miles distant, Parmenion rode warily at the head of the Macedonian infantry with Alexander alongside him. Throughout the night the Spartan had listened to reports from the scouts concerning the Persian positions. Believing Alexander to be fleeing from him, Darius – as Parmenion had hoped – had become careless. His vast forces numbering more than 200,000 were camped by a river south of the town of Issus, and it was here that Parmenion intended to force the battle; for the flatlands south of the town extended for only a mile and a half, and it would be difficult for the Persians to use their numerical advantage to envelop the Macedonian flanks.

Alexander was unnaturally quiet as they rode, and none of the officers felt inclined to break the silence.

This was the moment of truth and every man, marching or riding, peasant or noble, knew it. It was not even the question of victory or defeat – save in the minds of the generals and captains. Today would see each man face the prospect of death or mutilation. News had spread of the size of the force opposing them and Alexander had toured the camp – talking to the men, exhorting them, lifting them. But even such charismatic encouragement seemed thin and as wispy as the mist on this cold morning.

The land ahead widened, the hills to the east flattening and the mountains receding behind them, and Alexander ordered the infantry to fan out on to the plain. Led by the silver-bearded Theoparlis, the Shield Bearers – elite foot-soldiers trained by Parmenion – moved out to the right, leaving the Macedonian infantry under Perdiccas in the centre. Allied soldiers and mercenaries remained on the left and the advance continued on a wide front, the men marching now in ranks eight deep.

Alexander and his officers rode along the line to the west where the allied cavalry and Thessalians fanned out from the centre like the wings of an eagle.

At last Alexander spoke, guiding Bucephalus alongside Parmenion's mount. 'Well, my general, the day is finally here.' He grinned and reached out to clasp Parmenion's hand in the warrior's grip, wrist to wrist. 'We will meet again in victory – or in the Elysian Fields.'

'Victory would be preferable,' answered Parmenion, with a wry smile.

'Then let it be so!' agreed the King, tugging on the reins and galloping to the far right, his Companion cavalry and Lancers streaming behind him.

Parmenion rode back to the column of lightly-armoured archers, marching behind the phalanxes. The men were Agrianians from Western Thrace, tall and wolf-like, mountain men carrying short, curved hunting bows of bonded wood. The archers were fine fighters – calm, unflappable and deadly in battle. Calling their officer to him, Parmenion ordered the bowmen to angle their march to the right into the mist-clad foothills.

'Darius will almost certainly send cavalry to outflank us. Harry them. Turn them back if you can. If you cannot, then make sure they suffer great losses.'

'Yes, sir,' answered the man. 'We'll send them running.' He gave a gap-toothed grin and loped off towards the east, his men filing out behind him.

The Spartan rode back to the cavalry on the left, his eyes scanning the long line of flat beach to the west. He swung to Berin, the hawk-faced Thessalian prince who had fought beside him at the Crocus Field so many years before. Berin was grey-bearded now, but still lean and strong, his face tanned to the colour of old leather. The Thessalian smiled. 'They may try to attack on the flat by the sea,' he said. 'You want us to ride out there?'

'No. Take your men behind the infantry and dismount. I do not want you seen until the enemy are committed to a flank attack.'

Berin gave a casual salute and led his men back along the line. Dust was rising now behind the marching men and the Thessalians dismounted and hung back, protecting the delicate nostrils of their mounts. Some even spilled precious water on to dry cloths, wiping dust from the mouths of their horses.

The army moved on. In the distance the Persian defences came into sight, across a narrow ribbon of a river where earthworks had been hastily thrown up, pitted with stakes.

Brightly-garbed Persian cavalry could be seen moving through the foothills on the right, but Parmenion forced himself to ignore them, trusting to the skills of the Agrianian archers to contain them. Slowly the advance continued, Parmenion angling the 2,000 allied cavalry further to the left and ordering the men to spread out.

As he had hoped, a large force of Persian horsemen forded the river, heading west towards the beach. His trained eye watched them streaming out from the enemy right, three thousand, four, five, six . . .

Ptolemy moved alongside Parmenion. 'Can we hold

them?' asked the young man nervously. The Spartan nodded.

'Order Berin and his Thessalians to mount.'

Parmenion swung his gaze back to the centre, where the Macedonian infantry were almost at the river. Now was the testing time, for there was no way the men could cross the water and maintain formation. And they faced a solid mass of well-armed and armoured Persian Guards and at least 5,000 renegade Greek mercenaries, many from Boeotia and Thebes, men with deep hatred for the Macedonian conquerors.

Parmenion was confident that his wild Thessalians could turn the Persian cavalry on the beach, protecting the left, and had great faith in the skills of the Agrianian archers guarding the foothills on the right. But everything now depended on the Macedonian cavalry breaching the enemy centre. For, if the Persians were allowed to sweep forward, sheer weight of numbers would cleave like a spear through the eight deep ranks of the infantry.

The Spartan cleared his throat, but could not raise enough saliva to spit. All rested now on the courage and strength of Alexander.

*

Alexander tightened the straps on the iron buckler at his left forearm, then knotted Bucephalus' reins. From here on he would control the war-horse only with his knees. Philotas called out and Alexander turned to see Persian cavalry on the right moving into the foothills. Glancing back, he saw the bowmen moving out to intercept. He hawked and spat, clearing the dust from his mouth; then drawing his sword he raised it high above his head and kicked Bucephalus into a run for the river. The Companion cavalry, led by Philotas, Cleitus and Hephaistion, raced after him. Arrows and stones flashed by the King's head as he charged, but none of the missiles touched him as Bucephalus splashed into the water, sending up great arches of spray.

Thousands of Persian horsemen rode to meet the Macedonian attack, and Alexander was the first to come into contact. With a wild cut he hammered his blade into the shoulder of a silk-clad rider and the man fell screaming into the mud-churned water.

The Persians wore little armour save brocaded breastplates, and the Macedonians surged through them to the far bank.

'Kill! Kill! Kill!' roared Alexander, his voice carrying above the ringing clash of battle. As the King pushed on a lance clanged from his breastplate, tearing loose a gold-embossed shoulder-guard. Alexander ducked under a slashing sabre and disembowelled the attacker.

At the top of the slope the King reined in his mount and cast a swift glance to his left. Darius' renegade Greek mercenaries had counter-charged against the Macedonian infantry and the two forces were battling at the centre of the shallow river, all formations lost. Behind the Greeks stood the Persian Royal Guards, poised to follow the mercenaries into the attack. Instantly Alexander realized that were they to enter the fray now the Macedonian centre would be sundered.

Swinging Bucephalus, Alexander charged at the Guards, the Companion cavalry desperately trying to support him. It was a move of dazzling courage and the Macedonians struggling in the water saw their King, single-handedly it seemed, cleaving his way towards the Persian centre.

A great cry went up and the phalanxes surged forward.

Alexander, wounded on both arms, continued his advance, for he had caught sight of his enemy, Darius, standing in a golden chariot drawn by four white horses. The Persian King was tall and fair, his golden beard long and tightly curled. Upon his head was a conical crown of gold set upon a silver helmet. A white silk scarf was bound about his face and neck, flowing down over a cloak of silver thread.

'I see you, Usurper!' bellowed Alexander. Hephaistion and the Companion cavalry came alongside the King, protecting his flanks, but once more Alexander urged Bucephalus forward. The Persian Guards fell back before the ferocity of the charge, a great heaving mass of men jostling before the chariot of their King.

On the far side of the field, Berin and his Thessalians had broken through the Persian ranks and were sweeping to the right in a bid to reach Alexander.

Dismayed by the onslaught, the Persians struggled to form a fighting square around Darius. Alexander saw the Persian monarch snatch up a spear and try to turn his chariot to face the invader, but the white horses – alarmed by the noise and the smell of blood and death – panicked and bolted, drawing the golden chariot clear of the field. Darius fought to control the maddened beasts, but it was beyond his powers and the chariot sped towards the north.

Seeing their King apparently fleeing the battle, many of the Persians fled with him, opening huge gaps in the ranks. Thessalian riders burst through them to link with Alexander.

Within moments the battle became a rout, Persian foot-soldiers running for the hills, throwing away swords and shields as they went. Whole regiments which had not yet come into the battle retreated back towards the relative safety of the town of Issus.

As the sun reached noon only the last of Darius' Royal Guards offered any resistance, but these few were swiftly overcome and slain. Just under 3,000 renegade Greek mercenaries laid down their weapons and offered to surrender to Alexander. But the King refused.

'You have betrayed your nation,' he told their messenger. 'You have fought on the side of the Usurper against the avenging army of Greece.'

'But we are mercenaries, sir,' the messenger replied, his face pale under his tan. 'It is our way. Darius offered to hire our services and we served him loyally. How can you call us traitors when we are only following our calling?'

'He paid you to fight,' answered Alexander coldly. 'So fight. Pick up your weapons and earn your pay.'

'This is madness!' cried the messenger, turning to seek support from Alexander's generals.

'No,' hissed the King, '*this* is madness.' And stepping forward he rammed his dagger into the man's neck, forcing the blade up under the chin and into the brain. 'Now kill them all!' he screamed.

Before the mercenaries could gather up their weapons the Thracians and Macedonians surrounding them rushed in, hacking and cutting. Drawing his sword Alexander ran in among them, his blade plunging into the back of the nearest renegade. With a wild roar the entire army descended on the mercenaries, cutting and stabbing until not one enemy soldier was left standing.

One by one the Macedonians fell back from the slaughter until only Alexander, blood-drenched and screaming, ran among the dead seeking fresh victims.

A terrible silence settled on the army as they watched the King's frenzied dance of death among the slain. Hephaistion, who had taken no part in the slaughter, walked forward to speak softly to Alexander, who sagged into his friend's arms and was helped from the field.

Lindos, Rhodes, 330 BC

Aida was content as she sat under the shade of an awning, her gaze resting on the glittering sea far below. The castle here was built on a towering cliff above a small village that nestled between two bays. From where she sat Aida could see only the smaller bay, a sheltered cliff-protected bowl where ships could anchor to escape the winter gales that raged across the Aegean.

A trireme was beached in the bay, its huge sail furled, its three banks of oars drawn in. It sat on the beach like a child's toy and Aida watched as several sailors leapt ashore and an officer began the long walk up the winding cliff-path to the castle.

The sea air was fresh and Aida drew in a deep breath. She could taste the Dark God's power upon her tongue, feel his swelling presence in the air around her, blowing on the sea breeze from Asia. She licked her lips, revelling in dreams of tomorrow.

There were those who talked of good and evil. Foolish notions. There was only strength and weakness, power and helplessness. This was at the heart of all the Mysteries she had so painfully learned during her long, long life.

Earth magic could prolong life, extend strengths, earn riches for the man or woman who understood it. But earth magic required blood and sacrifice; it needed screaming souls to feed it.

This much had been understood since the first rays of the first dawn. Throughout history the wise had known of the power of sacrifice. But only the true initiates understood the nature of the power released.

Yes, you could kill a bull and gain a particle of power. But a man? His fear just before death would swell the particle, filling it with dark energy, releasing Enchantment into the air.

Aida's dark eyes looked to the east, across the wide waters. Thousands upon thousands of men had died there a year ago, at Arbela, slain by the ever-victorious Macedonian army. Darius the King was dead, murdered by his own disenchanted men as they retreated. Alexander was crowned King in Babylon.

Alexander, King of Kings. Alexander the god . . .

No, she realized, not yet the god. Still the mortal fought to hold back the power living within him.

But not for much longer . . . She closed her eyes, her spirit soaring across the blue sea to the city of Susa, where Alexander sat upon a throne of gold studded with rare gems. He was dressed now in flowing silks, a cloak of golden thread upon his shoulders.

Aida hovered unseen in the air before him. 'Master!' she whispered.

There was no response, but she could feel the pulsing force of the god within him. Alexander was like a man clinging to a rock-face far above the ground, his arms tired, his fingers cramping. She could sense his fear. His soul had proved stronger than Aida would have believed possible, holding the god from his destiny – and such a destiny! Once he was in full control his powers would grow, radiating far beyond the frail human shell he inhabited. The might of Chaos would then surge across the earth, drawn into every living being, every tree and rock, every lake and stream.

And then those who had served him faithfully would gain their reward: a life of eternal youth, an infinity of pleasure, an intensity of experience and sensation never before attained by those of human birth.

Soon would come the blessed day.

Each victory, each death by Alexander's hand, added strength to the darkness within him.

Not long now, thought Aida.

Returning to her body she leaned back on the couch, reaching for a goblet of wine. The sun was dipping now towards the west and she felt its rays hot upon her legs. Standing, she pushed the couch further back into the shadows before stretching out again.

Soon the messenger would be here, hot and tired from walking the steep cliff-path. She had written to Alexander, begging leave to come to his court where she could offer the benefit of her sage counsel. Once there she could speed the process, adding the necessary narcotics to his wine, lessening his will to resist.

Such joys awaited . . .

Her thoughts turned to the woman Derae and she found her good mood evaporating. Old fool! She had been so dismissive, seemingly so content trapped within that frail, arthritic shell.

'How content are you now,' whispered Aida, 'now that the worms feast on your flesh? You understood nothing. All your healing and your good works! You merely fed upon the Enchantment of the world, giving nothing back. If we were all as you, then the Enchantment would die. What would the world be then? A sprawling mass of humanity with not a shred of magic upon it.'

She shivered at the thought. A young red-haired acolyte moved before her, bowing deeply. 'There is a man to see you, mistress,' she said. 'An officer of Alexander.'

'Bring him to me,' ordered Aida, 'and fetch wine.'

The girl backed away. Aida smoothed her gown of black silk and waited. A young man, tall and dark-bearded, stepped into view. His breastplate was black, edged with gold, and held a white-plumed helm in his left hand. His face was handsome, burnished bronze by the Asian sun, and showed not a trace of sweat from the long climb to the castle.

He bowed. 'I am Hephaistion, lady. I am sent by Alexander to bring you to his court.'

She looked into his dark eyes and disliked him immediately. Though she despised men, Aida had come to rely on their adoration. But Hephaistion was unaffected by her beauty. It irked her, but she did not show it. Instead she offered the young man a dazzling smile.

'I am honoured,' she said, 'that the Great King should invite me to Susa.'

Hephaistion nodded. 'Your home here is beautiful,' he said. 'May we walk the walls?'

Aida disliked strong sunlight, but Hephaistion was known as Alexander's closest friend and she had no wish to offend him. 'Of course,' she told him. Taking up a wide black-brimmed hat, she stood and led him to the northern wall. From here they could see the wider of the two bays of Lindos and watch the gulls swooping and diving above the small fishing boats returning from the sea.

'The King is troubled,' said Hephaistion. 'He believes you can be of great help to him.'

'Troubled? In what manner?'

Hephaistion sat back on the parapet. 'There are two Alexanders,' he said softly. 'One I love, the other I fear. The first is a kindly friend, understanding and caring. The second is a ruthless and terrifying killer.'

'You are speaking very frankly, Hephaistion. Is that wise?'

'Oh, I think so, my lady. You see, he told me about your stay in Pella and the . . . aid you gave him.'

'Aid?' she asked, nonplussed.

'How you helped him to take the throne.'

'I see.'

'I think you do,' said Hephaistion softly, his dark eyes holding to her gaze. 'When the King received your letter, he asked me to come to you . . . to thank you for all you have done for him. He gave me two instructions. Both were different, but I am becoming used to that.'

'What were these instructions?'

'Firstly, as I have said, he asked me to bring you to him.'

'And the second?'

'Well, that brings me to a problem. Perhaps you could help me with it?'

'If I can,' she told him.

'As I told you there are two Alexanders, and each of them gave me separate instructions. Whose should I follow? The friend . . . or the one I fear?'

'It is always wise,' said Aida carefully, 'to respond with caution to orders from men one fears. The friend can be forgiving. The other will not.'

Hephaistion nodded. 'You are very wise, lady.' Leaning forward, he took her arms and lifted her to sit on the parapet wall. 'Wise, and beautiful. I shall take your advice.'

'Then our relationship has begun well,' she said, forcing a smile.

'Indeed it has,' he agreed, 'and ended well.'

'Ended?' Aida's mouth was dry and she felt the beginnings of fear.

'Yes, lady,' he whispered. 'For, you see, my friend asked me to bring you to him. The other Alexander told me to kill you.'

'That cannot be. I am his loyal servant, I always have been. He would not order my death. You are mistaken, Hephaistion. Now let me down. I have had enough of this nonsense.'

'Perhaps you are right,' he told her. 'It is so hard sometimes to tell them apart. But in Pella you helped him to kill a child; you even convinced him he should eat its heart. I don't believe my King has need of your counsel.'

'Listen to me . . .' she began. But Hephaistion's hand took hold of her legs, tipping her back into space.

Aida felt herself slide clear of the wall.

Far below her the jagged rocks waited, and her screams echoed over the village.

*

Hephaistion leaned over the parapet to watch Aida fall – her body spiralling down, her shrieks carried away on the wind. It seemed to the Macedonian that she looked like a huge crow, her black robes fluttering like broken wings. He watched her strike the rocks, heard her screams cut off, then saw a flock of gulls descend upon her, their white forms slowly masking the black robes.

Stepping back he took a deep breath. He had never killed a woman before, but he felt no regrets. Her evil had been almost palpable and he was sullied by touching her.

He had told her the truth, in part at least. Alexander had admitted to fearing her and wishing her dead – yet later, his voice cold, he had ordered her brought to court. During the two years since the bloody slaughter at the Issus Alexander had spoken often of his fears, of the dark force eating away at the centre of his soul. Hephaistion knew more of the King's secrets than any man – even Parmenion, who now commanded a second Macedonian army and rarely saw Alexander.

It was Hephaistion in whom Alexander confided, and Hephaistion who recognized when the Dark God was close to the ascendant. The King's voice would grow cold, his eyes distant. Then he was chilling . . .

As on the night in the captured city of Persepolis when he had led a drunken mob of torch-bearers to destroy one of the great wonders of the world, the beautifully carved wooden temple to Ahura Mazda containing the works of the prophet, Zoroaster. Hephaistion had stood by, stunned, as Alexander hurled oil over the ox-hides on which the words of the prophet were written in gold.

Twenty thousand hides, the most treasured possession of the Persian people, destroyed in one night of debauchery, billowing flames clawing at wooden carvings which had lasted for centuries under a Persian sun.

Alexander remembered nothing of it the following morning.

Then had come the Night of the Spear.

A late-night feast had ended with the cavalry general, Cleitus, asking the King why he had taken to wearing Persian robes and insisting on the Persian practice of forcing his subjects to prostrate themselves before him, kissing the ground at his feet.

Alexander was embarrassed by the question, for there

were several Persians present and Hephaistion knew that, though the King did not like the ritual, he was endeavouring to act like a Persian monarch, honouring their customs. But he had never asked his Macedonian officers – nor any Greek – to prostrate themselves before him.

Cleitus was drunk, and unhappy at being asked to sit away from the King's right hand, his place being taken by a Persian general.

Hephaistion had tried to pull Cleitus away from the table, urging him to return to his tent and sleep off his drunkenness, but the old cavalryman pushed him away and stumbled towards the King, shouting: 'I served your father, you arrogant puppy, and I never had to kiss his feet. Damned if I'll kiss yours!'

Hephaistion saw Alexander stiffen and watched in sick horror as his eyes grew pale. Never before had the transformation happened publicly and he ran towards the King, desperate to get him away from the revellers. But he was too late. Alexander stepped back, seized a spear from a guard and thrust the iron blade through Cleitus' belly. Blood gushed instantly from the old man's mouth and he fell back, the spear tearing loose from the wound. For several moments the stricken man writhed on the floor, screaming. Then, with a gurgling, choking cry he died.

A stunned silence followed.

Alexander blinked and staggered as Hephaistion reached his side, taking his arm. 'What have I done?' whispered Alexander. 'Sweet Zeus!' Turning the spear upon himself he tried to fall upon the blade, but Hephaistion wrestled it from him. Two guards came to his aid and the weeping King was helped from the tent.

The following day, his hair covered with ash, Alexander led the funeral procession behind Cleitus' body. Instead of following the Macedonian custom of burning the corpse and placing the bones in a ceremonial casket of gold, he had ordered Egyptian embalmers to preserve the body, intending to have it placed in a crystal case and displayed in a specially built tomb of marble.

The King's grief was obvious to all and the soldiers, who

loved Alexander, forgave him swiftly. But his officers, having seen him murder a loyal brother, were silent, and Hephaistion knew their thoughts. Who will be next?

The embalming of Cleitus was a memory Hephaistion would never forget.

A slender Egyptian moved to the body carrying a box of cedar wood from which he produced a long, narrow spike, bent and forked at the tip.

'What is he doing?' Hephaistion asked the King.

Alexander's reply was detached, his voice distant and cool. 'He must remove the internal matter of the skull to prevent it rotting. So that the face is unmarked, he will insert the spike in the nostril and hook it into the brain, dragging it out.'

'I need to know no more,' snapped Hephaistion, turning and rushing from the room.

Later he made Alexander promise that if he, Hephaistion, ever fell in battle, he was to be buried in the Macedonian way.

The gulls moved away from the broken body on the rocks below and Hephaistion stepped back from the parapet and walked from the cliff-top castle down the long winding path to the small bay. The trireme's captain – a short, stocky Rhodian called Callis – met him on the beach.

'Will she be long?' he asked. 'The tide is turning and we need to sail within the hour.'

'She will not be travelling with us, captain. Sadly, the Lady Aida is dead.'

'What a wasted journey,' said Callis, cursing. 'Ah well, it will be a relief to the men. No sailor likes a woman aboard. And they say she was a witch who could foresee the future.'

'I do not think that was true,' said Hephaistion.

By dusk the trireme was sailing east on the busy trade lane to Cyprus, a stiff breeze billowing the great sail, the oars drawn in, the oarsmen resting at their seats on the three rowing decks. Hephaistion sat on a canvas-topped chair at the stern, eyes locked to the land sliding slowly by them.

First Caria, then Lycia, once so hostile but now merely small outposts of the Empire of Alexander.

He remembered the ceaseless forced marches under Parmenion four years ago as the Macedonian advance troops sought to avoid major clashes with the Persian forces. How right the Spartan had been. Had he fought the Persians and won, then Darius would undoubtedly have gathered an even larger force and Alexander would have arrived in Asia to find himself confronted by an irresistible enemy. The lands of the Persian Empire were more vast than Hephaistion could ever have imagined, its people more numerous than the sand grains of the beaches he could see to the north.

Even now, after almost six years of war and Alexander's winning of the crown, there were still battles to fight – against the Sogdianians of the north, the Indians of the east and the Scythian tribesmen of the Caspian Sea.

Parmenion had marched a second Macedonian army to the east, winning two battles against superior numbers. Hephaistion smiled. Even close to seventy years of age, the Spartan was still a mighty general. He had outlived two of his sons: Hector had died at the Battle of the Issus three years ago, while Nicci had been slain at Arbela fighting alongside his King.

Only Philotas remained.

'What are you thinking?' asked Callis, his huge arms resting on the tiller.

Hephaistion glanced up. 'I was watching the land. It seems so peaceful from here.'

'Yes,' agreed the sailor. 'All the world looks better from the sea. I think Poseidon's realm makes us humble. It is so vast and powerful and our ambitions are so petty alongside it. It highlights our limits.'

'You think we have limits? Alexander would not agree.'

Callis chuckled. 'Can Alexander sculpt a rose or shape a cloud? Can he tame an angry sea? No. We live for a little while, scurrying here and there, then we are gone. But the sea remains: strong, beautiful, eternal.'

'Are all seamen philosophers?' Hephaistion asked.

The captain laughed aloud. 'We are when the sea surrounds us. On land we rut like mangy dogs, and we

drink until we piss red wine. What war will you be fighting
when you get back?'

Hephaistion shrugged. 'Wherever the King sends me.'

'What will he do when he runs out of enemies?'

'Does a man ever run out of enemies?'

Susa, Persia, 330 BC

The moment had come, as he had long known it would, and Philotas felt a sudden coldness in his heart. His father had been right all along. His mouth was dry, but he did not touch the wine set before him. Today he wanted his head clear.

Alexander was still speaking, his officers gathered around him in the throne-hall at the palace of Susa. One hundred men, warriors, strong and courageous, yet they kept their gaze to the marble floor, not wishing to look up into the painted eyes of the King.

Not so Philotas, who stood with head held high watching Alexander. Gold ochre stained the King's upper lids and his lips were the colour of blood. The high conical crown of Darius, gold and ivory, sat upon his head, and he was dressed in the loose-fitting silken robes of a Persian emperor.

How had it come to this, Philotas wondered?

Alexander had conquered the Persians, drawing the defeated army into the ranks of his own forces and appointing Persian generals and satraps. The Empire was his. He had even married Darius' daughter, Roxanne, to legitimize his claim to the crown.

And what a sham that was, for not once had he called her to his bed.

Philotas' gaze flickered over the listening officers, whose

faces showed their tensions and their fears. Once more Alexander was talking about treachery amongst them, promising to root out the disloyal. Only yesterday some sixty Macedonian soldiers had been flogged to death for what the King called mutiny. Their crime? They had asked when they could go home. They had joined the army to liberate the cities of Asia Minor, not to march across the world at the whim of a power-crazed King.

Five days before that, Alexander had had a vision: his officers were set to kill him. The vision told him who they were, and six men were garrotted – one of them Theoparlis, the general of the Shield Bearers. Philotas had not liked the man, but his loyalty was legendary.

Ever since Hephaistion's departure the King had been acting strangely, given to sudden rages followed by long silences. At first the generals had affected to ignore the signs. Alexander had long been known to possess unusual Talents, though always before such behaviour had been short-lived. But now it seemed that a new Alexander had emerged, cold and terrifying.

In the beginning the officers had talked among themselves of this transformation, but after the killings began there grew among the Macedonians such a fear that even friends no longer met privately in case they should be accused of plotting against the emperor.

But three days ago had come the final lunacy.

Parmenion and the Second Army had at last taken the city of Elam. More accurately, the ruling council of the city had negotiated a surrender. Parmenion sent the city's treasury – some 80,000 talents of silver – to Alexander at Susa. Alexander's reply had been to order the killing of every man, woman and child in Elam.

Parmenion had received the order with disbelief and had sent a rider to question its authenticity.

Philotas had been summoned to the palace along with Ptolemy, Cassander and Craterus. They had arrived to find Alexander standing over the body of the messenger.

'I am surrounded by traitors,' Alexander declared. 'Parmenion has refused to obey the orders of his emperor.'

518

Philotas gazed down on the body of the messenger, a young boy of no more than fifteen. The lad's sword was still in its scabbard, but Alexander's dagger was buried in his heart.

'You have always spoken against your father, Philo,' said Alexander. 'I should have listened to you earlier. In his dotage he has turned against me. Against *me*!'

'What has he done, sire?' Ptolemy asked.

'He has refused to punish Elam for its rebellion.'

Philotas felt himself growing cold, a numbness spreading through him. All his life he had believed that one day he would be a king – the knowledge sure, set in stone, based on the promise of the only person who had ever loved him, his mother Phaedra. But, during the last year, the stone of belief had slowly crumbled, the cold breeze of reality whispering against it, scattering his hopes, destroying his dreams. Lacking the charisma of a Philip or Alexander, or the intellect of a Parmenion, he could not even inspire the troops he led into battle. Self-knowledge came late to him, but at last even Philotas had come to recognize his mother's folly.

No kingdom. No glory. His father had been right: he had built his future upon a foundation of mist. What now, he wondered? If he remained silent, then Parmenion would be slain and he, Philotas, would remain as a general of the King. If not, he would be taken and murdered . . . and Parmenion would still be killed. His mouth was dry, his heartbeat irregular. To die or not to die? What kind of a choice was this for a young man, he wondered? 'Well, Philo?' asked Alexander.

Philotas saw the King's eyes upon him . . . and shivered. 'Parmenion is no traitor,' he answered without hesitation.

'Then you are also against me? So be it. Take his weapons. Tomorrow he shall answer for his betrayal before his comrades.'

Craterus and Ptolemy had marched Philotas to the dungeons below the palace. They had walked in silence until Ptolemy reached out to pull shut the cell door.

'Ptolemy!'

'Yes, Philo?'

'I wish to send a message to my father.'

'I can't. The King would kill me.'

'I understand.'

The room was small, windowless and dark as pitch with the door bolted. Philotas felt his way to the pallet bed and stretched out upon it.

Nicci and Hector were both gone now, and tomorrow the last son of the Lion of Macedon would join them. 'I wish I'd known you better, Father,' said Philo, his voice quavering.

Despite his fears Philo slept, and was awakened by the sound of the bolts being drawn back on the door. A shaft of light filled the cell and the Macedonian blinked as armed men pushed their way inside.

'Up, traitor!' ordered a soldier, seizing Philo's arm and hauling him from the bed. He was pushed out into the corridor and marched back to the throne-room where his fellow officers waited in judgement.

Alexander's voice echoed in the vast hall, shrill and strident, his face flushed crimson. 'Philotas and his father owe everything to me – and how do they repay me? They plot and they plan to supplant me. What is the penalty for such treachery?'

'Death!' cried the officers. Philotas smiled. Only a few days ago his had been one of the voices shouting for the death of Theoparlis.

Slowly Philo rose to his feet, all eyes turning to him.

'What do you say, prisoner, before sentence is carried out?' asked Alexander.

'What would you have me say?' responded Philo, his voice steady, his gaze locked to the unnaturally pale eyes of the King.

'Do you wish to deny your villainy, or to plead for mercy?'

Philo laughed then. 'There is not one man in this room save you who believes that Parmenion would ever plot against you. For myself I have nothing to offer by way of defence. For if a man as loyal as Theoparlis could be found guilty, then what chance does Philotas have? I have followed you and fought battles alongside you – battles that my father won for you. My two brothers died to ensure you would sit upon that throne. I should have no need to defend myself. But let it be clearly understood by all present that Parmenion is no traitor. You ordered him to take a city – and he took it. Then you ordered that every man, woman and child in that city should be put to death as an example to other rebels. That he would not do. Nor would any other decent Greek. Only a madman would order such an atrocity.'

'Condemned out of his own mouth!' roared Alexander, rising from the throne and advancing down the room. 'By all the gods, I'll kill you myself.'

'As you killed Cleitus?' Philotas shouted.

Alexander's dagger swept towards Philo's throat, but the Macedonian swayed to his right, the blade slashing past his face. Instinctively he struck out with his left fist, which cannoned against Alexander's chin. The King fell back, the dagger falling from his hands. Philo swept it up and leapt upon him, bearing him to the marble floor. Alexander's head cracked against the stone. The point of the dagger in Philo's hand touched the skin of Alexander's neck, and Philo bunched his muscles for the final thrust.

Alexander's eyes changed colour, swirling back to the sea-green Philo remembered from the past.

'What is happening, Philo?' whispered the King, his voice soft. Philo hesitated . . . then a spear rammed through his unprotected back, ripping into his lungs and heart. He reared up, and a second guard drove his blade into the dying man's chest.

Blood gushed from Philo's mouth and he slumped to the floor beside the semi-conscious Alexander. The King rose shakily, then backed away from the corpse. 'Where is Hephaistion? I need Hephaistion!' he cried.

Craterus moved alongside him. 'He is gone, sire, to Rhodes, to fetch the Lady Aida.'

'Rhodes?'

'Let me take you back to your rooms, sire.'

'Yes . . . yes. Where is Parmenion?'

'In Elam, sire. But do not concern yourself. He will be dead by tomorrow. I sent three of our finest swordsmen.'

Alexander groaned, but for a moment he said nothing. He could feel the Dark God fighting back inside him, storming the bastions of his mind. Yet he held on and drew in a deep breath. 'Get me to the stables,' he ordered Craterus.

'The stables? Why, sire?'

'I need to stop them, Craterus.'

'You cannot ride out alone. You have enemies everywhere.'

The King looked up into the earnest young man's eyes. 'I am not insane, Craterus. But there is . . . a demon inside me. You understand?'

'A demon, sire, yes. Come and rest. I will send for the surgeon.'

'You don't believe me? No, but then why should you? Leave me!'

Alexander pushed Craterus away and ran down the long corridor, emerging into the bright sunshine of the courtyard. Two sentries snapped to attention, but he ignored them and continued to run along the tree-lined road to the royal stables.

Bucephalus was in the eastern paddock and his great head lifted as he saw the King. 'Come to me!' called Alexander. The black stallion trotted to the fence and Alexander opened the gate, took hold of the black mane and swung himself to Bucephalus' back.

There were shouts from the west and the King turned to see Craterus and several of the officers running after him.

Alexander kicked Bucephalus into a run and rode for the south-east, through the royal park and out on to the road to Elam. The city was some sixty miles away on the coast, the road petering out into rocky tracks and high hills.

There were robbers in the hills, savage tribesmen who looted many of the trade caravans from the east, but Alexander did not think of them as he rode. Instead he pictured the Spartan, remembering his gallantry in the lands of the Enchantment and his quiet counsel in the years that followed. Now there were assassins on their way to kill him.

Sent by me!

No, not by me. Never by me!

How could I have been so foolish, thought Alexander. The moment his father had torn the necklet from his throat he had felt the surging force of the Dark God. But he had believed he could control the evil, holding it back, using it when necessary. Now he knew that even that belief had been merely one more example of the cunning of Kadmilos.

Kadmilos! Even as he thought the name of the Beast he could feel the claws of power pulling at his spirit, drawing him down, the dizziness beginning . . .

'No!' he shouted. 'Not this time!'

'*You are mine,*' came the whispering voice from deep within him.

'Never!'

'*Always,*' came the response. '*Look on, Alexander – and despair!*'

The hidden doors of his memory opened and he saw again the murder of Philip, but worse than this he saw himself the night before, speaking with Pausanius and urging him to seek revenge. 'When I am King,' he heard himself saying, 'your rewards will be great indeed.'

'*Poor, naïve Pausanius,*' whispered the voice in his mind. '*How surprised he was when you leapt across the body of the fallen King and plunged your sword into his chest.*'

Alexander's spirit reeled from the shock. There was no doubting the vision. For years he had practised self-deceit, never daring to search for the truth. Other images swarmed into his mind – the death and mutilation of Philip's wife and son, the killing of Cleitus and Mothac, the murder of Theoparlis . . . loyal, trusting Theoparlis.

The King cried out as he rode and the demon within him laughed and rose.

'No,' said Alexander again, quelling the emotions of hatred and fear, hauling himself clear of self-reproach and guilt. 'Those deeds were yours, not mine.' His concentration deepened and he pushed the demon back.

523

'*You cannot resist me for long*,' Kadmilos told him. '*You will sleep, and I will rise.*'

It was true, but Alexander did not allow the fear to dominate his thinking. The cowardice of Kadmilos – his spirit fleeing as the point of Philo's dagger touched the skin of Alexander's throat – had given the King one last chance at redemption, and his thoughts were of Parmenion as he rode.

The great stallion galloped on, seemingly tireless, the drumming of his hooves echoing through the hills.

'Father Zeus,' prayed Alexander, 'let me be in time!'

The City of Elam, 330 BC

Parmenion awoke from a dream-filled sleep and sat up, pushing back the thin sweat-soaked sheet. The sky beyond the narrow window was streaked with grey as he climbed from the bed and padded across to the small table where last night's pitcher of wine still stood. It was almost empty, but he poured the dregs into a goblet and drained it.

He was about to return to his bed when he turned and caught sight of his naked body reflected in a mirror of polished brass. His hair was white now, and thin, his face lean and sharp, the hawk-nose more prominent than ever. Only the pale blue eyes were the same. He sighed and dressed in a simple *chiton* of silver grey, then belted on his dagger before walking down to the long gardens behind the house.

Dew lay upon the leaves and the morning was chill as he strolled the winding paths, halting by a ribbon of a stream that gushed over a bed of coloured crystals.

Seventy years – fifty of them as a general.

He shivered and walked on.

Parmenion. The Death of Nations. So many he could no longer find their names within his memory. The early days were the easiest to recall: the fall of Spartan power, the defeat of Illyria, Paionia and Thrace. The sack of the Chalcidice, the overthrow of Thebes . . .

But the last few years had seen the destruction of dynasties too many to recall: Phrygia, Cappadocia, Pisidia, Cilicia, Syria, Mesopotamia, Persia, Parthia. . . .

The stream opened out on to a wide pond around which statues had been set. A leopard, beautifully crafted and vividly painted, stood at the edge of the pool leaning its head forward as if to drink. A little distance away stood a striped horse, and beyond that several deer. All still, motionless, frozen in time.

The sun broke through in the east, the warmth touching the Spartan but not lifting his spirits. He walked on towards the eastern wall. There were alcoves there, fitted with carved wooden seats.

In the furthest of these Parmenion seated himself, looking back across the pond and up towards the great house with its rearing columns and red-tiled roof.

Some ten paces to his left sat a stone lion. Unlike the other animals in the garden, he was not painted; his great albino head was cocked to one side, as if listening, and the muscles of his flanks were magnificently rendered. Parmenion found the statue to be among the best he had ever seen, wondering why he had never noticed it before.

As the Spartan stared the lion suddenly moved. Slowly and with great grace it stood, and stretched its muscles of marble. Parmenion blinked and focused on the statue. The lion was still again, returning to its former position with head cocked.

'I am back,' said a soft voice. Parmenion turned his head and was not surprised to see Aristotle sitting beside him on the wooden bench. The man had not changed. In fact he seemed if anything a little younger, his grey beard streaked now with auburn hairs.

'Why did you create the lion?'

The *magus* shrugged. 'I like to make a dramatic entrance.' But there was no smile and his voice was subdued.

'Why have you come?'

'It was time.'

Parmenion nodded, though he did not understand.

'Alexander is losing his battle with the Dark God,' he said, 'and I am powerless to save him. He no longer listens to me, and the messages from his court are all of murder and madness. Can you help him?'

Aristotle did not answer at once, but reached out and laid his hand on Parmenion's arm. 'No, my friend. The Dark God's power is far greater than mine.'

'Alexander is my son. My flesh, my blood, my guilt. His evil is upon my hands. I should have killed him years ago.'

'No,' said Aristotle. 'The drama is not yet played out. I took the liberty of fetching this from your rooms.' The *magus* held out a small pouch of soft hide.

'It is useless now,' said Parmenion.

'Take it anyway.'

The Spartan tucked the pouch into his belt. 'You said it was time. So what is to happen?'

Aristotle leaned back, turning his face to stare up towards the house. 'Three men are dismounting at the main entrance. Soon you will see them striding down this path. Kadmilos – the Dark God – sent them. You understand?'

Parmenion took a deep breath and his eyes narrowed. 'I am to die,' he said.

A door opened at the rear of the house and three men began the long walk down the path by the glittering stream. Parmenion stood and turned to Aristotle.

But the *magus* had disappeared . . .

*

Parmenion walked slowly towards the three men. He did not know them by name, but had seen them with Alexander. Two were Parthians, dressed in oiled black leather tunics and long riding-boots, their dark hair cropped short to the skull. The third was a high-born Persian who had entered the King's service. The Spartan smiled as he saw that the man carried a sealed scroll.

'We have a message for you, sir,' called the Persian, increasing his pace. He wore loose-fitting silk troos and an embroidered shirt, beneath a cape of soft leather which hung down over his right arm.

'Then deliver it,' Parmenion told him. As the Persian came closer, Parmenion could smell the sweet, perfumed oil which coated his dark tightly-curled hair. He offered the scroll with his left hand, but as the Spartan reached for it the man's right hand emerged from beneath the cape. In it was a slender dagger. Parmenion had been waiting for the move and, sidestepping, he slapped the man's arm aside and drove his own dagger home into the assassin's chest. The Persian gasped and stumbled to his knees. The two Parthians leapt at Parmenion with swords drawn. The Spartan threw himself at them, but they were young men, swift of reflex, and he no longer had the advantage of surprise. A sword clove into his left shoulder, snapping the bone of his arm. Spinning, he hurled his dagger at the swordsman, the blade slicing home into the man's throat to tear open the jugular.

Something struck Parmenion in the lower back. It felt like the kick of a horse and there was no sensation of a cut or stab, but he knew that a sword-blade had plunged into him. Anger flared, for his warrior's heart could not bear the thought of dying without at least ensuring that his killer joined him on the path to Hades. Pain roared through him as the assassin wrenched the blade clear. The Spartan staggered forward and fell to the path, rolling to his back.

The Parthian loomed over him. Parmenion's fingers closed over a rock and, as the swordsman prepared himself for the death strike, the Spartan's hand flashed forward, the rock cracking against his assailant's brow. The man staggered back, the skin above his right eye split.

With a curse he ran at the wounded Spartan, but Parmenion's leg lashed out to sweep the Parthian from his feet. The man fell heavily, losing his grip on his sword. Parmenion rolled to his belly and struggled to rise. But for once his strength was not equal to his will and he fell.

He heard the Parthian climb to his feet and felt the sudden pain of the sword-blade as it pierced his back, gouging into his lung. A boot cracked against his head, then a rough hand tipped him to his back.

'I am going to cut your throat . . . slowly,' hissed the

Parthian. Dropping his sword the assassin drew a curved dagger with a serrated edge, laying it against the skin of the Spartan's neck.

A shadow fell across the killer. The man looked up . . . in time to see the short sword that hammered into his temple. He was catapulted across Parmenion's body and fell face-first into the stream, where his blood mingled with the water that rippled over the crystals.

Alexander knelt by the stricken Spartan, lifting him into his arms.

'I am sorry. Oh gods, I am so sorry,' he said, tears falling from his eyes.

Parmenion's head sagged against the young man's chest and he could hear Alexander's heartbeat, loud and strong. Lifting his arm, the Spartan pulled the pouch clear from his belt and pushed it towards the King. Alexander took it and tipped the contents on his palm; the gold necklet glittered in the sunshine.

'Put . . . it . . . on,' pleaded Parmenion. Alexander lowered him back to the ground and took the necklet in trembling fingers, looping it over his head and struggling with the clasp. At last it sat proud, gleaming and perfect.

Aristotle appeared alongside the two men. 'Help me to carry Parmenion to the eastern wall,' he said.

'Why? We should get a surgeon,' said Alexander.

The *magus* shook his head. 'No surgeon could save him. But I can. His time here is done, Alexander.'

'Where will you take him?'

'To one of my homes. I shall heal him, do not fear for that. But we must hurry.'

Together they carried the unconscious Parmenion to the white lion, laying him down on the grass beside the statue. The stone beast reared up upon its hind legs, growing, widening, until it loomed above them like a monster of legend. The belly shimmered and disappeared, and through it Alexander could see a large room with a vaulted window, opening on to a night-dark sky ablaze with stars.

Once more they lifted the Spartan, carrying him to a wide bed and laying him upon it. Aristotle took a golden stone from the pouch at his side, placing it on the Spartan's chest. All breathing ceased.

'Is he dead?' Alexander asked.

'No. Now you must return to your own world. But know this, Alexander, that the magic of the necklet is finite. It may last ten years, but more likely the power will fade before then. Be warned.'

'What will happen to Parmenion?'

'It is no longer your concern, boy. Go now!'

Alexander backed away and found himself standing in the sunlit garden staring back into the moonlit room within the statue. Slowly the image faded and the lion shrank, the great head coming level with the King – the jaws open, the teeth long and sharp. Then it sank to the earth and slowly crumbled, the stone peeling away like snowflakes, drifting on the breeze.

Behind him he heard the sound of running feet and turned to see Craterus and Ptolemy, followed by a score of warriors from the Royal Guard.

'Where is Parmenion, sire?' Ptolemy asked.

'The Lion of Macedon is gone from the world,' answered Alexander.

Babylon, Summer 323 BC

Seven years of constant battles had taken their toll on Alexander. The young man who had left Macedonia was now a scarred warrior of thirty-two, who moved with difficulty following a wound to his right lung and the slashing by a hand-axe of the tendons in his left calf.

His victories stretched across the Empire, from India in the east to Scythia in the north, from Egypt in the south to the northern Caspian Sea. He was a living legend throughout the world – adored by his troops, feared by the many enemies he had forced back from the frontiers of his new realm.

Yet, as he stood on this bright summer morning by the window of his palace rooms, he thought nothing of his reputation.

'Are you still set on this course, sire?' asked Ptolemy, moving forward to embrace his King.

'I have no choice, my friend.'

'We could seek the help of wizards – there are some in Babylon said to be most powerful.'

Alexander shook his head. 'I have travelled far to find a way to fight the Beast. All are agreed that I cannot defeat him. He is immortal, everlasting. And the power of the necklet is fading fast. Do you want to see the old Alexander return?'

531

'No, my lord. But . . . I wish Hephaistion were here. He would be able to advise you better than I.'

Alexander did not answer, but swung his head to stare from the window. It was the death of his beloved Hephaistion which had decided him upon this course of action. The Macedonian – the most trusted of the King's officers – had been found dead in his bed, apparently choked to death. Of the night in question, twelve weeks before, Alexander could remember nothing.

The surgeons had found a chicken-bone wedged in Hephaistion's throat, and it appeared that the officer had died while dining alone.

Alexander wanted to believe it. Desperately. For Hephaistion, above all his friends, had helped him during the seven years since Aristotle had taken Parmenion. As the power of the necklet faded, it was Hephaistion whose constant love and friendship had been the rock to which Alexander had clung when the Beast had been clawing at him, dragging him down.

Now Hephaistion was gone and the final battle was here.

'You will do as I bid – no matter what?' he asked Ptolemy.

'On my life I promise it.'

'No one must lay their hands upon . . . it.'

'Nor shall they.'

'You must go to Egypt. Make the land your own. Hold it against all the others.'

'There may be no war, sire. We are all friends.'

Alexander laughed. 'You are friends *now*,' he said. 'Leave me, Ptolemy. And tell no one what I plan.'

'It will be as you say.'

The general bowed once and turned to leave. Then suddenly he swung back to Alexander, embracing him and kissing his cheek. No more was said and, tears in his eyes, the officer left the room, pulling shut the door behind him.

Alexander walked to the table and filled a goblet with the wine he had prepared earlier. Without hesitation he lifted it to his lips and drank. Then moving to a bronze mirror on the far wall, he examined the necklet. There was little gold showing now; the interlaced wires had become black as jet.

'Just a little longer,' he whispered.

His servants found him lying on his bed at dusk. At first they moved around him, thinking him sleeping, but after a while one of them moved to his side, touching his shoulder.

'My lord! Sire!' There was no answer.

In panic they ran from the room, summoning Perdiccas, Cassander, Ptolemy and the other generals. A surgeon was called – a slim, wiry Corinthian named Sopeithes. He it was who found the pulse still beating at Alexander's throat. While no one was watching him, Ptolemy took the goblet containing the dregs of the drugged wine and hid it in the folds of his cloak.

'He is not dead,' said the surgeon, 'but his heart is very weak. He must be bled.'

Three times during the next five days a vein in the King's arm was opened, but at no time did he regain consciousness.

Time slipped by, and soon it became apparent to all that Alexander was dying. Ptolemy quietly made the arrangements Alexander had ordered, then he sat by the King's bedside.

On the twelfth night, with only Ptolemy beside him, Alexander's voice whispered out for the last time: 'Kadmilos.'

The Void, Time Unknown

Alexander sat at the mouth of the tunnel, a golden sword shining in his hand and casting its light upon the grey, dead soil of the Void. Some distance away, sitting upon a boulder watching him, was a twin Alexander dressed in silver armour, white hair framing his handsome face, ram's horns curving back from his temples.

'Poor Alexander,' taunted Kadmilos. 'He came to slay me. Me? He thought to use his pitiful sword against a spirit that has lived since before time. Look around you, Alexander. This is your future. No kingdoms here in this world of ash and twilight. No glory.'

'You are a coward,' the King told him wearily.

'Your words are useless, Human. Even if I allowed that sword to strike me I would not die. I am eternal, the living heart of Chaos. But you, you are pitiful. Your body still lives in the world of flesh, and soon I shall take possession of it. The drugs you swallowed will not deter me. It will be a matter of moments to nullify them. Then I shall heal your ruined lung and your wasted leg.'

'Come then,' offered Alexander, 'walk by me.'

Kadmilos laughed. 'Not yet. I shall walk the path to your soul when it pleases me. Look at your sword, Alexander. See how it fades. The last lingering Enchantment of the necklet is almost gone. When it dies, your blade will die with it. You know that?'

'I know,' answered the King. 'The priests of Zeus-Ammon warned me of it.'

'Then what did you hope to achieve?'

The King shrugged. 'A man must always fight for what he believes to be right. It is his nature.'

'Nonsense. It is a man's nature to lust, to long for all he cannot have, to kill, to steal, to plunder. That is why he is – and will always remain – a creature of Chaos. Look at you! By what right did you lead your armies into Persia? By what right did you impose your will upon the world? Your name will be remembered as a killer and a destroyer – one of my more glorious disciples.'

Kadmilos laughed again, the sound chilling. 'No arguments, Alexander? Surely you can summon some small defence for your actions?'

'I have no need of defence,' answered the King. 'I lived in a world governed by war. Those who did not conquer were themselves conquered. But I fought my enemies on the battlefield, soldier against soldier, and I risked my life as they risked theirs. I carry no shame for any action of mine.'

'Oh, well said,' sneered Kadmilos. 'Will you deny the surging passions aroused when you marched into battle, the lust for slaughter and death in your own heart?'

'No, you are wrong,' replied Alexander. 'I never lusted for slaughter. Battle, yes, I will admit to that. Pitting my strength and my will against my enemies – that gave me pleasure. But you it was who gained the most satisfaction from random butchery.'

Kadmilos stood. 'Your conversation is dull, Human, and I see your sword is now but a miserable shadow. Therefore we must end this meeting. Your mortal form awaits me.'

Alexander looked down at the fading sword, and even as he gazed upon it the weapon vanished from his hand.

'Enjoy your despair,' hissed Kadmilos, his form swelling, changing, becoming a dark cloud that flowed over Alexander, swirling into the tunnel and on towards the flickering light in the far distance.

The Void was empty now, save for a floating mist that seeped across the barren rocks. Alexander sighed, his heart heavy.

A figure moved from the mist, and the King saw it was Aristotle. The *magus* smiled and reached out to take Alexander's hand.

'Come, my boy, I cannot stay here long. But there is time enough to lead you to the Elysian Fields where your friends await.'

'Did I win? Did I hold him for long enough?'

'We will talk as we travel,' the *magus* answered.

*

The Spirit of Chaos surged into the body of Alexander. The eyes were open and through them Kadmilos could see a high, painted ceiling. He tried to move, but found the body paralysed. This was of small concern and he turned his powers inward, seeking out the poison soaked into the veins and nerves of the frail human form.

Foolish mortal, he thought, to believe that such a narcotic could foil the ambitions of a god. Swiftly he started to eradicate the drug. Feeling began to seep back into the body. He felt a cool breeze from a window to the left and a dull ache from the wounded leg. Ignoring the poison, he switched his attention to the injured limb, rebuilding the wasted muscle.

That was better! Pain of any kind was anathema to Kadmilos.

Returning to the poison, he cleaned it from lungs and belly.

Soon, he thought. Soon I shall awake.

He heard people in the room, but still the paralysis gripped the body. Footsteps sounded and he saw a shadow move into his range of vision. A dark-skinned man loomed over him.

'The eyes are incredible,' said the man. 'Truly he was blessed by the gods. It is a pity we cannot save them.'

'Are you ready to begin?' came the voice of Ptolemy.

'Yes, lord.'

'Then do so.'

Into Kadmilos' vision came a hand, holding a long spike forked at the tip.

'No!' screamed the Dark God, soundlessly.

The spike pressed hard into the opening of the left nostril, then drove up into the brain.

A City by the Sea, Time Unknown

Parmenion stared out over the harbour where great ships, larger than any he had seen, were docked, with curiously clad men moving about their enormous decks. Switching his gaze to the buildings surrounding the wharves, he marvelled at their complex design, the great arches supporting huge, domed roofs. Below in the narrow cobbled street he could hear what he imagined to be shopkeepers and stall-holders shouting about their wares. But the language was unknown to him.

He turned as Aristotle entered. The *magus* had another name here, and another appearance. His hair was long and white, a wispy beard grew from his chin, and he wore a long coat of velvet and trousers of embroidered wool.

'How are you feeling?' asked the *magus*.

Parmenion swung away from the window. Against the far wall was a mirror of silvered glass and the brilliance of its reflection still stunned the Spartan, though he had looked upon it many times during his five days in Aristotle's home.

He was healed of his wounds and the image in the mirror showed a young man in the prime of health – tall, slender, with a full life ahead of him. The clothes he wore were comfortable, but unnecessarily fussy he thought. The voluminous white shirt, with its puffed-out sleeves slashed with sky-blue silk, looked very fine, but the material was not strong. One day in the harsh Persian sun or the bitter rains of Phrygia, and the garment would be worthless, as indeed would be the ridiculous skin-tight leggings. And as for the boots! They were raised at the heel, making walking difficult and uncomfortable.

'I am well, my friend,' he answered, 'but what will I do in this place? I understand none of its customs, and the language I hear from the streets below is strange to me.'

'You will not be staying here,' Aristotle told him. 'Now that you are strong again I shall take you to a better world – one which I think you will enjoy. But that is for later. Tonight we will eat fine food and drink strong wine, and all your questions will be answered.'

'You have learned the truth? You know what happened?'

'Yes,' answered the *magus*. 'It has taken a little time, but I think you will find the wait was worthwhile.'

'Tell me.'

'Have patience. Such tales are best left for the evening.'

Throughout most of the afternoon Parmenion waited, but towards dusk he wandered through the house seeking the *magus*. In the north of the building was a flight of wooden stairs leading to a brightly-lit studio below the roof. Here he found Aristotle sitting at an easel, sketching a dark-haired woman who sat on a high-backed leather chair before him.

As the Spartan entered the woman smiled and spoke. He did not understand her words and merely bowed. Aristotle laid down his charcoal and stood. He said a few words to the woman, who stretched her back and rose. The *magus* walked her to the door, leading the way downstairs, then returned to the studio.

'I did not realize it was so late,' he said, reverting to Greek.

Parmenion was standing before the sketch. 'It is a good likeness. You have great talent.'

'Centuries of practice, my boy. Come, let us eat.'

After the meal the two men sat in comfortable chairs by an open leaded-glass window through which the stars could be seen glittering like diamonds on sable.

'What happened to Alexander?' asked Parmenion.

'He died some seventeen hundred years ago,' the *magus* answered, 'but in death he won his finest victory.'

'How so?'

'The Dark God took control of his body at the end. But Alexander had ordered it embalmed.'

'What difference could that make?'

'Kadmilos was spiritually joined to the body of Alexander. He could only be released from it when the body was destroyed by fire or consumed by carrion eaters, or rotted to nothing. But embalmed? Alexander's body would never rot and Kadmilos was trapped.

'When the King died there was a civil war among his generals. Ptolemy stole the embalmed body and took it to Egypt, to Alexandria, where he had a huge mausoleum built to accommodate it. For centuries men came from all over the world to gaze upon the still, perfect form of Alexander the Great. I myself stood before it with an emperor of Rome five hundred years after Alexander died. And Kadmilos was still a prisoner within. I could feel his evil pulsing through the crystal that held the body.'

'Is it still there?' Parmenion asked.

'No. Barbarians sacked Alexandria hundreds of years ago. But the priests of Alexander carried the crystal coffin into the mountains and buried it there, deep and far from the gaze of men. No one knows where now it lies. Save me, of course . . . for I found it. The body is still perfect, the Chaos Spirit trapped – perhaps for eternity.'

Parmenion smiled. 'Then no more will demon-possessed kings bring evil upon the world?'

'Not this demon, at least,' answered Aristotle, 'but there are others. There will always be others. But their powers do not rival those of the Dark God.'

'Poor Alexander,' whispered Parmenion. 'His life was cursed from the beginning.'

'He fought the demon with great courage,' the *magus* said, 'and he knew friendship and love. What more could a man want? But let us think of you . . .'

'Where can I go?' asked Parmenion, with a sigh. 'What is there for me, Aristotle?'

The *magus* chuckled. 'Life. Love. It is time, I think, to say our farewells. There is someone waiting for you.'

'Who?'

'Who else but Derae?'

'I never went back. That was decades ago.'

Aristotle leaned forward, clapping his hand to the Spartan's shoulder. 'It is only Time. Have you learned nothing?'

The Gateway, Sparta, 352 BC

Derae drew the woollen cloak more tightly about her as the clouds covered the moon and the night winds swirled.

Six hours had passed since Parmenion walked back through the shimmering Gateway to the unknown world beyond. She shivered and stared up at the cold stone pillars. The *magus* had asked her to wait here, but now she was alone beneath the empty sky.

'Derae!' called a voice, soft as the whisper of a distant memory. At first she thought she had imagined it, but it came again, tiny but insistent.

'I am here,' she answered aloud.

Something shimmered at the edge of her vision and she saw two ghostly shapes – faint, almost transparent – standing before her on the hillside. It was difficult to make out their features, though she could see that one was male and the other female.

'Who are you?' she asked.

'Close your eyes,' came the faraway voice. 'Use your powers.'

'I have no powers.'

'Trust me. Close your eyes and draw us in.'

Fear sprang into her heart, but she quelled it. What harm could they do to her? Was she not a Spartan, strong and proud? Closing her eyes she concentrated on the voice. It grew a little stronger and she recognized the *magus*, Chiron.

'I have someone with me,' he said, 'and I have a favour to ask.'

'Name it,' she told him.

'I want you to open your mind and allow her to enter your heart.'

'No!' answered Derae, suddenly fearful.

'She will leave when you request it,' he assured her.

'Why are you doing this?'

'For love,' he told her.

Instantly she became aware of the second spirit. 'It is her! You are trying to kill me. It was all a trick, wasn't it? Parmenion loved her and now she wishes to steal my body. Well, she cannot have it! You hear me?'

'That is not true,' he said gently. 'But it is your choice, Derae. Look into your own heart. Would you steal the body of another?'

'No,' she admitted.

'Not even to save your life?'

She hesitated. 'No,' she said firmly. 'Not even for that.'

'Then why would she?'

'What do you want of me?'

'Let her come to you. Speak with her. She will ask nothing from you. But through her memories you will see Parmenion – his life, his dreams.'

'And then?'

'If you wish it, she will depart from you and I will take her to another place.'

'She's dead, isn't she?'

'Yes.'

Derae fell silent, then opened her eyes to look once more upon the stone Gateway through which her love had passed.

'I will speak to her,' she said softly.

A great warmth flowed through her, images tumbling into her mind –a different Sparta, another life, a temple, a turbulent ocean of sick, injured, diseased or dying people, begging, praying, a lifelong struggle against the evil of Kadmilos. Derae reeled under the weight of those memories and felt herself slipping into a daze.

543

Light blazed, the sun shining high above a hillside.

'Thank you,' said another voice and Derae blinked, for sitting beside her was a woman in white, young and beautiful, with red-gold hair and wide green eyes.

'You are me,' said Derae.

'No – not quite,' the woman replied.

'Why have you come?'

'Aristotle . . . Chiron . . . found me. He said it would warm my soul to know you. He was right.'

Derae felt a great sadness growing within her. 'Your dreams were never realized, were they?'

The woman shrugged. 'Some were. But there are those who walk through life and never know love. They are the ones to pity.'

'He is coming back to me,' said Derae. 'But it is you he wanted, you he loved. I am only a . . . copy.'

'Not at all,' the woman assured her. 'You are everything he could want; you will be happy.'

'Why did Chiron bring you to me? What does he want me to do?'

'He wants us to become one.'

'Two spirits in one body?'

'No. There can be only one. He believes we can merge, one soul with two paths of memory.'

'Is that possible?' Derae asked.

The woman spread her hands. 'I do not know. But if you have doubts, then do not attempt it. There is no need for you to do this for me. Parmenion will soon be here, and your lives together will be rich and fulfilled.'

Derae looked at her twin and reached out her hand. 'Let us try,' she said.

The woman looked surprised. 'Why? Why would you do this?'

'Would you not do it for me?'

The woman smiled. 'Yes, I would.' Their hands met and the light faded.

Derae found herself sitting once more in the moonlight in the shadows of the Gateway. There were no ghosts and no voices, and the stars were bright above her. Taking a deep breath, she summoned her memories.

For a time she sat unmoving. The corridors of the past were branched now and there were two histories to scan. She remembered her life as a child in the Sparta of the Enchantment, and also as a young woman in the world of Parmenion. The years spiralled on, from youth to the first grey hairs, and she recalled with a shiver her arthritic joints, felt again the constant pains of old age, the fading of her powers. *Her powers?* I had no powers, she thought. Of course I did, she reminded herself. They were developed by Tamis when first I came to the Temple. But I had to give my sight to acquire them.

I have never been blind! An edge of panic touched her, but the memories flowed on, filling her mind, covering her like the warm blankets of childhood.

'Which one am I?' she asked aloud, but there was no answer. The memories were all hers – and identity was based, she knew, on memory.

It was not just the years of healing at the Temple that she could recall, but all the emotions and yearnings that had accompanied those years. Yet, similarly, she could remember vividly her time as Sparta's Queen with the first Parmenion, and her childhood with Leonidas.

'Which one?' she asked again.

Glancing down she saw a small white flower with fading petals, its time finished, its beauty disappearing. Reaching out, she held her hand above it; the petals swelled with new life. All confusion left her then.

'We are One,' she whispered. 'We are Derae.'

The panic faded, to be replaced by a quiet longing. Her gaze swung to the hill above her and the twin columns of stone.

The Gateway shimmered with golden light and a tall young man stepped out on to the hillside.

Bibliography

ANDRONICOS, M., *Sarissa* (Bulletin de Correspondance Hellenique 94).

ARISTOTLE, *Ethics* (trans. J. A. K. Thomson, introd. Jonathan Barnes, rev. ed. Penguin Classics 1976).

ARRIAN, *Campaigns of Alexander* (trans. Aubrey de Selincourt, rev. J. R. Hamilton Penguin Classics 1971).

AUSTIN, M. M. & VIDAL-NAQUET, P., *Economic and Social History of Ancient Greece* (Batsford 1977).

BENGTSON, H., *The Greeks and the Persians* (Weidenfeld 1968).

CASSIN-SCOTT, *The Greek and Persian Wars* (Osprey 1977).

CAWKWELL, G., *Philip of Macedon* (Faber 1978).

COOK, J. M., *The Persian Empire* (Dent 1983).

DEMOSTHENES AND AESCHINES (trans. A. N. W. Saunders, introd. T. T. B. Ryder, Penguin Classics 1975).

DIODORUS SICULUS, *Books 15–17* (Loeb).

ELLIS, J. R., *Philip II and Macedonian Imperialism* (Thames and Hudson 1976).

FLACELIERE, R., *Daily Life in Greece* (Macmillan 1966).

HAMMOND, N. G. L. & GRIFFITHS, G. T., *History of Macedonia Vol. II* (OUP).

HATZOPOULOS, M. B. & LOUKOPOULOS, L. D, *Philip of Macedon* (Heinemann 1981).

JENKINS, I., *Greek and Roman Life* (British Museum Publications 1986).

KEEGAN, J., *The Mask of Command* (Cape 1987).

KERENYI, C., *The Gods of the Greeks* (Thames and Hudson 1951).

LANE FOX, R., *Alexander the Great* (Omega 1973).

————, *The Search for Alexander* (Allen Lane 1980).

MAY, C., *The Horse Care Manual* (Stanley Paul 1987).

PLUTARCH, *Lives* (trans. J. and W. Langhorne Routledge).

RENAULT, M., *The Nature of Alexander* (Penguin 1975).

RUTTER, N. K., *Greek Coinage* (Shire Archaeology 1983).

SEKUNDA, N., *The Army of Alexander the Great* (Osprey 1984).

STARR, C. G., *The Ancient Greeks* (OUP 1971).

SYMONS, D. J., *Costume of Ancient Greece* (Batsford 1987).

WYCHERLEY, R. E., *How the Greeks Built Cities* (Macmillan 1962).

XENOPHON, *The Persian Expeditions* (Penguin Classics).